"For years I've dre
but no man wante

Now Tristan knew Caroline's motives. They were pure and painfully simple. She wanted to be a mother.

She paced up to him with her eyes blazing. "I'd do anything—even marry you—for the sake of two beautiful children. Does that confession satisfy you, Major Smith?"

A wry smile lifted his lips. "You're a brave woman, Caroline."

"I'm not brave at all," she murmured.

"I think you are," he answered. "I'd be pleased to marry you...for the sake of the children, of course."

The moment called for a handshake. They were sealing a business deal. But Tristan couldn't bring himself to offer merely his hand. Neither could he kiss her, not even as a token of friendship. Moving slowly, he touched her cheek. "You should call me Tristan."

Victoria Bylin
and
Rhonda Gibson

Marrying the Major
&
The Texan's
Twin Blessings

LOVE INSPIRED
INSPIRATIONAL ROMANCE

LOVE INSPIRED®

INSPIRATIONAL ROMANCE

Recycling programs
for this product may
not exist in your area.

ISBN-13: 978-1-335-23990-7

Marrying the Major & The Texan's Twin Blessings

Copyright © 2020 by Harlequin Books S.A.

Marrying the Major
First published in 2011. This edition published in 2020.
Copyright © 2011 by Vicki Scheibel

The Texan's Twin Blessings
First published in 2015. This edition published in 2020.
Copyright © 2015 by Rhonda Gibson

This edition published by arrangement with Harlequin Books S.A.

For questions and comments about the quality of this book, please contact us at CustomerService@Harlequin.com.

Love Inspired
22 Adelaide St. West, 40th Floor
Toronto, Ontario M5H 4E3, Canada
www.Harlequin.com

Printed in U.S.A.

CONTENTS

Victoria Bylin fell in love with God and her husband at the same time. It started with a ride on a red ◄ motorcycle and a date to see a Star Trek movie. A recent graduate of UC Berkeley, Victoria had been seeking that elusive "something more" when Michael rode into her life.

Michael's career allowed Victoria to be both a stay-at-home mom and a writer. She's living a dream that started when she read her first book and thought, "I want to tell stories." For that gift, she will be forever grateful. Visit her website at victoriabylin.com.

Books by Victoria Bylin

Love Inspired Historical

The Bounty Hunter's Bride
The Maverick Preacher
Kansas Courtship
Wyoming Lawman
The Outlaw's Return
Marrying the Major
Brides of the West

Visit the Author Profile page
at Harlequin.com for more titles.

MARRYING THE MAJOR

Victoria Bylin

Which of you, if your son asks for bread,
will give him a stone? Or if he asks for a fish, will
give him a snake? If you, then, though you are evil,
know how to give good gifts to your children,
how much more will your Father in heaven
give good gifts to those who ask him!
—*Matthew 7:9–11*

This book is dedicated to my sons, Joseph Scheibel and David Scheibel. One's traveled the world and the other is a soldier. They both influenced this story. Love to you both!

Chapter One

Wheeler Springs, Wyoming, October 1876

Tristan Willoughby Smith didn't like to be kept waiting, and he'd been waiting for three days for the arrival of the quinine he needed to treat his malaria. He'd also been waiting for the arrival of the Bradley sisters. He'd hired the youngest, Miss Caroline Bradley, to be the governess to his children. He'd hired the elder sister, Miss Elizabeth Bradley, to serve as a nurse and advisor for the treatment of the disease he'd contracted in the West Indies.

Tristan had a high tolerance for the fevers that came with malaria, but he had no patience at all with tardiness. A former major in the British army, he expected people to do what he told them.

He expected such obedience from his children.

He expected it from the men who worked his cattle ranch.

Mostly he expected such discipline from himself.

He also expected discipline from the stage line scheduled to deliver the quinine he needed to control his fevers. With his hands on his hips, he stared down the wind-blown street that made up the heart of Wheeler Springs.

The stage was three days late. He'd contracted the disease four months ago. The year before it had taken his wife, Molly, leaving him alone to care for their two children. To protect them from the disease, Tristan had come to Wyoming with Jonathan Tate, his best friend and former second in command. Wyoming was as far from malaria—and his home in England—as Tristan could get. It was also eighteen hundred miles away from the Philadelphia pharmaceutical company that manufactured the quinine. If the quinine was lost, he'd be in dire straits.

As much as Tristan needed the medicine, he needed Caroline Bradley even more. The new governess didn't know it, but he had plans for her that went beyond tutoring his children. He had plans for Jon, too. If malaria put Tristan in an early grave, his best friend would be the executor of his will and guardian of his children. Under no circumstance did Tristan want his children returned to his family in England. As the third son of a nobleman, Tristan had no importance. That fact had been drilled into him by his father, Harold Smythe, the Duke of Willoughby, and he didn't want Freddie and Dora growing up under the same cloud.

He also wanted them to have a mother, especially if the malaria took his life. Whether Tristan lived or died was up to God, a being he viewed as a Supreme Commander who gave orders without discussion. Tristan would submit to God's decree, but he couldn't bear the thought of leaving Freddie and Dora without a family. That's where the new governess came in. It was high time Jon settled down. If Tristan died, he expected Jon to marry her and give the children a mother. He'd ruled out the oldest sister for this particular job. The Bradley sister, named Elizabeth, was twelve years older than the younger one, and in her letters she'd stated her dedication to nursing. The governess, however, had written eloquently about her love of children.

The wind kicked a tumbleweed across the street. For the first day of October, the air held a surprising chill. Or had the chill come from within, the first sign of yet another attack of illness? Tristan glanced up at the sky. The fevers usually started late in the day, and the sun had yet to reach its peak. Still, the chill was enough to show him that he couldn't wait any longer to find out what had happened to the stage. A military man, he sized up the obstacles between the railhead in Cheyenne and Wheeler Springs.

The Carver gang could have held up the stage.

Indians could have attacked.

An afternoon storm could have washed out the road and taken the stagecoach with it.

Tristan had a fertile imagination—a blessing to a poet but a curse for an army officer and a bigger curse for a man with malaria.

The door to the stage office swung open and Jon strode forward. He was forty-two, seven years older than Tristan, but he hadn't lost an ounce of the muscle that made him a formidable captain in the West India Regiment. Neither had he lost the dour expression he wore around everyone except Tristan's children. Five-year-old Dora had Uncle Jon wrapped around her little finger, and Freddie, almost ten, lived in the man's shadow.

Jon had gone to speak with Heinrich Meyer, the owner of the inn that served as the stagecoach stop. Looking at his friend, Tristan felt a familiar dread. "It's bad news, isn't it?"

"Yes, sir."

In private, Jon had stopped calling Tristan "sir" five years ago. The formality signaled trouble. In a habit from his days in uniform, Tristan laced his hands behind his back. "Go on."

"The bridge over the gorge is out."

Tristan blanked his expression, but his belly clenched. Two days ago a storm had ripped through Wheeler Springs. Runoff from the hills would turn the Frazier River into a torrent. The first time he'd ridden over the bridge that spanned the gorge, he'd called it a rickety abomination. Without the bridge, the stagecoach would have to take a longer route from Cheyenne or return to the city to await repairs. Even more worrisome, the coach could have been washed into the gorge. He imagined it lying on its side in the river, the quinine crystals saturated and useless. He thought of the governess and her sister injured or dead.

"We need to find the coach," he said to Jon.

"And quickly." His friend lowered his voice. "The Carver gang is in the area."

The Carvers had advanced from rustling cattle to robbing banks and stagecoaches. They were tough, crass and mean. The thought of the governess and her sister being trapped between Wheeler Springs and Cheyenne and at the gang's mercy made Tristan's neck hairs prickle.

"Get the horses, will you?" He'd have preferred to take a wagon to carry the women and their belongings, but the downed bridge made it necessary to go on horseback.

Jon gave him a quelling look. "You're not well. I'll go with Heinrich and his son."

"I'm fine."

"No, you're not."

"I am," Tristan said evenly. "I have to be. I'm almost out of quinine and you know it."

"And if you get feverish?" Jon knew how to be honest

but respectful. "You'll be more of a burden than a help. Stay here, Tristan."

"Absolutely not."

"But—"

"Don't argue with me." Tristan hadn't lived his life sitting on the sidelines, and he didn't intend to start now. He'd felt worse and done more. "Not only do I need the quinine, but the new governess and her sister are possibly stranded between here and Cheyenne. They're my responsibility. I'm going and that's final."

"If you say so, *sir*."

Jon emphasized *sir* not as a sign of respect but as a way of telling Tristan he was being a fool. If Tristan became ill, Jon would be stuck with him. An obvious solution loomed. He'd simply refuse to fall ill. He glanced at the sky. If they rode hard, they'd reach the river before dusk. "Get supplies. We'll leave immediately."

"I figured you'd be stubborn." Jon looked peeved. "Heinrich sent his son to ready the horses."

Shoulder to shoulder, the men paced to the mercantile. While Jon ordered supplies from the storekeeper's wife, Tristan weighed the facts. The ride to Cheyenne took two full days, three if the weather muddied the roads. A stagecoach station sat between the city and the town. He and Jon could be gone a week, maybe longer.

He had to get word to Bert Howe, the ranch foreman, and Evaline, his housekeeper and the woman tending to Freddie and Dora. Tristan had no worries about the ranch, but he worried greatly about his children. They tended to be nervous about his whereabouts. He had to get word to them that he'd be gone longer than expected. He kept a house in Wheeler Springs, and he knew just the man to deliver the message. Noah Taylor was Tristan's houseman, Evaline's husband and a former sergeant in the West India Regiment.

"I need to speak with Noah," Tristan said to Jon. "Someone has to let Bert and Evaline know what's happened."

Jon nodded and went back to purchasing supplies. Tristan crossed the street at a rapid pace, glancing up at the sun and wondering again about the sheen of sweat on his brow. He hated being ill. It turned him into the skinny boy who'd grown up on his father's massive estate.

England had stopped being home the day he'd walked out of his father's study. As a third son, he'd known early that he had limited prospects. He just hadn't expected his father to be so blunt about it...or so cruel.

You have no place here, Tristan. Join the army. Become a clergyman. I don't care what you do.

That parting had been fifteen years ago. Tristan had never been interested in religion. In boarding school he'd been taught to believe in God as a father. If the Almighty was anything like the duke, Tristan wanted nothing to do with him. He accepted God's power, submitted to His authority, but felt no love for Him. Instead of joining the church, he'd used a portion of a large inheritance from an uncle to purchase a commission in the British Army. To make the break from his father complete, he'd changed the spelling of his name from the aristocratic "Smythe" to the more egalitarian "Smith." Tristan missed England, but he'd never go back to his father's estate. If the malaria claimed him as he feared, he wanted to buried at the ranch he called "The Barracks."

Of course he didn't want to be buried at all. He wanted to see Freddie become a man and Dora a wife and mother. Given a choice, he'd die an old man with a soft belly and a head full of gray hair.

But he didn't have a choice. God controlled his fate the way a commander waged a war. Tristan could only lead the battles in his control, which meant ensuring his children wouldn't be returned to England. It wasn't likely the duke would have an interest in Freddie, and it was certain he'd consider Dora a worthless girl, but Tristan had still made legal arrangements to name Jon as guardian. Silently he gave thanks he hadn't been born first. His oldest brother, Andrew, was heir apparent. He'd married Louisa Hudgins, the woman Tristan himself had hoped to wed. She and Andrew had probably produced a dozen children by now. Tristan's second brother, Oscar, would have married as well, though he'd been legendary for his romantic capering.

Putting his thoughts aside, Tristan strode to his town house. Stepping through the front door, he called to Noah. The man stepped immediately into the foyer. Tall and black, he carried himself with the military bearing he'd earned in the West India Regiment. The WIR was composed of free blacks and led by white officers from England. Most of the officers considered the post undesirable, at best a stepping-stone to another assignment. Tristan had felt otherwise. In his own way, he knew how it felt to be judged inferior. He'd led his men with pride and they'd fought with courage. When Tristan made the decision to settle in Wyoming, he'd invited Noah to work for him.

"Good morning, sir." Noah spoke with the singsong tones of the Caribbean. "Any word on the stagecoach?"

"The bridge is out. Jon and I are going to look for the passengers." He didn't mention the quinine. Needing medicine stung his pride, and Noah already knew the importance of it.

The former sergeant gave him the same look he'd

gotten from Jon. "If you'll excuse me, sir. Is that wise? You're not well, and—"

"I'm well enough." Tristan hated being questioned, a fact Noah knew better than most men. That he'd dared to bring up Tristan's health showed both respect and caring.

Tristan took the command out of his voice. "I need you to get word to The Barracks. The children will be worried."

"I'll see to it."

"Thank you, Noah." Tristan turned back to the door.

"Sir?"

"Yes?"

"Mrs. Harvey just delivered a letter." She was the postmistress and very conscientious. "It arrived with last week's stage. She apologized for misplacing it. I put it in the study."

"Who is it from?"

"Pennwright, sir."

Pennwright was his father's long-time secretary, a man who joked that his name had doomed him to his occupation. When Tristan had been sent to boarding school, Pennwright had written regularly. The correspondence had started at the duke's direction, but it had continued for years out of affection.

"I'll look forward to it when I return," he said to Noah.

"Yes, sir."

Satisfied, Tristan walked to the livery where he found Jon waiting with their mounts and two packhorses. If they found the women, the females would have to ride to Wheeler Springs. As for their possessions, they'd take what the horses could carry. When the bridge was repaired, he'd send a wagon for the rest. He welcomed the thought of having such a problem. The alternative—that they'd find the coach destroyed and the driver and women dead—couldn't be tolerated.

Looking grave, Jon handed him the reins to his favorite horse. Tristan preferred a spirited mount and the stallion he'd named Cairo had speed and intelligence. A sleek Arabian, Cairo was black with a matching mane and tail. The stallion obeyed Tristan, but he did it with an air of superiority.

Jon rode up next to him on the gray mare he favored. She wasn't old, but Tristan had named her Grandma because she rode like a rocking chair.

As he turned Cairo down the street, the sun hit him in the face. He swiped at beads of perspiration with his sleeve, then nudged Cairo into an easy canter. With the fever lurking in his body and the Bradley sisters in places unknown, there was no time to waste. Jon rode next to him, letting Tristan set the pace.

Three hours passed with no sign of the stage. The sun peaked and was halfway to the horizon when they arrived at the downed bridge. Tristan slid wearily off Cairo, shielded his eyes from the sun and scanned the gorge for the downed stagecoach. He saw only boards from the bridge wedged between rocks and the sparkling water racing past them.

Relief washed over him. "They didn't get this far."

"So it seems."

"We need to push on." Tristan inspected the sides of the gorge. A trail led to the river and stopped at a sandy bank. The men climbed back on their horses and headed for the crossing with Tristan in the lead. The storm had turned the path into slick mud, but they arrived at the river's edge without mishap. Cairo didn't hesitate to wade into the current, but Grandma needed coaxing. When Tristan reached the far bank, he turned and saw his friend urging the skittish horse to take one step at a time. He hoped the river would recede before they had to cross it again, hopefully with the stage driver and the two women. When Grandma found firm footing, she bolted out of the water.

Jon grinned at Tristan. "The old girl did it."

"Barely," Tristan acknowledged. "For a minute, I thought you'd have to carry her."

Jon smiled at the joke, then looked down the road. Tristan followed his gaze with the same questions in mind. Had the stage come this far and turned back? Had it gone off the road before reaching the bridge? He also had to consider the Carver gang. Fighting fever, Tristan acknowledged the cold facts. Anything could have happened. The quinine could already be lost, and the women could be hurt or trapped or worse.

With no time to waste, he barked an order at Jon. "We still have daylight. Let's go."

He nudged Cairo into a comfortable trot. Jon stayed with him, but at dusk Tristan admitted defeat. They hadn't seen a single sign of the coach. With the fever nipping at him, he gave in to Jon's suggestion that they strike camp for the night. They'd start looking again in the morning.

Caroline Bradley awoke on the hard ground with a jolt. Dawn had broken with startling splendor, but it wasn't the golden light that roused her from a troubled sleep. It was the snap of a twig, then the frustrated muttering of a male voice. She clutched the shotgun she'd found in the boot of the stagecoach. She'd slept with it for two nights, and she knew how to pull the trigger. If the Carver gang had come back, she'd use it.

Three days ago she and Bessie had left Cheyenne for

Wheeler Springs. They'd had the coach to themselves, so they'd passed the hours speculating about Tristan Willoughby Smith, his children and what life would be like on a cattle ranch. Not once had they imagined the stagecoach being robbed by the Carver gang. Thanks to the sacrifice of the driver, they'd escaped while he'd challenged the outlaws with his pistol. She and Bessie had run for their lives and hidden in a ravine, listening as the Carvers killed the driver and ransacked their trunks and other shipments. When the outlaws finished, they'd stolen the horses and pushed the yellow coach into the ravine.

Cracked and lying on its side, the old Concord had offered adequate shelter from the sun, very little from the rain and none from the frightful howling of wolves.

In the scramble down the hill, Bessie had sprained her ankle. By herself, Caroline had piled rocks on the dead driver, then she'd salvaged what she could of their possessions. In the course of her efforts, she'd found a crate addressed to Major Smith from the Farr, Powers and Weightman Chemical Laboratory in Philadelphia. It had been opened and the contents had been dumped without care. In the pile of broken bottles, she'd seen a label marked "Sulphate of Quinine." Knowing the value of the medicine, she'd salvaged seven of the twelve bottles. They were wrapped in an old nightgown and hidden in the stagecoach for safekeeping.

She knew the major was ill, and she'd assumed he had a chronic illness or a war injury. Now she wondered if he was suffering from malaria. It had been a scourge during the war that had destroyed the South. Bessie had served as a nurse during the conflict, and she'd complained often that illness killed more men than mini balls. Major Smith, it seemed, was a very ill man. Seeing the medicine, Caroline had thought of his motherless children. Who would love them if they lost their father? Malaria was a fickle disease. It could take a man's life in a day or linger in his blood for years.

Outlaws had the same penchant for randomness. Aware of the slow, measured steps coming toward her, Caroline weighed her options. Bessie's ankle meant they couldn't run. Neither could they hide. Huddling against the undercarriage of the coach, she whispered into her sister's ear. "Bessie, wake up but don't move."

Her sister's eyelids fluttered open.

The footsteps were closer now. A bird took flight from a cottonwood. Caroline wanted to fly away, too. Instead she clutched the shotgun. The steps came closer. She heard the slide of dirt and rock as he reached the bottom of the hill, then the thump of leather on dirt as he paced toward the coach. A squirrel leapt from one branch to another, springing high and then landing with a bounce. Leaves fell like dry rain. With each step the stranger came closer to the coach until all noise stopped. Caroline took a breath and held it. Nothing stirred. Not a bird. Not a breeze. Bessie lay still, watching with wide eyes and signaling her with a nod to be brave.

Leaping to her feet, Caroline aimed the shotgun at the man's chest. "Who are you?"

He looked at her as if she were no more dangerous than a gnat. Refusing to blink, she stared down the barrel at a man who looked more like a scarecrow than an outlaw. Tall and gaunt, he had hair the color of straw and eyes so red-rimmed they seemed more gray than blue. His clothes hung on his broad shoulders, but there was no mistaking the fine tailoring. She took in the creases around his mouth, his stubbled jaw and finally the boots that reached to his knees. Black and spit-shined, they didn't belong to a shiftless outlaw.

She couldn't say the same for the pistol in his hand. It was loose and pointed downward, but she felt the threat. She dug the shotgun into her shoulder. "Throw down your gun!"

He raised one eyebrow. "I'd prefer to holster it, if you don't mind."

That voice…it reminded her of a fog bell coming out of a mist, a warning she remembered from the Carolina shore, the place of her birth and the reason for her name. She heard the trace of an accent she couldn't identify, not the boisterous timbre of an Englishman or a German, but the muted tones of a man who'd worked to leave the past behind.

When she didn't speak, he holstered the gun then looked at her with his hands slightly away from his body, taking in her appearance with a flick of his eyes. Caroline knew what he'd see… A woman with an average face and an average figure, past her prime but young enough to want a husband. For a few months she'd once been secretly married, but he'd see a spinster. A woman desperate enough for a family that she'd decided to become a governess. If she couldn't have children of her own, she'd borrow them.

First, though, she had to get rid of this unknown man studying her with both fascination and fury.

"Get your hands up!" she ordered.

He kept them loose at his sides. "Perhaps—"

"Raise them!"

He let out a sigh worthy of a frustrated king. "If you insist."

Slowly he raised his arms, holding her gaze with a force that nearly made her cower. When his hands were shoulder-high, palm out so she that she could see the aristocratic length of his fingers, he lowered his chin. "Perhaps, Miss Bradley, you'd allow me to introduce myself?"

The accent was no longer muffled. Thick and English, it held a command that made her lower the shotgun. She didn't need to hear Tristan Willoughby Smith say his name to know she'd just met her future employer, and that she'd impressed him...in all the wrong ways.

Chapter Two

"Major Smith!"

Tristan arched one brow at the stunned brunette. "May I lower my hands now?"

"Of course." Most people groveled when they realized they'd stepped on his toes. Caroline Bradley snapped to attention but not in the way of an underling. She looked him square in the eye. "I'm sure you understand my reaction. As you can see, the stagecoach was robbed."

"Yes."

He wished now they hadn't stopped at dusk. As luck would have it, they'd camped less than a mile away. By the morning light he'd spotted in the debris a woman's shoe and a nightgown that had been mauled by dirty hands. Certain the two Miss Bradleys had been on the coach, he'd left Jon to search through the crates and had maneuvered down the ravine. He'd spotted the yellow coach lying on its side but hadn't seen the women. Until Miss Bradley had gotten the jump on him, he'd believed the sisters had been abducted by the Carvers or left for dead inside the coach.

Looking at her now, the one he assumed to be the governess, he decided the timing of his arrival had been fortuitous. If he'd arrived in the dark, she'd have shot him. The elder Miss Bradley—the nurse—was struggling to stand.

Tristan stepped around the overturned coach and offered his hand. "Allow me."

"Thank you," she replied.

When the elder Miss Bradley reached her feet, the younger Miss Bradley put her arm around her waist to steady to her. Tristan couldn't address both women as "Miss Bradley." In his mind he'd think of them as Caroline and Elizabeth. If only one sister was present, he'd address her as Miss Bradley. When they were together, etiquette required him to address the eldest as Miss Bradley and the younger as Miss Caroline. Looking at the women, he easily discerned the difference in their ages and spoke to the nurse. "I presume you're Miss Elizabeth Bradley?"

"That's correct, sir."

He looked at the governess and wished the rules of etiquette weren't quite so clear. Calling this pretty woman by her given name struck him as too personal, even when he prefaced her name with "Miss." He studied her with a stern eye. "I'll address you as Miss Caroline. Is that acceptable?"

A populist gleam twinkled in her wide eyes. "Simply Caroline would do."

"Hardly."

"Then whichever you'd prefer, Mr. Smith."

"It's Major Smith."

He'd been out of the army for months, but he hadn't adjusted to being Mr. Smith. In England he'd have been Lord Tristan, a title that gave him indigestion but sounded normal to his ears. As much as he wanted to deny it, titles and ranks were in his blood.

Maybe that's why Caroline's tone struck him as insubordinate. Even more annoying, she reminded him of Louisa. Not only did she have a lively glint in her eyes, but she also had Louisa's ivory skin and brunette hair. It was an utter mess at the moment, a tumbling pile of curls that had once been meant to impress him. He knew from her letters that she had a suitable education, but he hadn't expected the keen intelligence he saw in her brown eyes. Or were they green? Hazel, he decided. She had eyes that mirrored her surroundings, and today they'd been muted by the grayish sky. He couldn't help but wonder if her eyes had once been brighter or if they had faded with life's trials.

He'd taken a chance hiring a stranger to raise his children, but he had little choice. He hoped Jon would see Caroline's attributes as plainly as he did. His friend would certainly notice her female curves. Any man would—including Tristan, though the awareness had to remain fleeting.

She stood with her chin slightly raised, silent but somehow conveying her irritation with him. Tristan didn't like being challenged even with silence, so he paused to examine the overturned coach. He didn't expect to see the crate of quinine, though he held to a sliver of hope.

The new governess cleared her throat. "Sir?"

"One moment," he ordered. "Jon will be here shortly. There's no point in repeating yourself."

"Who's Jon?" she asked.

He glared at her. "He's second in command at The Barracks."

"A barracks? I thought you owned a ranch."

"I do," he said with aplomb. "*The Barracks* is a nickname. I assure you, Miss Caroline. You'll live in a perfectly proper house."

She gave him a doubtful look but said nothing.

Tristan cupped his hand to his mouth and called for Jon. "I've found the women. Get down here."

When he looked back at the two Miss Bradleys, the eldest was giving him a look he could only describe as scolding. Tristan's own mother had died when he was five, but he'd seen his wife give that look to Freddie. Tristan didn't like receiving it from an employee.

The new governess reflected the same disapproval. "Major, you should know—"

"Not now."

"But I have something to tell you!"

"I know enough," he snapped at her.

He must have established his authority because she sealed her lips. He looked up the hill, saw Jon navigating the incline and waited in stony silence for his friend to arrive. Tristan couldn't stop himself from wondering about the quinine. If the Carvers knew the value, they would have stolen it. Judging by the mayhem on the road, at the very least they'd smashed the crate. Without sufficient quinine, his next bout of fever would be a brute.

As Jon came down the hill, Tristan saw the look his friend wore after a battle when bodies lay askew and the price of victory was its most obvious. He hadn't found the quinine.

The man strode to Tristan's side, acknowledged the women with a nod, then spoke in a quiet tone. "I found the crate. It's been smashed. The bottles are broken or missing."

"I see."

"I'm sorry," Jon murmured. "There's nothing to salvage."

The younger woman cleared her throat. "Major Smith—"

"Miss Caroline!" He bellowed to make a point. "Do you *always* interrupt with such enthusiasm?"

"Only when it's important."

She said no more, leaving it up to him to humble himself and ask. "If you don't mind, it will have to wait. I'm expecting an important shipment. Jon is looking for—"

"Quinine," she said quietly.

Instead of scolding her again, Tristan stared into her shimmering eyes. "Go on."

"Part of the shipment was destroyed, but I salvaged seven bottles. They're hidden in the stagecoach."

He said nothing because being in her debt was humbling and he didn't know how to be anything but a man in command. Malaria had turned the tables on him. The disease was in charge, and it had been since he'd left the West Indies. Now Caroline Bradley was in charge. He didn't like being beholden to anyone, especially not a woman with brunette hair and intelligent eyes. Molly had been gone for more than a year. He missed her terribly, but his own illness had forced him to cope with the loss quickly. He had only one focus—to provide a family for Freddie and Dora in case of his death.

Jon offered Caroline his hand. "You must be one of the Bradley sisters. I'm Jonathan Tate. I keep Major Smith in line."

Tristan watched the woman's eyes for a flicker of interest. Jon was twelve years older than she was, but women found him appealing. More than once Tristan's second in command had been called a pussycat, while Tristan had been called "sir" by everyone including his wife and children.

Caroline Bradley shook Jon's hand, then introduced her sister. Apparently, the elder Miss Bradley went by Bessie. Tristan should have been doing the honors, but he disliked social pleasantries. They reminded him too much of the stilted formality of his childhood.

"It was terrible," the eldest Miss Bradley said about the robbery. "One minute we were riding along at a reasonable clip, and the next we were flying around the curves. The driver made it around a turn and stopped the coach. He told us to run for our lives."

"What happened to him?" Tristan asked.

"They shot him," Caroline said quietly. "I did my best to bury him, but his family might want to do better. His name was Calvin."

Tristan knew Calvin. He'd worked briefly at The Barracks. He had no family, but Tristan wouldn't leave him in an unmarked grave. He turned to Jon. "When we get to the ranch, send someone to take care of the body."

"Yes, sir."

Tristan turned back to the women. "Was there someone riding shotgun?"

Caroline shook her head. "There was supposed to be a second driver, but he didn't show up. Calvin made the decision to go alone." She gave him a deliberate look. "He was anxious to deliver the quinine."

Calvin would have known the importance of the medicine. Yet again, Tristan was beholden to someone. The debt couldn't be repaid except to live in a manner worthy of the sacrifice. That meant showing kindness to Caroline and her sister. Looking at her now, he saw a courageous woman who'd survived a robbery, buried one man and saved another by salvaging the medicine. Needing to focus on something other than her attributes, he changed the subject. "Do you know who robbed the stage?"

Bessie answered. "Calvin mentioned the Carvers before we left Cheyenne."

"That's the assumption," he acknowledged.

Caroline had the haunted look of a soldier reliving a battle. "The robbers ransacked the stagecoach. We heard them making threats, so we hid. We couldn't run because Bessie twisted her ankle."

Tristan couldn't stand the thought of the Carvers harming either of the women.

Bessie squeezed her sister's hand. "The good Lord had an eye on us."

Tristan doubted it. In his experience, God ignored the needs of human beings as surely as the duke had ignored his third son. Where was God when Molly lay shaking with fever? Neither did God care about little Dora, who still cried for her mother, or for Freddie, who didn't cry at all. Tristan had seen too much death to deny the hope of an afterlife, but he didn't see God in the here and now. He especially didn't see a loving Father when fever made him delusional and his bones caught fire.

Bessie indicated the area around the coach. "As you can see, we've been camping. Caroline saw to everything."

He studied the patch of ground sheltered by the coach. Caroline had done a commendable job of salvaging essentials from the wreckage. She'd built a fire, used a pot to fetch water from a stream and neatly organized food they'd brought from Cheyenne. The campsite was a testament to ingenuity, neatness and order, all traits Tristan admired. Nonetheless, he imagined the women would prefer his house in Wheeler Springs to another night in the open. They'd have to move quickly to arrive by nightfall, especially with packhorses laden with their possessions. He did a quick calculation and decided the women could ride together on Grandma. Jon could manage a packhorse, while the other carried what it could.

"We should be on our way." He turned to Bessie. "Miss Bradley, how severely is your ankle injured?"

"It's just a sprain." She looked at Jon. "I can walk up the hill if someone will give me a strong arm."

Jon turned on the smile that made him a pussycat. "I'd be delighted—"

"No," Tristan interrupted. "I'll escort Miss Bradley up the hill. You help Miss Caroline break down camp. Make sure you're careful with the quinine." Tristan would have preferred to carry it himself, but he felt wobbly.

Jon focused on the pretty brunette. "I'm at your service, Miss Caroline."

"Thank you, Mr. Tate."

"Call me Jon." He shot Tristan a sly glance. "Only the major insists on formalities."

The woman smiled. "Jon it is. For the sake of simplicity, Bessie and I go by our first names. You're welcome to call me Caroline."

Jon nodded graciously and Caroline smiled.

Though pleased by their budding friendship, Tristan felt envious. What would it be like to seek a woman's attention? To woo her the way he'd wooed Molly? They'd had a stellar courtship, even if he said so himself. He hoped Jon would show the same ambition for Caroline. If Tristan's plan worked, they'd fall in love and get married. If the malaria bested Tristan, they'd raise Freddie and Dora, and his children would have a family.

At Caroline's direction, Jon went to work gathering their meager possessions while she retrieved a bundled nightgown that presumably held the bottles of quinine. Tristan stepped to Bessie's side and offered his arm. "Shall we?"

"Thank you, Major."

As he helped the injured woman up the hill, he admitted to a sad fact. He didn't have to slow his pace to match hers. In fact, she'd slowed down for him. He glanced over his shoulder and saw Jon laughing with the pretty brunette. In other circumstances, he'd have given his friend a run for his money for the woman's attention… and he'd have won.

Caroline liked Jon, but Major Smith struck her as a pompous, arrogant, pigheaded fool. If he hadn't been so rude, she'd have told him about the quinine the instant she recognized him. She didn't expect her new employer to be overly friendly, but she'd hoped for common courtesy. She didn't like Major Smith at all.

Watching as he escorted Bessie up the hill, she saw the slowness of his movements and turned to Jon. "How long has Major Smith had malaria?"

"Four months." Jon stopped gathering blankets and looked up the hill. "He won't tell you anything, but you should know what he's been through. If you have questions, you should bring them to me. I know him as well as anyone. We served together in the West India Regiment. He's been to Africa, India, all over the world."

"And England," she added.

"Yes, but not for a long time." Jon's expression hardened. "That one is his story to tell. What you need to know is that he lost his wife a year ago. Molly was a peach. We all loved her."

"Was it malaria?"

"Yes. It struck hard and fast. She died within a week. Tristan wanted to leave the West Indies for the sake of the children, but his transfer request wasn't approved. He had no choice but to stay until he caught the disease himself."

Caroline ached for the entire family. "The children must be terribly frightened."

"They are," Jon replied. "Dora cries at the drop of a hat. It'll break your heart. Freddie doesn't show his feelings, but they're deep. He's like his father in that way."

Caroline glanced at the arrogant man struggling to climb a hill. "How sick is he?"

He hesitated. "I've seen Tristan at his best and at his worst. He's a fighter. If anyone can beat the malaria, he can."

He hadn't answered her question. "Is today his best or his worst?"

"It's typical."

Later Caroline would ask Bessie about the course of the disease. "How did he come to be in Wyoming?"

"It's as far from swamps and England as he could get."

Caroline understood his aversion to swamps. His dislike of England baffled her, but she knew Jon wouldn't explain. She followed his gaze to the top of the ravine where the major had just crested the ridge. Caroline didn't know why God hadn't answered her prayers for a family of her own, but she saw a need here. Major Smith didn't like her, but his children needed someone who wouldn't leave them.

She wondered if he'd made arrangements for a guardian in case he succumbed to malaria. She couldn't bear the thought of growing to love these children and losing them to a distant aunt or uncle. She turned to ask Jon more questions, but he'd finished gathering their things and had tied them in a blanket. "Do you have the quinine?"

She indicated the bundled nightgown. "I'll carry it."

With the pack of clothing slung over his shoulder, he offered his elbow. "Shall we join them?"

"Yes, thank you."

Holding the quinine in one hand, she took his arm with

the other. When the path narrowed, they broke apart and she climbed alone. It seemed a fitting way to end the ordeal in the canyon. Soon she'd be in Wheeler Springs. She'd be able to take a bath and sleep in a bed. She'd meet Major Smith's children, and she'd have people who needed her. Feeling hopeful, she stepped from the ravine to level ground and saw Bessie and Major Smith at her trunk. In addition to clothing and a few personal treasures, it held her sister's medical bag. Bessie needed it to give the major a dose of quinine.

"I'll get it," Caroline called.

She didn't want Major Smith looking at her things. It struck her as too personal, plus she'd hidden the one photograph she had of her husband. Their marriage had been secret, and she had always used her maiden name. Charles had been a black man and a crusader, a gentle giant and a man of great faith. He'd died at the hands of a mob because he believed in educating all children regardless of color—and because he trusted people too easily.

Caroline had no idea what Major Smith would think of her choices, and she didn't care. She would always admire Charles and had no regrets, but it hurt to be an outcast. She didn't want to fight that battle again, so she hurried to the trunk before the major could look inside. She handed Bessie the quinine bottles, lifted the medical bag and unbuckled it. Jon walked up to them with a canteen in one hand and a tin cup in the other. Major Smith took the cup and looked at Bessie. "The quinine, please."

Bessie opened a bottle and poured a dose of crystals into the cup. "Quinine is most effective when mixed with alcohol. I have some in my bag."

Caroline opened a tightly corked flask and handed it to the major. He poured a swallow in the cup, returned the bottle to her, then swished the liquid to absorb the crystals. He downed it in one swallow and turned to Bessie. "You're experienced with malaria."

"I'm afraid so," she answered. "I nursed hundreds of soldiers during the war."

Caroline put away the bottle, set the medical bag in the trunk and glanced around for a wagon to take them to Wheeler Springs. Instead of a wagon, she saw four horses. Two were saddled. Two carried supplies.

"I don't see a wagon," she said.

"There isn't one," the major replied. "The bridge over the gorge is out. We'll use one of the packhorses for your things. Jon can ride the other one, and you and your sister can share the gray."

A shiver started at the nape of Caroline's neck and went to her fingertips. Horses terrified her. She and Bessie had grown up in Charleston where their father had been a doctor. They'd been city girls. What little riding she'd done as a child had been slow and ladylike. She hadn't enjoyed it, but she hadn't become terrified of horses until the night she'd seen her husband lynched. As long as she lived, she'd never forget the sudden bolt of a horse she'd believed to be gentle.

No way could she ride to Wheeler Springs. She had neither the skill nor the confidence to sit on a horse. Neither did she have the courage. How she'd make that clear to Major Smith, she didn't know, especially when he was looking at her as if he'd just had the best idea of his life. What that idea was, she didn't know. She only knew this man was accustomed to giving orders, and he expected them to be followed.

Chapter Three

Tristan saw a chance to bring Jon and Caroline together and took it. "On second thought, perhaps you'd prefer to ride with Jon? I'll take your sister, and we'll use both packhorses to transport your belongings."

The eldest Miss Bradley nodded in agreement, "That's a fine idea, major. Our possessions are modest. Perhaps we can bring everything with us."

Caroline didn't seem to concur. She was gaping at him with wide-eyed horror. Surely she wasn't so modest she couldn't see the practicality of his suggestion? Tristan frowned. "Is there a problem?"

"Well…yes."

He waited five seconds for her to explain. Considering he didn't wait for anyone except Dora, five seconds was a considerable compromise. When the new governess failed to find her tongue, he lowered his chin. "Spit it out."

The elder Miss Bradley gave him a critical look. "My sister is afraid of horses."

"*Afraid* of horses!" Tristan couldn't help but sputter. "I own a cattle ranch. How does she expect to travel?"

Caroline glared at him. "You hired me to care for your

children, not round up cows. I expect to walk or ride in a carriage or wagon."

Tristan looked at Jon. "How far is it to Wheeler Springs?" He knew quite well, but he wanted her to hear the answer from Jon, who she seemed to like.

Jon's brow wrinkled in sympathy. "It's a good thirty miles."

She turned ashen. Tristan almost felt sorry for her. He'd been afraid many times in his life, ironically less often on the battlefield than in his own home. He'd been afraid of his father when he was boy, and he'd been afraid when Molly had fallen ill. Now he was afraid of the malaria. He tried to offer consolation. "You're obviously a resolute woman. You'll be fine with Jon. He's an excellent horseman."

"I'm sure he is. It's just that…" She shuddered. "There's no choice, is there?"

He shrugged. "You could walk."

Bessie touched her sister's shoulder. They exchanged a few quiet words, then the nurse turned to him. "I think it would be best if my sister and I shared the gray as you first suggested."

Tristan preferred his second idea, but he was tired of arguing. "Very well. Let's get moving."

When Caroline hesitated, Jon gave her the reassuring look he often gave Dora. "The horse's name is Grandma. She couldn't be gentler."

She managed a smile. It was tentative and sweet and so full of courage Tristan wanted to give her a medal. But they really didn't have time to dawdle if they wanted to get home before dark. "We need to go."

She glared at him. "I need to finish emptying the trunk."

Without waiting to be dismissed, she took her sister's

medical bag out of the trunk and set it close to her feet. Tristan had to admire her priorities. Except for Molly, the women he'd known would have reached for their jewelry before the medicine. Bessie reached into the trunk to help, but Caroline shooed her away. "Rest your ankle," she murmured. "We have a long ride."

So did Tristan and he already felt done in. He wanted to encourage the camaraderie between Jon and Caroline, so he offered Bessie his arm. "Come with me."

He escorted her to a flat boulder where they sat and watched the packing. Almost clandestinely, Caroline lifted a framed picture from the folds of her gowns. She put it with the precious quinine, then handed the bag to Jon. "This requires special attention."

"Of course," he answered.

Tristan called to his friend. "Bring it here. I'll carry it." He trusted Jon, but he didn't trust the packhorse to cross the river without balking. Tristan wanted the medicine in his care alone.

Caroline shot him a look. He figured the photograph was of her parents, though he wondered if it told other tales. Seated on the rock, he watched her expression as Jon set the bag at his feet and returned to help her. In a separate drawstring bag she stowed a black-bound volume he supposed was her Bible, a smaller book bound in cloth and what looked like a doll. She gave the bag to Jon and said something. Looking pleased, he tied the bundle to Grandma's saddle.

Just as Tristan hoped, the two of them quickly developed an easy rapport. Thirty minutes later, a packhorse was bearing all the women's possessions.

The time had come to mount up. Tristan leveraged to his feet and offered Bessie his hand. Together they ambled to the horses where Jon and Caroline were standing in front of Grandma. Jon was stroking the horse's nose, but it was the woman at his side who needed comforting. Looking tentative, she raised her hand to pet the horse.

Surprised, Grandma raised her head. Jon controlled her, but no one was there to control Caroline. She skittered away like a leaf in the wind.

The terror in her eyes reminded Tristan of Dora and how she came to him in tears after Molly's death. Dora expected people to help her. Caroline clearly had no such hope. She was staring at Grandma as if she were looking at a mountain. He felt sorry for her, but she had to get on the horse.

Jon motioned to Bessie. "Let me help you up first."

Leaning on Tristan's arm, Bessie limped to Jon's side, gripped the horn and put her good foot in the stirrup. With Jon's help, she landed gracefully in the saddle. Grandma didn't mind at all.

Jon looked at Caroline. "Are you ready?"

She looked close to tears, but she marched back to the horse like a soldier facing his second battle, the one where experience replaced ignorance and a man discovered his true mettle. Looking at her, Tristan wondered if she'd been thrown before. He could understand her reluctance to try again. He'd felt that way about love after Louisa rejected him.

Molly had mended that hole in his heart. It had threatened to open again with her passing, but she'd been adamant with him.

Don't you dare leave our children without a mother! I want you to marry again.

He'd made the promise, but he'd done it halfheartedly. He *would* give his children a mother, but she'd be Jon's bride, not his. Never his. The malaria had seen to that.

He studied Caroline as she listened to Jon, noting the

tilt of her chin and the way she held her shoulders. Her demeanor struck a chord of admiration. So did the way she swung up behind her sister in a flurry of petticoats and courage. When she rewarded Jon with a quiet thank-you, Tristan felt a surge of jealousy. Jon had his health. He had a future, and if the woman's smile was any indication, he'd have a wife as Tristan hoped and now envied.

Annoyed with himself, he lifted Cairo's reins from a tree and swung into the saddle as if he were a healthy man and not a feverish weakling. Frowning, he called to Jon. "Let's go."

He led the way, keeping the pace slow for the ladies but itching to nudge Cairo into a run. He wanted to leave his weakness behind—the illness, his worries—but he couldn't. All he could do was ride at a leisurely pace, listening to a pretty woman laugh at Jon's banter. The pleasantries should have given Tristan comfort. Instead he had to grit his teeth against the urge to one-up Jon with stories of his own.

For two hours he said nothing. When they arrived at the downed bridge, he turned to look at the women. Bessie had a steady way about her, but Caroline went chalk-white at the sight of the trail zigzagging down the canyon wall. Without a word, he led the way on Cairo with Grandma following and Jon at the rear with the second packhorse in tow. He could hear Caroline's unsteady breathing, but she didn't utter a word.

When they reached the water's edge, Tristan turned again to look at the women. Bessie had the stalwart expression of a veteran soldier. He suspected she'd experienced more difficult challenges than crossing a river. Caroline, however, could have been looking at a man-eating grizzly. Tristan followed her gaze to the rushing current. The knee-high water hadn't gone down since yesterday. Cairo could handle it, but Grandma would be skittish.

He slid out of the saddle. "I'll ferry the women across."

It was the first time he'd spoken in two hours. Caroline stared as if she'd forgotten him. "Are you sure it's safe?"

"Positive."

Jon dismounted, then lifted her off Grandma's back. She landed in front of him with her hands resting lightly on his shoulders. Envy poked at Tristan again. Next Jon assisted Bessie, and the four of them stood in a square of sorts. As if the women weren't present, Tristan addressed Jon. "I'll take Miss Bradley first. You'll wait here with Miss Caroline. When I take her across, follow on Grandma with the packhorses."

To Tristan's consternation, Caroline took a step back and turned away from them. He followed her gaze to the river and saw a tree branch floating by. Bessie put an arm around her sister's waist and murmured something. The younger woman murmured back loud enough for Tristan to hear. "I can't do this," she said. "It's just too much."

Bessie patted her back. "I know, but it's just a river. You can do it."

"But I don't *want* to!" Her voice rose in volume and pitch. "First we get robbed. Then you sprained your ankle and the wolves kept howling—" She shuddered. "When is it going to *stop?*"

Tristan ached for her because he felt the same way about his illness. It wasn't the river that had Miss Bradley in a knot. It was days, weeks, maybe years of frustration.

He stepped up behind her. Wondering if he'd lost his mind, he touched her shoulder. "Caroline?" He deliberately left off the "Miss."

She startled like a deer, then faced him. "I'm sorry, Major. It's just—"

"I understand."

He could have been speaking to Dora, but his daughter wouldn't have tried to be brave. She'd have reached to be picked up, fully expecting him to protect her. Caroline had no such expectation.

Her doubt challenged him. "The river isn't deep. I'm confident Cairo can handle it."

"Who's Cairo?"

"My horse."

She turned to look at the stallion. In the shadows of the canyon, his coat glistened black and his muscles were deeply defined. Poised and ready, the horse towered over Grandma.

"He's huge," Caroline murmured. "And he looks fast."

"He's practically a nag," Tristan said, joking. "The old boy can barely walk." He meant the horse, but she looked at *him*.

Anger flared in her eyes. "You're making fun of me."

"No," he said gently. "I wanted to make you smile. You can be assured that you'll be safe."

"I just don't know."

"I do," he said, deadpan. "No one disobeys me. Not even Cairo."

Jon laughed out loud. "Tell that to Dora."

"Well, yes," he acknowledged. "Dora has a mind of her own."

"So do I." Caroline squared her shoulders. "But there's no choice."

She'd spoken the same words earlier, and it bothered him. He wanted to tell her there was always a choice, but he hadn't chosen malaria. He hadn't chosen to lose Molly. Sometimes, there was no choice but to accept the inevitable. Today, though, he had a choice to make. He could be a sympathetic friend or an unfeeling tyrant. Before

Caroline could object, he took her hand and tugged her to Cairo. The horse stood with the expectation of royalty. Tristan took a peppermint from his pocket and offered it on his flat palm. Cairo took the treat, bobbing his head as he tasted the mint.

Caroline laughed. "Your horse eats candy."

"Yes." Tristan took another piece of peppermint from his pocket and handed it to her. "Hold it flat like I did."

"I couldn't—"

"Like this," he said, unfolding her fingers.

When she didn't argue, he put the peppermint in her palm and held her hand under Cairo's nose. The horse took the treat with the gentleness Tristan expected. More amazed than terrified, she turned to him. They were face-to-face, a breath apart. If he'd been a healthy man, he'd have wondered about kissing her. Not now, but later when he knew her better. But malaria had bent his life into a question mark. He could be gone in a week or a month…or he could live a long life. Looking at Caroline, he thought of his promise to Molly to remarry, and he imagined keeping it.

Blushing, Caroline looked away. "Let's go while I have the courage."

"Certainly."

Tristan pulled himself into the saddle, took the reins and guided Cairo to a flat boulder. Understanding his intention, she followed and climbed on the rock. He took his boot out of the stirrup and offered his hand. Nervous but determined, she placed her foot in the stirrup, grasped his fingers and looked into his eyes.

"On the count of three," he said. "One…two…three."

He pulled her up and over the horse. She landed with a plop and instinctively wrapped her arms around his waist, squeezing as if she'd never let go. For that moment, the malaria didn't matter. Tristan felt strong and capable. He might not live to see another Christmas, but he could get Caroline safely across the river.

"Are you ready?" he asked.

"Yes, Major."

He'd have preferred to be called Tristan, but a barrier had to be maintained. With Caroline clinging to his waist, he nudged Cairo into the current. The horse plowed into the river until the water rose above his knees. Ripples splashed against Tristan's thigh, and the hem of Caroline's skirt became sodden. She was trembling against his back, struggling to breathe evenly and holding him like she'd never him go.

"You're doing wonderfully," he said.

"We're halfway, aren't we?"

"Exactly."

They were dead center and in the deepest part of the river. Tristan looked up the canyon and saw a tree branch floating in their direction. He held Cairo back to let it pass, but the current aimed the branch straight at them. When Cairo sidestepped, Miss Bradley squeezed the breath out of him.

"We're fine," he said gently. "Just hang on."

He nudged Cairo to take another step. The horse refused to budge. Looking down, Tristan saw a submerged tangle of limbs and leaves. It was caught on the horse's hoof, and Cairo didn't like it.

Caroline trembled against his back. "Why aren't we moving?"

He thought of his boast that no one would dare disobey him. The stallion, it seemed, had decided to prove him wrong. Tristan would win this test of wills, but it would come at a cost. He put his hand over Caroline's stiff fingers. "Cairo needs a little encouragement. I'm going to dig in my heels. I want you to be ready because he's going to jump forward."

"Oh, no," she whimpered.

She held even tighter to his waist. Just before he nudged Cairo, the horse sidestepped again. The branch came with him and he started to rear. "Hang on," Tristan called to her.

He needed both hands to control the horse. Cairo whinnied in irritation, then reared up with the intention of stomping the branch. To Tristan's dismay, Caroline slid off the horse in a tangle of skirts and petticoats. With a splash, she landed in the river.

Chapter Four

The water went over Caroline's head with a whoosh. She couldn't see or breathe. She could only feel the sudden cold and the current grabbing at her skirt. The stallion was bucking and stomping. If she didn't get out of the river, she'd be pulled downstream or trampled. She tried to stand but stumbled because of the weight of her clothing.

"Get back!" the major shouted.

He had his hands full with the unruly horse. She didn't know why it had bucked, but the medical case was slapping against its side. She had a horrible vision of it coming loose. Major Smith would lose the quinine, and she'd lose her only picture of Charles. Bracing against the sandy bottom, she pushed to her feet. She wanted to run for the shore, but if the case tore loose she'd go after it.

Cairo reared back and whinnied. She half expected Major Smith to land in the river with her, but he moved gracefully with the horse, aligning his body with the stallion's neck and back. Behind her she heard Jon sloshing toward them on Grandma. Being caught between two horses terrified her more than drowning, so she hoisted her skirts and ran downriver.

She stumbled a dozen steps, tripped on her hem and went down again. Rocks pressed into her knees and she cried out. She kept her head above water, but her skirt was tangled around her legs. Seemingly out of nowhere, male hands gripped her arms and lifted her from the current.

"Caroline." She heard the major's voice, the accent thick as he set her on her feet. "It's all right. I've got you."

She felt the strength of his arms and the sureness of his stance. As he steadied her, she wiped her eyes with her sleeve and became aware of his body shielding her from the current. She had no business noticing him in a personal way. She was merely an employee, a woman who was afraid of horses and had fallen in the river.

She pulled back from his grasp and staggered away. "I'm all right."

He splashed closer, reaching for her. "Let me walk you to the shore."

"No!" She didn't want to feel his arm around her waist. "Go take care of your horse."

"Jon has Cairo."

She looked past him to the shore where Jon and Grandma were leading Cairo up the sandy bank. The black horse had calmed, but he still looked on edge… much like the major. He stepped closer to her, his hand extended as if he were giving her a peppermint. "Come now," he said with authority. "There's nothing to be afraid of."

"Oh, yes there is!" She was afraid of *him,* afraid of her feelings because she couldn't help but appreciate the nobility of what he had done. With malaria symptoms, he had no business jumping into the river to help her. He should have taken his horse to shore and let Jon come to her rescue. Instead he'd risked getting a chill. Even more revealing was the compassion in his eyes. He looked both sincere and commanding, a man of courage who understood fear. She could imagine soldiers following him into battle, trusting him to lead them to victory.

She wanted to trust him, too. It had been so long since she'd had a man in her life that she could rely on. Charles had died seven years ago. After losing him, she'd become a pariah and no man had wanted her. It had been Bessie's idea to move to Denver. There they'd found Swan's Nest, a boardinghouse for women in need, and Caroline had found the faith to love again but not a man to love. She'd continually failed to measure up, though her friends had all found husbands.

Adie Clarke had married Joshua Blue, an unlikely but wonderfully happy match between a woman with a secret and a minister with regrets. Pearl Oliver had found a husband in Matt Wiley. A victim of violence, Pearl had married a lawman dedicated to justice and his little girl. And then there was Mary Larue. Two months ago she'd married outlaw J. T. Quinn, a man from her past whom she'd loved for years.

Caroline didn't begrudge her friends their happiness, but she very much wanted a family of her own. She wanted to belong somewhere, anywhere. That was what she'd hoped to find when she'd answered the major's advertisement. But now she wondered if she'd made a mistake. If she was *still* making a mistake, trusting too soon, believing she could rely on the major. In Denver she'd been safe. Since leaving Swan's Nest, she'd been robbed and nearly drowned. God had let her down, and so had Major Smith when his horse reared. She glared at him. "I thought no one disobeyed you, not even your horse!"

"Cairo startled—"

"He bucked me off!"

"Yes," the major said gently. "He became tangled in a branch and startled."

That voice… He could have gentled the wildest of creatures with that tone, the singsong of his accent. Suddenly she wanted to cry. She didn't blame the major for Cairo getting spooked, but neither would she forget that she'd fallen. She'd trusted him and suffered for it. Not only could she have drowned, but also he might have been harmed trying to save her.

"Accidents happen," she said bitterly. "I'm well aware of that."

"Yes," he said. "I apologize again. If you'll allow me to walk you to the shore, we'll rest for a bit while you dry off."

She didn't want to rest only to struggle through a long, tiring journey when the rest was over. She wanted to be safe and dry in a home of her own. She wanted an ordinary life in a place where she belonged. But she couldn't have any of that. She only had herself. Ignoring his offered hand, she met his gaze. "Thank you, Major. But I can manage."

She gathered her wet skirts and trudged to the shore, walking slightly upriver and feeling the tug of the current. He came up beside her but didn't speak. After she'd gone twenty paces, each more draining than the last, he looped his arm around her waist. She felt secure. She felt protected. And she was madder than a wet hen that she wanted to be more than a governess, more than an employee and a woman who'd fallen in the river.

As they slogged through the current, Major Smith acknowledged Jon with a reassuring wave. Mounted on Grandma, Jon recrossed the river to fetch Bessie and the packhorses, leaving Caroline and the major to make their way to the shore. When they reached the bank, he stepped away from her. Except for Cairo tied to a willow, they were alone. Caroline shivered with the chill. As soon as Jon brought the packhorses, she'd put on dry clothes.

With his back to her, Major Smith opened the medical bag to check the quinine. She thought of the picture of Charles. He'd see it. Good, she thought. If he had questions, he could ask. If he had prejudices, she wanted to know it.

"Is the quinine safe?" she asked.

"Yes." He looked deeper in the case. "Your photograph is unharmed, as well."

Would he ask who was in the picture? Did he expect her to give details that were none of his business? When he turned and looked into her eyes, she felt like a private in the presence of a general, but she refused either to cower or snap to attention.

Major Smith spoke first. "I was an officer in the West India Regiment. Have you heard of it?"

"No, sir."

"The West India Regiment is part of the regular British Army. It's led by men like myself, sons of England—" he said *England* as if it tasted bad "—but the soldiers are locals from the Caribbean Islands. They're free black men, Miss Bradley. I don't know who the gentlemen in your photograph is or what he means to you, but I presume he is—or was—someone important to you."

She'd been expecting rejection, prejudice. Instead she'd found another reason to like Major Smith. Wondering if the day could get any worse, she looked into his eyes and saw a loyalty that stole her breath, leading her to open her heart. "Charles was my husband. He died seven years ago."

"I'm very sorry."

"He was lynched," she said before she could stop herself. "It was ugly and violent, and I saw it happen. That's why I'm afraid of horses. The men who did it put him on a broken-down nag. Someone told me later they didn't intend to kill Charles. They just wanted to scare him." Her voice dropped to a hush. "They wanted to scare me, too. But the horse went wild. It bucked and Charles...died."

Major Smith held her gaze. "I've seen men die. It changes a person."

"Yes."

"And I've lost my wife," he added. "That changes a man, as well."

Caroline nodded because she truly understood. "I'm sorry for your loss, Major Smith."

"Likewise, Caroline."

He'd left off the "Miss," a fitting acknowledgment of the new accord between them. He also pronounced her name Caro-*line*. Most people called her Caro-*lyn*. It made her feel different from the woman she'd always been.

They looked at each other a long time, then both turned away to remember or think. Caroline was surprised at the sudden sense of kinship she felt with this man who had seemed at first to be so brusque and domineering. There was a kindness to him she hadn't expected. It was enough to make her hope that this journey hadn't been a mistake. Perhaps she truly had found a place where she could belong.

Still, she wouldn't get her hopes up yet. She knew too well how badly it would hurt if they were dashed once more.

To her relief, Jon arrived with Bessie and the packhorses. Her sister slid off the mare, ran to Caroline and hugged her. "You could have drowned."

"Or been trampled," she added.

"Let's get you in dry clothes," Bessie said firmly. "Then you can put the scare out of your mind."

Caroline agreed about needing dry clothes, but she doubted today's ordeal would ever leave her thoughts. Somewhere between one side of the river and the other, she'd seen a new side of a man with whom she had believed she had nothing in common, a man from another class and another continent…a man who might finally be able to give her a home. It was a heady and frightening thought. Shivering, she went with Bessie to find a private spot to change. It was a long way to Wheeler Springs. She dreaded getting back on a horse, but she'd be fine with Bessie and Grandma. As for Major Smith and Cairo, the horse scared her and so did the man.

When the women were out of sight, Tristan thought of his own wet clothes. He was soaked to his thighs, but the sun and constant wind would dry the fabric. Feverish or not, he was more concerned about getting Caroline to Wheeler Springs without another incident. She'd most likely want to ride with her sister on Grandma, but Tristan had experience with both fear and horses. Fear had to be faced, and horses had to be controlled. Caroline had to get back on Cairo or her fear would fester. It had nothing to do with any wish on his part to keep the lady close, of course. No, he was convinced it was simply the logical response any employer might have toward a phobia on the part of a brave, stubborn, lovely employee. Turning to Jon, he saw his friend retying the bundle of clothing. "Caroline's badly shaken," he said. "But she needs to ride with me, at least for a time."

"I suppose so," Jon agreed.

"Of all the fool things," Tristan muttered. "Cairo's good in water. That branch came out of nowhere."

"We almost had two women in the river." Jon's brows lifted with admiration. "I had to stop her sister from going in after her."

"I hadn't noticed."

"I did." Jon's lips tipped into a smile. "You're a good judge of character, Tristan. The Bradleys are exceptional women. I expected the nurse to be a dour sort, but she's quite pleasant."

Tristan thought about his plan to match his friend with Caroline. Jon and Bessie were closer in age and possibly in temperament. The nurse would make a fine substitute mother, but he wanted his children to have someone young and spirited, someone more like Molly...someone with the courage to buck convention. Molly had done it when she'd defied her family and joined him in the West Indies. Caroline had done it when she'd married a black man.

Normally reticent, Tristan wouldn't have mentioned the photograph but he'd been surprised. He'd also been impressed by the defiant tilt of her chin. She was exactly the kind of mother he wanted for his children. If not for the malaria, he'd have been looking forward to riding with her on Cairo. Instead he found himself glaring at Jon.

His friend shot him a concerned glance. "You're looking rather dour, yourself. Are you feeling ill?"

"I'm fine."

"You're always *fine*," Jon said, mocking him. "If you're not up to ferrying a frightened woman, I'm sure the Bradleys would do well on Grandma."

Common sense told Tristan to agree. Male pride made him frown at Jon. "If the day comes that I can't handle a horse, I'll be ready for the grave."

"I didn't mean the horse," Jon said rather cheekily. "I meant the woman."

Tristan glared at him.

"You seem to be getting along quite well," Jon said too casually. "She's quite pretty, though of course you didn't notice."

Of course Tristan had noticed, but a man in poor health had no business courting a woman's affections. He was about to suggest Jon take Caroline on Grandma when the women approached from the bushes. Caroline had fashioned her hair into a braid and looped it around her head in a crown of sorts. The sun glinted off the dampness, giving it a sparkle. She'd put on an old calico, a gown he guessed to be comfortable and a favorite. She looked none the worse for wear. In fact, she looked lovely with flushed cheeks and a determined lift of her chin.

When the women reached the horses, she addressed him directly. "We're ready, Major."

"Yes, I see."

She turned to Grandma, where Jon was waiting to help Bessie into the saddle. His friend lifted a brow at Tristan, questioning him about the riding arrangements.

Tristan cleared his throat. "You'll be riding with me."

She faced him, her mouth slightly agape. "I don't think—"

"I do. We all know the adage about getting back up on a horse."

"And I will," she replied. "I'll ride Grandma with my sister."

Tristan put his hands behind his back, a pose he assumed to intimidate new privates. "May I be blunt?"

"Of course."

"Not only do I think it's wise for you to overcome your fear, I'm afraid I have a point to prove…to Cairo."

She wrinkled her brow. "Your horse's behavior isn't my concern. My safety is."

"Which leads to my second point." His tone stayed firm. "I'd like a chance to prove that Cairo isn't as dangerous as you've assumed. It's rather important, really. If you're to be living on a ranch, you need to be comfortable around animals."

"I don't mind animals," she replied. "But your horse—"

"He reacted to a fright," Tristan answered. "Surely you can understand. He'd like a chance to redeem himself." Tristan didn't want to admit it, but he had the same need. He glanced at Jon for help and saw a bemused look on his friend's face and then a twinkle in his eyes. Looking roguish, Jon addressed Caroline. "I can attest to the major's abilities as a horseman."

She glanced at her sister. Bessie gave a little shrug. "It's up to you."

Pale, Caroline turned back to him. "I don't think—"

"I do," he said gently. "The river is tricky for a horse. The road to town isn't."

She looked at him for several seconds. What she was gauging, he didn't know. Was it his ability, or her own courage? In the end, she walked in his direction. "I suppose you're right. I'll go with you on Cairo."

"Very good." Why he was so pleased, Tristan couldn't say. Neither did he know why he shot Jon a triumphant look, the kind they'd shared before he'd settled down with Molly, when they'd been young lieutenants and full of themselves.

As Caroline approached Cairo, Jon helped Bessie climb on Grandma, then mounted the packhorse. Tristan mounted Cairo, took his boot out of the stirrup and held out his hand. Without a rock to stand on, she had to leap and stretch, which is just what she did. She held his waist like before, but without the cinchlike grip. In silence he turned Cairo and headed down the road at a walk.

Clop. Clop. Clop.

She sighed.

Clop. Clop. Clop.

Tristan looked over his shoulder. "How are you doing?"

"Fine."

She sighed again. He said nothing. After a mile, she spoke over his shoulder. "Major Smith?"

"Yes?"

"How long will it take us to get to Wheeler Springs?"

"At this pace, about three days." When she laughed, he thought of lively piano music and the celebrations after battle. It felt good to know he'd restored her humor. Encouraged, he spoke over his shoulder. "Do you think you can handle going a little faster?"

She hesitated. "I suppose so. I'm eager to get to town."

"So am I," he replied. "I'm going to give Cairo a nudge. If you feel at all uncomfortable, just say so."

"Set the pace, Major."

When he urged Cairo into a slow jog, Caroline tightened her grip on his waist to keep from bouncing. He was tempted to ask if she wanted to go faster, but if she agreed then he knew she'd hold on tighter. He needed to keep her at arm's length the way an officer lived apart from enlisted men. That's how he'd think of Caroline Bradley...as a private in his personal army. Or maybe a sergeant because she'd be raising his children. With that thought in mind, Tristan rode with the pretty governess in resolute silence.

Chapter Five

Caroline couldn't fault the major's logic about having her ride with him on Cairo, but she felt like a sack of potatoes, one in danger of sliding to the ground and splitting open. With her arms belted around his waist, she heard every beat of Cairo's hooves. She distracted herself with questions about the man before her. Why had he come to America instead of returning to England? What had his wife been like? And the malaria… How did he cope with the fevers? And what provisions had he made for his children?

Unable to stand the silence, she decided the children were a safe subject and surrendered to curiosity. "Major Smith?"

"Yes?"

"I'd like to hear about Freddie and Dora."

He hesitated. "You already know their names and ages."

"Yes, but I'd like to know *about* them. What do they like to do?"

"They're children, Miss Bradley. They entertain themselves."

Miss Bradley made it clear his earlier kindness was

to be forgotten. It annoyed her but not nearly as much as his refusal to talk about his children. He seemed cold again, even austere. Having lost their mother, Freddie and Dora needed their father's attention, and if his current behavior was any indication, he seemed unwilling to give it. If *she'd* been blessed with children, she'd have cherished every smile, every new adventure.

She rode with the major in silence, staring straight ahead until they reached the livery stable marking the beginning of Wheeler Springs. A row of buildings included a barber and bathhouse, a dress shop and a mercantile with its doors propped open. The shopkeeper stepped outside with a broom. Seeing their arrival, he waved a greeting.

Major Smith answered with a nod, a gesture that reminded Caroline of a returning soldier in a parade.

Across the street she saw a café with yellow curtains, and she thought of the wonderful food at the café run by Mary Larue, now Mary Quinn. At her wedding, Mary had placed her bouquet firmly in Caroline's arms, a gesture Caroline knew to be futile. For whatever reason, God had said no to her prayers for a family of her own. Instead He'd brought her to Wheeler Springs to love the Smith children, a cause she intended to embrace.

Halfway through town, the major turned Cairo down a road that led to a three-story house with paned glass windows, a wide porch and a cupola. Square and painted white with green trim, it reminded her of the houses in Charleston.

"Where are we?" she asked the major.

"My town house. We'll leave for The Barracks in the morning."

Once broken, the silence between them felt sharper than ever. Where was the man who'd helped her out of

the river? The one who gave peppermint to his horse?
The closer they rode to the house, the more rigid the
major became until she felt as if she were holding on to
a lamppost. They were still several paces away when
the front door burst open and a little girl came charging
across the porch. Dark hair framed her face and accented
her rosy cheeks.

"Daddy!" she cried.

The major heaved an impatient sigh. "I gave orders
for the children to stay at The Barracks."

The thought of children being *ordered* to stay away
from their father struck her as heinous. Why would he do
such a thing? She wanted to take him to task, but she was
in no position to initiate such a conversation…at least not
yet. She settled for a calm observation. "Dora is lovely."

He said nothing.

"You must be very proud of her."

"I suppose."

Appalled by his apparent indifference and moved by
Dora's obvious need, Caroline tried again. "Does she like
to play with dolls?"

He said nothing, though he hadn't looked away from
his little girl. Did he know what a gift he had in this precious child? Caroline wanted to lecture him, to warn him
that such gifts could be snatched in a blink, but then she
realized that he knew it. Major Smith was afraid to love
his children because he was afraid of dying and leaving
them to grieve.

Caroline watched over his shoulder as a boy with the
major's blond hair and stiff posture joined his sister at the
top of the two steps connecting the porch to the ground.
"That must be Freddie," she said more to herself than the
major. "He's a handsome lad, isn't he?"

Major Smith reined Cairo to a halt. "You should be

aware, Miss Bradley, that I expect orders to be followed. And I left specific instructions for the children to remain at the ranch."

She couldn't resist a bit of defiance. "Apparently not everyone obeys you, at least not when children miss their father."

Without turning or twitching, the major spoke in a tone just for her. "Courage becomes you, Miss Bradley. Rudeness does not. I suggest you mind your own affairs and leave me to mine."

He'd snubbed her, rightfully so, considering her position in his household. Stranded on his horse, she wanted to escape his nearness but feared sliding off and ending up in a heap. She settled for releasing her grip on the major's waist and looking for Jon. He rode up next to them, swung off the packhorse and helped her down with a gentleman's ease.

"There you go," he said in a friendly tone.

"Thank you."

Bessie halted Grandma next to the packhorse. After Jon helped her sister dismount, Caroline asked him to retrieve a small bundle from their possessions. It held gifts for the children and she wanted to present them now. Assuming Major Smith would introduce her, she waited while he tied the reins to the hitching post.

She turned her attention to the children. Dora's eyes were wide with curiosity. Freddie reminded her of his father, both in looks and in temperament. He had a stoic expression, a sign he'd learned sadness and loss too young. Dora needed a smile and a hug. Freddie needed to know she'd respect his quiet nature. Already Caroline felt challenged by the differences in the children.

Major Smith indicated she should step forward. For the first time since leaving the river, she had a clear view of his face. Creases fanned from his blue eyes, deeper and more numerous than she'd seen this morning. The line of his mouth pitched downward in a frown, or maybe it was a grimace against exhaustion. He wasn't a well man, and the trip to the stagecoach had cost him. Compassion tempered the frustration she'd felt toward him moments ago.

She came forward as he'd indicated, watching the children for their reactions. Freddie snapped to attention. Dora leaned against her brother and acted shy. Caroline was glad she'd brought the doll. Little Dora desperately needed something to hug.

The major spoke in a firm voice. "Good afternoon, children."

"Good afternoon, Father," Freddie answered.

Dora hid her face against her brother.

"Come forward, please," the major said. "I'd like you to meet Miss Caroline Bradley, your new governess."

Freddie took Dora's hand and guided her forward. The protective gesture touched Caroline to the core and reminded her of how the major had gently guided her out of the river. His cold attitude to the children hadn't always been a wall between them. She suspected that losing his wife and facing an illness had changed him.

When the children reached the ground, they stopped four feet in front of her. Freddie looked up at his father, a soldier ready to take orders. Dora looked at her toes, a little girl who didn't know what to do. Aching for her, Caroline stepped forward and dropped to a crouch so she could look into the child's eyes. They were blue like her father's and no less haunted. A harrumph told her she'd crossed the major, but she didn't care. *He* could be cold and distant if he wanted, but Caroline had no such inclination.

She smiled at the shy little girl. "You must be Dora."

Still looking down, the child nodded.

"That's a pretty name," Caroline said gently. "And you're wearing such a pretty dress. I bet you like to play with dolls."

Her head bobbed up and she nodded.

"Good," Caroline declared. "So do I."

The major spoke to her back. "Miss Caroline, I don't think—"

"I do." Ignoring him, she opened the drawstring bag and gave Dora the doll. "I made this for you."

The major's voice boomed behind her. *"Miss Bradley!"*

He sounded ready to court-martial her, but she had to give the book to Freddie the way she'd given the doll to Dora. She took the volume from the bag, stood tall and handed it to the boy. "This is for you, Freddie."

The major had said little about the boy's interests, so she'd taken advice from Mary Quinn's young brother and selected a science book with easy experiments. "We can use kitchen items to make a volcano. That should be fun."

Freddie's eyes lit up, but he looked to his father for direction.

Not wanting the boy to be a pawn, Caroline faced the major. She recalled how he'd ignored her when she'd wanted to tell him about the quinine. It went against her nature to be rude, so she gave him a wistful smile. "Forgive me, Major Smith. I was just so excited to meet your children. I'm sure you understand."

She'd meant to bridge the gap between the major and Freddie and Dora. Instead she felt as if she were in the middle of the river again, only this time Major Smith needed to be led to shore. He looked both stunned and bitter about his poor health. Caroline couldn't abide his attitude toward Freddie and Dora, but neither would she do him the dishonor of being blunt. His children were present, and Bessie and Jon were watching them with more than idle curiosity.

She softened the moment with a winsome smile. "I *do* apologize, Major Smith. With your permission, I'd like to speak to Dora and Freddie for a just another moment."

He made a sweeping motion with his arm. "By all means, Miss Bradley. Speak as long as you'd like. Take all afternoon…take all night."

Ignoring the sarcasm, she crouched next to Dora. "I thought we could name your new doll together."

Dora's bottom lip pushed into a pout, trembling until she finally spoke. "I want to name her Molly."

Freddie elbowed his sister. "You can't!"

"Why not?" Dora whined back.

"Because that was *Mama's* name."

The boy had the cold tone of an undertaker, but Caroline wasn't fooled. He'd built a wall to protect his bruised heart. Dora's innocent attempt to keep her mother's memory alive hit the wall like a battering ram. Behind her the major inhaled deeply, a sign he wasn't as indifferent to his children as he wanted to appear. Hoping to smooth the waters, she touched Dora's shoulder. "Molly's a fine name. It would honor your mother, but we need to consider your father and Freddie, too. We can give the doll two names, a special middle name and one for everyday."

"Do you have two names?" Dora asked.

"I do," Caroline answered. "I'm Caroline Margaret Bradley. Margaret is after my grandmother."

Dora looked at her father. "What's my other name?"

A five-year-old shouldn't have needed to ask that question. She should have been loved and schooled in family memories. When the major hesitated, she wondered if he knew the answer.

He finally cleared his throat. "Your full name is The-odora Constance Smith. Constance was your mother's sister."

Dora's eyes got wide. "I can't write all that!"

Caroline took the child's hand and squeezed. "I'll teach you."

Standing, she turned to Freddie. The boy's expression was strained, a mirror image of his father. She'd have to work to win him over, but she firmly believed God had brought her to this family for a purpose. Not only did the children need a mother, but they also needed a father who wasn't afraid to love them.

She motioned for Bessie to come forward. "This is my sister, Miss Elizabeth Bradley. You can call her Miss Bessie." Hoping to earn Freddie's interest, Caroline spoke to him directly. "She was a nurse in the war."

Freddie tried to seem bored, but his brows lifted with curiosity. Bessie greeted the boy, then said hello to Dora. Both children enjoyed the attention.

Caroline thought the first meeting went well. She turned to express her pleasure to Major Smith and saw a frown creasing the corners of his mouth. He dismissed the children with a terse order to go back inside, instructed Jon to report their arrival to the stage office, then motioned for Caroline and Bessie to enter the house. In the entry hall she saw a tall black man. When he broke into a smile, she thought of Charles.

"Good evening, Miss Bradley." He greeted her with a slight bow. "Welcome to Wheeler Springs."

Major Smith stood to the side. "Ladies, this is Sergeant Noah Taylor. Noah, I'd like you to meet the Bradley sisters, Miss Bessie and Miss Caroline."

She and this man were peers and equals, employees

of the major. Caroline extended her hand. "Please call me Caroline."

"Yes, Caroline."

He greeted Bessie with equal aplomb. Behind him a black woman emerged from the kitchen. Tall and graceful, she looked at Major Smith with a mix of dignity and frustration. "Good afternoon, sir."

Major Smith answered with a nod. "Ladies, this is Evaline. She's Noah's wife and will show you to your rooms."

"Yes, sir," she said. "But first I must apologize."

He raised one eyebrow. "Does this have something to do with my children being here?"

The woman dipped her chin. "I know you left orders to keep them at The Barracks, but they were lonely for you."

Caroline loved Evaline on the spot. She'd risked a scolding to do right by the children. The major claimed no one disobeyed him, but his housekeeper had the freedom to follow her conscience. The major gave orders, but he wasn't unreasonable. Deep down, he cared about people. It showed, if one knew where to look.

Looking wry, he traded a look with Noah. "I seem to have lost all authority."

The man grinned. "No, sir. Just with Evaline."

The major harrumphed but made no effort to scold the woman. Instead he seemed to forget all about the transgression. "See to it the Bradley women have bathwater and whatever else they need." He turned back to Caroline. "Supper will be served at seven o'clock. The children will be present."

"Yes, sir," she answered.

Evaline indicated the stairs. "This way, ladies."

The housekeeper led the way with Bessie behind her and Caroline bringing up the rear. When she reached the landing, she looked down. At the same instant, the major looked up. Their gazes locked in a test of wills. She'd defied him when she'd spoken to the children, and he'd let her. Neither had he chastised Evaline. The major conducted himself with acerbic authority, but his final decisions showed respect, even a deep caring, for his friends and family. Why would he be so cold on the outside when he plainly loved Freddie and Dora?

They looked away from each other at the same time. Silent but determined to bring joy to this troubled household, she followed Evaline and Bessie up the stairs.

It was a sad day when a man's housekeeper disobeyed him and he let her. It was an even sadder day when he couldn't control the governess, or even his own children. Wondering why he bothered to issue orders at all, Tristan went to his study, shut the door and dropped down in the leather chair. It squeaked, yet another act of defiance against his desire for quiet.

He couldn't be angry with Evaline. He'd been happier to see Freddie and Dora than he could admit. But he'd held true to his resolve to keep his distance. With the malaria threatening his life, he had to stay strong for them. They had to learn they could live without him. The decision had seemed wise until Caroline skewered him by giving Dora the doll. He'd known how much his daughter missed her mother, but he hadn't realized how alone he'd left his children. It took discipline to stay strong for them, but that's what a father did…what an officer did. When everyone else succumbed to tears and flashes of temper, an officer kept his wits about him.

At the moment Tristan's wits were in tatters. He needed another dose of quinine, but he hadn't taken the bottles from Bessie's medicine bag because he'd been dis-

tracted by the children. Neither did he have easy access
to the small supply he'd brought from The Barracks. It
was upstairs in his bedroom, and he didn't want to pass
his houseguests in the hall. He'd wait, but only for a bit.

To fortify himself, he picked up the letter that had been
delivered before he'd left. Pennwright's neat script was
badly smudged, but he expected the man's dry humor
would be intact. He sliced the envelope with an opener,
removed a single sheet and began to read.

Dear Tristan,
I'm writing to you with a heavy heart. Both of your
brothers are dead.

Tristan read the opening words again, then a second
time. As the ramifications sunk in, his insides shook the
way they did before weapons were drawn for battle. The
shaking signaled danger and the loss of life…his life…
the life in Wyoming he wanted for his children. With his
brothers dead, he'd become his father's heir and the next
duke of Willoughby. The clock in the entry gonged six
times, a death knell to accent Pennwright's perfect script.

As if surveying a battle report, he took in the rest of
the letter. Andrew had died of cholera, and he'd left no
sons or daughters. Tristan immediately thought of his
widow, Louisa, alone and grieving without even children to comfort her. She'd broken his heart when she'd
married his brother, but he held no bitterness. He only
wondered why she jilted him and if somehow he'd failed
her. Oscar had died a week after Andrew. Pennwright's
explanation chilled Tristan to the bone.

He died from a gunshot to the head. Your father is
calling it a hunting accident.

Tristan knew his brother well enough to read between the lines. Oscar had called hunting the sport of fools. He didn't like horses, exercise or perspiration. With a heavy heart, Tristan acknowledged what hadn't been written. Oscar's "hunting" accident had likely been suicide. Tristan viewed the deed as cowardice, but he understood why Oscar had done it. A man of little discipline, he'd have become the duke's whipping boy.

Pennwright's next words carried no surprise, but they jarred him nonetheless.

You, Tristan, are now heir to your father's title and holdings. He wishes you to return to England immediately to assume your duties.

If Tristan had been healthy, he might have gloated at the irony. The son his father had dismissed as worthless now had value to him. But Tristan wasn't well… Chances were good his father would outlive him, and Freddie would fall under the man's influence. The thought chilled Tristan to the bone.

The duke could issue whatever orders he pleased, but Tristan wouldn't snap mindlessly to attention. He had to protect his son. The duke had turned Andrew into a pampered poodle and Oscar into an alley cat. Tristan refused to be paraded like a pet, nor would he allow Freddie to be turned into Andrew or Oscar.

In the same breath, he recognized the profound responsibility of being a duke. He'd been born a third son, but he'd become a leader of men. By blood and British law, he had a duty to the people of Willoughby and wanted to fulfill his obligation with honor.

But he was also a father and he had to protect his son. Tristan was the only defense between Freddie and the duke. He refused to allow his son to be used and manipulated. Dora would suffer, too. His daughter would be valued solely for her worth as a future wife, not for the charming little girl she was. As long as Tristan and his father were both alive, he had time to come up with a strategy. There was no need to rush back to England, at least not yet.

Weary to the bone, he left Pennwright's letter on the desk and headed to his room. After supper he'd speak to Jon about ways to protect Freddie. Tristan was a good strategist, but Jon had a more creative mind. First, though, he needed quinine.

He entered his suite and shut the door with a click. He took the dose of medicine, then washed his hands and changed into attire befitting a meal with the new governess and her sister. The women would talk throughout supper and so would his children. Jon would be charming, and Tristan would be stoic. With a bittersweet longing to be well again, he headed for the dining room, wearing the stiff upper lip he was so very tired of maintaining.

Chapter Six

Caroline had never had a better-tasting meal in her life…or a more awkward one. She was sitting to the right of Major Smith and across from Bessie. Jon was next to her sister, and Freddie was next to Jon. Little Dora sat in a child's chair to Caroline's right.

The instant she sat, Caroline had been determined to bring an air of cheerfulness to the meal. Jon and Bessie had been willing participants in the banter, but the major ignored everything except the food on his plate. He could have been eating in separate quarters, which she suspected he'd have preferred to Jon's joking and the laughter of his children. How could he not smile at Dora's face as she tasted the raspberry tart Evaline had made for dessert? Did he know Freddie imitated his every mannerism? Someone needed to open his eyes to the love he was denying his children. She wouldn't do it tonight. His skin had the pallor of exhaustion, and he'd eaten more lightly than she would have expected. She couldn't help but worry about him.

Unexpectedly Noah appeared in the doorway to the dining room. "Sir?"

"Yes, Noah?"

"I apologize for interrupting, but a courier delivered this letter." He handed the envelope to the major. "He won't leave until you reply."

"That's odd," Jon said for them all.

Attempting to be nonchalant, the major opened the letter and began to read. His eyes flicked to the bottom of the page, then back to the top. As he read, his face turned into stone. Caroline glanced at Jon for a hint of understanding and saw his mouth tighten with apprehension.

Freddie broke the silence. "What does it say, Father?"

"It doesn't concern you." He stood abruptly and headed for the door, the letter dangling from his fingers.

Dora called after him. "Daddy! What's wrong?"

If he heard the child, he'd chosen to ignore her. And if he hadn't, he should have. These children had lost their mother and lived in a fragile world, one that could be easily shattered by their father's thoughtless behavior. Caroline put her napkin on the table and stood. She looked first at Dora. "I'm going to talk to your father, okay? I'll find out what's wrong."

Dora nodded too quickly.

Caroline looked at Freddie and saw criticism but spoke anyway. "I'll be back in a few minutes."

"You shouldn't go," the boy said coldly. "He won't like it."

Caroline ached for him. He was trying to earn his father's love through rigid obedience. It wouldn't work. The person who had to change wasn't Freddie. It was the major, and she intended to confront him. No matter what the letter said, he should have given his children more consideration.

After a glance at Bessie and a nod from Jon, she went to the entry hall. She saw Noah and the major speaking to a man she didn't recognize. No voices were raised, but she felt the tension as plainly as the sun on a hot day. Ducking into a room off the hall, she watched as the courier left. The major told Noah he needed air and went out the door. When Noah went back to the dining room, Caroline followed the major.

Tristan made a beeline for the carriage house. He needed to think about the contents of the letter still loose in his hand, and he wanted to be alone while he did it… or at least away from inquisitive women and little girls eating raspberry tarts, away from Jon who'd read his expression too easily and Freddie who'd forgotten how to laugh. Cairo was all the company he could stand in light of the news he'd just received. His father was in Cheyenne. He'd ordered Tristan to send two carriages—one for himself and his traveling companion and the other for his staff. He didn't name his companion, and Tristan hadn't quizzed the courier. It would be just like his father to travel with a mistress. Needing time to think, he had sent the courier back to the hotel with instructions to wait for a reply in the morning.

What Tristan would do he didn't know. But he'd learned to think before taking action, to make a battle plan before firing off a shot that would lead to a war he couldn't win. The war with his father was one he couldn't lose.

Stepping into the carriage house, he lit a lantern and read the man's demands a second time.

Perhaps you did not receive Pennwright's letter. I can think of no other reason for your lack of attention to your duties now that your brothers are dead. As the heir apparent, you are now the Marquess of Hayvenhurst, and I have come to escort

you home to England. Send two carriages to the
Dryer Hotel. I expect them immediately.

I am traveling with a female companion, some-
one who may surprise you.
Harold Smythe, Duke of Willoughby
P.S. I understand from Pennwright that I have a
grandson. I look forward to making his acquain-
tance.

The mention of Freddie sent ripples of anxiety from
Tristan's spine to his fingertips. He'd written proudly to
Pennwright about his children. Not once had he imagined
his father would show an interest, but the duke had apparently quizzed the secretary. Now Freddie had value.
So did Tristan, and he found the equation disgusting. He
paced down the row of stalls, pivoted and paced back to
the door.

It opened a crack and he stopped. Female fingers
curved on the wood, pushing slightly so that the hinges
creaked and the opening let in a draft of air. Caroline
slipped into the circle of light by the door. He'd had
enough of employees ignoring his orders, enough of *her.*
All through supper she'd prodded him to engage his children in small talk, an activity he found painful in Molly's
absence. He'd hired her to take care of his children, and
he expected her to do her job.

"*What* are you doing here?" he demanded.

Cairo added his support by snorting.

Miss Bradley startled but didn't retreat. Whatever she
wanted to say, she felt strongly enough to venture into a
barn populated by horses.

"We need to speak about the children," she said.

"Not now."

"Sir, they're frightened." She moistened her lips, a gesture he found oddly distracting. "The way you left—"

"I had business."

"But they don't understand," she said patiently. "When a child loses a parent, the world becomes a dangerous place."

"Miss Bradley!" Her name exploded from his lips. "Do you think for *one moment* that I *don't care* about my children? Do you think you know them better than I do? Do you think you have the *right* to come out here and tell me that my children are upset because their mother is dead? Do you think I don't *know* that?"

She went pale.

"You have no such right!" Tristan waved the letter. "You have no idea what is about to befall this entire family!"

Her eyes glistened with genuine worry. "What happened?"

Tristan fought for a modicum of self-control. Not once in his years as an officer had he lost his temper. He considered the lack of decorum a weakness. Tonight he'd shamed himself. "It's none of your concern."

"I'd be glad to listen."

"No!"

She stood unmoving, staring with those hazel eyes that offered a comfort he couldn't accept.

"Tend to the children," he ordered. "It's their bedtime."

Instead of executing an about-face, she took a step closer. "I really am a good listener."

"I beg to disagree," he said in a superior tone. "If you were a good listener, you'd be walking back to the house instead of pestering me."

She stopped two feet away from him, a picture of womanhood in a russet-colored gown that matched the autumn hue of her irises. She'd put up her hair in a coif of loose curls, and her jaw had the strength of polished ivory. She looked determined and resolute but not cold or hard. Instead, she seemed to radiate sympathy and concern for him and his family. This woman had a heart for children. Judging by her first marriage, she cared about the downtrodden and needy. Tristan didn't like being on that list, but he knew she saw him in that light because of the malaria.

She looked calmly into his eyes. "I'll go, Major. But I'd be obliged if you'd do me one small favor."

He wanted to bark an order, but her gentleness held his temper captive. "What do you want?"

"Say goodnight to your children."

As simple as it was, the request tore at his gut. Molly had been the one to read to the children and listen to their prayers. She had also prayed for *him*... He'd prayed for her, but his words had been perfunctory until the end, when he'd begged God for mercies that hadn't been given. Tristan hadn't been surprised. God and the Duke of Willoughby had a lot in common. They both issued commands without feeling. Tristan had feelings, strong ones, but he didn't quite know what to do with them when it came to Freddie and Dora. With death breathing over him, he feared they'd suffer more if he loved them without drawing lines. Memories brought comfort, but they also caused pain. Even so, Molly would have been frustrated with how he'd been acting. She'd have been as concerned as Caroline, and she'd have been cheering for the governess.

"All right," he agreed. "I'll be in shortly."

The smile on her face couldn't have been more lovely. The light encircled her within a gentle glow, and he wondered what he might have done if he'd been a well man.

Molly had been clear. *Don't grieve too long, darling. I want our children to have a new mother.* Now he lived on the brink of death himself and understood the clawing need to provide a family for Freddie and Dora. He also knew the depths of grief and the coldness of an empty bed. If he ever loved again, it would be in the distant future when the disease had been beaten and he could live a normal life.

He was staring at Caroline—admiringly, though he hoped he looked stern—when Jon walked into the carriage house. His eyes went first to the governess, then to Tristan. Surprise registered, then concern. "What's going on?"

Tristan strode to Jon, handed him the letter and aimed a look at Caroline, silently ordering her to leave. Good manners must have trumped her curiosity because she headed for the door.

"Wait," Jon said to her, indicating the letter. "You should know about this."

Didn't *anyone* follow his orders? Tristan glared at Jon. "It doesn't involve her."

"I beg to differ," he said mildly. "If your father's going to show up at The Barracks, it will be *everyone's* business. Whether you like it or not, Tristan, you're the next Duke of Willoughby. You're also ill, which makes Freddie the heir presumptive."

Caroline's eyes turned into saucers. "You're a *duke?*"

"No!" he shouted.

"Technically, he's a marquess, or maybe an earl." Jon looked at Caroline with understanding. "As an American, you're probably not familiar with the British nobility. As the heir apparent, Tristan will use one of his father's lesser titles, a courtesy title if you will. His father is Harold Smythe, the Duke of Willoughby."

Caroline stared at him in disbelief. "I had no idea you were a duke!"

"I'm not," Tristan retorted. "And when I advertised for a governess, I wasn't heir apparent. My ties to England weren't important."

"They are now." Jon faced Caroline. "Tristan isn't fond of his father. It's his story to tell, but he left England to get away from his family. Because the duke had two elder sons remaining, he didn't interfere. But now that the major's brothers are dead, he is next in line. And after him, Freddie."

The poor woman looked torn between executing a curtsy and raising her chin in good old American defiance. She chose a middle road. "If you're a nobleman, should I still call you major?"

"Good grief!" Tristan erupted. "Of course, you should call me 'major.'" He glared at Jon. "Stay out of this. What's happened is no one's business but mine."

"If you believe that then you're a fool."

"Jon—"

"Be quiet, Tristan." He turned to Caroline. "The duke is a powerful man. He's also known to be pompous and prone to vices. He'll stop at nothing to get what he wants. If he learns Tristan is ill, he'll want Freddie."

Caroline turned to him with a quizzical look. "Is your father really that difficult?"

"Yes." He had no desire to elaborate.

She looked skeptical. "If I understand correctly, you haven't seen your father in years. Perhaps he has changed."

"He hasn't." Jon spoke for them both. "The duke belongs to a world you don't understand, and it has fixed his character in a way that makes him unfit to spend time with any child."

Tristan knew she'd push for answers. "I'm going to be blunt, Miss Bradley. My father has no time for anyone but himself. He turned my eldest brother into a weak man. My middle brother committed suicide rather than become his puppet. My father is critical and vain and a master of manipulation. As you know, my health is precarious. I do *not* want him influencing either of my children."

Jon broke in. "I have to agree with Tristan. The tone of the man's letter—plus Oscar's suicide—indicates he's as calculating as ever. In light of Tristan's illness, we have to protect the children."

Caroline gave Tristan a look of pity, then turned to Jon. "You both know better than I do. How can I help the major?"

When had Jon become the chief strategist? Tristan bristled. "I'm standing right here. I *do* have a say in all this."

"Of course," Jon acknowledged. "But you're too close to the problem. I can be objective. Does the duke know you're ill?"

Jon had a point. "Not to my knowledge."

"That's good," Jon said. "We have to keep him from suspecting you're in poor health."

The thought of his father discovering his weakness made Tristan sweat.

Caroline interrupted. "Bessie's a nurse. We'll have to explain her presence."

"That won't be hard," Jon explained. "She could have been hired for the children."

"What about people in town?" she asked. "Is it common knowledge Major Smith is ill?"

"I'm afraid it is," Tristan answered.

"Good point," Jon said to her, ignoring him yet again.

"We need to get the duke to The Barracks immediately. The staff won't talk."

Tristan hoped not. The men and women he employed were loyal to him, but the duke would be bringing his own servants. They'd be watching him. "I don't see how to keep the illness a secret. If the malaria strikes, he'll know it." He gave Jon a hard look. "If I die, what happens then?"

Jon spoke in a hush. "We hide the children."

"Where?" Tristan couldn't imagine a place where Freddie and Dora would be safe.

"America's a big country," Jon answered. "The duke is a man of great influence, but even *he's* no match for an entire continent."

Tristan had his doubts. Did Jon plan to keep moving with the children? How would he make a home for them?

Caroline interrupted. "I could take them to Denver. I have friends who'd help us."

Stunned by the offer, Tristan looked into her eyes. He didn't doubt her sincerity. She'd braved her fear of horses to come to the carriage house to scold him for the children's sake. He knew she truly wanted to help them and he trusted her. He wished he could have trusted his father, but like God, the duke cared nothing for individuals, only for his own purposes.

"It would work," Jon said to him. "The Bradley sisters are Americans. They can live anywhere and not be noticed. Even better, Caroline's the perfect age to be considered the children's real mother."

Tristan thought of Molly. For years she'd urged him to make peace with his father, but she hadn't known the depth of his tyranny. If she had, she'd have been begging Caroline to hide Freddie and Dora. Jon's plan had merit, but it also had pitfalls. Tristan saw an obvious one. "She can't just run off with the children. If my father were to find them, he'd accuse her of kidnapping."

"I agree," Jon said with gleam in his eyes. "That's why you need to marry her."

"*Marry* her?"

"*Marry* me?" she echoed.

"Don't look so shocked," Jon said, sounding impatient. "A marriage in name only would give Caroline legal standing. It's perfect, really. Even taking your name is a benefit. What could be more common than Caroline Smith?"

Tristan shook his head. "That's a ridiculous idea."

"Is it?" Jon asked.

"Of course." Tristan had an uncomfortable awareness of the woman standing by the door, listening to the vehemence in his rejection. He didn't want her to take the rebuff personally, so he faced her. "I apologize for Jon. As you can see, he's lost his mind."

"I don't think so." She spoke gently, but her eyes were blazing as she turned to Jon. "I'd like to speak to Major Smith in private."

"Certainly." Jon headed for the door without giving Tristan a glance.

So much for being in charge… He'd been abandoned by his second in command. Tristan had waged war and tamed wild stallions. He'd fought fevers and delirious dreams. Looking at Caroline, her heart brimming with concern for his children and her eyes wide and bright, he prepared to do battle with the most dangerous enemy of all—a well-intentioned female.

As soon the door creaked shut, she faced him. "I'm considering Jon's suggestion."

"But why?"

"I can see how worried you are. You'd do anything to stop your father."

"I would."

"And I know you love your children." She gave him a forthright look. "If you didn't, you wouldn't be considering what Jon suggested."

He felt as if she were spinning him in circles. "Who says I'm considering it?"

"*Are* you?"

Yes, but he refused to admit it. "I can't possibly ask you to be my wife."

"You didn't ask," she reminded him. "Jon did, and I'm inclined to agree with him. As he said, it's a legal arrangement, one that's only slightly different than being a governess. The difficulty lies in the future." She gave him a meaningful look. "If you recover, we'd have to stay married or attain an annulment. With the children—"

"An annulment would be complicated," he replied. "They'd be hurt."

"Yes." She squared her shoulders. "If you survive the malaria—which I believe you will—would you return to England?"

"Eventually, but I have some flexibility as long as my father's alive."

"I see." She bit her lip. "Your obligations complicate the situation. I'm obviously not capable of being a duchess—"

"That's irrelevant," he said sharply. "I'm far more worried about dying than I am about living."

If he died, she'd be hiding his children and a marriage in name only would protect them all. If he lived, he could stay in America as long as his father remained healthy. Even so, he didn't want Caroline to be locked into a marriage she didn't want. He kept his voice even. "I realize

going to England is above and beyond what you're prepared to offer. For that reason, among others, I'd insist
on maintaining the possibility of an annulment."

"Of course," she murmured.

An annulment would give Caroline a way out of the
marriage. The children had to be considered and their
immediate needs outweighed a hypothetical problem in
the future, but he still wanted to be sure that Caroline's
chance for future happiness was protected. If he died, an
annulment wouldn't be necessary. And if he lived, she
could be rid of him soon enough. He brushed the depress-
ing thought aside, but an equally disturbing one rose in
its place. He didn't take marriage lightly. If they took
vows, he'd keep them. Looking into her eyes, he saw the
distinct possibility that he'd *want* to keep them. They'd
been together less than a day, but they'd exchanged several letters beforehand and he'd been impressed by everything she'd done.

He didn't know what the future held and neither did
she. He only knew he had to protect Freddie and Dora
from his father, and he had to protect Caroline from being
hurt. Her offer to marry him suggested she was vulnerable to the feelings that plagued every human being, and
he worried she'd regret her kindness.

"It's a generous offer," he said to her. "But I can't take
advantage of your goodwill."

"Why not?"

He didn't want to admit to his potential feelings, but
the possibility of affection, or the lack of it, had to be
addressed. "You've been married before. I presume you
loved your husband just as I loved Molly. A marriage in
name only strikes me as…inadequate."

She stood straighter. "Women marry for all sorts of
reasons."

"Of course." In England men and women alike married for money and prestige. In America, women married for survival. He'd seen the advertisements for mail-order brides in cheaply bound catalogs. Those creatures struck him as pitiful. Caroline struck him as remarkable. He didn't intend to accept her offer to marry him, but he wanted to know why she'd made it. "If you'll forgive my boldness, why would you settle for an arrangement of this nature?"

Color stained her cheeks. "That should be obvious."

"It's not." At least not to him.

She held out her arms in a manner that put her life on display. "Look at me, major. I'm almost thirty years old. It's true I'm widowed, but my marriage was clandestine. In the eyes of society I'm on the shelf. I have no children, no family except for Bessie. My prospects for marriage are nil."

He couldn't believe she thought so little of herself. "That's simply not true."

"Forgive me," she said with a touch of sarcasm. "But you're either blind or an incurable optimist."

How this woman could believe she had no hope for a husband was beyond him. She was lovely, smart, brave and kind. She wasn't a naive girl anymore, but that hardly mattered to a mature man. Tristan preferred a woman whose character had been tested, someone who understood that life had ups and downs. He looked boldly into her eyes. "I assure you, Caroline. I'm not blind. As for being an optimist, I plead guilty. A man with malaria has little choice but to hope."

Her eyes misted. "You're carrying a terrible burden."

"Yes."

She lowered her arms like a bird that had decided

not to take flight. "For the sake of the children, let me help you."

Never before had he admitted to the weight of his worries, but her kindness exposed his secrets. He didn't want to die. He loved his children and wanted to marry again. He and Caroline respected each other. What if their feelings ripened into love? What if he desired her and she desired him? As an ailing man, he'd vowed to never love again—or be loved—because he knew the pain of losing a spouse. If Caroline lost her heart to him and he died, she'd suffer.

Common sense told him to reject her kindness, but he was worried enough to consider her offer. Then a troubling thought occurred to him. Every angle had to be considered, even the ugly ones. He didn't think she was marrying him for his money, but he had to be sure. "There's another side to this. I'm a wealthy man. And after my father's death, I'll be even wealthier. If you think you'll inherit—"

"I don't," she said firmly. "If you think money can buy happiness, you're naive."

"I think no such thing, but perhaps you do."

"Absolutely not!"

"Then why do this?" he demanded. "What do you want?"

"A family!" she cried. "I want children and Christmas dinners and bedtime stories. For years I've dreamed of having a family, but no man wanted me."

Sadness gave her eyes a crystalline sheen. He felt like a louse for goading her into a humiliating confession, but he counted her discomfort as the cost of battle. Now he knew her motives. They were pure and painfully simple. Caroline Bradley wanted what most women wanted, what Molly had wanted and what his children needed. She wanted to be a mother.

Shamed but strong, she paced up to him with her eyes blazing. "As you can see, I'm a pathetic, childless spinster who'd do anything—even marry you—for the sake of two beautiful children. Does that confession satisfy you, Major Smith?"

They stood nose to nose, their breathing synchronous and close. Her chin was raised. His was pointed down. He could smell the soap she'd used to wash off the dust from the trip, and he saw the woman who'd bravely gotten on a horse after being bucked off. With a marriage in name only, he supposed she was getting on a horse of a different kind. She'd been hurt and rejected. He didn't want to be the man to trample her courage.

A wry smile lifted his lips. "You're a brave woman, Caroline. Perhaps the bravest I've ever known."

"I'm not brave at all," she murmured.

"I think you are," he answered. "If you're agreeable, I'd be pleased to marry you...for the sake of the children, of course."

"I'm agreeable," she replied.

The moment called for a handshake. They were sealing a business deal, not affirming a lifetime of love, but Tristan couldn't bring himself to offer merely his hand. Neither could he kiss her, not even on the cheek as a token of friendship. Moving slowly, as if she were a horse that needed a peppermint, he touched her cheek. He'd crossed a small but significant line, and he wanted to cross another. "You should call me Tristan."

"Tristan..." She said the name as if it tingled like the candy. "With your father in Cheyenne, we should move quickly, I think."

"Agreed." He'd need a license and someone to officiate. Wheeler Springs didn't have a church, only a monthly service when a minister visited from Laramie. Judge Abbott would have to do. "I'll make arrangements with the justice of the peace. Will that be acceptable?"

Sadness flitted in her eyes, a sign that this marriage in name only was indeed less than adequate. "A civil ceremony seems appropriate."

"Agreed." They were making a commitment to each other, one they'd both honor, but it would be based on respect instead of that mysterious kind of love that united a certain man and a certain woman.

"So tomorrow then?" he asked.

"The sooner, the better."

She smiled but it didn't reach her eyes. The moment called for a kiss…a caress. This time he offered his hand. They shook. A business deal had been struck, so why didn't he want to let go of her soft fingers, and why did she look like she wanted to cry?

Chapter Seven

In the morning Tristan penned a letter to his father explaining he'd send transport when the bridge over the Frazier River was repaired, possibly in three weeks' time. He said nothing of his new position as heir apparent, nor did he mention his pending marriage. He hoped the duke would wait in Cheyenne, but he fully expected him to leave immediately, taking the longer, more eastern route that avoided the river.

He took the letter to the hotel and gave it to his father's courier, a young man he'd never met. When the fellow addressed him as "Marquess," Tristan corrected him.

"In America I'm to be addressed as Major Smith."

"Yes, sir." The young man looked shocked, but Tristan remained as neutral as Switzerland.

Next he went to the courthouse where he obtained a marriage license and made arrangements with Judge Abbott to perform the ceremony at noon. He left the courthouse feeling both confident and ill at ease. In a few hours, he'd be a married man again. He'd be committed to a woman he barely knew but somehow trusted. He couldn't help but be impressed by her, and the feeling worried him. He liked her far more than was a wise for a man with malaria and a call to return to England.

He was tempted to renege on the entire arrangement, but the needs of his children pressed him to make one last preparation for the ceremony. He returned to the house in town and went into the attic, where he'd stored a particular trunk. He hadn't taken it to The Barracks because it was too painful to open. He'd seen it for the first time fifteen years ago on his wedding night with Molly, and now it held his dead wife's treasures—the quilt she'd made for their bed, her wedding dress, a few trinkets and her jewelry.

As he opened the lid, he felt as if Molly were in the room with him. He touched the quilt and recalled the promise he'd made to remarry. With his head bowed, he spoke to her in his mind. He shared his doubts and worries, then he said goodbye to her as his wife and hello as a cherished memory. Molly would have approved of the marriage and she'd have liked Caroline, but he also knew she'd want more for him than a marriage of convenience. She'd want him to love again.

He couldn't allow it, not with the malaria nipping at him, but he felt peaceful with Caroline. He'd do his best for her, and that meant honoring their marriage. Mixed in Molly's jewelry was a diamond ring that had belonged to Tristan's mother. Square-cut with tinges of pink, the stone was mounted on a platinum band. The day his mother died, he'd seen the ring unattended and he'd taken it. As a boy, he'd hidden it. As a man, he had kept it as a fond reminder of the woman he'd barely known.

Molly had never worn it, though he supposed she'd owned it in a legal sort of way. In the same legal sort of way Caroline was about to become his wife. It seemed fitting to give her the ring, so he put it in his pocket and went to his room to dress for the wedding. The ceremony was a legal affair, he reminded himself, a formality equivalent to hiring a governess. Even so, he selected a jacquard vest, a flashy ascot he arranged in a puff and his finest frock coat. His clothing didn't matter, but he wanted to honor Caroline. The ring mattered to him greatly, and he hoped she'd like it.

"Am I doing the right thing?" Caroline murmured to Bessie as they walked to the courthouse. Situated on the edge of town, the new building was a short walk from the major's house. He and Jon were five paces in front of them, just barely out of earshot.

"Only you can know," her sister replied. "But it's not too late to change your mind."

All night long, Caroline had been assailed with doubts. Her worries had nothing to do with the children. Tristan's determination to protect them had convinced her they were at risk. Dora had been instantly affectionate, and Freddie needed her, too. The boy had a chip on his shoulder, but the toughness merely showed his grief for his mother. The children filled her with confidence in her decision. What made her quake were the feelings inspired by their father.

A marriage in name only seemed logical, but then he'd touched her cheek and her heart had betrayed her. How could she not admire a man who'd do anything for his children? She would need all the discipline she could muster to keep from losing her heart to him. If the malaria didn't take him away from Wyoming, England would. Caroline was an ordinary American, a woman with average abilities and looks. She had no business being married to a man destined to be a duke.

If she'd needed proof, which she didn't, her clothing

offered evidence. She'd come to Wyoming to be a nanny, not a bride and certainly not a duchess. Today she was wearing a gray moiré jacket, a navy skirt and a white blouse. There wasn't ruffle or frill in sight. She'd planned to wear the costume when she met the major for the first time. It was sleek and businesslike, which she supposed was as fitting today as it would have been for her position as a governess.

Except she wasn't going to be a governess. She was going to be a wife in name only and a mother to Tristan's children.

As the men stepped onto the boardwalk, Bessie gripped her elbow. "Are you *sure* you want to do this?"

It was the second time Bessie had asked her to reconsider a marriage. The first had been the night of her marriage to Charles. She'd been twenty-two years old and teaching the children of former slaves when he'd arrived in the war-ravaged town where she and Bessie had taken refuge. Born into freedom and schooled in Europe, he'd dedicated his life to the cause of education. She hadn't meant to fall in love with him, and he'd been even more reluctant. Love, though, had triumphed and she'd talked him into marriage.

I don't care about the risk. I love you, Charles.

You'll suffer, my dearest. We'll be judged.

I'll take that chance.

She'd been ready to pay the price for herself, but not once had she considered the cost to Charles. Bessie had tried to dissuade her, but Caroline had argued.

I don't care what people say.

But you'll have children—

We're saving money to move to Philadelphia. Life will be different there.

In the end, Bessie had stood with her in a church basement where she and Charles had spoken their vows in front of a young minister. Someone must have seen them, because gossip had erupted. Charles had been called uppity. A month later he'd been murdered and she'd become a pariah. She'd tried to continue his crusade for education, but the hate had been too much to bear on top of her grief. When Bessie suggested they travel West, Caroline had been glad to go. Privately she'd vowed to never again be an object of scorn.

Now here she was—an American woman about to marry an English nobleman—but it didn't matter. They had no future. If he survived the malaria and returned to England, they'd have to annul the marriage. Caroline was an excellent choice for a governess, and she made a decent wife under the circumstances, but a future duke would need a woman who was beautiful and accomplished. Caroline could only hope their effort to protect the children now wouldn't lead to worse heartbreak later. It was a risk Tristan had been willing to take, and she respected his opinion.

She took Bessie's hand and squeezed. "This is right. I'm sure of it."

Together they approached the courthouse. Tristan had gone ahead and was holding the door. Jon had hung back and now offered his hand to Bessie. Smiling her thanks, she took it. The two of them walked into the courthouse, leaving Caroline alone as if she really were a bride at the end of a processional. When she reached the door, Tristan offered his arm and together they went down the hall to an open door. Judge Abbott stood waiting for them in front of a judge's box.

A balding man with a beard, he cleared his throat. "Ladies and gentlemen!"

He'd shouted as if calling court to order. Startled, Caroline drew back. Tristan consoled her with a pat on her arm.

The judge's voice boomed again. "I have business elsewhere, so take your places."

The couples fell into position, the women on one side and the men on the other. Judge Abbott cleared his throat. "Since this is a legal proceeding, let's not waste time. Do you Tristan Willoughby Smith take Caroline Margaret Bradley to be your lawfully wedded wife?"

Caroline's mouth gaped at the abruptness. She hadn't been expecting poetry or even a prayer, but she would have liked more than a deaf old man barking orders.

Next to her, Tristan frowned. "I do."

Judge Abbott looked down his nose at her. "And do you Caroline Margaret Bradley take this man to be your lawfully wedded husband?"

"I do."

Had Tristan asked for this cold, heartless ceremony? She'd offered herself to be a mother to his children. Surely the promise deserved some recognition. If this was how he intended to treat her, she had to question her decision to marry him. With her stomach in knots, she turned and saw the angry set of his jaw.

He lowered his chin, aiming his eyes at the judge the way he might have pointed a pistol. "Your honor?"

"What is it, Major?"

"I'd like to say a word to my bride."

His bride... Her stomach flipped. Did he have the same confused feelings she did?

Judge Abbott glared at him. "Make it quick."

Tristan gave him a stern look, then faced her. When he looked down at her hands, she recalled his touch in the stable and the way he'd lifted her from the river. Gripping her gloved fingers in his bare ones, he looked into her eyes. "My dear Caroline, I'm honored by your generosity of spirit, your kindness and your concern for my children. I will return that regard to the best of my ability…as long as I am able."

He'd made no mention of love, of course. Their marriage would be based on respect and honor. Friendship would have to suffice. But with the kindness of his words, she was once more convinced she was making the right decision. She raised her face to his. "I promise to love your children as my own, to protect them from harm and to give them a future. I am honored to become a part of your family."

With their gazes locked, his grip tightened on her hands. The gesture confused her, in part because she yearned to hold on more tightly than she had the right to do. She wanted more than honorable promises. She wanted to be loved and to love in return, but the commitment they'd made would have to be enough.

She broke Tristan's stare and focused on the judge. The man eyed Tristan with annoyance. "Do you have a ring?"

"Yes, sir." Jon put something sparkly in Tristan's palm.

She hadn't expected a ring, and she certainly hadn't expected something with a diamond. With her eyes wide, she took in the silvery band and the flash of light from a pink-hued stone. Looking up, she saw a twinkle in Tristan's eyes. He'd surprised her and was obviously pleased.

"Your glove?" he said.

"Oh!" She tugged it off a finger at a time, then offered her hand. Tristan took the weight of it, then looked at Judge Abbott expectantly.

"Repeat after me," the man said. "With this ring, I thee wed."

Tristan turned back to her. "With this ring, I thee wed."

Looking down, he slipped the cool band onto her finger. It slid like liquid and warmed against her skin, a reminder of what marriage was meant to be—a circle of unending love. Today the ring symbolized promises of a less romantic nature, but she appreciated having it on her finger.

Judge Abbott cleared his throat. "I now pronounce you man and wife. Major Smith, you may kiss the bride."

She wished the judge had skipped the gesture. A kiss had no place in a marriage of convenience. Even so, she turned to Tristan, lifting her chin for the token caress. He must have felt the same hypocrisy because he kissed her cheek as if she were a maiden aunt.

Suddenly stiff, he stepped back. Bessie pulled her into a hug. "Are you all right?"

"I'm fine," she whispered.

Behind her she heard Jon congratulating Tristan and wondered if he felt as off balance as she did. He turned to her. "We should leave for The Barracks."

"Of course," she replied.

Their gazes mingled long enough to make her wonder what he was thinking, then he offered his arm and escorted her to the house. Bessie and Jon stayed several paces away, giving them room for a private conversation. They hadn't discussed anything about the marriage, and the ring made the commitment more personal than she'd expected. She wanted to know about their sleeping arrangements and how they'd tell the news of their marriage to the children. She wanted to discuss everything, but she didn't know where to start.

When the house came into view, she saw a carriage waiting by the front door and realized they were leav-

ing immediately for his ranch. Cairo stood next to the
rig, saddled and ready to ride. Dora and Freddie were
nowhere in sight.

"Where are the children?" she asked.

His brow furrowed. "I sent them ahead with Noah
and Evaline."

"I assumed we'd tell them about the marriage—"

"We will." He spoke in a friendly but businesslike
tone. "Come to my study at seven o'clock. I'll advise
them of the change in your status, then we'll have supper as usual."

Caroline gaped at him. "We're becoming a family.
There has to be a better way to tell them."

Judging by the look in his eyes, he didn't like the idea
at all. The creases around his mouth deepened. "What
did you have in mind?"

"I don't know exactly, but it seems right to tell them
with smiles on our faces." They'd reached the carriage,
so she stopped.

"They'll be informed. That's enough." He looked
vaguely uncomfortable. "There's another matter to discuss. It's of a personal nature."

"Ah, yes." She'd been expecting this talk and welcomed getting it over with. "Our sleeping arrangements."

"Exactly." He looked like the stern officer he'd been.
"There's a small room adjoining the master suite. The
spaces are attached by a closet. You'll have total privacy,
but we'll be able to speak alone whenever we wish. Will
that be acceptable?"

"Of course."

"Very well," he said abruptly. "Let's be on our way."

He handed her into the carriage then mounted Cairo.
Jon did the honors for Bessie, then climbed to the driver's seat. With Tristan in the lead, the four of them left

town. She wondered about Grandma and figured Noah and Evaline had taken the horse with them.

Neither Caroline nor Bessie spoke until the buildings were a mile behind them. Surrounded by grass and cottonwoods, high sky and wisping clouds, Caroline marveled at the beauty of an ordinary day…only the day was no longer ordinary. For most married couples, the date would be marked on a calendar and celebrated. Caroline had no expectation of celebrating this landmark with Tristan, but the memories were engraved on her heart.

Bessie touched her hand. "How are you feeling?"

"Good."

"I'm glad," she said. "I thought you might feel a bit glum."

"I'm fine." Caroline inhaled the crisp air. "I came to Wyoming to borrow a family, and that's what I'm doing."

"You've done more than borrow the major's children. You just married him."

"I know."

"I'm worried, Caroline."

"Why?"

"Jon told me more about Tristan's father. He'll be a formidable enemy if Tristan succumbs to the malaria."

A breeze stirred through the trees, a reminder of changing seasons and the approach of winter. "He seems better today."

"The major and I discussed his health at breakfast. He's been ill for some time, and that's a good sign. Malaria kills quickly or it lingers for months, even years. I suspect he has the variety that lingers."

"That would be good," Caroline replied.

"Yes, but he needs to continue on the quinine. I suggested he increase the dosage."

"Will he have enough?"

Bessie looked confident. "A new shipment is already on the way."

Caroline stared across a meadow that seemed to stretch forever. "He has to live. That's all there is to it."

"That's up to God."

Caroline knew that fact too well. Not only had she grieved Charles, but she was also single and childless against her will. She'd had a few battles with her faith, but in the end she accepted her circumstances. She had learned to look for the good in all things, though she could see no good at all in malaria, and she saw even less in a child's loss of a mother. Nor did she understand the tensions between fathers and sons. For whatever reasons, Tristan had been terribly hurt by his father. Caroline intended to give the older man a chance, but Tristan's warnings had been dire and sincere.

She turned to Bessie. "Do you think the duke is as difficult as Tristan says?"

"I don't know, but he's likely to be critical of this marriage…and of you."

"I imagine so," Caroline murmured. If Tristan's opinion of his father proved accurate, the duke would treat her with disdain. She'd encountered such conduct because of her marriage to Charles. She didn't relish enduring the spite again, but she could do it for the children.

"The duke can say or do what he wants," she said to Bessie. "My only concern is for Freddie and Dora."

"When will you tell them about the marriage?"

"Tonight."

Bessie huffed. "I hope he's not planning on briefing them as if it's a war effort."

"That's exactly what he's planning."

"You can't allow it," Bessie said. "If he orders them

to accept you, they'll resent you even more, especially Freddie. He'll think you're trying to replace his mother."

Caroline had no desire to replace Molly, but she very much wanted to be a family. She'd dreamed of having children her entire life. Her dream could come true, but only if Freddie and Dora shared it. She thought of being a child herself and saw a simple answer. She turned to Bessie. "Do you remember the game we played when we were little? The one where we dressed up in mama's things and pretended to be other people?"

"You called it the dream game."

"Tonight I'll play it with Tristan and the children."

The game would soften the news that the children had a new mother, and it would give Tristan a much needed glimpse into their hearts. More than anything Caroline wanted to unite him with his children. Judging from what she'd observed, he barely knew them.

She'd have to hurry once they reached The Barracks, but tonight's announcement wouldn't be made in the major's study, a room she felt certain would be dark, gloomy and lined with hunting trophies. Tonight they were going to celebrate with costumes, cake and laughter. This wouldn't be the wedding night she'd dreamed of, but it would be a new beginning just the same.

Chapter Eight

Tristan looked at the clock on the wall. It was two minutes after seven o'clock. He'd told Caroline to be in his study at seven sharp, and he'd given Evaline instructions to deliver the children five minutes later. Did *anyone* listen to him anymore?

Apparently not.

Intending to find Evaline, he stepped into the hall. As he turned, he saw the housekeeper coming in his direction. She wore an impish smile and a paper crown decorated with leaves and pine needles. Tristan gaped at her. "What in the world—"

"You're late, sir!"

How could he be late to a meeting *he'd* arranged? Noah came up behind Evaline. As he passed her, Tristan saw a dozen medals pinned to his chest. Some were medals the man had earned in the army. Others were made of tin and buttons and resembled playthings. To Tristan's consternation, Noah handed him a stick horse that had been painted black. "You better hurry, Major. You're late."

He took the horse without thinking. "Late to *what?*"

"Supper, of course." Noah assumed a formal pose,

but his eyes were twinkling. "Mrs. Caroline requested the meal be served on the veranda. She and the children are waiting."

Tristan glanced again at the medals on Noah's chest. Maybe he was seeing things. Occasionally the fevers made him delirious. Maybe he was having an attack and didn't know it. Perhaps he'd imagined the crown on Evaline's head. As for the stick horse in his hand, it felt real enough to remind him of his boyhood dreams of being the finest horseman in England. He scowled at Noah. "What's going on?"

"You'll have to see for yourself, sir."

"I intend to do just that." He strode past Noah and Evaline, down the hall and through the children's playroom to the veranda. Through a window he saw lanterns on the railing, each one casting a circle of yellow light into the dusk. The glow reminded him of making camp with his men. He'd enjoyed the camaraderie around a campfire, but today he felt none of that ease.

Noah stepped ahead of him and opened the door to the veranda, indicating he should pass with a sweep of his arm. Tristan noticed the makeshift medals again and stopped. "*What* are you wearing?"

"You'll have to ask Mrs. Caroline."

"I certainly will." He raised the stick horse as if it were a king's scepter and instantly felt ridiculous. Annoyed, he marched out the door and saw Caroline and the children seated around a small table set with the china Molly had loved.

Caroline stood. "Good evening, Major."

They hadn't yet told the children of their marriage, so she'd addressed him formally.

"Miss Bradley," he acknowledged. "Children."

Before he could fully take in the gown Caroline had

chosen, Dora ran to him. Instead of her usual pinafore, she was wearing a white dress with ruffles and pink ribbons. Molly had stitched it before she'd fallen ill. It had been for another child's birthday party, an event Dora had missed because her mother had died. Did the child remember? Tristan did… He'd found the dress with a needle still stuck in place, waiting for Molly to finish adding the trim. He didn't recall bringing it to The Barracks. Evaline must have packed it, though he felt certain Caroline had finished the ribbons and perhaps let out the side seams. The dress was a bit short, a sign that Dora had grown.

His daughter executed a curtsy. "Do you like my dress, Daddy?"

"It's lovely."

He hadn't seen Dora smile in a long time. To her the dress was a carnival of ribbons and lace, not a sad reminder of what she'd lost. Tristan looked at Caroline, wordless because he didn't know whether to thank her or scold her.

Dora tugged on his hand, the one not holding the stick horse. "We're having a party for us!"

"I see that." He disliked parties.

He glared at Caroline. When she answered with a smile, he felt like a curmudgeon. He had no idea what to say, so he turned his attention to Freddie. The boy was wearing his Sunday best but nothing outlandish. He looked as uncomfortable as Tristan.

Like father, like son.

The thought brought no comfort. Tristan wanted Freddie to enjoy life. Instead he was looking at Tristan the way Tristan had looked at the duke, stubbornly silent while yearning for approval. Whatever Tristan did, Freddie would copy him. If he disrespected Caroline, so would the boy. Aware his reaction would mark everyone at the table, he paused to give his wife of seven hours an opportunity to explain herself.

Her eyes brightened with the challenge and she stood, lacing her hands at the waist of a blue calico covered with a white apron. This morning her hair had been piled on her head in a mass of curls befitting a wedding. Now her brunette tresses were wrapped around her head in a braid. Compared to everyone else, she looked ordinary.

"What's going on?" he finally asked.

"We're playing a game." She spoke sweetly, but Tristan heard a dare in her voice. "Each one of us is dressed as the person we want to be someday. I thought we'd tell each other about our dreams for the future."

"I see."

"Sit down, Major." She indicated the chair across from hers. "We'll start with the children."

He wanted to get the silliness over with, but he had to admit her game had a certain charm. He'd been younger than Freddie when a groom in his father's stable had made him a stick horse like the one in his hand. He'd spent hours dreaming of being a cavalry officer. Looking at his children, he realized he had no idea what they dreamed of becoming. In his effort to protect them, somehow he'd stopped knowing them.

With his chest tight, he sat in the chair across from Caroline and propped the stick horse against the table. "Who goes first?"

"I do!" Dora jumped to her feet. "Guess what I am!"

"I have no idea," he said, teasing her a little.

"I'm a princess!"

"And a lovely one." He could hardly speak. Dora looked just like Molly, bright and eager and full of fun.

She'd lost her mother, yet somehow she'd remained a hopeful child.

Caroline smiled at the girl. "Why do you want to be a princess?"

She thought a minute. "Princesses live in castles and they have ponies."

"I see." Caroline turned to him with a shine in her eyes. "Shall we ask Freddie to go next?"

In the most gracious of ways, she'd handed over the reins for the party and acknowledged him as head of the family. Looking carefully at her outfit, he realized the game had a deeper purpose than entertaining the children or getting to know them better. They'd each worn something to symbolize their deepest wishes. Caroline had worn a dress a mother would wear while baking bread or wiping a child's tears. Uncomfortable with the game but wanting to honor her, Tristan looked Freddie up and down. The boy was wearing a white shirt and a black tie, dark pants and a coat he'd soon outgrow. He looked formal and owlish, far more serious than the typical ten-year-old boy.

Tristan tried to sound cheerful. "You're dressed for business, I think."

"In a way," the boy replied.

"Are you a lawyer?"

"No."

"A banker?" The weight of not knowing his son hit Tristan hard. He should have known the answer without asking.

Freddie looked hurt, but he covered it up the way Tristan had covered hurt at the same age. He looked bored. "I'm a scientist. And I don't like games."

Caroline ignored the slight. "Science is a worthy pursuit."

"It is," Tristan agreed. So were silly games that revealed a child's dreams. "Why do you want to be a scientist?"

"Because they find answers."

"To what?" he asked.

"To everything," Freddie announced. "Even the cure for malaria."

Tristan felt his son's fear like a kick. It nearly broke him. "That's a worthy goal, Freddie."

The boy stared straight ahead, every bit as stalwart as Tristan had become in his fight against the malaria. He wanted to give Freddie hope, but his tongue refused to move. Even more powerful was the urge to pull the boy into a hug and never let go. Instinct told him to do it. Years of restraint kept him rigid in his chair.

Why, God?

Tristan stifled the angry cry. Whether he respected God or not, he had no choice but to take the Commander's orders. Caroline's gaze flicked from his face to Freddie's and then back to his. Just as she'd needed rescuing when she fell in the river, he needed someone to pull him out of his confusing flood of emotion.

She tipped her head. "It's your turn, Major. Knowing how you feel about horses, the children guessed you'd wanted a horse like Cairo since you were a boy."

"I did," he said, feeling more tense than ever.

Dora smiled at him. "We painted the horse to look like Cairo. Do you like him?"

"I do."

"It's fun to pretend," Caroline said. "But it's even more fun when our dreams come true."

She looked directly at Tristan, prompting him to lead the way across the bridge she'd built to his children. Taking a breath, he took the first step in what would be a major change in their young lives. "Children, do you know what Miss Caroline wants to be?"

Dora looked at her with grave intensity, biting her lip as if her life depended on the right guess. Freddie looked bored, though Tristan saw worry in his eyes. "She's the governess," Freddie said coolly.

"No," Tristan said quietly. "Keep looking."

When she smiled, Dora's eyes got wide. "She's a… lady."

"She's that," Tristan said gently. "She's also dressed in her everyday clothes, the clothes a mother would wear. Caroline is going to be more than your new governess. We were married this morning. She's to be your new—"

"Friend," she interrupted.

Tristan bristled at the rudeness, then realized she'd saved him from a grave mistake. No one could replace Molly and she didn't want to try. He wished he could touch her foot under the table to acknowledge the correction. That's what he'd have done with Molly, and Caroline deserved the same gesture of apology. He offered a tiny nod, an acknowledgment that she knew best, then waited for her to continue.

She looked from Dora to Freddie. "Your father and I know this is a surprise, but we've given the situation a great deal of thought. We've been corresponding and—"

Dora flung herself into Caroline's arms and hugged her hard. Holding the child close, Caroline kissed the top of her brunette head.

Tears threatened to well in Tristan's eyes. He fought them off, but his heart turned into an aching bruise. He looked at Freddie, saw confusion on the boy's face and realized he had a choice. He could act like his own father and be cold, or he could treat his son the way he'd wanted to be treated at that age.

"Freddie," he said quietly. "Let's speak outside."

His son's frown deepened into a sneer.

Tristan stood and waited. Still Freddie didn't budge. The child was glaring at Caroline with an arrogance Tristan recognized all too well. He'd seen in it himself. Even more frightening, he'd seen it in his father. Somehow he had to undo the damage done by his months of coldness. He touched Freddie's shoulder and felt bone. Squeezing gently, he eased the boy off the chair and led him down the steps to a patch of weeds. With the sky turning purple, they stood face-to-face.

Looking into his son's eyes, Tristan said words he couldn't recall ever hearing from his own father. "I love you, son."

Freddie look stunned, embarrassed…and like a child. "You do?"

"Yes." He spoke with authority. "I'm proud of your dreams and intelligence, your desire to be a scientist and how you help with your sister. We all miss your mother. I certainly do—"

"But you're marrying Miss Caroline." The boy sounded offended.

"Yes." Peace in the house hung on his next words. "I admire her, Freddie. I respect her and trust her. Dora needs someone, and—" *So do you.* At the defiant look in Freddie's eyes, Tristan held back. His son was still a boy, but his journey to manhood would be fueled by respect. "We *men* need her, too. A woman is a gentling influence. I hope you'll accept Caroline as a member of the family, not as a mother, but as a friend. Perhaps you could call her Aunt Caroline."

In the boy's turbulent expression, Tristan saw grief for his mother, the longing for peace and another time-honored male tradition. Freddie wanted to fight and win.

The mask of indifference was gone. In its place was a
boy who didn't quite know what to do. "She makes good
pies," he finally said.

"She does?"

"She baked them before supper," Freddie explained.
"Dora helped and she let me have a taste."

Tristan liked pie. "Then perhaps we better get back
for the meal so we can have dessert."

"I guess so."

The boy hadn't agreed to call Caroline "aunt," but
Tristan counted the exchange as a start. Wanting to show
affection but not sure how, he clapped Freddie on the back
the way he slapped privates who'd done a good job. As
if something had been jarred loose, Freddie turned and
hugged him hard. "I love you, too, Father."

They didn't need to say or do anything else. In the
way of men, they went back to the veranda where the
females were seated at the table awaiting the arrival of
supper. Dora looked like a real princess, and Caroline
looked like a real mother, a bit worried but hopeful as
they climbed the steps. As soon as Tristan's foot hit the
veranda, Dora ran to him and hugged him. The three of
them—Tristan, Freddie and Dora—hugged for a very
long time, with Caroline watching from a distance, but
not joining them.

Just as she'd dreamed, Caroline was sitting at the supper table with a husband and children. The three of them
told her stories and she laughed, but it soon became apparent her success in uniting Tristan and his children
came with a single failure. The three of them were a
family. She didn't belong except as an observer. When
Evaline served the pie Caroline had made for dessert, the
three of them praised her baking but quickly returned

to remembering pies Molly had baked. Caroline didn't mind talking about Molly at all. The children's memories needed to be enjoyed. What hurt was being forgotten.

Tristan had finished his pie and was looking affectionately at Dora. The child had kept her dress clean, but she had a ring of cherry pie around her mouth. With Caroline watching, Tristan dipped his napkin in his water glass and cleaned her face, a bit awkwardly because he wasn't accustomed to such things, then he said, "I believe it's bedtime."

"Will you read to me?" Dora asked.

"Of course." He turned to Freddie. "Are you too old for bedtime stories?"

"I read to myself," the boy answered. "But you can say goodnight. Mother used to do that."

"Then that's what I'll do." Tristan turned to her, his eyes shining with love for his children. "Will you excuse us, Caroline?"

"Of course."

She managed a smile, but disappointment welled in her middle. He'd said nothing about returning to her. She'd wait a bit but not too long. She stood with the three of them, watching as Tristan hoisted Dora to his hip and followed Freddie into the house. The candles burned bright, but the darkness pressed at the edges. She wondered which story Tristan would read to Dora, and if the child had a favorite.

Next she imagined him knocking on Freddie's door. They'd trade a joke or a remark about the meal, then he'd say goodnight. In her dreams he came back to the veranda…he came to be with her.

The door creaked and her eyes opened. Instead of Tristan, she saw Evaline still wearing the crown that made her a queen. Caroline thought of Noah's medals and

his desire to be a commissioned officer. Their dreams
would never come true. Neither would hers, it seemed.
She thanked Evaline for the fine meal, then went upstairs
to the little room adjacent to Tristan's suite. In the dim
light, she took in the narrow bed, a white chest of draw-
ers and a rocking chair. The room was intended to be a
nursery. Caroline couldn't help but think of the children
she'd never conceive. She longed to rock a baby to sleep,
to hold it to her breast and feel its breathing turn deep.

It was her wedding night.

There would be no children. There would be no love,
physical or otherwise. There would be nothing but restless dreams. She scanned the room again, feeling the rise
of a lump and the taste of regret. "Oh, Lord," she murmured. "What have I done?"

Dropping into the rocker, she buried her face in her
hands and wept. This morning she'd been confident that
she belonged with Tristan and the children; now she felt
all the pain of being an outsider. Even worse, she'd seen
a side of Tristan she deeply admired. As annoyed as he'd
been by the dream game, he'd played along. When he
saw the wisdom of it, he'd embraced it. He'd hugged his
children and they'd hugged him back.

Fresh tears welled in her eyes. "Lord," she whispered.
"This is why You brought me here. I know it. But it hurts
to be alone."

Alone in a crowd…alone in a family.

She felt the stirrings of self-pity, then the pounding
of resentment. Abruptly she lifted her head. "I will *not*
be bitter… *I will not be bitter.*" She slid to her knees,
laced her fingers in a knot and prayed. "Father God,
bless Tristan and his children. Bring them close to each
other and close to You. Heal their sorrow and their fear."

Masculine footsteps interrupted her prayer. Already

she could recognize the cadence of Tristan's walk. It matched the beat of her heart as she listened, growing louder as he approached her room, then fading as he passed her door. Disappointment welled in her chest, but she pushed it aside. Considering the lines they'd drawn, a private talk in her bedroom would have been too personal. With the silence heavy, she fought the ache of loneliness by counting her blessings.

She was a wife instead of a governess.

The dream game had been a resounding success.

She liked Evaline and Noah, and Jon had befriended Bessie. And Tristan… The quinine had helped already. She thanked God for his improved health.

She had a roof over her head and food to eat, warm clothes and shoes without holes. She'd survived a stage-coach robbery, ridden a horse and not been drowned when she'd fallen in the river. She had much for which to be grateful, and yet she wanted more…she wanted a husband and a baby of her own. She couldn't stop the tears that welled. "Why, Lord?" she murmured. "Why can't I be satisfied—"

A soft knock startled her. Eyes wide, she stared at the door to the storage area between her room and Tristan's. It had to be him… He'd come to her.

Chapter Nine

Until tonight, Tristan hadn't realized how much like his own father he'd become. He'd distanced himself from Freddie and Dora for different reasons, but the effect had been the same. He didn't know his children the way he wanted to, especially Freddie, who was older and learning to be a man. The boy had copied Tristan's every move, every attitude, and until tonight, he'd set a poor example. He wondered what other mistakes he'd been making. He didn't know, but he knew someone who did and he'd left her alone on the veranda.

After leaving Freddie, he went back to the supper table. Someone had cleared the dishes and extinguished the candles, leaving nothing but shadows and the smell of wax. Inhaling the cool air, he realized he'd been gone close to an hour. Caroline had gone upstairs…alone.

It shouldn't have mattered to him, but it did. He very much wanted to include her in tonight's success. Feeling intrepid, he went to the kitchen where he piled a tray with the remaining pie, a knife, two plates and two forks. As quiet as a spy, he carried the tray to his suite, placed it by the fire and lit the logs in the hearth. When the flames settled into a steady dance, he went through the closet and tapped on her door. If she was asleep, he didn't want to wake her. Or maybe he did… Even a wife in name only deserved an acknowledgment on her wedding night.

After a moment, she opened the door a crack and peeked at him. "Hello, Major."

She'd slipped back into formality. What it signaled, he didn't know. "I thought we'd agreed on Tristan."

"Yes," she mumbled. "Of course."

Her hair was down, and she had brushed out the braid. Backlit by the lamp, the dark waves had a translucent quality that reminded him of the ocean at night. His eyes flicked to her hand, and he saw a hairbrush and the unbuttoned cuff of her nightgown.

"Am I too late?" he asked.

"For what?"

"To invite you to my room for more dessert." He suddenly felt silly in the closet. "It's later than I realized. Perhaps in the morning—"

"No!" she said quickly. "I was hoping we'd have a minute together."

He'd been thinking in terms of an hour, maybe two. Deep down, he wanted days with her, maybe longer. If their feelings grew, he'd want fifty years…except he didn't know if he had fifty years. He might not have fifty days.

Leaving the door ajar, she tied back her hair with a ribbon and slipped into a robe. As she punched into the sleeves, he glanced around the room and remembered its purpose. The room was meant to be a nursery. Tristan had purchased the ranch from a man with a young wife. They'd expected to raise a family, but she'd been unhappy and they'd left with their dream unfulfilled. Peering into the nursery, Tristan considered the dreams a woman would have…the dream Caroline had of being a mother. The inadequacy of their marriage struck him as cruel, but it would be crueler still to seek anything more than friendship. Not only did he not want a woman to grieve for him, he couldn't risk leaving a wife with a child he'd never see.

"Come with me," he said, issuing an order.

She opened the door wider, saw the narrowness of the closet and hesitated. He stepped back to let her pass and bumped his head on something sharp. Grimacing, he pressed his hand to his scalp and felt blood.

"Are you all right?" she asked.

"I'm fine." He hurried out of the closet, fetched a handkerchief from his bureau and pressed it to the cut. Blood quickly saturated the linen.

Caroline came up beside him. "Let me do that."

"I can manage."

Ignoring him, she put one hand on his forehead and the other against the handkerchief. Firm but gentle, her fingers made a vise of sorts. Reconciled to the wound, he bowed his head so she could maintain pressure. "I seem to have been attacked by a nail," he said drily.

"You might need a stitch."

"I don't want a stitch," he grumbled.

"Would you rather bleed all over your pillow?" she replied rather haughtily.

As a man who gave orders, Tristan knew when to surrender. "I suppose not." He raised his hand with intention of taking over the handkerchief. "I'll do that."

"Not yet. We should keep pressure on it."

Pressure on his head put a different kind of pressure on his heart. He'd forgotten how it felt to be the recipient of a woman's touch. Everything Caroline did brought healing of some sort. Tonight she'd made his family whole. He wanted that same wellness for his body, but she didn't have that power. God alone numbered a man's days. In Tristan's experience, He didn't much care about the in-between.

Annoyed, he put his hand on top of hers and pressed. "I'll hold it."

"But—"

"That's an order, Miss Bradley."

Startled, she slid her hand away from his and moved back. Tristan felt like a fool for knocking his head, but he felt even worse about the hurt in Caroline's eyes. She'd moved in front of the fire and was standing with her arms crossed and her hair falling down her back. Through the meal she'd been the picture of poise. Now she looked shaken and he felt like an ogre.

He tried to smile. "Forgive me, Caroline. I didn't mean to be harsh." How could a little cut cause so much trouble? "I asked you to my suite so I could thank you, and instead I end up in your care."

"It's just a cut," she murmured.

"Yes." He put on a rueful smile. "A cut to my pride and to my head. I don't like being in your debt."

"You don't owe me anything."

"I owe you a great deal." With his hand still pressed to his scalp, he indicated the divan. "Please sit down. I thought we could have more dessert."

"You liked the pie?" she asked.

"Very much." He wanted to talk about more than her baking skills. "Tonight you gave my family a wonderful gift. You deserve to hear about it."

She looked suddenly shy. "Perhaps tomorrow would be better. With your head and all—"

"Please don't argue."

"But—"

"Caroline..." He tried to sound firm, but her name

came out in a near whisper. "I may be ill, but I *was* an officer in the British Army. People *used* to do what I wanted. Indulge me, please."

Her lips curved into a smile. "Your friends want to take care of you."

"I suppose," he said. "But I seem to have lost all dignity."

"Not to me."

"You're being kind. What you did tonight was remarkable."

Pleasure gave her cheeks a rosy hue. "It went well, didn't it?"

"Very." He risked lowering the handkerchief. To his dismay, blood trickled down the nape of his neck. Annoyed, he put the cloth back in place.

"Sit down," she ordered.

Surrendering to the inevitable, he sat on the divan. With his neck bent and his eyes on the carpet, he heard the swish of her robe as she came to stand behind him. Her fingers combed through his hair to part it, then came to rest on the handkerchief. She blotted the fresh blood, then examined the cut with her fingers. A horrible thought made him cringe. His blood was tainted. Doctors believed the contagion came from swamps and not from people, but exactly how the disease spread had yet to be understood.

"Don't touch the blood," he said, feeling sick.

"I'm being careful." She pressed the handkerchief back in place. "You definitely need a stitch. Hold this while I get a needle and thread."

He did as she ordered, silently wondering what other holes in his life this good woman could mend. She had a gentle way of dealing with wounds and blood and sadness, a quiet acceptance of what had to be done. He admired her greatly, but he had to put a stop to such thoughts. Closing his eyes, he concentrated on the snap and hiss of the fire until he heard her return.

"I'm back," she said coming up behind him. "I'll need to shave some of the hair. Where do you keep your shaving tools?"

"In the washstand."

She went to the heavy piece of furniture and pulled out the chair for him. "Come and sit."

Tristan shaved standing up, and it felt odd to sit in a spindly chair he never used. Being careful to keep pressure on the cut, he removed his shaving tools from the drawer while Caroline poured water from the pitcher into the basin. The moment should have been awkward, but she had the demeanor of a nurse and he was accustomed to being a patient. She cleaned the cut, then used his razor to gently scrape away an inch of hair.

"This will hurt a bit," she said to prepare him.

"I've endured worse."

"Were you wounded in battle?" she asked as the needle pierced his scalp.

"A few times." A second stitch followed the first. "Malaria has proven to be a more formidable enemy."

The thread pulled the skin tight. She took a second stitch for good measure, made a knot and snipped. "The cut will ooze a bit, but you'll be fine."

He stood and faced her. "Yet again, I'm beholden to you."

"It's just a stitch," she said modestly.

"Yes, but tonight with the children was far more than 'just a stitch.' You opened my eyes, Caroline. I'm grateful."

"I merely put you all in the same room. Your hearts did the rest."

She'd said *your hearts,* meaning Tristan and his children. She hadn't said *our hearts.* After he'd made peace with Freddie and Dora, Caroline had become as invisible as the maid who laid the fire he'd lit. Once the memories had been set ablaze, he and the children had savored the warmth while Caroline had been left in the cold. Not anymore...not tonight. "You belong with us."

"Not really."

She'd restrained her hair with a ribbon, but the unruly strands framed her face. He saw the same spirit in her eyes, but it had been dulled by disappointments like the one she'd suffered tonight. He had no business touching her, but he raised his hand and brushed her jaw with his thumb. Wise or not, he kissed her cheek. The caress held all the tenderness in his heart, but it felt shy and incomplete. Looking into her eyes, he wondered if she felt the same inadequacy.

He lowered his hand. "Let's have some of that pie."

Slightly flushed, she sat on the divan, cut a generous slice and handed it to him as he sat next to her. She cut a smaller one for herself and picked up her plate. Their forks scraped the china in unison, a sign they were tasting the same sweetness and feeling the same awkwardness.

After a third bite, she set the plate on the tray. "Your children are lovely, Tristan."

"It's only been a day, but you seem to know them."

"Little girls aren't hard to understand. Freddie's more of a challenge."

"For me, too."

"It'll take time," she said. "But I hope you all become close."

"I hope *we* become close." When she looked at him ...de eyes, he realized his mistake. *We* hinted at the two of them. He had to clarify. "I mean the four of us, of course."

"Of course." She echoed his sentiment, but he'd seen the glimmer in her eyes. They'd known each other only briefly, first through letters and now by circumstance, but he felt a connection that went deeper than time. Suddenly restless, he went to the fireplace and jabbed the logs with an iron rod. She'd married him because she wanted to be a mother to his children. He felt an obligation to make her dreams came true. He just didn't know how to truly make her part of the family without the risk of their feelings growing stronger.

She lifted her chin. "I suppose we should discuss what to do when your father arrives."

He should have been pleased with her sensible attitude, but the shift in topic annoyed him. He didn't want to talk about his father. He wanted to sit next to her on the divan and watch the flames shrink into embers. He hadn't asked her into his room to talk about their strategy, but it was a safer topic than figuring out how to be a family.

He stayed on his feet. "With the bridge down, we have some time to prepare. The limited nature of our marriage is no one's business, but it's important for the sake of the children that we appear to be—" *in love* "—united."

"And happy," she added.

"Yes."

"Concerning your father, what do I need to know?" She sat with her hands folded in her lap, a willing student.

"Officially his name is Harold Smythe, Duke of Willoughby. Willoughby is a place. You should address him as 'your grace.'"

"'Your grace,'" she repeated.

"Yes." The title sounded awkward on her American lips and foreign to his ears. "In England, as a third son,

I was addressed as Lord Tristan. As heir apparent, I've been assigned a courtesy title from my father's lesser titles. I won't use it in America."

"If you *did* use it, what would it be?"

"Tristan Willoughby Smith, Marquess of Hayvenhurst."

She looked befuddled. "I think I prefer 'major.'"

"So do I." He smiled at her. "You're officially Caroline Bradley Smith, Marchioness of Hayvenhurst."

Her cheeks paled. "I feel like Dora finding out her middle name. I can hardly say it, let alone write it out."

"You'll do fine."

She shook her head. "I know how to be a mother, but a marchioness is another matter altogether. How long do you think he'll stay?"

"I don't know." A day was too long in Tristan's opinion. "I have no intention of returning with him to England, but he'll attempt to persuade me. One of us has to give in. It won't be me."

He thought of the gnarled branches of the Smythe family tree. Some had died of natural causes; others had to be pruned for the health of the tree. In that regard he'd cut himself off from his father, but the roots were very much intact. Freddie was the newest branch on the tree, and he needed protection Tristan couldn't give if he died. To hide his concern and sadness, he turned his back to Caroline and stared into the flames.

He heard the swish of her robe, then felt her hand on his arm. "I've been wondering. What happened to your mother?"

"She died of influenza. I was five."

"I'm so sorry."

"So am I," he said quietly. "The ring I gave you, it was hers."

"I'm honored." She hesitated. "I'll return it when—" She didn't finish. *When he died...when she ended the marriage.*

Tristan's heart clawed at his chest. He cared about the ring, but he cared more about the children. "If I die—"

Her fingers tightened on his arm. "Don't talk like that."

"We have to be realistic. If I die, leave immediately."

Her eyes dimmed. "May I say something?"

She'd speak her mind whether he granted permission or not. "Go ahead."

"Bitterness is a kind of poison. For a time I was bitter about Charles. I only made myself unhappy."

"What are you saying?"

"Perhaps there's another way to deal with your father."

"Such as?"

"Kindness… Charity."

He shrugged off her hand. "Those are lovely sentiments, but you don't know the duke."

"No, I don't. But I know you worry about the influence he may have on the children. The only way to counteract his behavior is through your own. Compassion instead of disdain. Acceptance instead of manipulation. You cannot control the duke's behavior, but you can control your own. You can choose to set an example for Freddie and Dora by treating everyone—even the duke—with courtesy and respect."

Tristan remembered himself in short pants, standing in his father's study awaiting discipline for a mild prank. The duke had caned his bare backside until he was begging for mercy. Could he repay that treatment with courtesy and respect? He doubted it. But one thing he did know about his father's treatment of him, the humiliation had turned him into a fighter. Being a fighter turned him into a soldier. Soldiers fought and sometimes died. They protected those in their care. Tristan thought of his children. He'd protect them and so would Caroline, but who would protect *her?* The duke would belittle her at every turn. He'd insult her and point out her faults. His visit would be difficult for everyone, but especially the woman he would view as a future duchess, particularly if she followed her own advice and returned his insults with kindness. No, if she would not protect herself, he'd do it for her. Tristan knew what he had to do. "We'll begin lessons tomorrow."

"Lessons in what?"

"How to be a marchioness." He didn't want her to change. He liked her the way she was, but he knew the power of symbols and protocol. They could shield her from some of the duke's scorn.

He tried to read her expression but couldn't. In one instant anger flashed in her eyes. In the next, she looked like a nervous child at a piano recital. Being married to a nobleman clearly didn't appeal to her. She hesitated, then stood. "We need to deal with your father's expectations, so whatever you say will be fine. It's late. If you'll excuse me—"

"Of course."

She headed for the door to the closet, pausing before she stepped into the dark. "Goodnight, Tristan."

"Goodnight, Caroline."

He might have approached and kissed her cheek, but she closed the door, leaving him to wonder if their wedding night had seemed as inadequate to her as it did to him.

Caroline closed the door to her room and thought about Tristan's plan to make her into a marchioness. How could a woman like herself—someone who had clerked in a store and liked to bake pies—become a noblewoman? After removing her robe, she blew out the lamp and slid into the narrow bed. The evening had been a peculiar mix of triumph and disaster. She was thrilled with Tristan's connection to his children, and she had dared to hope the four of them would become a family.

Then he'd spoken of his father and titles, and she'd been reminded that he belonged in England. She'd felt like a fish out of water...a fish about a thousand miles from any water at all. She'd never belong in Tristan's world, not as a wife and not as a marchioness. If he survived the malaria, he'd want an annulment. Whatever hope she had for the marriage to ripen into love had to be denied. She pulled the covers up to her chin.

Lord, where are You?

She closed her eyes against the dark, but her throat tightened with longing. She wanted to be settled and content. She'd wanted to be a wife and mother. She'd been hopeful until Tristan mentioned giving her lessons. Sleep stayed away, but she didn't bother playing the dream game. Instead she wept for what she'd never have and the woman she couldn't be.

Chapter Ten

A week passed with Caroline slipping into a quiet routine. Along with Evaline she planned meals for her family. She baked pies, saw to the children's lessons and made sure they washed behind their ears. Dora happily called her Aunt Caroline, but Freddie didn't call her anything. Whether he resented her place in the family, or whether the resentment came from being ten years old with a dislike of schoolwork, she didn't know.

She'd also slipped into a routine with Tristan. At night he tucked the children into bed, then they met in his suite and sat by the fire. She'd told him more about Charles, and he'd spoken of his life in England, his military accomplishments and the pain of losing Molly. In those quiet hours they became friends...more than friends. She tried to deny her feelings, but she had to admit Tristan was a man she could easily love.

The admission frightened her because his feelings were unreadable. Sometimes he teased and flirted with her. Other times he treated her like a maiden aunt. Did she interest him or bore him? She didn't know, but she disliked what he called her "duchess" lessons. In the droll tones of a professor, pacing as if giving a lecture, he'd schooled her in titles, etiquette and English history, Smythe family lore and the Willoughby holdings. He'd also suggested she learn how to ride, something she steadfastly refused to do. While she enjoyed Tristan's attention, she cringed at his effort to turn her into someone she wasn't, someone she couldn't be.

She was happiest with the children, and that's where she was now. She and Dora were pinning a hem on a new pinafore.

"Aunt Caroline?" the child asked.

"Yes, Dora?"

"Do you think Daddy will get well?"

Caroline's breath caught in her throat. "I hope so."

"I want to know for sure." Her voice came out in a squeak.

As much as Caroline wanted to hide behind easy assurances, the child deserved the truth. "He's getting better thanks to the medicine." She inserted another pin. It pricked her finger and drew blood. "Miss Bessie is hopeful and so am I."

Dora stood on the box like a statue, her shoulders straight and her chin firm. "Mommy said God would look out for us."

"He does."

"I'm glad," she said simply.

The faith of a child… Caroline envied it. She'd once believed with the same ease, but she'd learned that not all prayers were answered the way she wanted. Instead of a family of her own, God had given her this precious child and her troubled brother. As for their troubled father, she didn't dare hope for more than she had.

A terrified cry came from downstairs "Miss Caroline!" The voice belonged to Evaline.

Caroline imagined Tristan lying in a heap in his study,

delirious with fever. He seemed well last night, but he hadn't joined the family for breakfast. She assumed he'd gone for an early ride on Cairo, but now she worried. She lifted Dora off the box and set her on her feet. "Wait here."

"No!" The child clutched Caroline's skirt. "I'm scared."

Caroline didn't dare bring her downstairs. Seeing Tristan passed out would only frighten the girl more. She settled for giving Dora a firm hug. "Wait here, sweetheart. I'll be back as soon as I can."

"I want my daddy!"

"Of course you do." Caroline smoothed back the child's messy braid. "Let me see what's happening, then I'll come back. Okay?"

With her bottom lip trembling, Dora nodded. Caroline kissed her forehead and hurried to the stairs. What she saw from the landing made no sense at all. Evaline was fanning the face of a woman lying in a heap on the floor. She was on her back with her head in Evaline's lap. Her dark hair was curled on the housekeeper's white apron and her gown made a puddle of black silk. A young woman, presumably a lady's maid, stood in the corner with her back pressed against the wall.

Evaline looked up at Caroline with wide eyes. "This woman fainted!"

"Who is she?"

"My daughter-in-law." The voice was male, unfamiliar and distinctly British. Caroline looked at the door, where she saw a tall man in an expensively tailored coat and a top hat. He had blue eyes that matched Tristan's, blond hair threaded with gray and Tristan's nose and chin. Instantly she recognized the Duke of Willoughby. With a woman unconscious, she had no time for introductions. "Good afternoon, sir."

Belatedly she recalled Tristan's instructions. She should have called him 'your grace.'"

He looked at her as if she were a bug. "You must be the children's nanny."

"No, your grace," she said, still coming down the stairs. "I'm Tristan's wife."

"Molly?" He gaped at her. "I thought you were dead."

"I'm Caroline," she answered. "And I suggest we save the explanation for later. Your daughter-in-law needs medical attention."

Crouching at the woman's side, she put her hand on her forehead. As the duke's daughter-in-law, she had to be Louisa, Andrew's widow. Tristan had detailed the family tree in their late-night talks, but he'd said little about Louisa except that she'd married Andrew. The heat of fever instantly dampened Caroline's palm. "She's burning up."

The woman moaned but didn't open her eyes. Caroline turned to Evaline. "Do you have smelling salts?"

"In the kitchen."

"Fetch them." She looked back at the unconscious woman. Not only was she burning up, but blisters also were erupting on her forehead and neck. Bessie had a better eye for disease, but Caroline knew contagion when she saw it. With a chill running down her spine, she looked at the duke. "Has your daughter-in-law been exposed to smallpox?"

"Heavens no!"

His denial was too quick to be trusted. "But you took the train from the East Coast. Was it crowded?"

"Yes, but—"

"So you don't really know. She could have—"

"She has a name." The man stood even taller, glaring at her with an intensity that unnerved her. "This is Marchioness Andrew Smythe. I don't care that we're in

America! She's to be addressed as 'Marchioness Andrew.'"

"Formalities can wait, sir. I'm concerned for her health." *And the health of my family.*

"I assure you," he said coldly. "The marchioness did *not* contract smallpox. I wouldn't allow it."

Did this man think he could control a deadly and infectious disease? Tristan had described him as difficult. Caroline had to agree. Unwilling to argue with him, she spoke to the lady's maid. "Do you know if she's been exposed to anyone who's been sick?"

"No, ma'am." The girl couldn't have been more than seventeen.

Caroline felt sorry for her. "Would you see to her trunks, please? They'll need to go upstairs."

"Yes, ma'am."

The girl curtsied and slipped through the door. Caroline removed a handkerchief from her pocket and wiped Louisa's brow. If the woman had smallpox, the entire household would be in danger. The disease killed nearly half the people who became infected, and it left the survivors badly scarred. Silently Caroline gave thanks she'd told Dora to wait upstairs.

Evaline arrived with the ammonia carbonate. "Stay back," Caroline said quietly. "It could be smallpox."

"Lord, have mercy!" Evaline cried.

"I'm not sure." Caroline indicated the line of bumps. "But the blisters are worrisome. We need Bessie."

Evaline wrung her apron. "She and Mr. Jon went riding today. They're looking for those healing herbs she talks about."

"Send Noah to find them. And summon Tristan, please."

"Yes, Mrs. Caroline."

"And Evaline?" She looked at the housekeeper with a silent plea. "Dora's in the sewing room. She's frightened."

"I'll go to her." The housekeeper headed up the stairs.

"Speak to her, but don't open the door," Caroline called after her. "Whatever you do, keep her upstairs."

When Evaline reached the landing, she turned and the women locked eyes. They both knew what an illness, even a mild one, could do to Tristan. Swallowing hard, Caroline went back to tending her patient. The more information she had, the more she could help Bessie. Before uncorking the smelling salts, she took Louisa's pulse. It was strong and steady.

Without looking up, she spoke to the duke. "Did she have breakfast this morning?"

"How should I know?" He grumbled. "I had eggs and toast in my room. The eggs were cold, and the toast was dry. The hotel in that little town is deplorable. I barely slept."

The man was a self-obsessed fool, a benefit if he'd stayed in his room and not asked anyone in town about Tristan or the children. She uncorked the smelling salts and held the vial under the woman's nose. Louisa inhaled once, twice, then startled into consciousness.

"What happened?" she said in a weak voice.

"You fainted," Caroline replied.

"I'm so sorry to be a bother."

She tried to sit up, but Caroline nudged her flat. "You need a few minutes to recover. My sister's a nurse. She'll be here soon."

The woman's eyes lit up. "Are you Dora's nanny?"

"No," Caroline answered for the second time. "I'm Tristan's wife."

"Molly?"

The poor woman looked as if she thought she'd died

and really was seeing Molly. Caroline took pity on her. "I'm not Molly. My name is Caroline. Tristan and I married just recently."

"Oh, I see." Sorrow filled her eyes.

The duke grumbled behind them. "I should have been informed."

Louisa glanced up at the duke, her eyes shiny with fever or sudden tears. Caroline couldn't discern the difference, but news of her marriage to Tristan had saddened this woman. Perhaps the circumstances had renewed her grief for her own husband. Caroline spoke in a hush. "I'm very sorry about Andrew."

Something knifelike flicked in her sparkling blue irises. "Thank you."

The duke interrupted. "Where is the marquess?"

"Who?" Intimidated, Caroline forgot her lessons in titles and etiquette.

"Lord Tristan, of course!" the duke bellowed.

The pomposity irked her. "We're in America, your grace. He goes by 'major.'"

Louisa arched a brow, whether out of shock or pleasure Caroline didn't know. The duke said nothing, but his silence carried a threat. Caroline looked back to the ailing woman. "I'm sure Tristan will express his regrets for your loss."

Louisa's eyes filled with longing, then she squeezed Caroline's hand. As their fingers touched, her gaze went to the ring on Caroline's finger. The pink diamond spoke far louder than words, and Louisa looked up. "I wish you and Tristan nothing but happiness, Marchioness. We were good friends, you know. We grew up together. We were…close." Fresh sorrow dimmed the woman's eyes.

Judging by her obvious melancholy, this woman and Tristan had been more than childhood playmates. What exactly did "close" mean? And why hadn't Tristan done more than mention Louisa's name in passing?

Louisa managed a tiny smile. "Does Tristan still love horses?"

"Very much."

"He wanted to breed Arabians," she murmured.

Louisa closed her eyes, leaving Caroline to weigh the unexpected information. Louisa, it seemed, had known Tristan extremely well...well enough to know his hopes and dreams. She'd come to America expecting to find him widowed. What else had she expected? It seemed to Caroline Tristan had left out more than a few important details about his sister-in-law. Why hadn't he spoken of her? He'd schooled Caroline in the names of his brothers and cousins, his grandparents and servants to whom he'd been close. He'd described everyone except Louisa, who was beautiful, poised and gracious, even while lying on the entry floor. The woman was clearly born to be a duchess, while Caroline had been born to bake pies.

She studied Louisa's flushed face. "How long have you been ill?"

"A few days, I suppose."

"Have you had headaches?" Caroline asked. "Perhaps nausea?"

The duke interrupted. "What kind of question is that?"

Caroline looked over her shoulder, raising her chin until her eyes met his cold stare. "It's a necessary one, your grace."

He lowered his chin. "A *lady* doesn't speak of such things," he said, implying Caroline wasn't a lady.

Her temper flared, but she held it in check. Turning back to Louisa, she saw that more bumps had emerged at her hairline.

Evaline came back to the entry through the back hall,

an indication that she'd spoken to Dora and used the back-stairs to send Noah in search of Bessie. "Dora's quiet now," she said to Caroline. "I sent Freddie to get his father. Noah's going after Jon and Miss Bessie."

"Good."

Lady Louisa spoke in a hush. "What's wrong with me?"

"I don't know yet." Caroline thought of all the things the rash could indicate. Smallpox was the biggest worry, but other diseases—measles in particular—had to be considered.

"I'm so sorry," Louisa murmured. "I should have stayed at the hotel. The children—" She sealed her lips, then implored Caroline with a bleak stare. "If something happens to Dora or Freddie, I'll never forgive myself."

She'd used the children's everyday names, a sign she cared about them. "Let's wait and see," Caroline replied.

With another look, the two women moved from acquaintances, and possibly rivals, to allies. No matter the cost, the children had to be protected. When Louisa's eyes fluttered shut, Caroline knew she was praying the same prayers that had run through Caroline's mind for the past five minutes.

The duke cleared his throat, an unnecessary gesture used solely to gain attention. Caroline looked up and over her shoulder. He had a gaunt face, a liver spot on his neck and a critical arch to his bushy brows. Her initial reaction to the man was distaste, but she couldn't ignore the concern in his eyes. Whether the concern came from a fatherly affection for Louisa or from what he hoped to gain by using her, Caroline didn't know.

She had expected to be challenged by Tristan's father. She hadn't expected to compete with a beautiful woman from Tristan's past. In Denver Caroline had always been second-best. In Louisa's company, she was second-best yet again. Considering Tristan's silence, it seemed possible, even likely, that he had feelings for Louisa. They shared a past, and it had been romantic enough to bring Louisa to Wyoming. With Andrew gone and Tristan widowed, nothing stood between them—except his unconsummated marriage to a lowly American.

The front door swung open and Tristan strode into the entry hall. His gaze whipped from the duke to Louisa. He didn't see Caroline at all. She'd become invisible to him. He had eyes only for the woman lying on the floor, looking up at him with such adoration Caroline could hardly breathe.

Ten minutes ago Tristan had been in the barn grooming Cairo when Freddie had come running through the double doors.

Grandfather's here! I want to meet him!

The use of the name shouldn't have troubled Tristan, but it did. Approaching the house with Freddie at his side, he'd told the boy to mind his manners and wait outside. Climbing the steps, he'd mentally rehearsed his first words to his father in fifteen years. *Good afternoon, your grace. Shall we speak in my study?*

He planned to tell his father he'd do his duty when the time came, but that he wouldn't be returning to England until necessary, the implication being he wanted nothing to do with his father, living or dead. He hoped the insult would send the old man packing.

Tristan had been ready for the duke. He hadn't been at all prepared to see Louisa. The sight of her paralyzed his lungs. He'd once loved this woman. He'd been hurt when she rejected him and confused when she refused to see him. The tender feelings had faded with time, but he

had wondered for years why she left him, if he'd somehow failed her or if she'd truly loved Andrew.

Watching her now, he could feel his plans for his father derailing.

Louisa lying prostrate on the floor complicated the
situation. Molly had filled his heart completely and he'd
recovered from being jilted, but the wound had closed
over a knot of guilt. For years he'd wondered if he'd failed
to rescue her from a plot of some kind, or if her love for
Andrew had been sincere. Her dark clothing indicated
mourning, so he stepped forward to offer condolences.

"Stop!" Caroline cried.

He didn't appreciate being ordered around in front of
his father. "What is it?" he said coldly.

"Louisa is ill."

The ramifications chilled him as surely as the fever
heated his blood. With his weakened system, he couldn't
afford another infection. His brow furrowed. "How ill?"

"I don't know," Caroline said in a hush. "We're waiting
for Bessie, but the pustules indicate a pox of some sort."

Fear for himself turned to terror for his children. He'd
seen outbreaks of smallpox in the West Indies. He'd been
vaccinated, a privilege of being an officer, but his children had no such protection. He was familiar enough with
the disease to know the symptoms. He looked down at
Louisa's face, forcing himself to see the blisters on her
hairline rather than her pleading eyes. The bumps were
scattered and small. They didn't look like smallpox to
him, but he knew a sure sign of the disease.

He looked at Caroline. "Does she have pox on her
hands?"

"I didn't look."

Louisa looked at her hands herself, then held the one
she'd offered to him palm out. "Both hands are clear."

"Then it's not smallpox." Crouching at her side, he clasped her hand. "It's most likely chicken pox, which, as I recall, I had and you didn't."

"That's right," she murmured.

Time had changed her appearance, but she'd only become more beautiful. It had changed Tristan, too. While he treasured the gold of pleasant memories, he hadn't forgotten the pain of unanswered questions or the immediate problem of his father looming behind him. "This is quite a surprise," he said to her.

"For me, too." She wrinkled her nose as if she were still a little girl. "I seem to have fainted in your entry hall."

"I can see that."

"It reminds me of the day I fell off Bonfire."

Bonfire was the mare she'd ridden when they'd explored his father's estate as adolescents. An excellent horsewoman, Louisa had fallen just once but she'd landed in a stream and gotten covered with moss. It had been a silly accident, one where they'd ended up laughing and kissing for the first time. It had been his first such experience...hers, too. A smile curved on his lips. "That was quite an event."

"Yes." Averting her eyes, she withdrew her hand. "Your wife is taking good care of me."

Caroline... He'd forgotten her in his relief over the pox, but he looked at her now. Her eyes were full of questions, dark and guarded in a way he'd never seen before. In their late-night talks he'd barely mentioned Louisa, yet here he sat holding the woman's hand, speaking in a jaunty tone and trading memories like the old friends they were.

"Caroline," he said too boisterously. "This is my sister-in-law."

"We've met," she said.

"Yes, of course." Feeling foolish, he stood and looked down at Louisa. "I employ a nurse for the children. I'm sure she's well versed in chicken pox."

He looked to Caroline, both for confirmation and to include her, but she focused her eyes on Louisa. "Evaline went to get her. She's my sister. Her name's Bessie and she's far more knowledgeable than I am. I'm sorry to have given you such a scare."

"Nonsense," Louisa replied. "I fainted in your entry hall. If anyone owes an apology, it would be me. You've been sweet and exceptionally understanding."

Caroline looked more ill at ease than ever. Tristan wanted to intervene, but she found her tongue first. "We'd planned for the duke and his companion to stay in the guesthouse, but you should be near Bessie. Can you climb the stairs?"

Louisa tried to sit up. "I'm a bit wobbly…"

Tristan offered his hand. "Allow me to assist."

Louisa took it and he pulled her upright, keenly aware of his father's eyes on his back. If his sister-in-law's presence was an indication, his father was already attempting to manipulate him. The old man had known of Tristan's infatuation with Louisa. Tristan strongly suspected she was being used to lure him back to England. The manipulation made Tristan sick. If Andrew had been a pampered pet, Louisa had been reduced to bait.

He felt sorry for her. "Caroline will take care of you," he said gently.

"Of course," his wife agreed.

He wished Evaline were present so he didn't have to treat her like a servant. "Do we have a guest room ready?"

"Yes, Major."

He didn't blame her for the formality, but it irked him. He'd schooled her in etiquette, but he hadn't expected her to treat *him* any differently. It also put a chink in the united front he wanted to present to his father. The lapse worried him. He could only imagine how insulting the duke had been to Caroline upon his arrival. And now she had to deal with chicken pox. Louisa would be well mannered, but Freddie and Dora would likely fall ill and be irritable.

Even as he explained away her attitude, Tristan knew he was ignoring the obvious. A woman from his past had just walked into his life, and he'd reacted like a smitten adolescent. No wonder Caroline had put up her guard. He'd insulted her and belittled their vows. He felt inept and wanted to explain, but he couldn't follow her up the stairs. Their talk would have to wait until tonight, both for the sake of appearances and because he had to deal with his father.

When the women reached the top of the stairs, he turned to the duke with deliberate slowness. "Good afternoon, your grace."

"Good afternoon, Marquess." The duke drawled out the title. "You look well."

"I go by 'major,'" he said coldly. "And I'm quite fine, thank you." The malaria had stayed away for more than a week. He'd been feeling much better since Bessie increased the quinine, but he felt edgy from lack of sleep and his temper tended to flare.

The duke arched a bushy silver brow. "You've forgotten your manners, Tristan. Not only did you fail to advise me of your marriage, but you also didn't introduce me to your bride."

"I assure you, I didn't forget. Subjecting my wife to

your scrutiny was less important than caring for Louisa. You should have stayed in Cheyenne until she was well."

The man huffed. "She's not that ill."

"I beg to differ." Tristan spoke as if he were dressing down a soldier. "She fainted and she's contagious. Two children reside in this household. How long has Louisa been ill?"

"How would I know? I have concerns of my own."

"You haven't changed a bit, have you?" Tristan wasn't surprised. The duke always put himself first.

"Neither have you," the man retorted. "But the circumstances *have* changed. You'll return to England immediately."

"No.

"You have no choice in the matter."

"Yes, I do," Tristan said mildly. "I can't stop being your son, but I won't return to England to be at your beck and call. I'll assume my responsibilities when necessary and no sooner."

"It's necessary now."

"It will be necessary when you pass on." Refusing to argue, Tristan crossed the entry to the door and turned the knob.

His father bellowed at him. "Tristan!"

As if he were a boy, he stopped. Like the officer he'd become, he made a slow turn that demanded respect. When he didn't receive it, he glared at his father. "What is it?"

"I want to meet my grandson."

Such a meeting was inevitable, but Tristan dreaded it. "You'll meet Freddie at supper." Of course there had been no mention of Dora.

"I want to meet him now," the duke insisted.

Tristan bristled. "You might have authority in Willoughby, but you have none at The Barracks."

At that moment, the front door flew open. Freddie burst into the entry hall, proving yet again that no one, not even his children, followed Tristan's orders.

Chapter Eleven

"Grandfather!" The boy had eyes only for the old man, and the old man had eyes only for him. Tristan could have been a coatrack for all that he mattered.

Looking ridiculously pleased, the duke offered Freddie his hand. "Frederick! It's a pleasure to meet you at last."

The boy beamed at the attention. "Hello, Grandfather."

Tristan's first instinct was to wedge himself between Freddie and the older man. If Tristan succumbed to the malaria, Freddie would replace Andrew in the duke's "affections." He'd be turned into a pet. Tristan couldn't allow his son to become spoiled, but intervention would exact a price. Freddie might become rebellious, and the duke would certainly be indignant. Tristan also understood Freddie's hunger for family. The boy had no cousins, no uncles or aunts aside from Louisa, whom Freddie had never met. A grandfather should have been a welcome addition to the boy's world. Sadly, Tristan had no illusions about the kind of love Freddie would receive from the duke. The roots of the Smythe family tree had been infected with selfishness, scheming and manipulation. The duke cared far more about his legacy than he did about the needs of a child. Even now the man was studying Freddie as if he were livestock.

"Look at that blond hair!" he declared. "You're clearly a Smythe."

Yes, but Freddie had his mother's nose. He also had Molly's inquisitiveness. Freddie was...himself. He was also a child and susceptible to flattery. "Freddie, you're excused," Tristan said firmly. "You'll see your grandfather later."

The duke huffed. "Come now, Tristan. Allow the boy to stay. We have much to discuss. After all, he's a future duke."

Freddie's eyes popped wide. "I am?"

Tristan had told his children nothing of his title and family. It had been irrelevant until his brothers died, then he'd felt the weight of his illness. "We'll speak later," he said to the boy.

"But Father—"

"Freddie—" His voice held a warning. To his relief, his son held back an argument. Tristan softened his tone. "We'll speak later. Find Noah and see if he needs help putting up the horses and carriages."

The duke raised his brows in seeming shock. "Surely you have servants for such tasks?"

Freddie liked helping on the ranch. He never argued about chores, but he was looking at Tristan quizzically. "Do I have to?"

"Yes, you do."

The duke smirked. "You'll love England, my boy. We have an entire staff just for the barns. You won't have to lift a finger."

Freddie looked at him, wide-eyed. "No chores?"

"Not a one."

Tristan interrupted. "That's quite enough, your grace."

The man's plan couldn't have been more obvious—undermine Tristan's authority and steal Freddie's affection. As much as Tristan wanted to walk away from his father, he had no choice but to sit down with the man and lay down some rules.

The duke smiled possessively at his grandson. "Do what your father says, Freddie. We'll have plenty of time together."

The boy seemed to grow six inches. "I'm glad you're here, Grandfather."

"So am I, Freddie."

Tristan couldn't say the same. As the boy left, Tristan indicated the hall leading to his study. "We need to talk."

"Yes, we do."

Ramrod straight, the duke paced down the hall. Tristan followed until they reached the study. He indicated the duke should enter first. As the man passed him, Tristan thought about what his father would see. Paintings of Arabian stallions covered the walls. The carpet had been imported from Persia, and military memorabilia decorated a dozen mahogany shelves. He had hundreds of books, everything from poetry to mathematics. Burgundy drapes hung from the windows, and comfortable chairs and a divan made a half circle in front of a stone hearth. The room told Tristan's story, though he felt certain his father would show no interest.

Predictably the duke crossed to Tristan's desk without once turning his head, then without asking permission, he helped himself to a cigar from a crystal humidor. The cigars were a gift from the men in the West India Regiment, and they'd become a treasured souvenir.

Ignoring his father's presumption, Tristan sat behind his desk. The duke dropped down on the chair across from him, causing the leather to squeak. It squeaked again as the man rolled the cigar in his fingers, silently ordering Tristan to light it.

Tristan wouldn't do it. He enjoyed a good cigar, but he didn't enjoy his father's company. The fact saddened him. Just as Freddie longed for a grandfather, Tristan wanted a father who'd offer advice and understanding, someone who'd care that he was struggling with malaria and had lost his wife, that he was raising his children and trying not to fall in love until he could claim a small piece of the future. The duke was his father by blood, but the family tree was diseased in a way that made them strangers.

The duke continued to roll the unlit cigar between his fingers. "Again you've forgotten your manners—"

"Not at all."

"—*and* your responsibilities." His eyes narrowed. "You can't possibly remain in America. I raised you to do your duty."

"You didn't raise me at all." Tristan had been closer to the groomsmen in the stable, even the cook, than he'd been to his own father. Now the man acted as if he owned him.

"You're my heir," the duke insisted. "You'll do what I say."

Tristan showed Cairo more respect. "I'll do what I believe is best for everyone involved."

The duke rolled the cigar between his fingers, daring Tristan to be a gentleman and light it. It was a trap of sorts. Lighting it was an act of compliance. *Not* lighting it made him a petulant child. Either way, his father was pulling the strings as if Tristan were a puppet. Those strings had to be cut, so Tristan smirked. "I don't recall offering you a cigar."

"You didn't."

"They're Cuban. A gift from my men."

"Then I'll take another for later." The duke opened the humidor, took two cigars to make a point and put them inside his coat. Staring at Tristan, he removed a match from his pocket, struck it against his shoe and lit the cigar clamped between his lips.

Tristan smelled sulfur and thought of the battlefield. He'd fought for his country and he'd been willing to die for it. He would do no less to protect his family. It was too soon to send Caroline away with the children. Their departure would alert the duke to the problem of his health. Neither could Tristan stand to give up even a minute with them. He and Freddie were just getting to know each other, and Dora wouldn't understand at all. She'd feel abandoned and rightly so.

If his father wouldn't leave and the children had to stay, Tristan had only one choice. He'd live in close quarters with his enemy. As a military man, he could do it. The boy who'd longed for his fathers' attention had grown up and become a father himself, one who'd protect his children at any cost.

Tristan took a cigar of his own, lit it and blew a ring of smoke, watching it dissipate to suggest he was bored. Finally, he said, "I'm sorry about Andrew and Oscar."

"Thank you."

"Pennwright provided the details." Tristan thought of the note in the secretary's familiar hand. His own father hadn't told him of the deaths of his brothers, and even now the duke accepted sympathy without offering it in return. Tristan hadn't seen his brothers in years, but the three of them had shared the rituals of childhood, pulling pranks and wrestling with each other. They hadn't been close, but they shared the same blood.

His father puffed heavily on the cigar, causing the end to burn hot before it withered to ash. When the tip looked ready to break apart, he tapped it into a candy dish not meant for ashes. "I'm going to be blunt, Tristan. Andrew was the finest son a man could have. His death left me in shock…and somewhat unprepared. Oscar, as you know, was a terrible disappointment."

And what was I to you?

The question stayed unasked, in part because Tristan knew the answer. If Andrew had been a pampered poodle and Oscar a cur, Tristan had been a puppy wagging for attention.

Suddenly far away, the duke looked admiringly at the signet ring that never left his finger. "Andrew was a mirror image of myself. He exceeded every expectation I had…except for one." He raised his gaze to Tristan with the suddenness of a bullet. "Your brother failed to produce a son, but that no longer matters. You've given me Freddie. He looks like me, don't you think?"

The man's vanity knew no bounds. "Freddie looks like himself."

"Yes, but he's clearly a Smythe."

So was Tristan. Again he'd been overlooked as a branch on the family tree. "And your point?"

The man's gaze sharpened with the intelligence that made him dangerous. "We've had our differences, Tristan. When you failed to reply to my letter, I came expecting you to be as rude as you've been. I was hoping, however, that duty alone would prompt you to return immediately to England."

Even if he'd been healthy, Tristan would have delayed returning to England. He had a duty to fulfill, and he'd been born and bred to be loyal, but he didn't want his father to have any control whatsoever over his children. His illness made the obligation treacherous, and he didn't want the duke to know about it. The old buzzard would circle until Tristan died, then he'd take Freddie for his own.

Tristan blew another ring of smoke. "I'll meet my obligation when it's time. You seem well enough to me."

He man harrumphed. "Of course I'm well enough."

"Then there's no hurry," he said lazily. "As you can see, I have responsibilities here."

"None that matter," the duke declared. "Sell this ridiculous ranch at once."

"No."

"I insist."

Tristan knew better than to argue with the duke. Stalling offered the wisest course. "I'll consider a trip in the spring. There's no point in a winter voyage."

The older man's brows knit together. "I can't stay until spring."

"Of course not." The sooner his father left for England, the safer Freddie would be. "I imagine you and Louisa are eager to return home."

"Louisa." He spat her name. "She's useless to me now. She's nothing but a mannequin, always has been."

Inwardly Tristan balked at the insult. The girl he'd known in England had been good-natured and fun. She'd also been intelligent. Calling her a mannequin said far more about the duke than it did about Louisa. He couldn't stop himself from defending her.

"I'd hardly call Louisa *useless*."

The duke gave him a speculative stare. "You ruined my plans by marrying that American woman. How long has it been?"

There was no point in hedging. "A little more than a week."

The man tapped the cigar on the candy dish. "If I

didn't know better, I'd think you married her to embarrass me. She'll never be accepted, you know."

Tristan thought of the reasons for their marriage and the option of an annulment. He enjoyed the duchess lessons because of Caroline's good humor, but she clearly had no desire to assume the role. He wished she did. The more time he spent with her, the more he appreciated her natural goodness. If he hadn't been ill, he'd have viewed the limitation of their marriage in a very different light. As things stood, he couldn't allow the marriage to go beyond friendship. If they fell in love and he died, she'd grieve. If he lived, she'd become the Duchess of Willoughby, a fate with other costs.

The duke leaned back in the chair, his eyes narrowing like a sleepy cat. "In their own way, women are useful. Louisa's still quite lovely, don't you think?"

Tristan heard his father's sly tone and recoiled. If he denied noticing Louisa's beauty, he'd be a liar. If he agreed with his father, he'd be disrespectful to women everywhere. He answered by silently puffing on the cigar.

The duke mirrored his actions. "As I recall, you were once in love with her."

"I also enjoyed sardines for breakfast. I outgrew that habit."

"Nonetheless, a man never forgets his first conquest."

Tristan had kissed Louisa, but she hadn't been a conquest. He'd been with just one woman, his wife. He refused to let the insult stand. "Louisa wasn't a conquest. She deserves respect."

"But you wanted her."

Tristan had heard enough. "What are you suggesting?"

The duke set the stump of the cigar in the dish. "Divorce your worthless American wife and you can have Louisa."

"I have no reason to divorce Caroline." *And every reason to love her.* The thought sobered him. He couldn't love Caroline, not yet. Maybe not ever. But neither could he deny the hope that he'd recover and that someday she'd want to be his duchess. He had to stop his father's criticism now. "I care deeply for my wife. She's a good woman."

"No, she isn't." His father huffed with disgust. "She's unsuitable. She's crass and rude and—"

"That's enough."

The duke frowned. "You always were intractable. Suit yourself. Don't divorce her. You can keep Louisa as your mistress."

Tristan had expected such a remark. The duke kept one mistress in London and another in Paris. Even when Tristan's mother had been alive, he'd broken his vows. Tristan believed in marriage and he'd honored Molly with his fidelity. He'd give Caroline the same respect. "I'm not interested in a mistress," he said drily.

"You will be."

Tristan held in the retort. If his father sensed weakness, he'd move in for the kill. "This is none of your concern."

"I'm the duke," he said, matter of factly. "You're my heir. Everything you do is my concern. When I give an order, you'll follow it."

"No, sir. I will *not*."

"Why you—" the duke clenched his teeth. "You're an abomination! If Andrew had lived, I wouldn't have to put up with you!"

What did a son say to such outward disdain? Tristan didn't know, but a realization slowly dawned... As a boy he'd cowered in his father's presence and feared his punishment. Looking at the duke now, he saw a pompous fool, a man with an inflated notion of his own importance and the inability to care for others. The duke wasn't infallible. He wasn't God. He wasn't even close.

Tristan had to wonder… If God didn't have anything in common with the Duke of Willoughby, what was He like? Tristan thought of Caroline's dream game and how she'd seen into the hearts of his children. He recalled the gentle way she stitched the cut on his head and how she'd cried with him over Molly. In spite of losing her husband, she had a childlike faith in God's goodness and it sustained her. That kind of faith could sustain him, too.

Tristan felt as if he were shedding a too-tight skin, but he instantly went on alert. No matter what he felt, or didn't feel, for his father, Freddie had to be protected. That required all his attention and complete vigilance. He kept his voice mild. "Is there anything else, your grace?"

"Yes." The duke waited, silently commanding Tristan to kowtow to him. As an officer, Tristan had the patience to wait all day.

Finally the duke spoke. "Freddie is a future duke. He should begin training."

As if he were a dog. His military control kept Tristan calm. "Freddie is a boy. He doesn't need *training.*"

"Of course he does."

"He's not a pet, your grace. He's an active, happy child. I won't allow you to influence him."

"But I'm the duke."

"And I'm his father."

The old man seemed not to hear. "The boy has my build, don't you think?"

Tristan said nothing.

"And my coloring, too." The duke's eyes gleamed. "My hair was as blond as his until it turned gray."

Tristan also had light hair, not that his father ever noticed. "Is there anything else, your grace?"

His father stood. "I expect my accommodations are
ready?"

"Yes. You'll be staying in the guesthouse." Jon usually occupied it, but he'd moved to the bunkhouse for the
duration of the visit.

Tristan rose and came around the desk. He followed
his father out of the study to the entry hall, then stepped
in front of him and opened the door. His father's valet
had been waiting outside, and together the men went to
the guesthouse.

Shutting the door, Tristan thought about the tactics his
father would use to gain Freddie's affection. He'd spoil
the boy with gifts. He'd praise him until he was barking
like a trained seal. Tristan's blood burned in his veins,
a reminder of his illness. He had to stay healthy, and he
had to hide his condition from his father.

He also had to protect Caroline. If he didn't school
her properly, his father would flay her alive. She'd also
seen him take Louisa's hand. His feelings had been tiny
embers from the past. They'd flared in an unexpected
breeze and immediately died, but Caroline would recall
the sparks. He hadn't told her about Louisa because the
episode embarrassed him. No man liked being jilted. But
after what Caroline had witnessed, she deserved to know
what had happened.

The memory raised old questions. Had Louisa left
him because she loved Andrew? Or had he failed to rescue her from some sort of trouble? If he'd failed to help
her, he didn't want to repeat the mistake. He wanted to
speak with her, but she was ill. He'd have to wait for answers from Louisa, but tonight he'd give answers of his
own to Caroline.

* * *

"I'm sorry to be such trouble," Louisa said to Caroline as she climbed into bed. "My lady's maid can tend to my needs when she returns."

The girl had gone downstairs to fetch tea and a bowl of broth. Caroline had sent her. "I don't mind helping."

Louisa sighed. "If I'd known I had chicken pox, I'd have never left Cheyenne. I hope you don't come down with it."

Caroline had no such worries. "I've had it and so has my sister." Even more important, Tristan had had it as a child, though Caroline was still reeling from how she'd learned that small fact. He'd been close to this woman, even closer than she'd first thought. Had he loved her? Judging by how easily he'd taken Louisa's hand, it seemed more than possible. It seemed likely.

Louisa pulled the covers over the nightgown Caroline had loaned her because her trunk hadn't yet been delivered to her room. Bessie hadn't returned, but Caroline expected her any minute. Until the nurse arrived, she felt duty-bound to stay with Louisa.

She dipped a cloth in cool water and squeezed it nearly dry. "This will fight the fever."

Louisa slumped against the pillow. "I've been a terrible disruption to you."

Caroline put the folded cloth over Louisa's brow. "Don't worry about the children. If they get sick, we'll manage."

"You're too kind," Louisa said gently. "I wasn't apologizing for the chicken pox. I want you to know, I respect your marriage. In no way do I want to interfere—"

"It's all right," she said too quickly.

"No, it's not." Louisa removed the cloth from her brow. "How much has Tristan told you about his father?"

"Quite a bit." It was Louisa he'd neglected to mention.

"Then you know he's a conniver." She averted her eyes. "He had…expectations for Tristan and me."

"I wondered," Caroline murmured.

"Tristan must have told you about us."

He hadn't, but Caroline was too embarrassed to admit her ignorance. She took the cloth and dampened it again. "You're ill. We should speak later."

"No," Louisa insisted. "I have to get this off my chest. Would you give Tristan a message for me?"

Caroline stopped wringing the cloth. "What is it?"

"Tell him I'm sorry."

"For what?"

"Everything…" Louisa closed her eyes. "You're right. I'm too ill to think clearly. I shouldn't have said anything. I'm sorry, Caroline…so sorry." Tears leaked from her eyes.

Questions swarmed in Caroline's mind, but she couldn't quiz an ailing woman. It was Tristan who needed to explain, but what right did she have to confront him? He'd promised her nothing but respect. If he chose to keep secrets, he had that right. More troubled than she wanted to be, Caroline studied Louisa's face. The woman was pretty, even beautiful with her delicate nose and wide eyes. Her dark hair made a cloud on the pillow, and her figure had womanly curves any man would desire. She had poise, grace, intelligence and honor. She'd make a fine duchess, a position Caroline had no ability to fulfill.

It wasn't the first time she'd felt second-best to another woman, but it was the first time she'd felt that stab of inadequacy as Tristan's wife. If they hadn't already been married, what would he feel for Louisa? The noble thing to do—the honorable thing—was to immediately offer Tristan an annulment. If he had feelings for Louisa, she didn't want to stand in his way. Neither did she want to wait around for *him* to reject *her*.

Only the children stood as a barrier. She couldn't stand the thought of losing her adopted family, but neither could she return to being a governess after more than a week of being a mother. As she worried about the future, Louisa slipped into a restless slumber. Several minutes passed, then a soft knock sounded on the door.

"Come in," Caroline said.

Bessie stepped into the bedroom and closed the door behind her. "I hear we have a guest with chicken pox."

"We do." Caroline told her about Louisa's symptoms but nothing about Tristan's reaction to the woman…or her own. She needed time to sort her thoughts, but she also needed to know if Freddie and Dora had already had the childhood disease. "I need to speak to Tristan about the children. Do you need anything before I go?"

"I'm fine," Bessie said. "Jon's taking care of the herbs we collected."

"Did you find what you wanted?"

"I had an amazing time." Bessie's cheeks were pinker than usual, presumably from time in the sun, but Caroline had to wonder if Jon's company had something to do with the spark in her sister's eyes. The two of them often walked together after supper. Caroline wanted to hear more but not in front of Louisa.

"We'll talk later," she whispered.

Excusing herself, she headed downstairs to look for Tristan. He was nowhere to be found, but she learned about the duke's whereabouts from Evaline. He was safely tucked into the guesthouse.

"That man is full of himself," the housekeeper complained.

"I know," Caroline said. "But we have to put up with him. Louisa is much nicer."

Evaline sighed with sympathy. "That woman's going to be itching very badly. I hope the children don't get sick."

"I do, too," Caroline replied. "Have you seen the major?"

"He left a while ago."

She thought of the places he could be. Most likely he'd gone to the horse barn. She didn't want to be around horses, but she needed to speak with him. "Thank you, Evaline."

As she headed for the door, the housekeeper called after her. "Do I need to do anything special for dinner? The duke seems very hard to please."

Caroline thought a minute. She and Tristan had been eating supper on the veranda with the children. She loved their meals, especially the tone of Tristan's voice as he offered grace. She'd felt a new gentleness in him, a new hope. Tonight he had duties as his father's heir. "Tristan and I will eat with the duke in the dining room. If you'd see to the children, I'd appreciate it."

"Yes, ma'am."

Evaline returned to the kitchen, and Caroline paced through the front door and into the yard. In the distance she saw Jon approaching with a basket in each hand. They were full of stems, grass and flowers, an indication Bessie had indeed been successful in her hunt for medicinal herbs. Judging by Jon's dashing smile, they both enjoyed the expedition.

Their paths crossed in a patch of sunlight near the guesthouse. Caroline greeted him with a smile of her own. "You don't look like a man who's been ousted from his home."

"I'm not," he replied. "I gave it up willingly."

"That was kind of you."

He shrugged. "The less Tristan sees of his father, the better. Who's the woman he brought?"

"She's Andrew's widow."

Jon's brow shot up. "Louisa is here?"

"You know her?"

"Not personally, but—" He paused, clearly weighing his words. "Tristan will have to explain."

"No, he doesn't," she said quickly. He didn't owe her anything at all. They had a legal agreement for the purpose of protecting his children. Apart from that common concern, they were from different worlds. Tristan read Shakespeare. Caroline read her Bible, but little else. She'd grown up cooking for her father and sister. Tristan had grown up with servants who tended to his needs. He'd distanced himself from his father, but his feelings for Louisa were another matter entirely. Caroline's mind went down a sad and familiar road. How many times had she been interested in a man to have him set her aside for someone else?

"Caroline? Did you hear me?"

Jon's voice pulled her back to the sunlight. "I'm sorry. What did you say?"

"I asked how Tristan handled the initial meeting."

"With Louisa?"

He gave her a sad, patient look. "I was asking about the duke, but it seems Louisa upset you even more."

"Oh, no," she protested. "I'm fine."

"You don't look fine."

"I am." She gave an offhand laugh. "Why wouldn't I be fine? You know as well as I—my marriage to Tristan is a formality. Louisa is a lovely person. And she's Eng-

lish. If he cares for her, that would be—" Suddenly tears
welled and she had to bite her lips.

"That would be utterly stupid," Jon said.

Caroline wished she hadn't spoken to him. She wished
she'd stayed in her room until she'd sorted her thoughts.
She waved off his concern. "Tristan and I have a legal
commitment. Nothing more. If you'll excuse me, I need
to ask him if the children have had chicken pox."

"He's in the horse barn," Jon answered.

They walked in opposite directions, leaving Caroline alone with her worries. She was halfway to the stable when Tristan emerged from the building with a man
she didn't recognize. Presumably the fellow had arrived
with the duke. He wore a stylish frock coat and had ramrod posture. Sideburns made his face plump and cheerful. Even from a distance she could see Tristan enjoying
himself. The stranger seemed to be telling a joke with
arm gestures and odd posturing.

When Tristan doubled up with laughter, her heart
sank. He had bitter feelings toward his father, but he fit
comfortably into his father's world.

Caroline didn't.

But Louisa did… She fit perfectly.

With her chest tight, she turned and walked back to
the house. She didn't want to lose the children, but neither would she stand in the way of Tristan's happiness.
If he had genuine feelings for Louisa, she'd remove herself from his life. She'd accept being second-best…again.
Feeling like a moth in a bevy of butterflies, she hurried
back to the house.

Chapter Twelve

Tristan had enjoyed a spirited reunion with Pennwright, but the rest of the day had been impossibly irritating. It was now late into the night. Alone in his bedroom, waiting for Caroline to come upstairs, he thought about his father's obnoxious behavior.

The misery had started with the duke's arrival at the dinner table. He'd walked into the dining room with his own valet, as if he were going to ask the man to taste-test the food for poison. He'd complained about Evaline's cooking and had demanded his own pitcher of gravy. The children had eaten earlier with Bessie, and Jon had joined them rather than endure the duke. To Tristan's consternation, Freddie had come into the dining room and announced he'd been invited by his grandfather.

Tristan didn't have the heart to deny his son, though he now regretted the decision. The duke had fawned over the boy, flattering him with as much intensity as he insulted Caroline. Her conduct was impeccable, but he belittled her table manners. He had inspected the water goblets for spots and the silverware for tarnish. He'd even berated her for interrupting him when she'd merely taken a deep breath.

Tristan had intervened, but he couldn't control his father's tongue. When the man wasn't making rude comments, he droned on about himself and England, excluding Caroline while enticing Freddie.

The meal had ended two hours ago, and the duke had retired to the guesthouse. Bessie had long ago seen to the children and Louisa. Caroline seemed to have disappeared. He'd been expecting her for an hour now, but still she hadn't come upstairs. Not only did he want to apologize for his father's rudeness, but he also had to tell her about his former feelings for Louisa.

When the clock on the mantel chimed eleven times, he wondered if she'd slipped into her room without him noticing. With his father staying in the guesthouse and Louisa bedridden, she didn't have to use the main door to his suite, as they'd planned. Frustrated, Tristan paced through the storage room and tapped on her door.

No answer.

He tapped again more forcefully. "Caroline?"

Hearing nothing, he opened the door and stepped into the cubbyhole of a room. In the moonlight coming through the window, he saw the untouched coverlet on her bed and a Bible left open on her desk. He wondered when she'd read it and if she'd been seeking wisdom or comfort. He didn't know, but words he'd memorized as a child came to him.

Our Father, Who Art in Heaven
Hallowed be Thy name

The verse had made him angry as a boy, but now he felt a longing to understand God the way Caroline did. She didn't see Him as a distant commander-in-chief. She saw the kind of father Tristan had never known but wanted to be. Tonight she'd also seen the illness in the Smythe family tree. She'd been belittled by the duke the way Tristan had been belittled as a boy. He had to find her.

To signal he wanted to see her, he left both doors to the closet open, then stepped into the hall. He glanced at Bessie's door, saw no light and figured she'd gone to sleep. He walked ten paces to Louisa's room, paused and listened to the silence. She, too, seemed to be sleeping. Dora's room was dark, and so was Freddie's. Caroline wasn't in the house.

Wondering if she'd been cornered by the duke, Tristan reconnoitered the downstairs as if searching enemy territory for a prisoner of war. Every room was empty, so he headed to the veranda. With still no sign of Caroline, he walked to the railing and found her at last. She was alone in the garden, thirty feet away and walking through the fallow rows. Moonlight rained down on her, giving shape to a shawl covering her shoulders and the neat arrangement of her hair. She reminded him of the deer that came and nosed the dead plants, scavenging for food when there wasn't any.

He thought of Molly and her request that he remarry. He'd kept his promise, but he hadn't fulfilled it completely. Molly would have wanted him to honor Caroline with all the love a wife deserved. She'd have wanted Freddie and Dora to have brothers and sisters. With the moon bright on Caroline's face, Tristan admitted to wants of own.

He wanted to be free of the malaria.

He wanted to love again.

He wanted to honor his duty as the future Duke of Willoughby and be the best husband and father a man could be. He wasn't sure how to do all those things at the same time, but he knew what *not* to do. Keeping his emotions in check wasn't the answer. He'd learned the lesson playing the dream game.

"Help me, Lord," he murmured. "I want to be well again. I want—" He felt like Dora asking for a cookie or Freddie dreaming of becoming a scientist. Like his children, Tristan had visions for a future that seemed beyond his grasp, but just as *he* was capable of giving Dora a cookie and paying for university for Freddie, his heavenly Father had the ability to handle the problems beyond Tristan's control. With a hopeful heart, he prayed. "Father God, I want Caroline and the children to be happy and safe. I want to love them as a husband and father."

It had been more than a week since he'd had a bout of fever. The daily quinine was helping. Tonight he felt good. He felt strong…and he very much wanted to be the husband Caroline deserved. Only he didn't have that right. Until he could be sure of his health—at least *more* sure—he had to convince her of his loyalty without overstepping the lines they'd drawn. He'd start by telling her about his past with Louisa.

He ambled down the path to the garden, deliberately kicking a pebble so she'd hear him and wouldn't startle. Deep in thought, she still didn't notice him. When he was five feet away, he spoke in a hush. "Caroline?"

Gasping, she faced him. "Tristan!"

"I've been looking all over for you." He didn't mean to scold her, but he was disappointed that she'd been avoiding him.

"I'm sorry," she said. "I—I needed air."

"So did I."

He saw no reason for small talk. "I'd like to tell you about Louisa."

"You don't owe me an explanation," she said hurriedly.

"In fact, I've been thinking. There's something I need to say."

A gentleman acquiesced to a lady. Caroline had endured a difficult day and deserved to vent her spleen. "I'm listening."

"Today was…challenging."

"Very."

She ambled down the row, looking at the sky as she gathered her thoughts. He wouldn't rush her. After an evening with his father, she could take all the time she needed. He stayed at her side as she walked, her skirt brushing the ridges of empty earth. With her face tilted up to the stars, she finally spoke. "I'm wondering if perhaps we were too hasty to get married."

He'd been expecting her to complain. Instead she'd taken the duke's insults to heart. "What are you saying?"

"You don't need me, Tristan. I saw how you looked at Louisa—"

"Caroline, stop." He clasped her arm. "It's true that Louisa and I were once in love. She jilted me for Andrew and I still don't know why. I stopped loving her years ago. There's nothing between us."

"But there could be," she murmured.

"I'm not married to Louisa," he said with authority. "I'm married to *you*."

"Not really."

"We took vows," he reminded her.

"Yes, but it's the physical union that truly binds a man and woman. As long as we haven't consummated the marriage, you're free to obtain an annulment. Perhaps we should consider it."

He didn't want to consider an annulment. He wanted to be a healthy man with a future. But he wasn't. "Is that what you want? To end our marriage now?"

She didn't answer, leaving him to weigh the events of the day. His father had harassed and belittled her. She'd also come face-to-face with a woman from his past. Even sick with the chicken pox, Louisa was English and aristocratic, kind, educated and poised. She'd been born and bred to be a duchess, whereas Caroline's talents went in other directions. He could understand why she felt dispirited, and he wished he had the words to soothe her anxieties.

Finally she spoke to the sky. "Your father is a cruel man, but that doesn't mean he isn't right about certain things."

"Such as?"

"I'm not fit to be your wife."

"That's utter nonsense. My father's impossible. You shouldn't listen to him."

They were near the end of the row. The branches of a tree cast a tangled shadow and she stopped. "Your father spoke the truth tonight. I'm not schooled in English ways. Like he said, I'm a lowly American. You could do better."

"I think not."

She looked into his eyes. "Please don't patronize me, Tristan. You hired me to be a governess, not your wife. You come from a world I don't understand. Someday you'll be the Duke of Willoughby—"

"If I live."

"You will," she said with confidence. "Every day you're stronger. Earlier I saw you with a man down by the barn—"

"That was Pennwright," he interrupted. "My father's secretary."

"You were at ease."

"Yes. He's an old friend."

She took a breath. "So is Louisa. Don't you think you should give your feelings a chance?"

"No!"

He didn't know what to make of her willingness to step aside. She loved his children, yet she was willing to sacrifice herself for the happiness of others. The offer struck him as generous, noble…and pathetic. He wanted her to fight for what she wanted, not give it up in a misguided act of martyrdom. He understood why she'd be reluctant to be a duchess, but did the gesture mean she didn't have feelings for him? There was a sure way to find the truth. If he kissed her as sincerely as he wanted, he'd know her heart. But they'd also set foot on a rickety bridge to the future, one missing planks and strung with old rope. With his health precarious, he had no business leading her into that kind of danger. At the same time, he had to convince her of his loyalty.

"I want to tell you more about Louisa," he said. "Let's go inside."

"You don't have to explain—"

"Caroline." He clasped her biceps. "I *want* to explain, though I'm not sure I can. I was twenty. She was seventeen. We'd spoken of marriage and had an understanding. Out of the blue, she became engaged to Andrew."

"I'm sorry."

"I tried to speak to her, but her family sent her away. To this day I don't know if I somehow failed her or if she failed me."

Caroline touched his cheek. "That must have been devastating."

"It was, but it happened a long time ago. I haven't thought of Louisa in years. I'd like to know why she married Andrew, but I'm very aware that I'm married to you.

You need to know that I honor my commitments, especially when they pertain to marriage."

They were back where they'd started, leaving Caroline
with the same question. Just how much of a commitment
had Tristan made to her? She couldn't help but wonder if
his feelings for Louisa were as dead as he indicated. She
didn't expect them to pick up where they left off. Fifteen
years was a long time, but she could imagine them falling in love all over again.

She'd experienced Louisa's graciousness for herself.
Before supper she'd checked to see how the woman was
doing. At least a hundred more pustules had erupted, including one on the tip of her nose. Louisa had joked about
having polka dots and had entertained them by making
funny faces. Not only did Caroline like the woman, she
admired her. Louisa was Tristan's equal, his mirror image
with feminine beauty in the place of male strength.

It hurt to face facts, but Caroline refused to deny the
obvious. She was second-best. They both knew it. She
turned to Tristan. "Louisa admires you greatly."

"And I admire her," he said with British aplomb.

"You were good friends. You could be friends again,
even more than friends. Don't you think you should give
those feelings a chance?"

He waited so long to answer that she knew she'd asked
a hard question. "That's what I thought," she said. "You
need time."

"I certainly do *not!* I know my own mind, and I don't
love Louisa." He looked into her eyes. "Time is the one
thing I may not have."

He meant the malaria. "You're much improved. Bessie's optimistic that you'll make a full recovery."

"I hope she's right."

"So do I." Watching him in the moonlight, she saw a hesitation that matched her own. "You could be missing something wonderful because you're afraid. Give Louisa a chance. Be brave."

It hurt to speak the truth, but she refused to look away. She had loved Charles and seen him murdered, but she cherished their time together. She'd lost her mother as a child and her father to a heart ailment, but she had an abundance of happy memories. During the war, she'd seen women bury sons, brothers and husbands. Life was precarious for everyone. Love had to be cherished.

Hoping to share her courage, she smiled at Tristan. "I'm right, you know."

"Yes," he agreed. "But not about Louisa."

"About what then?"

"About us…"

In his eyes she saw the desire for a kiss. He cupped her jaw with his palm, his thumb brushing her cheek with a tenderness that could have been given to a child…or a wife. She stayed as still as the fallow ground, waiting, wondering, hoping…until footsteps on the path to the house caused them both to pull back.

Chapter Thirteen

Tristan pulled Caroline under the cottonwood at the end of the garden. The shadows hid them from view, but he could hear the whisper of her breath in the darkness. Had his father stepped outside for a late-night cigar? Tristan had no desire to deal with the duke. He'd been about to kiss Caroline and he resented the intrusion.

Drawing her close, he heard the drone of conversation. He recognized Jon's voice and relaxed. He couldn't make out the words, but Jon sounded buoyant. When Bessie's laughter drifted in their direction, Tristan knew his friend was up to his charming ways. Looking over his shoulder, he saw the couple heading for a stone bench at the other end of the garden.

Caroline whispered, "We should make our presence known."

"Or we should leave," he said quietly.

They turned together, bumping arms as he gripped her hand. They'd taken a single step when a feminine gasp caught Caroline's attention and she stopped. When she turned to look at the couple, so did Tristan. Jon was kissing Bessie, and he wasn't being shy about it. Neither was Bessie reserved in her response.

Caroline pressed her hand to her mouth. Her fingers tightened in his and she started to shake with a suppressed giggle. Tristan had to clench his jaw to keep from letting out a laugh of his own, a reaction that would put an ignoble end to a kiss that was getting longer…and longer…and longer. He needed air. So did Caroline. Gripping her hand, he led her to the path and they hurried to the house while Bessie and Jon were lost in the kiss.

Tristan guided Caroline to the veranda where they gasped for air, laughing until she slumped against him. They were closer than they'd ever been. Closer than when she'd ridden with him on Cairo… Closer than when she'd stitched his head and he'd kissed her cheek.

Until now he'd held back because of the malaria, but tonight it seemed right to match his mouth to hers and that's what he did. The kiss was tender but wise, a mix of questions and promises that tasted sweeter with each passing moment. He imagined a future bright with love, a house full of children and a porch with rocking chairs where they'd grow old together.

The thought stopped him cold. He felt better than he'd felt in weeks, but the malaria still lurked in his blood. Kissing Caroline was a promise of sorts, one he feared he couldn't keep. Suddenly tense, he stepped back. "Go upstairs."

She put her hand on his chest. "Are—are you coming with me?"

Neither of them was ready to go beyond a kiss, but they both understood the potential. He shook his head. "I'm staying here."

"Then I'll stay, too."

"No, don't."

"But—"

"Please, Caroline. Just go."

She stepped back, her head down and shoulders hunched. He knew she felt rejected, even inadequate. Sending her away after a kiss was a terrible thing to do, but allowing their feelings to grow before he could be sure of his health could cause the worst pain imaginable.

"It wasn't the kiss," he said without touching her. "It's—" He didn't know what *it* was. He only knew he'd gone too far too soon. For Caroline's sake, he had to win the war raging in his blood before he gave in to the feelings he could no longer deny. He loved her, and he wanted their marriage to be far more than adequate. He wanted it to be…spectacular.

Caroline fled through the house to her room. She lit the lamp and turned it low, but even the soft light was harsh after kissing Tristan in the dark. Blinking, she saw the open doors between her room and his and closed them. Even if he knocked, she wouldn't answer. She'd been wounded tonight, like a bird that had flown bravely from a cage only to smack into a window. Beyond the glass she'd seen a glorious future. She'd dared to believe Tristan had feelings for her. She'd been sure of it when he kissed her…then he'd set her aside.

She no longer thought he still loved Louisa, but something was keeping them apart. Either he doubted her ability to be a duchess, or he expected to die from the malaria and didn't want her to grieve. With either choice, the facts stood. He'd kissed her and rejected her. The kiss had been soft and tender and so sweet she'd believed they were falling in love. But then he'd pulled back. Dropping down on the rocker, she looked at the ring on her finger. The diamond sparkled with a pinkish glow, but it didn't belong to her, not really. She'd always be second-best to women like Louisa.

Fighting tears, she pressed her palms to her cheeks. "Not again, Lord," she whispered.

How much rejection could a woman take? Tonight she and Tristan had crossed a line. She couldn't imagine going back to being his friend, a wife in name only, when she'd experienced his kiss. She needed to ask God to guide her, but the prayer choked her. She'd never felt so unwanted and unworthy in her entire life. He denied feelings for Louisa, but what man wouldn't be attracted to a woman of Louisa's perfection?

A knock on the hall door startled her. Rather than come through the storage room, it seemed Tristan had put more distance between them by approaching from the hall. "Go away," she said in a low voice.

"It's me," Bessie whispered. "I have to talk to you."

Caroline had no desire to speak with anyone, especially not her sister who'd just been thoroughly kissed. She couldn't bear to think of the excitement in Bessie's tone, but they were sisters. "Come in," she said, rising to her feet.

Bessie slipped inside, her face flushed and her eyes bright. "I hope I didn't wake you, but if I don't talk to someone I'll go crazy."

Caroline reached around her and closed the door. "I think I know why."

"How—"

"I saw you with Jon."

Bessie pressed her hands to her face. "This is awful!"

"Why?" Caroline would have given a year of her life to have Bessie's problem.

"I'm too old to feel this way!"

"No, you're not." Her sister was forty-one. "Who says you have to be young to be in love?"

"I do."

Caroline laughed, but it hurt. "I imagine Jon disagrees."

"He's impossible!" Bessie closed her eyes. "But the way he kissed me... Oh, my!"

Caroline laughed again. It hurt even more than the first time, but she was happy for her sister. She only wished Tristan hadn't held back. She couldn't allow herself to love him, not when he didn't love her back. But it was impossible not to dream of a future with him. With the malaria, Louisa and his obligations in England, their situation was complicated. Bessie had no such impediments. There wasn't a reason in the world she and Jon couldn't fall in love, except for Bessie's silly notion that she was too old.

"I'm happy for you," Caroline said simply.

"Happy?" Bessie plopped down on the rocker. "How can you be happy? I'm *terrified!*"

Caroline laughed. "Trust me, sister. That terror turns into something good. I've been in love before. You haven't."

Gripping the arms of the chair, Bessie pushed off. The rockers creaked like a runaway wagon. "I'm too old for this silliness."

Caroline sat on the bed across from her. "That's a lame excuse and you know it. How old is Jon?"

"He's a year older than I am."

"Do you think *he's* old?"

"No."

"Then neither are you." For once Caroline had more experience than her older, wiser sister. "Trust me, Bessie. You won't regret taking a chance with Jon. Even if you get hurt, it's worth the risk."

Bessie inhaled deeply. "That's good advice. I hope you take it for yourself."

"What do you mean?"

"I've seen how the major looks at you. I understand the limitations of the marriage, but anyone can see he has feelings for you."

Caroline didn't want Bessie to see the defeat in her eyes, so she turned her attention to the window. She thought of that uncaged bird hitting the glass. Beyond it lay everything the bird wanted, but it had no way of escape. "If Tristan has feelings for me, he regrets it."

"What do you mean?"

"He kissed me tonight—"

"Oh!" Bessie declared. "Then I'm right."

"No, you're wrong. He sent me away without a word of explanation." In quiet tones, she told her sister about Tristan's past with Louisa. "Either he's afraid of the malaria, or he's confused about Louisa. I don't think he still loves her, but I think he *could* love her again. She'd be a far better duchess than I'd be."

"That's rubbish!"

"It's true." Caroline stood and went to the window. It overlooked the garden. The moon was higher now, visible but too small to cast any meaningful light. The cottonwood had lost its leaves a week ago, and now the branches were empty and fragile. She touched the glass.

Bessie stood and came to stand beside her. "If I didn't know what you'd been through with Charles, I'd call you a coward."

Caroline's fingers curled on the cold glass. She considered herself brave when necessary, but some fights were lost before they started.

Bessie kept her voice low. "I don't blame you for giving up on Tristan. You're right about Louisa. Even with the chicken pox, she's the picture of grace. She's smart and pretty. I'm sure the kids will love her. Why, she's just plain old perfect. No wonder Tristan had feelings for her. You know, she—"

"Stop!"

"I was about to say that she reminds me of someone."

"Who?"

"You." The women turned at the same time. They were eye to eye, but what caught Caroline's attention was the mirror on the wall behind her sister. It reflected Caroline's pale face and Bessie's hair, mussed from Jon's touch. Fear and risk collided on the silver glass. The uncaged bird refused to be fooled again.

"I'm not that strong," Caroline said firmly.

"I think you are." Bessie lowered her hands. "For someone who just gave me a lecture on courage, you're acting like a mouse."

"I'm being cautious."

Considering her first marriage, she had to weigh the costs. When she'd married Charles, she'd claimed to be brave enough for anything, and they'd both suffered. She didn't want to go down that road again, but neither could she imagine *not* going down it. Hope and fear went hand in hand. She wanted to choose hope, but her insides were shaking.

Mustering her faith, she smiled at Bessie. "You're right. I'm being timid. I don't really know what Tristan's thinking, and I'm not sure he even knows."

"He probably doesn't," Bessie went back to the rocking chair. "He's recovering from malaria, but it's a long road. As for Louisa, I don't believe for a minute he's still in love with her."

"Maybe not," Caroline agreed. "But he could fall for her again, I'm sure of it. Even *I* like her."

"I do, too," Bessie admitted. "You two don't have to be rivals, but you *do* have to fight for Tristan."

"How?"

Bessie's eyes took on a silvery glint. "You have to prove to yourself that you can be the wife he needs, and you have to be willing to go to England. He's already teaching you what you need to know. The problem is that you don't believe you can do it."

"I know I can't," she insisted. "I like being ordinary, and I can't stop being an American."

"That's true," Bessie acknowledged. "But you're also a woman of faith. You dared to love Charles against the odds—"

"And look what happened."

Bessie's eyes shimmered. "You just told me love is worth the risk. Is it?"

"Yes, but—" Caroline bit her lip. "What if I embarrass Tristan? He can do better than me. Look at Louisa—"

"I'm looking at *you,* and I'm seeing a woman who needs to fight for the man she loves. We've both trusted God through good times and bad. We're scared right now, but don't you think God knows what's happening?"

"Yes, but—"

"You're still afraid."

"Yes! I'm terrified," she admitted. "You make my situation sound simple, but it's not."

"I think it is," Bessie countered. "God put Esther into the king's court for 'a time such as this.' He brought you to Wyoming for a purpose, and He brought me. I have to believe He'll give us both the strength we need to live in a way that honors Him."

Caroline had said similar things to Tristan when she'd urged him to be brave. The thought of being his duchess completely unnerved her, but she had the faith to take the first step of the future God had planned just for her.

"What should I do?" she said to Bessie.

Her sister smiled. "I think you should learn to ride a horse."

"A *horse!*"

Bessie chuckled. "Why not? Tristan would love to share that part of his life with you."

"That's true," she admitted. "But I'm terrified—"

"Which scares you more? Learning to ride or losing Tristan forever?"

She whispered, "Losing Tristan."

"That's your answer," Bessie said quietly. "It's my answer, too. Not only did Jon kiss me, he asked me to marry him."

"He did!"

Bessie's cheeks turned bright pink. "I didn't give him an answer, but I will tomorrow. And it's going to be yes."

"Are you sure?" Caroline asked. "You haven't known him long."

"We've waited our entire lives for each other. We're too old to waste another minute. What do you think of a June wedding? Perhaps Adie and Pearl and Mary could come?"

"That would be wonderful." Caroline hugged Bessie tight. She couldn't have been happier for her sister, but she had to admit to a bittersweet moment. With Bessie's engagement, Caroline would soon be the only woman from Swan's Nest who wasn't happily married. A marriage in name only was no marriage at all. But she didn't have to settle for so much less than what God intended marriage to be. If Tristan had feelings for her, she could learn to be a duchess. She could be brave and get on a horse.

Releasing Bessie, she shared a smile with her sister. "I'm happy for you. Jon's a lucky man."

"So is Tristan," Bessie said quietly. "But you need to—"

"Fight for him," Caroline finished.

"Yes."

She managed a tiny smile. "Do you think he'd give me riding lessons?"

Her sister smiled. "I'm sure of it."

They talked about a wedding dress for Bessie and a riding outfit for Caroline. When the clock chimed midnight, they hugged and said goodnight. Tomorrow she'd ask Evaline to help her sew a riding habit. The outfit would take time to complete, but she didn't mind the wait. She'd be praying for courage. More than anything, she wanted to prove to herself and Tristan that she could be the wife he needed.

Chapter Fourteen

Kissing Caroline changed everything for Tristan. By mutual agreement, she'd stopped coming to his room for duchess lessons. He missed her, but he couldn't continue the charade of a loveless marriage until he came up with a plan. He'd withdrawn from the war zone in order to size up the enemy. The war wasn't with Caroline or himself. It was with the malaria. After four days apart from her, he decided on a strategy. If he could go a full month without a fever, starting now, he'd court his wife properly. If the kiss they shared was an indication, and he believed it was, her feelings were as strong as his. He had to get well. It was that simple.

He also had to convince her that she'd make an excellent duchess. They wouldn't return to England immediately, maybe not for years, but someday he'd take the mantle of authority and he wanted her at his side. His father felt otherwise, and he'd made his objections clear.

He'd also continued to show a keen interest in Freddie, and the boy had eaten up the attention. Tristan understood all too well. Pampered poodles did tricks for treats, and the duke was doling out praise with a heavy hand.

Tristan wanted his father to return to England, but

he couldn't broach the subject as long as Louisa was ill. According to Bessie, Louisa had the worst case of chicken pox the nurse had ever seen. Louisa had conveyed through Bessie that she wasn't ready for visitors, but she hoped to speak with Tristan as soon as she recovered. Considering he'd lived with the mystery of their parting for fifteen years, he didn't mind the delay.

He was far more concerned about Caroline, who was looking at him from across the breakfast table with a pensive expression. She had finished her meal except for her coffee, which he now knew she drank with one heaping spoonful of sugar. After lowering the cup, she put her napkin on the table but didn't excuse herself, a sign the wall between them was about to come down.

He set down his cup of tea and waited.

Caroline put her hands in her lap.

He smiled.

She smiled back. "I have a favor to ask."

"Of course," he answered. "What can I do for you?"

"I want to learn to ride."

He couldn't have been more surprised if she'd announced she could fly. "You do?"

"Yes." She sat straighter. "Evaline finished my riding habit last night. We can start today if you're free."

"I'm free, but—" He felt like he had water in his ears. "Why are you doing this? You don't like horses."

"You do."

"Yes, but there's no need for you to trouble yourself."

She looked deflated, but then she bucked up. "If you don't want to teach me, I could ask Jon—"

"No," he said quickly. "I'm just surprised."

"In a bad way?"

"Not at all." He was surprised in a good way…a very good way. Since he'd started counting the days without a fever, he'd marked four days off the calendar. He had moments of feeling poorly, but he hadn't been pasted to his bed like a corpse. He'd gone even longer if he counted back to the trip from the river, but on his mental calendar he had twenty-six days before he could open the doors between their rooms.

Teaching Caroline to ride gave him a welcome excuse to be with her. "I assume you'll want to ride sidesaddle?"

"Actually, no."

She stood and he saw her riding costume, a tailored jacket with a split skirt. The garment was unusual, and he wondered how she'd come up with it. It would preserve her modesty but he knew how his father would react. He'd call her a hoyden. Tristan thought she looked both lovely and practical. For a rancher's wife, riding astride made perfect sense and he'd have suggested it himself. She could have worn a pair of his trousers for all he cared about propriety, but he worried that his father would mock her without mercy.

"A split skirt is…unusual," he said.

"Evaline made it for me." Looking at him, she held out the sides. "You don't approve?"

"Quite the contrary." He skimmed her with his eyes. "It's very practical."

It was pretty, too. The fawn color contrasted with her dark hair and made her eyes light brown. He also saw the stubborn tilt of her chin and recalled taking her across the river. He wanted to make the lessons a resounding success, and he had an idea. He rose to his feet. "Shall we meet at the barn in an hour or so?"

"That would be fine."

He dismissed her with a nod. "I'll see you there."

As she left the room, he watched the sway of her skirt. He didn't know what the future held, but he planned to enjoy every minute of the morning. He admired Caroline's courage. He also knew that making her comfortable around animals in general would go a long way to making the lessons a success. He left the table and headed for the front door.

As he reached for the knob, his father stepped into the house. "I'm here for Louisa."

Tristan had heard from Evaline that she'd recovered enough for an outing. "Where are you going?"

"I thought we'd see some of this land of yours. Pennwright tells me it's quite impressive."

Tristan knew better than to trust the duke's praise, but for a moment he was a boy again, hungry for his father's attention. Wiser now, he addressed his father as a man. "If you'd like a guide, I'll ask Jon to show you around."

"I was hoping you'd accompany us."

"I have a prior commitment."

"I see." The duke looked speculative. "I suppose a guide won't be necessary. It'll be a short ride."

Tristan's neck hairs prickled the way they did before cannon fire. He had the feeling he was missing something, but a direct challenge to the duke would only lead to subterfuge. If he hadn't made plans with Caroline, he'd have gone with his father to keep an eye on him.

The rustle of skirts drew his gaze to the stairs. "Good morning!" Louisa said brightly.

With a sweep of his eyes, Tristan took in her royal-blue skirt and jacket, a lace jabot and a black top hat with a swathe of tulle to hide her face, no doubt still bearing marks of her illness. It was a tribute to her poise—and perhaps her need to get out of the house—that she'd decided to go for a ride in spite of her imperfect complexion.

"Good morning," Tristan answered. "You're looking well."

"I feel wonderful." She beamed a smile at him. "I was hoping to run into you this morning."

The duke reached for the doorknob. "Don't let me interrupt, my dear. I'll meet you on the porch."

The duke was never considerate. He'd left them alone for a reason, and Tristan feared he knew what it was. The duke wanted Louisa to tempt him so he'd return immediately to England. The ploy wouldn't work, but he welcomed the chance to speak with her.

Graciously she tipped her head to the duke. "Thank you, your grace. This won't take long."

"Take all the time you need, Marchioness." The duke used the title naturally, though Louisa was officially a dowager and the title belonged to Caroline. His departure left Tristan alone with Louisa for the first time in years.

She lowered her voice. "Could we speak in your study?"

"Certainly." He indicated the hall, waited for her to pass and then followed her to his office. When she stepped inside, he indicated the divan. Instead of sitting, she shut the door he'd intentionally left open. He, too, wanted privacy but not at the risk of provoking curiosity or worry for Caroline. There was no reason to think she'd come looking for him, but he couldn't ignore the possibility.

"I'd prefer to keep the door open," he said quietly. Already the meeting felt clandestine.

"I don't trust the duke," she whispered. "His valet could be lurking."

Tristan had to agree. Leaving the door shut, he stood directly in front of it. He'd open in it in a heartbeat if anyone approached, especially if he recognized the tap of Caroline's boots. Being alone with Louisa was a potential insult to his wife, and he didn't want to hurt her feelings.

Instead of sitting, Louisa stayed on her feet. With her chin high, she lifted the veil from her face so that he could see her eyes along with polka dots left by the fading chicken pox. She held her chin high. "For fifteen years I've prayed that you'd forgive me for what I did."

"I have," he answered. "Though I have to admit, I'm not sure what I'm forgiving."

"Oh, Tristan—" Her voice broke.

He'd once loved this woman. He still did—but only as a sister. Protective instincts compelled him to comfort her, but he stayed by the door. Until he could be sure she wasn't being used by the duke, he'd keep a firm and polite distance. "You left me for Andrew."

"I had no choice."

Caroline had used the same words about crossing the river. "There's always a choice, Louisa. And there's always a cost. I bear you no ill will, but I'd like to know why you did it."

"You know my father gambled."

"Yes." So did the duke, the difference being the duke could afford to lose and Louisa's father couldn't.

Louisa steadied herself with a breath. "My father ran up a terrible debt. Your father offered to cover it, but only if I married Andrew."

"Why would he do that?"

Louisa bit her lip. "I'm ashamed to tell you."

She turned and went to the window, giving Tristan a moment to consider the facts he'd evaluated a hundred times before. He'd been in love with Louisa, but she hadn't been highly sought after. Her father had a lesser title than the duke, and her family was known to be in debt. Her one asset was her beauty. If she and Andrew had produced children, they would have been lovely to behold. And that, Tristan realized, was why his father had essentially bought Louisa for Andrew. She'd been no better than broodmare.

He felt sick for her. "My father gave you to Andrew because you're beautiful."

"Yes."

"But you had no children."

Louisa turned abruptly to the window. "I didn't know about Andrew until our wedding night."

"Know what?"

She continued to speak to the window. "Andrew preferred the company of his male friends in London. He was a homosexual."

"I see." Tristan had heard rumors about his brother, but he'd written them off as gossip.

Louisa still had her back to him. "That's why we failed to produce an heir. He had no interest in me."

"He had no interest in *women*," Tristan corrected. "That's why my father forced the marriage. Andrew needed a push, and you were the perfect pawn."

At last Tristan understood why she left him. If she'd refused to marry Andrew, the duke would have ruined her father and her two sisters would have suffered. The conversation answered one question but raised two others. Had the duke deliberately picked Louisa because he knew Tristan would be hurt? Not likely, Tristan decided. The duke hadn't cared about him at all.

The second worry had burdened him for fifteen years. "I should have found a way to speak with you. I should have helped you—"

"Oh, Tristan…" She turned away from the window but didn't approach him. "There was nothing you could have done to stop your father. We were young. Even if I'd come to you, we couldn't have run away. I had a duty to protect my family, especially my sisters."

"You paid a high price."

"Yes, but I'm done paying my father's debt. Your father brought me on this trip as your reward for returning to England. Your American wife disrupted that plan, but he has another one and it's despicable. I will tell you now that I will do *nothing* to come between you and Caroline. I've hurt you enough already."

"It's over and done," he replied. "I married Molly and had a wonderful time of it."

"I'm glad."

So was Tristan. "You've had a far harder life, I'm afraid."

"Yes, but I'm done being used. The duke instructed me to break up your marriage, but I won't do it."

She couldn't have done it even if she tried. His feelings for Caroline grew with each passing day. If the malaria stayed away as he hoped, he'd be free to tell her he loved her.

Louisa's expression turned wistful. "Please don't misunderstand, Tristan. It's not that I don't care for you. If you'd been free to marry, I'd have been glad to test the waters. But you're not free. You're married to a charming woman who loves you very much." She lifted one brow. "And If I'm not mistaken, you're being neglectful."

"What do you mean?"

"Husbands and wives often choose to maintain separate bedrooms, but a wife rarely chooses to sleep in a tiny little room that's clearly meant to be a nursery."

"How do you know it's a nursery?" he said, scowling. "Is it?"

He said nothing, which told Louisa everything.

"That's what I thought," she said cheekily. "I caught a glimpse of the tiny space when your housekeeper left the door open while cleaning. Something's amiss. I don't know why you're not showing your wife proper attention, but it's plain you're keeping her at arm's length. I've been watching her, Tristan. She cares for you, and I believe you care for her. What's wrong?"

Old friend or not, Louisa didn't have the right to such

an intimate observation. "My marriage is none of your business."

"Yes, but I consider Caroline a friend, and I know how it feels to be a neglected wife. Don't make that mistake."

He didn't want to neglect Caroline at all. He wanted to spend the rest of his life with her, but he had to be sure he had a future. "I have my reasons."

"Whatever they are, you're hurting Caroline."

Tristan said nothing. If he told Louisa about his illness, she might accidentally reveal the information to the duke. "Thank you for your concern, Louisa. The circumstances are complicated."

"As are mine," she said. "Which leads to the other reason I wanted to speak with you in private. I need your help."

"In what way?"

"I need a husband." She gave him a winsome smile. "Since you're not available, I'm considering Stuart Whitmore. Do you know him?"

"I do." Whitmore owned a ranch thirty miles from The Barracks. Like Tristan, he was the youngest son of a duke. Unlike Tristan, he had a reputation as a rake. Rumor had it his father had banished him to America.

"He's an interesting fellow," Tristan acknowledged. "A bit of a scoundrel, but he's done well for himself."

"He's also in need of a wife." She lifted one brow. "We met in Cheyenne. I thought perhaps you could hold a house party and invite him?"

Tristan had failed to rescue Louisa once before. He saw a chance to help her now, but he had to consider the cost. A gathering meant having his father stay longer at The Barracks, and it would require Caroline to test her mettle as a hostess. If the party failed, he might lose her completely. But if it succeeded—and he was sure it would—she'd gain some of the confidence she needed to be a duchess.

Battles weren't won by being timid. "That's a grand idea," he said. "I'd like to get to know Whitmore better myself."

"Excellent!" She smiled. "He has family visiting from England. We can invite them all."

Tristan nodded in agreement, but his protective instincts began a backbeat of caution. Whitmore's father was Darryl Whitmore, the Duke of Somerville. He was known to be an impressive man, and the Duchess of Somerville could be as haughty as Tristan's father. Entertaining Whitmore and some Americans would have presented a challenge to Caroline. Providing entertainment for English nobility was far more daunting.

"Who exactly is visiting?" he asked.

Her eyes sparkled. "The Duke of Somerville passed away two years ago. The dowager doesn't care for her daughter-in-law, so she decided to visit her youngest son in America. She's traveling with her two nieces."

"The dowager is quite formidable," Tristan acknowledged.

"She is," Louisa agreed. "I'll need your help to impress her."

"We'll also need male guests for the two nieces."

"I'm sure Mr. Whitmore has friends."

"No doubt," Tristan agreed. "I'll speak to Caroline later today. In fact, I'll suggest she invite friends of her own."

Before he'd ended their late-night talks, she'd told him about her friends in Denver and a place called Swan's Nest. He knew that Adelaide Clarke had married a Boston preacher named Joshua Blue, and Mary Larue had recently married a famous gunslinger. Even Tristan had heard of J. T. Quinn. She'd also visited Pearl and Matt Wiley in Cheyenne before arriving at The Barracks. Not only did Tristan want to meet the people Caroline loved, he also saw an opportunity to finish what they'd started at the courthouse in Wheeler Springs. If he stayed healthy, they could repeat their wedding vows in front of people she loved, with Reverend Blue presiding.

Louisa's eyes twinkled with hope that had nothing to do with him. "I know Stuart's a rake, but he quite charmed me in Cheyenne. Your father disliked him intensely."

Tristan laughed. "All the more reason to invite him to a party."

"I'm afraid the dowager might be difficult," she said apologetically. "She's quite willing to speak her mind."

Tristan thought of Caroline. He could teach her etiquette and history, but she'd need more than knowledge to contend with a cranky dowager. She'd need confidence with a touch of audacity and a sprinkling of wit. He'd help her as much as he could, but the battle would be hers. He considered begging off the house party, but he saw a benefit to Caroline facing the dowager in their own home surrounded by friends.

Louisa interrupted his thoughts. "I should be leaving for that ride with your father. I detest the man, but I'm pitifully dependent at the moment."

"Not for long, I hope."

He opened the door and guided her into the hall. She paused to adjust the veil on her hat, then she tugged on the black gloves she'd had in her pocket. As he crossed the threshold, he saw Caroline in the entry hall. Her back was to them and she was opening the door. Had she come to his study first? Had she heard them talking? Tristan refused to allow even the faintest stain on his loyalty to her.

"Caroline!" he called in a loud voice.

She faced him with an eager expression. At the sight of Louisa, her eyes widened with surprise then narrowed with dismay.

"Hello," she murmured to them both. "Louisa, you're looking well."

"Thank you." She went to Caroline and gripped her hands. "You have a wonderful husband, Caroline. Treasure him."

She gave a last look to Tristan, one he knew was a goodbye, then she left him alone with his wife.

Caroline watched Louisa slip through the door in a cloud of royal-blue linen. As the door creaked shut, she turned back to Tristan and saw both a challenge and an admission in his eyes. He'd been alone with Louisa in his study. She'd expected the old friends to have conversations, but the moment had a secretive air. She felt excluded and forgotten.

Turning back to him, she forced a smile. "I'm sorry to interrupt."

Tristan strode across the entry hall and took her hands in both of his. "You didn't interrupt a thing."

"But—"

He looked as if he wanted to kiss her. Instead he gave her a stern look and let go of her fingers. When he stepped back, she felt utterly foolish for imagining a kiss and averted her gaze to the floor. She saw boot prints, wondered who'd left them and wished she'd left the house five minutes sooner.

Tristan cleared his throat. "Louisa has asked us for a favor."

Caroline lifted her face, but she still felt foolish. "What is it?"

"She'd like us to hold a house party." Tristan described how Louisa had met Stuart Whitmore and explained about the man's family. The thought of entertaining a dowager duchess nearly sent Caroline running to her room. She'd mustered her courage to learn to ride. Having a house full of women as poised as Louisa was more than she could imagine.

"I'm not ready for that much company," she said to Tristan. "I'll embarrass you."

"That's not possible."

She managed to laugh. "I think it is."

Both commanding and imperial, he held her in place with a piercing blue gaze. The air smelled of his shaving soap, and his freshly scraped jaw remind her of a marble bench in the garden at Swan's Nest. She'd often sat there to pray, smelling roses and dust and wishing for a man like Tristan to love her. Upstairs she heard Evaline speaking to Dora. Footsteps charged down the hall and she looked up. The little girl was nowhere in sight, but Caroline felt all the ties of being a family. If she wanted to keep her adopted family, she had to fight for them. She had to prove her abilities to herself and a house full of English nobles.

"All right," she said. "We'll give that party.

"Very good." He sounded like an officer praising a private who'd managed to properly shine his shoes. "Louisa can help you with the invitation for the Whitmores. She knows their names and titles. I thought you'd also like to invite your friends from Denver."

Caroline very much wanted to see Adie, Mary and Pearl, but they didn't know she'd gotten married and she didn't want to explain the circumstances. Neither were her friends accustomed to the ways of people like the Duke of Willoughby. "It would be awkward."

"Nonsense." Tristan frowned. "They're your friends and they're welcome here. Invite them."

"I'd rather not."

A peeved expression crossed his face. She'd disregarded his request, something a good soldier didn't do, but she couldn't face her friends. They'd want to hear about the courtship that hadn't happened and the marriage that existed solely for legal reasons. Just as problematic, they'd come if she asked and the trip to The Barracks was long and difficult. Pearl was expecting a baby in a couple of months. Just before Caroline left Denver, Mary had whispered that her monthly was two weeks late.

She could see Tristan's dissatisfaction, but she wouldn't change her mind. Instead she changed the subject. "When should we send the invitations?"

"Immediately," he answered. "We've had excellent weather, but it won't last. I'll have the invitations hand delivered to the Whitmores. I imagine the guests will stay a week. We'll need entertainment…music and games, maybe charades. And for course, there will be riding for everyone."

"Riding?" she said meekly.

"Absolutely. Nothing strenuous for the women, just an easy tour of the ranch. For the men, we'll have a hunt, perhaps jousting."

"Jousting!"

"Only for the men," he said, laughing. She loved the sound of it, but she had more doubts than ever that she could be the wife he needed. He gave her another stern look. "Let's begin those riding lessons."

"Yes," she murmured.

Mustering her courage, she walked with Tristan out the door and to the stable where a very large and intimidating horse awaited her, a fitting reminder of the challenges to come.

Chapter Fifteen

They walked side by side to the barn, with Tristan talking about the house party and Caroline wondering if he'd lost his mind. The more he said, the more worried she became. She had no idea how to entertain in the fashion he seemed to expect. He assured her Evaline and Noah would see to the accommodations and food, but as Tristan's wife, she'd be accountable.

So far Evaline had yet to serve a meal that didn't give the duke a bad case of indigestion. With an additional six people visiting—Whitmore, the dowager duchess, the two nieces and two gentlemen who had yet to be determined—Caroline would have her hands full. The women would bring lady's maids, and Whitmore and the gentlemen would possibly have valets. Caroline counted bedrooms and decided to ask Evaline and Sophie Howe, the foreman's wife who helped with cleaning, to prepare every available bed. The servants would have to double up, but she didn't think they'd mind.

Suddenly nervous, she glanced at Tristan's profile. His blond hair was combed back into a peak, and his skin had a healthy glow. Dressed in a blue chambray shirt, dark trousers and shiny black boots that came to his knees, he had the air of the nobleman he was. No one would ever guess he had a potentially fatal disease, but it could still be in his blood. A new worry twisted through her mind. If he became ill during the party, it would be impossible to hide.

"I'm worried," she said suddenly.

"About what?"

"If you become ill while we have guests, what will happen?"

His jaw stiffened. "I don't plan on becoming ill."

She wanted to press for an answer but didn't. No man liked being reminded of weakness, and Tristan especially disliked it.

He gave her a friendly smile. "I'd much rather focus on your riding lessons."

Caroline would have preferred playing dolls with Dora or even catching frogs with Freddie, but she put on a brave face. When they reached the barn, Tristan indicated the door to the tack room. He guided her inside, then shut it behind them. Without the sunlight, the room turned into a palette of grays and browns. They were standing so close she could smell his shaving soap over the scent of hay. She'd been prepared to walk into the barn where she'd see Cairo and Grandma. She didn't know what to think when he crouched down and reached into a wooden box.

"What's going on?" she asked.

"I have a surprise for you."

She couldn't imagine what it would be. "I'm not fond of surprises."

"You'll like this one." Standing tall, he held a ball of butterscotch fur against his chest.

"It's a kitten!" she declared.

"Take it." He turned to give her room to lift it. As she

grasped the tiny creature, her fingertips grazed the cotton of Tristan's shirt and she looked up. He seemed not to react to her touch, but he inhaled softly as he slid the kitten into her palms. Snuggling the cat against her chest, she looked down at its face. The tiny thing had a black dot of a nose, pale green eyes and a tail that swished with feline nonchalance. She guessed it to be six or seven weeks old and eager to get on with life. She also discerned the cat to be female. "She's adorable."

"She's yours."

"Really?"

"We can use a mouser in the house." His lips quirked. "But mostly she'll be a pet. Dora loves kittens."

"So do I." Caroline lifted the tiny thing and rubbed noses with it, then she looked at Tristan. "I thought I was here for a riding lesson."

"You are." He took back the kitten. "In fact, you've just had the first one."

"I have?"

"I've discovered you like animals…and animals like you." He scratched the kitten's tiny head with his index finger. When it stretched, Caroline thought of a flower opening in the sun. "Let's call her Daisy."

"Whatever you'd like."

He put Daisy back in the box with her mother and siblings. "We'll leave her here until you go back to the house. It's time for the second lesson."

He opened the door into the barn, indicating she should lead the way. Breathing deep, she followed him into the cavernous space. The smells took her back to Wheeler Springs and the carriage house where she'd agreed to become his wife for the sake of the children. She'd been accepting of the limitations and she still was, but today she felt longings she couldn't deny. She cared about Tristan for a hundred different reasons.

He loved his children.

He was respected by his friends.

He was loyal, kind and courageous. How could she not have feelings for this man who'd been so understanding of her fears? Just as he'd probably hoped, the kitten had given her a bit of confidence. Feeling brave, she walked with him to the center of the barn. A horse stomped its foot. Another chuffed so loudly she jumped. Instinctively she reached for Tristan's hand.

He clasped her fingers and smiled. "This way," he said, indicating a stall at the end of the barn. She glimpsed a carved sign above the door. Instead of letters, she saw strange shapes. Pointing to it, she asked, "What does that mean?"

"It spells 'Cairo' in Arabic."

She stopped in her tracks. "I can't ride Cairo. He's too big. He's—"

"You're not riding Cairo," he said gently. "I am. But there's someone else for you to meet."

She dug in her heels. "I thought I'd be riding Grandma. Bessie says she's gentle."

"She is." His eyes twinkled. "We'll get to Grandma."

"But—"

He stopped in the aisle and faced her. "Trust me, Caroline." He took her other hand, again stroking her knuckles with his thumbs.

She'd become accustomed to the caress. It calmed her… It pleased her. Finally she nodded. "All right."

He led her to the stall at a leisurely pace. The top half of the gate was open, and she expected Cairo to stick out his giant head and look down at her. The horse didn't appear. Feeling brave, she let Tristan tug her close enough to peer over the half door. Instead of the fearsome stallion, she saw another animal altogether. "That's a goat!"

"Her name is Hannah." Tristan sounded pleased. "She's Cairo's best friend."

"My father kept a nanny goat in Charleston. It was my job to milk it." She looked up at Tristan and smiled. "Goats have a bad reputation, but they're rather sweet if they know who's in charge."

He opened the door to the stall. "Go on in."

She went up to Hannah, who gave her a friendly push with her head and bleated at her. Laughing softly, Caroline rubbed the goat's ears as she looked over her shoulder at Tristan. "Hannah's sweet. Why is she with Cairo?"

"Goats have a way of calming skittish horses."

"And skittish women?"

"I hope so," he replied. "Is it working?"

"I believe it is."

"She helped Cairo quite a bit," Tristan explained. "He didn't take kindly to being shipped across the Atlantic and again from the West Indies to here. Hannah keeps him company. I thought you'd enjoy getting to know her."

"I am," she admitted. "I'm having a good time."

Sunlight glinted through the window at the top of the stall, turning Tristan's straw-colored hair into shining white. Once pale, his cheeks were brown with the sun and his eyes were the brightest blue she'd ever seen. If she'd been seeing him for the first time, she'd have never guessed he'd been ill. Any doubts she had about learning to ride vanished at the sight of this brave man who'd fought for his country, his health and his family. If he could face an uncertain future, she could learn to ride.

She looked into his eyes. "I'm ready for the third lesson."

"Good." As he gave Hannah a last pat, Caroline stepped

out of the stall. Tristan closed the gate, then led her to the stall directly across from the one holding the goat. She looked over the gate, saw a pony and laughed. "Now that's a horse I could ride!"

"This is Biscuit.

He was light brown with a whitish mane and tail. "Because of his coloring?" she asked.

"I suppose. Dora named him."

"Does she ride him?"

"Yes, she does. Quite well as a matter of fact." A father's pride rang in his voice. "Let's give him some carrots."

Tristan fetched the treats from a crate. He showed her how to feed the pony by gripping the carrot and then flattening her hand to avoid a mishap involving teeth and fingers. Biscuit took the carrot from his hand and chewed happily. When he finished, Tristan handed her a carrot. "You do it."

Caroline followed his example, laughing as Biscuit's lips tickled her palm. When the pony pulled back his head to chew, she looked up and saw Tristan leaning on a post, watching her with frank appreciation. He looked both pleased and proud, and she blushed. "You've been wonderful, Tristan. I thought today would be hard, but you've made it delightful."

"Do you feel ready for Grandma?"

"I do."

"She's saddled and waiting in the corral." He held out his arm. Taking his elbow, she fell into step at his side. Together they passed the stalls, most of them holding horses that even she could see had excellent bloodlines. Tristan ran a cattle ranch, but he had the heart of a horseman. It was easy to imagine his horses being prized as the finest mounts in America.

She looked at him and smiled. "Your Arabians are beautiful."

"I think so," he said without modesty. "I had plans for breeding them, but—" He shook his head, unwilling to go down a road that led to uncertainty.

She tightened her grip on his bent elbow. "Bessie says you're doing well. You haven't had a fever in days."

"That's no guarantee that it's gone."

She expected him to pull away, but he drew her closer as they walked through the barn, their paces matching until they reached the door. Breaking away from her, he lifted a wide-brimmed hat from a nail and pulled it low. Side by side, they stepped into the yard where sunlight fell from the sky, warming the day with the start of an Indian summer. As relaxed as a cat, he led her to the corral where Bert Howe was holding Grandma. Next to the horse she saw a mounting block. She thought of how Tristan had pulled her onto Cairo and how she'd held his waist.

Today she'd be alone. Shivering with nerves, she told herself to be brave.

"You'll do fine," Tristan said with assurance.

He stopped her at the gate to the corral. In short sentences, he gave her basic instructions for mounting, holding the reins and positioning her feet. The next thing Caroline knew, she was sitting astride Grandma, clutching the saddle horn and feeling wobbly.

Tristan adjusted her stirrups. "Think of Grandma as a rocking chair with legs."

"She's a very *high* rocking chair!" Caroline almost hiccupped. "*And* she has a mind of her own."

"Move with her and you'll be fine," he said calmly. "Now take the reins and hold them like I showed you."

She did as he said, but her stomach felt queasy.

Satisfied with her posture, he swung up on Cairo with a grace she envied. Sitting next to him, she felt awkward and stiff.

"Are you ready?" he asked.

"I am."

When he instructed her to lift the reins, she obeyed. So did Grandma, and they took off at a leisurely walk. It was more than leisurely, Caroline decided. It was so slow she felt silly. Tristan didn't seem to mind, but Cairo chuffed in irritation until his master spoke to him. Riding along the fence, Tristan spoke to Caroline in the easy tone he'd used on Cairo. They talked about nothing in a way that relaxed her. As if it were just part of the conversation about the weather, Tristan told her how to urge Grandma into a faster walk. The mare perked up and so did Caroline.

For the next half hour they stopped and started, walking slow and then fast. Tristan gave instructions, and she gave the commands to Grandma. When she noticed him admiring her, she beamed a smile. "You're a good teacher."

"You're an excellent student."

"Could we go faster?"

"We can," he said, hesitating. "But trotting is quite different from walking. I suggest we do it tomorrow."

"I can handle it," she said, feeling confident.

"Very well." He told her how to work her knees to do something called posting, and to expect some bouncing until she found the rhythm, then he backed Cairo away from her. "Watch me."

He urged the stallion into a trot. Man and horse looked like a single creature, moving in perfect time. He made riding look easy and her confidence rose another notch. When Grandma shifted her weight, Caroline felt the roll in her back and swayed easily. The horse really did feel like a rocking chair.

Tristan rode up next to her. "You've done well today. Are you sure you're ready for more?"

"I'm positive."

Following his instructions, she put Grandma into a trot. To her horror, the comfortable rocking chair turned into a bone-jarring, teeth-rattling monster of a horse.

"You're doing fine," Tristan called from atop Cairo. "Use your legs."

"I-I-I'm t-t-trying!"

"You'll get it."

She straightened her spine and attempted to use her legs the way he'd instructed, but she was still bouncing like a ball on a string. Gritting her teeth, she focused straight ahead.

Tristan stayed beside her. "That's enough for today. Rein in Grandma."

Relieved to have the lesson over, she slowed the horse to a walk. Her legs ached so badly she wondered if she could stand, but she was smiling with pride as Grandma followed Cairo to the gate. Tristan climbed down from the stallion with a natural grace.

She expected him to help her off Grandma, but he was staring at something in the distance. She followed his gaze and saw the duke, Louisa and Freddie riding toward them, each one sitting tall and looking at ease, especially Louisa. Perched on a sidesaddle, she was the picture of grace. She was exactly the kind of woman Tristan deserved, and she had his full attention.

With her head high, Caroline prayed the house party would be a success. If she failed Tristan, she'd insist on the annulment. She'd lose everything and everyone she'd come to love, but she couldn't imagine a life of daily failure. The children, especially Freddie, would suffer because of her. In a way she'd already lost Bessie. With her engagement, her sister would stay with Jon.

With all the courage she could muster, Caroline squared her shoulders as Louisa, the duke and Freddie reined their mounts to a halt at the fence.

Louisa smiled back with warmth.

The duke ignored her.

Freddie stared at her with such dislike she felt a chill. Something had happened with the duke. She felt sure of it and braced herself for an unpleasant situation.

Chapter Sixteen

"We have company," Caroline said in a high voice.

Tristan immediately sensed her nerves. "Yes, we do."

He had noticed Louisa first. It was impossible *not* to see that bright-blue riding habit, but it was Freddie who had his attention now. The boy usually wore dungarees like the cowhands. Today he was sporting black pants and a miniature frock coat, most likely stitched by the duke's valet. He'd also chosen an English saddle and was sitting ramrod straight, a living picture of the boy Tristan had once been.

Tristan shifted his gaze to his father. He and Freddie were wearing the same haughty expression. The roots of the family tree ran deep, feeding even the youngest, most tender branches. Looking at the two of them, Tristan made a silent vow. Where the duke had sowed tyranny, Tristan would plant a desire to serve others. Where his father had been severe, he'd be gentle. And where the duke condemned others for no reason, Tristan intended to plant seeds of love for God, family and country.

Looking at Freddie, he realized that coping with malaria had changed him. In his weakness, Tristan had been reduced to a child again, and this time he'd felt a Father's love in the concern of his friends, his children and especially Caroline. In some ways he'd been as petulant as Freddie, issuing orders that no one followed, and yet no one had stopped caring for him. It seemed to Tristan that God had a very difficult job. Not only did his children need love, they needed to be protected from themselves and others.

Right now, Freddie needed to be protected from the duke. No matter how much the boy balked, Tristan could not allow him to mimic his grandfather's arrogance. If Freddie spoke rudely to Caroline, Tristan would correct him immediately.

Louisa spoke first. "What a lovely ride we had! Tristan, your ranch is spectacular."

"I'm glad you enjoyed the ride," he said mildly.

"Yes," Caroline echoed.

The duke pretended to stifle a yawn.

So did Freddie.

Tristan's hackles rose, but he wouldn't go to war over a yawn. Louisa lifted the veil from her hat, giving him a clear view of her eyes. "I've had a lovely day, but I'm quite tired. If you gentlemen will excuse me, I'll return to the house."

"Of course," Tristan replied. "Freddie will see to your horse."

The boy huffed. Freddie never huffed. He occasionally whined, but he didn't put on airs. Today he had the nerve to look down his nose at Tristan, then he said, "Don't we have *servants* for that, Father?"

Tristan said nothing for a full ten seconds. The pause was to give Freddie the opportunity to obey on his own and save his pride. When the boy huffed again, Tristan spoke with deceptive mildness. "At The Barracks, a man tends to his own horse. He also tends to a lady's horse without being asked."

Still Freddie didn't move.

Tristan's voice dropped lower. "And when I give an order, it's followed. You'll take care of all three horses, or you'll be confined to your room for three days."

"But *Father*—"

The duke interrupted. "Come now, Tristan. My time with the boy is limited, and we're quite ready for lunch. Perhaps Jon—"

"No." Tristan clipped the word. Next to him Grandma bobbed her head, a reminder that Caroline was silently observing the exchange. He wondered what she was thinking, but he didn't want to trade a look in front of Freddie. Louisa watched him with sympathy, as if she understood too well how it felt to be undercut by the duke. The next move was Freddie's.

The boy stayed in the saddle, unaware that he'd become a rope in a game of tug-of-war. Tristan watched as Freddie feigned disinterest. Silently he willed his son to slip from the saddle and do as he'd been told. Instead Freddie locked eyes on Caroline. "You're riding like a man," he said with disgust.

Tristan erupted. "Freddie! That's enough."

Caroline wisely stayed calm. "Yes, I am. It's quite practical."

Louisa broke in. "Caroline, you'll have to share the pattern for your split skirt. Don't tell anyone, but I, too, ride astride on occasion. It's far more practical for jumping."

The duke laughed out loud. "Jumping! She can barely stay on that nag of a mare."

"That's uncalled for, your grace." Tristan kept his

tone civil but just barely. Caroline deserved respect, and Grandma was far from a nag.

"It's true," Freddie said pompously. "We saw her trying to trot. Grandfather said she looked like a broken doll."

"Freddie!" Tristan's voice boomed. "Apologize this instant."

"Why should I?" the boy whined. "She was supposed to be the *governess,* not my mother. If she wasn't here, you'd take us to England. We could live in Grandfather's house and we'd have—

"That's enough," Tristan said. "It's also a lie."

Caroline stayed quiet. It wasn't her place to defend their marriage. It was his. "Caroline is my wife. For that alone, I insist on respect."

"Grandfather says she's common." The boy sounded smug.

"Your grandfather's opinion is both unwanted and incorrect." Tristan was speaking to Freddie, but he directed his gaze to the duke. He wanted to order the man to leave The Barracks immediately, but he'd promised to help Louisa. Seething inside, he aimed his gaze at his son and spoke with deadly calm. "Frederick Willoughby Smith, you will apologize *this instant* or face punishment."

"Tristan—" Caroline spoke so softly he barely heard her. "Perhaps Freddie and I should speak in private."

"No."

"But perhaps—"

"Caroline!" He regretted snapping at her, but he couldn't allow his authority to be questioned in front of his son...or his father. "I'll discipline my son, thank you very much."

"Of course." She sounded compliant, but he heard the tremor in her voice. Should he have said *our* son? That claim would have fueled Freddie's resentment, however, and it went against the honesty Caroline herself advocated. Whether the quaver in her voice had come from anger or hurt, he didn't know. Later he'd apologize for snapping, but first he had to finish with Freddie.

He stared at the boy until he saw the start of a crack in his resolve. Just when he thought Freddie would give in, the duke let out a petulant sigh. "I've had enough of this silliness, Tristan. It's time you—"

"Gentlemen!" Louisa raised her voice. "Perhaps you can agree to disagree."

Tristan said nothing.

The duke snorted but didn't argue.

"Good." Louisa turned to Freddie. "I'm feeling quite tired. If you'd tend to my horse, I'd be most grateful."

Freddie looked positively smitten. "I'd be honored, Aunt Louisa."

On the surface the situation had calmed, but Tristan felt a riptide of disrespect pulling them into deeper waters. Freddie had been invited to address Caroline as "Aunt" several days ago, and he hadn't used the endearment. Louisa had defused a tense situation, but she'd badly upstaged Caroline. To add to his wife's sense of inferiority, Louisa performed a gracious dismount while Caroline sat perched on Grandma. Freddie and the duke climbed off their horses. With Tristan already on the ground, Caroline alone was on her horse. She'd have to dismount with an audience.

Hoping to give her dignity, he explained the situation to the three onlookers. "This is Caroline's first time alone on a horse."

"How wonderful!" Louisa exclaimed.

The duke wore a smirk. "We saw *that* from afar."

Caroline looked at the duke, then at Louisa and finally

at Tristan. He gave her careful instructions for the easiest dismount, which unfortunately was inelegant. "Remove both feet from the stirrups," he said. "Then lean forward and swing your right leg over Grandma's rump."

With a surprising grace, she swung her leg over the horse and slid to the ground. She did just fine until her feet hit the dirt and her knees buckled. In a tangle of stockings and split skirts she fell against him. He circled her waist with his arm. If they'd been alone, he'd have enjoyed holding her close. They'd have laughed about the stumble and he'd have praised her courage. With Louisa and his father watching, the moment was simply embarrassing.

When she wobbled, he wondered if she'd twisted her ankle. "Are you hurt?"

"Only my pride." And her confidence, he feared.

She steadied herself then looked defiantly at the duke. Louisa had stepped to the fence and was standing with her gloved hands laced on the top rail. "You did wonderfully, Marchioness."

She'd used the title to show respect. Tristan appreciated the gesture, but he feared Caroline would feel mocked. He arched a brow at Louisa. "We're informal at The Barracks."

"Of course," she said. "Forgive me."

Caroline had regained composure. "There's nothing to forgive. I hope you enjoyed your ride."

"Very much," Louisa said quickly. "The land is—"

The duke intruded. "*I* found the landscape rather tedious. England is much greener, and we don't have this miserably hot weather in October."

"Wyoming and England are lovely in their own ways," Louisa said diplomatically. "I understand you call this time of year an Indian summer?"

"Yes," Caroline said to Louisa. "Tristan tells me we're hosting a house party in a few weeks. The warmer weather will be ideal."

Louisa smiled her gratitude. "I'm quite excited. I hope you and Tristan will take the opportunity to celebrate your marriage."

Caroline shook her head. "There's no need—"

"Oh, but there is." Louisa gave Tristan a meaningful look, one meant to remind him of his obligation as a husband. She meant well, but Caroline could easily misinterpret Louisa's look as a shared secret, which it wasn't. When Tristan didn't speak up, Louisa continued to make her point. "You've been married such a short time. A celebration is in order…a grand one, I think."

The duke harrumphed. "That's hardly necessary."

His implication was clear. He didn't think the marriage warranted public acknowledgment, and he wanted to snub Caroline. This was no time to be timid. Tristan spoke with complete calm. "Not only is it necessary, your grace, it will be an honor to introduce my new wife to a family as distinguished as the Whitmores."

He put his arm around her waist, felt the tension in every muscle and knew she'd have preferred riding Cairo to facing a house full of English nobles.

Caroline tried to appear nonchalant, even haughty, but her voice betrayed her nerves. "I hope you all enjoy the visit with the Whitmores."

"I'm sure we will," Louisa said gently. "Thank you, Caroline."

"It's our pleasure," she said evenly.

Tristan loved Caroline and he wanted her to succeed. A public acknowledgment of their marriage would make a quiet annulment impossible, but he didn't care. He had no intention of annulling the marriage or allowing Caroline to fail so badly that she'd insist on it.

He looked into her eyes. "The party is going to be a resounding success. I'm sure of it."

When she lifted her chin, he saw the woman who'd pulled a gun on him in the canyon. She'd been shaking inside, but she hadn't showed her anxiety. He sensed the same reluctant determination now, and he knew without a doubt his American bride had the courage to be a duchess…only she didn't know it.

Tristan did some mental calculations and decided to hold the party in three weeks. With a little luck, the good weather would hold. They had to move fast, so Tristan started giving orders.

"Caroline will write the invitations. I'll see that they're delivered to the Whitmores by one of my men.

She looked pale but nodded.

"Louisa, if you'd help with the entertainment, I'd be obliged."

"Of course." Her cheeks turned rosy. "Do you have a piano?"

"No, but we have some talented musicians in the bunkhouse. I'll arrange for music." He'd heard impromptu concerts. The men were enthusiastic if not classically trained, and he rather liked the idea of the duke having to cope with a fiddle-playing cowboy and zealous banjo player. Bert Howe played the guitar and he did it well. Tristan thought of whirling Caroline around the room in a waltz. By the end of the house party, he'd know if he'd beaten the malaria. He could ask her to dance without guilt or fear. In the middle of a waltz he could kiss her and confess that he loved her.

"We'll have dancing," he said firmly.

Caroline inhaled sharply but said nothing.

Tristan looked at his father. Considering how he'd mocked Caroline, he deserved a comeuppance and Tristan knew how to give one. No one gave the duke orders, but Tristan had no reluctance. "Your grace, you'll be in charge of the hunt for the men."

The duke looked peeved, then sly. "Perhaps another form of entertainment is in order… Something the ladies would enjoy."

"Such as?" Tristan asked.

"An American horse race." He looked pointedly at Caroline. "Your wife can show off her new skills."

Tristan clenched his jaw. His father was cleverly setting a trap. "I don't think that's a good idea."

"Why not?" The man's eyes were marble-hard. "Louisa would enjoy it, and I believe the Whitmore nieces are quite skilled. Your wife is learning, isn't she?"

"Yes, but—"

Caroline interrupted. "A race is a fine idea, your grace. My skills aren't up to such a test, but our guests will enjoy it."

The duke gave her a pitying glance. "For once, the marchioness and I agree. She's not up to a ride."

Despite the veneer of agreement, his words were meant to demean. Louisa gave Caroline a sympathetic look. The duke gloated. To Tristan's pride, Caroline kept her chin up as she answered him. "I'm looking forward to entertaining your friends, your grace. I hope they enjoy themselves."

"So do I," he said in a deadly tone. "The Dowager Duchess of Somerville is an impressive woman and an old friend. I don't want her inconvenienced."

"Of course," Caroline agreed.

Tristan vaguely remembered the dowager as a woman with thin platinum hair, a taste for emeralds and an acerbic sense of humor. As an ally, she was superb. As an enemy, she was lethal. For Caroline, the house party would be ripe with opportunities for both triumph and humiliation.

The duke excused himself with a curt nod. Louisa smiled sympathetically then followed him, leaving Tristan alone with his wife and the painful awareness that she'd just been thrown to a pack of aristocratic wolves. His father was the alpha male, the leader who'd run her off if she couldn't compete. If Louisa rode in his silly race, Caroline would be forced to ride, as well. Her riding lessons, it seemed, were just getting started.

Caroline had had her fill of riding lessons, Louisa's perfection and Tristan's insistence that she could be someone she wasn't. She had no desire to celebrate their nonexistent marriage, especially not in Louisa's shadow. The woman couldn't have looked more elegant in her riding costume. Even with the marks on her face, she was lovely. Her beauty came from the inside, along with the poise of a woman born to nobility…a woman who could ride sidesaddle without the slightest wobble.

In her split skirt, now dusty and wrinkled, Caroline felt like a gawky schoolgirl. Only a bit of pique had enabled her to stand up to the duke. Tired and saddle-sore, she wanted to go to her room. Recalling Tristan's lecture to Freddie about caring for his horse, she turned to him. "Do I need to tend to Grandma?"

"Not today." His eyes were gentle on her face, but she felt as if he were scouring her for a likeness to Louisa.

With a nod, she left him with Grandma and Cairo and turned to the gate. Tristan clasped her arm and she turned. "What is it?"

"That race," he said quietly. "My father's going to torment you with it."

"I expect so."

"I could insist on a traditional hunt. He'll still make remarks, but you wouldn't have to resist as strongly."

Was he making the offer to protect her? Or was he afraid she'd embarrass herself and him? If Louisa and the duke wanted to showcase Caroline's inadequacies, he'd found the perfect stage for an inept performance. She couldn't ride, and she didn't know very much about fine clothing or art and the symphony. Her favorite meal was chicken and dumplings, not pheasant. She liked to bake pies and eat supper as a family. She also had her pride, and she'd come to love this man who couldn't stop being an English noble anymore than she could stop being average.

"You don't have to protect me," she said quietly.

"I do. It's my duty."

Feeling clumsier than ever, she started to walk away. He called after her, "Another riding lesson tomorrow?"

She'd never be an accomplished rider, but she wanted to be adequate. She faced him. "That would be fine."

He dismissed her with a nod, but she saw pride in his eyes. She also saw hesitation. Was he worried she'd embarrass him? Or was he afraid for his health? She wanted to ask him, but she had worries of her own. If she failed to hold her own with the Whitmores, she'd ask for the annulment to protect them both.

Sick with dread, she entered the tack room and fetched Daisy. With the kitten against her chest, she walked to the house with thoughts of Hannah, Biscuit and the way she'd stumbled into Tristan's arms. Her legs ached, and her ears echoed with insults from Freddie and the duke. Cuddling Daisy, she circled to the back of the house to the veranda. She wanted to take refuge in her room, but Dora saw her and came running.

"Aunt Caroline!" she cried. "Let's play the dream game!"

She couldn't bear the thought of repeating the game, not with her own dreams dying, but she neither could disappoint Dora. Crouching down, she cradled Daisy in her hands. "Look what I have."

"A kitten!"

"She's going to live in the house."

Dora stroked the tiny feline while it meowed. After a time Caroline shifted Daisy to the crook of her elbow and stood. Gripping Dora's hand, she walked with her to the divan and pulled her into her lap. They played with Daisy until Dora remembered her original request. "I want to play the dream game."

Fortified, Caroline stroked the child's hair. "Do you still want to be a princess?"

When she shook her head no, Caroline knew something was wrong. She raised Dora's chin with her fingertip. "You look sad. What's the matter?"

"Freddie says we're going away."

Caroline could imagine the dreams the duke had planted in the boy's mind. "Where did he say you were going?"

"To England with Grandfather." She flung herself against Caroline's chest. "I don't want to go to England. I want to stay here with you and Biscuit…and my kitten."

Caroline held back a frown. What kind of person manipulated children? Until now she'd held the small hope that Tristan and his father would reconcile. He hadn't asked for her opinion, but she would have counseled him to be respectful in the spirit of "honor thy mother and father" and to pray for the ability to forgive the man who'd hurt him. She believed in those principles, but respect and forgiveness didn't require Tristan to put his children in the hands of a selfish manipulator.

She held Dora close. "Your daddy won't let anyone take you away."

Her lip quivered. "Is he still sick?"

"Yes, but he's getting better."

Dora snuggled closer. "I don't like Grandfather, but Aunt Louisa is nice. We played dolls last night."

Was there *anyone* who didn't think Louisa was perfect? Caroline couldn't possibly compete with her.

Dora snuggled closer, petting the kitten as she looked up at Caroline. "I like Aunt Louisa, but she talks funny."

"She's from England. I like how she sounds."

"I like how *you* sound." Dora's eyes blurred with angry tears. "I don't want two aunts. I want you to be my mama."

Caroline had no business encouraging such a deep attachment until she could be sure of the future, but how could she deny Dora this simple request? She couldn't. "I'd like that very much."

"Mama." She spoke firmly, as if stamping the word on her heart. She said it again, stamping it on Caroline's.

"I love you, Dora."

"I love you, too."

The child snuggled in her arms. Daisy was wedged between them, a ball of soft fur while Caroline's nerves twitched with worry. She had deep feelings for Tristan. She loved her borrowed children and didn't want to lose them, but neither did she want Tristan to look at her as second-best. With Dora's love fresh in her heart, she had more reason than ever to overcome her fear.

Silently she prayed. *Help me, Lord... I don't want to hurt this little girl, but I'm not capable of being a duchess.*

No comfort came in the silence, only a sure and quiet stretching of her faith. God had so loved the world that

He'd given his only Son for the benefit of all mankind. When a father loved his children, he sacrificed for them. When a man loved a woman, he fought for her. And when a woman loved a man, she waged the same battle.

With her eyes shut tight, she thought of Tristan's arm around her waist. She remembered the kiss in the garden and the look in his eyes when he handed her the kitten. She also heard the bitterness in his tone when he mentioned his illness and saw his pride when she'd done well on Grandma. Every instinct told her his feelings were as deep as hers, which left a single solution to her dilemma. She had to make the house party a resounding success.

Chapter Seventeen

The next three weeks passed in a blur of riding lessons, menu planning and visits from the Wheeler Springs dressmaker. To her surprise, Caroline enjoyed the riding lessons in particular. With Tristan's help, she learned to post with some gracefulness, and she enjoyed galloping Grandma around a grassy meadow. She had no fear of the gray mare at all, and she'd made friends with Cairo thanks to dozens of peppermints.

The riding lessons gave her a pleasant break from the house party preparations. If it weren't for Louisa, Caroline would have been overwhelmed. She hardly knew where to start, but Louisa had planned far more elaborate occasions and was taking delight in having a purpose and a protégée. She gladly schooled Caroline in titles and etiquette, laughing when Caroline professed utter confusion. She'd also insisted that Caroline have a completely new wardrobe. Her lady's maid had provided patterns for the latest fashions, and the two women had spent hours selecting fabrics and styles.

With the Whitmores scheduled to arrive any minute, Caroline took a last look at herself in the mirror, then breathed a prayer of thanks for Louisa. The hours together had made them confidantes who were rooting for each other. If Louisa didn't win Stuart Whitmore's heart, she'd be a worthless member of the duke's household, a hanger-on unless she returned to her family, an option that would render her dependent on the good graces of a penny-pinching brother-in-law. Even more important, Louisa had been taken with Whitmore's charm and physicality. Having been trapped in a loveless marriage, she wanted a husband as full of daring as she was.

Caroline hoped her friend would be successful. Any minute Stuart Whitmore would arrive with his mother, her nieces and two English gentlemen. As hostess, Caroline was wearing the fanciest day dress she'd ever had. It was fit for a duchess, but it made her feel like someone she wasn't. She touched the curls piled on her head. Louisa's maid had done her hair in a style that was elaborate, to say the least.

"Mrs. Caroline?"

She turned to the open nursery door and saw Evaline. The housekeeper looked stately in her new uniform, a black dress with a crisp white apron.

"Yes?" Caroline replied.

"The first guests have arrived."

"Thank you, Evaline."

Caroline went down the stairs with a stomach full of butterflies, silently rehearsing the formal greetings she'd practiced with Louisa. The dowager duchess was a stickler for such things. Praying she wouldn't make a fool of herself, she stood aside as Noah opened the door.

Instead of the dowager, she saw Adie Blue. Behind Adie she saw Josh holding the hand of their toddler son. Caroline burst into tears. Just seeing the Blues would have been a joy, but Mary and Jonah "J.T." Quinn walked in behind them. Most surprising of all, she saw Pearl heavy with child. Her husband, Matt, was holding their son on one hip while guiding their six-year-old daughter with his other hand. When Bessie walked into the fray from the hall, the flock from Swan's Nest was complete.

Behind them all, Caroline saw Tristan watching the reunion with a smile. He'd done this to surprise her, and she was grateful.

"How did you get here?" she said to Adie between tears. "How did you know—"

"Your *husband* sent invitations," Adie said pointedly.

Caroline hadn't told them about her marriage. Now she wondered how much they knew and felt nervous.

Bessie touched her arm. "Tristan asked for my help. I wrote the letters and Jon delivered them."

"And it's a good thing!" Always bold, Mary pulled her into a hug. "How dare you get married without us!"

"It's not— It's—" She bit her lip. "It's not that simple."

"We want to hear all about it," Pearl declared. "I say we crowd in your bedroom and you tell us everything. It'll be just like Swan's Nest."

Maybe, but her bedroom would reveal more than she wanted. Bessie interrupted, "Come to my room. I have news, too…something I didn't put in the letter."

Adie, Pearl and Mary waited expectantly, but Bessie had the patience of Job. "Let's get you settled, then we'll visit."

Caroline turned to Evaline. "You knew they were coming, didn't you?"

"Yes, ma'am." The housekeeper beamed. "The major asked me to prepare the third floor. It'll be a bit crowded up there, but we'll manage." With the arrangements they'd made for the Whitmore contingent, the house would be overflowing.

In a flurry of skirts, the women went upstairs with

Evaline leading the way and Caroline bringing up the rear. She wanted a word with Tristan, but he'd been joined by Jon and was speaking with the men. She'd have to thank him later.

It didn't take long for the friends to settle into their rooms. In less than an hour, the five women were together in Bessie's room with Pearl on the bed propped on pillows, Adie and Mary in side chairs, Bessie perched next to Pearl and Caroline at the foot of the-bed in the rocker she'd carried from the nursery.

"I want to hear everything," Adie insisted. "Why didn't you write to us that you'd gotten married?"

"Because it's a marriage in name only," Caroline said quietly.

Mary raised a brow. "That's not what it seems like to me. He went to a lot of trouble to send for us, and he did it for you."

Pearl nodded in agreement. "I was worried because of the baby, but he offered to pay for a doctor to accompany us. I told him no." She rested her hand on her belly. "The baby's not due for two months, but he offered because he cares about you."

"It's complicated," Caroline said.

Adie's gaze traveled from her face to her coiffed hair to the dress trimmed with more ribbon then she'd owned in her entire life. "You're dressed like a queen. What aren't you telling us?"

Caroline hesitated. "I'm not a queen, but in a strange way, I could someday be a—" She couldn't say *duchess* because she didn't believe it.

Bessie stepped in. "Caroline's trying to tell you that she's the future Duchess of Willoughby. Tristan is more than a retired army officer. He's the third son of a duke. When his brothers died, he unexpectedly became his father's heir. The house party is Caroline's chance to prove she's worthy of such a position."

"Of course she's worthy!" Mary declared.

"I know that." Bessie smiled. "So does Tristan. The person who doesn't believe it is Caroline."

Pearl gave her a sympathetic look. "It's a big step, isn't it?"

"It's huge," Caroline acknowledged. "And I'm so… ordinary."

"You're far from ordinary." Adie spoke with confidence. "You're the woman God made you to be. This gathering is going to be huge success. Not only do you have your husband pulling for you, you have all of us."

"That's right," Pearl agreed. "But you have to stay brave."

Coming from Pearl, the words had authority. The blonde had been the victim of a violent crime and had overcome her fears to find love. The baby in her belly was a testament to sorrow enduring for a night and joy coming in the morning.

Caroline looked next at Mary. She'd lived with a terrible secret. In his mercy, God had turned her shame into redemption for a hardened gunslinger. Caroline thought of the news Mary had whispered when they'd said goodbye. She raised her eyebrows with the question. "Are you—?"

"Yes." Her smile lit up the room. "Jonah's been wonderful. He's running the café so I can rest. The smell of bacon—" Mary winced. "Just thinking about it makes me sick!"

"Me, too," Pearl offered.

The women all looked at Bessie. Adie spoke for them all. "Tell us your news."

The oldest of the women, Bessie never expected to

marry. She loved being a nurse and considered it her calling. She looked from friend to friend, her cheeks growing pinker by the moment. "I met a man," she finally said. "His name is Jon."

Pearl spoke up. "He delivered the invitations. I like him."

"So do Josh and I," Adie replied.

Mary chimed in. "He and Jonah traded stories for half the night. He served in the British Army, didn't he?"

Bessie blushed harder. "He was a captain."

Caroline prodded her. "And?"

Suddenly shy, Bessie looked more like a girl than a middle-aged woman. "He asked me to marry him."

The women leaned forward, holding their breath for Bessie's answer until she smiled. "I said yes."

Hugs and questions abounded. Bessie and Jon had planned to have a spring wedding, but when the questions were over, Bessie agreed to ask Jon about moving the wedding up to the end of the house party so that her friends could attend and Josh could perform the ceremony.

"Oh!" Pearl cupped her tummy with both hands. "The baby kicked."

Adie put her hand on Pearl's belly. So did Mary and Bessie. They were all close enough to touch without standing. Caroline felt a million miles away until Pearl met her gaze. "Come here and feel the baby."

Rising to her feet, Caroline rested her hand on Pearl's tummy. The baby rolled under her touch, filling her with an old longing to bear a child of her own. She blinked and thought of the dream game. This dream could come true, but only if Tristan overcame his fear of dying and she proved herself worthy of being a duchess.

She closed her eyes. *Please, God. Keep him healthy and help me succeed.*

When the baby settled, the women broke apart and talk turned to plans for the house party and the other guests. No further mention was made of Caroline's troubled marriage, but she knew the women of Swan's Nest would be praying for her.

Tristan didn't like being surprised, but he greatly enjoyed surprising Caroline with the arrival of her friends. The entire day had been one victory after another. The Whitmores had arrived two hours later, and she'd welcomed them graciously. The evening meal—home-style American food—had been flawlessly prepared, and Caroline had made the dessert herself. Predictably, his father had complained about the raspberry pies, but the Whitmore crowd had been polite. Even the dowager duchess, a woman known for her sharp tongue and atrocious wigs, had refrained from comment.

Tristan had been proud of his wife and grateful to her friends. Reverend Blue was particularly erudite. Either his faith or his Boston upbringing—maybe both—gave him the ability to defuse the duke's snobbery. Matt Wiley and Jonah Quinn entertained everyone with stories about outlaws and bank robbers, a subject of great interest to the Whitmore nieces and the two men Stuart Whitmore had brought to round out the numbers. Terrence Pierce and Reggie Blackstone were Englishmen considering investments in the beef market. Jon and Bessie completed the table, along with Louisa and the duke.

Best of all, Tristan had been free of fever for twenty-six days. In four more days—less than one hundred hours—he could declare his love for Caroline. By then the house party would be a resounding success, and she'd have the confidence to be a full partner in his complicated life. Just four more days without fever... Just a dozen or so successful meals, a few rides through the hills, a dance and then they'd be free to venture into new and uncharted territory. First, though, he had to get through the remaining one hundred hours.

With the meal complete, he was bantering with the men in his study, watching the minutes tick by on a mantel clock. The men were enjoying cigars and talking about everything from cattle prices to American firearms. The women were in the front room, speaking of babies and whatnot. The evening would have been perfect if his study hadn't been so warm. Sweat was beading on his brow, an uncomfortable reminder of the fevers.

He moved away from the group. Turning his back to them, he looked out the window. The Indian summer filled the day with summer heat, but the evenings usually had a crisp chill. Tristan cracked open the window and felt the draft, but it failed to cool his brow. A shiver raced down his spine and settled in his bones. He was aching from head to foot, and his head was pounding with the familiar threat of delirium.

Dear God, no! Don't let this happen... Not now.

He couldn't deny the return of the malaria. He'd been so close to victory. Now he saw defeat as plainly as the shiny glass keeping back the night.

Where was God? Why hadn't He answered Tristan's prayers? No answer came, only chills that made him as weak as a child. But he wasn't a child... He was a man with duties, children and a wife. He had to beat the malaria. If God didn't see fit to heal him of the disease, Tristan would fight it by himself.

He had to speak to Caroline in private. Instead of sharing today's success, he'd remind her of the promise she'd made to hide Freddie and Dora from his father. With a house full of guests, his illness would be noticed. They could buy time with vague excuses, but the risk of his father learning of the malaria grew with each passing hour, and with that knowledge came increased danger to Freddie.

The duke was in the study now, attempting to dominate the conversation but being ignored by Quinn and Wiley, who were immune to his sense of privilege. Chills shot down Tristan's spine, a reminder he'd soon be nauseous. He closed the window, then he ambled to the group by the hearth. "Gentlemen, please stay and enjoy yourselves. I have some personal business to tend to."

Caroline's friends and the Whitmore contingent nodded and went back to their cigars.

The duke watched him like a hawk.

Jon put out his cigar. "I could use some air. I'll step outside with you."

Trying to appear steadier than he felt, Tristan left the study with Jon trailing him. When they were out of earshot, Jon stopped him. "It's back, isn't it?"

"Yes."

"I'll get Caroline."

"Thank you." Tristan had to speak with her about the children, but he had no intention of accepting her care as a patient. Tonight he'd planned to praise her for the start of the house party. He'd imagined kissing her goodnight before she went to the nursery. Instead he'd be ordering her to prepare to leave The Barracks. He turned his back on Jon and went up the stairs to his suite. Sweating profusely, he took off his coat and flopped faceup on the bed. Staring at the ceiling, he waited for the fever, the delirium, the nausea. Worst of all, he waited for Caroline with the intention of issuing the hardest order of his life.

* * *

Like the rest of the women in the front room, Caroline saw Jon motion to her through the door. She made apologies and they stepped into the hall.

"It's Tristan," he said quietly. "The fever is back."

"It can't be…" She could hardly breathe.

"He's upstairs," Jon explained. "He wants to see you."

"Of course." Her mind went in a dozen directions. She had to protect the children, but she couldn't leave Tristan. As long as he was alive, she'd be at his side.

Jon held her gaze. "I'll advise Bessie after the women retire for the night. She'll come to his room."

"Thank you."

"Stay brave, Caroline. Tristan's a fighter."

"I know." She also knew God alone numbered a man's days. Silently, she prayed for mercy, then she went back to the front room and spoke to the women. "Ladies, if you'll excuse me. I'm needed upstairs."

"Of course," Louisa said graciously. "I hope the children are all right."

"They're fine," she answered. "The problem is nothing new." Sadly, she'd spoken the truth.

The Whitmore girls offered understanding. The dowager raised a brow but said nothing. Adie, Mary and Pearl knew better than to quiz her in front of the others. Later she'd explain and ask them to pray. Bessie answered with a raised brow. *Do you need me?*

Caroline shook her head no. She'd leave informing her sister to Jon.

With her stomach in a knot, she hurried up the stairs. She'd been worried about Tristan since supper, but she'd taken the sheen in his eyes for pride. Now she recognized the start of a fever. She went to his room and entered from the hall, cracking open the door without knocking. A lamp tossed a circle of light against the wall and onto the floor. It spread to the bed, a monstrous thing that seemed to swallow Tristan alive. He raised his chin and looked at her. "We have to talk about the children."

"We will," she said. "But only if it's necessary."

"It is."

"Maybe not." Perching on the edge of the mattress, she put her hand on his forehead. "You're feverish, but you're not burning up."

"It just started." His jaw clenched. "In an hour or so, I expect to be delusional."

"You don't know that."

He heaved a sigh. "This could be it, Caroline."

"You're borrowing trouble."

He reached for her hand. "Promise me you'll hide Freddie from my father. Jon will help you—"

"I'll keep my word."

She squeezed his hand, released it and went to the washstand to fetch water. He couldn't die. He simply couldn't. She loved him and hadn't told him. If he died, she'd have to flee with the children, fulfilling her marriage vows in the saddest of ways. "We need to keep you cool. Have you taken quinine today?"

"I took a dose before dinner."

She returned with the washbowl, set it on the night-stand and dampened the hankie stashed in the pocket of her fancy gown. If she needed more cloth to cool the fever, she'd tear the garment into rags. She put the hankie on his forehead then filled a glass with water from a pitcher. She carried it to him then issued an order of her own. "Drink this."

"It won't help," he muttered.

"It won't hurt," she countered. "Sit up and drink."

He gave her a harsh look, one she welcomed because

it showed he was strong enough to fight. He sat up and took several sips, avoiding her gaze as she plumped his pillows. When he finished the water, he propped himself up. "You can leave now, but send Bessie."

"No."

"Caroline—"

"Don't you dare boss me around!" She was tired of being polite. She'd been walking on eggshells for hours, worrying she'd misspeak or trip on her gown. She wanted to shout at Tristan to fight the malaria. Instead she silently begged God to heal the man she'd married…the man who didn't know how she felt.

"I love you," she blurted to Tristan. "Don't you dare die on me!"

Awareness flickered in his eyes. He smiled, but feebly. "I love you, too."

"You do?"

"Yes, very much." He reached for her hand. "That's what makes this night so hard. If I could have gone a month without fever, I'd have asked you to marry me again, this time simply because I love you and want you for my wife."

"A month?" She didn't understand. She'd been in Wyoming five weeks and he hadn't been bedridden once. "When did you start counting?"

"Twenty-six days ago. We had a hundred hours to go."

"A hundred hours!" Tears welled in her eyes. "I don't care about a hundred hours. We love each other. We can fight the malaria together."

"And if I die?"

She cupped his feverish face. "I'd rather love you for a single day than not at all."

"I wanted to protect you," he said quietly. "I didn't want you to grieve—"

She wanted to shake him. "I would have suffered more not knowing you loved me and *still more* if I hadn't said the words to you."

It occurred to her that like Tristan, she'd drawn a line for herself, a mark in the sand that could be erased as easily as it had been made. Whether the house party succeeded or failed, she loved him. By testing herself, she'd acted out of fear, not faith.

"We're a couple of fools," she said meekly.

"What do you mean?"

"We've wasted days when we could have been together."

His jaw tightened. "It wasn't a waste, Caroline. I'm determined to protect you. I couldn't risk leaving you with child—"

"I'd welcome your baby!" She wanted a baby from the man she loved more than anything.

His eyes glinted. "Aside from that," he continued, "there's also the matter of my obligations. If I live, are you saying you'll come with me to England?"

She knew the cost. As an American, she'd never fit in. At best she'd be a curiosity. At worst, an embarrassment. But if she said no, she'd be something she couldn't tolerate. She'd be a coward. And she'd be giving up what she wanted most in the world—the chance to be a wife to the man she loved, and mother to his children. The same faith that required Tristan to fight the malaria would give her the strength to be the wife he needed.

"Yes," she answered. "I'll go with you to England."

As soon as the words left her lips, her insides tightened into a knot. She'd taken a chance when she'd married Charles, and he'd paid with his life. She couldn't stand the thought of failing Tristan, especially when he was looking at her with such hope. The moment called for a kiss, but neither of them wanted the tenderness to be held back by illness.

Tristan spoke first. "I suppose I'm in God's hands now. I can't say the thought is comforting."

"I understand." She knew too well that God didn't answer every prayer the way she wanted. "We'll just have to wait and see."

"Yes."

And so they waited…

Chapter Eighteen

With Caroline at his side, Tristan closed his eyes and relished the coolness of her hand. He'd been down this road before, but he'd never gone down it with so much at stake. If he died, Freddie would be the next Duke of Willoughby. Moreover, Tristan's death would break Caroline's heart, and she'd have to flee with the children. He had a house full of guests who'd all be gossiping about her sudden departure.

An hour passed.

Then two hours.

Caroline stayed at his side, making small talk as she cooled his brow with the cloth. When his shirt became damp with sweat, she helped him into a dry nightshirt. They were married. She had the right to tend to his needs, and that's what she did. It felt as natural as breathing, and he dared to hope that God wouldn't leave him in this bed to die.

A knock sounded on the door.

"That must be Bessie." Caroline stood and headed for the door. Before she reached it, the duke strode into the room. If his father smelled death, he'd circle like a buzzard.

Tristan whipped the cloth from his brow and sat up. "What do you want?"

Caroline gasped. "How dare you walk in here!"

Ignoring her, the duke eyed Tristan. "So it's true. You're in poor health."

He said nothing.

"I've been watching you, *Marquess*." The duke used the title to control him, but Tristan refused to react.

"What have you seen?" he asked casually.

"My valet overheard you speaking to Jon." He studied Tristan's face with the indifference of a man judging the health of prize bull. "I gather you're quite ill."

If he hid the facts, he'd appear weak. "It's malaria."

His father's expression shifted from haughty to grim. "I'm sorry."

"Are you?" Tristan asked.

The duke glared at him. "Of course I'm sorry. I don't want the future Duke of Willoughby to be a sickly invalid."

There wasn't an ounce of sympathy in his father's countenance. No compassion whatsoever for Tristan's suffering or his fears. To the duke, he was a commodity, someone—even a *thing*—to be used for selfish gain. Tristan thought of his feelings for Freddie and Dora. He'd die for his children. The duke wouldn't give his life for anyone. Until Tristan had value, the duke hadn't given him a second thought...but God had. Thanks to Caroline, he'd come to see that a father's love wasn't distant and commanding. A father disciplined and he taught, but he also played the dream game and he encouraged his children to love and laugh and be themselves.

Nothing could excuse the duke's coldness, but Tristan had been wrong to put God in the same camp. Perhaps the duke had been as poorly treated as Tristan. How deep did the twisted roots of his family tree go? And what did a man do to ensure that future trees—his sons and daughters—would grow straight and tall?

He loved.

He loved his children the way God loved mankind. He listened to them. He protected them. He forgave them for their weakness. In that moment, Tristan saw his father not as the Duke of Willoughby, but as a damaged child. The words he blurted startled them both. "I forgive you, Father."

"You *what?*"

"I forgive you." Peace flooded through his body like a cascading river. It wrapped around old rocks of bitterness, dislodging some and leaving others submerged and forgotten. He glanced at Caroline and saw tears in her eyes. It didn't matter what his father said or did. Tristan was at peace with his past. As for the future, he'd trust Caroline to use her best judgment. Forgiveness didn't mean handing his son over to a tyrant.

The duke's face hardened. "Deathbed confessions don't interest me. If you survive, I expect you to return to England at the end of this silly little gathering."

"And if I die?"

"Then Freddie is mine."

He'd been expecting such an answer, but Caroline inhaled sharply. "How dare you speak like that! You should be worried about your son! He's—he's—" She clamped her lips.

"He's dying."

"No, he isn't," she said more calmly. "The quinine is working. Bessie says—"

The duke huffed. "She's a stupid woman."

"She's a trained nurse!" Caroline shouted back.

Tristan wanted to cheer. If she could stand up to his

father, she could stand up to anyone. He admired her courage. Determined to stand with her, he lumbered to his feet. "Get out."

"Not yet." The duke studied Caroline thoughtfully. "Why did you marry a sick man? Do you think you'll inherit his money?"

She gasped. "That's just plain wicked!"

Tristan's blood heated beyond the fever. "I'm ordering you to leave, your grace. You have authority in England, but you have none in my home."

The duke stayed focused on Caroline. "You married quickly…and privately." He looked pointedly around Tristan's bedroom. "I don't see a single feminine touch. Not a hairbrush… Not a robe to cover your nightgown, my dear."

Tristan's flesh crawled at his father's mocking tone. The man was scheming and Tristan needed to know what ugly snake he'd unleash on them. "What are you suggesting?"

The duke looked at Caroline like a wolf stalking a lamb. "You're not sharing a bed, are you?"

Caroline said nothing.

Tristan glared at him. "I won't dignify that remark with a reply."

"You don't have to. The rumor alone will suffice."

With his eyes glinting, the duke turned to Caroline. "Tristan's progeny will carry my blood. If you're not woman enough to command his interest—"

"Get out!" Tristan roared.

"As I was saying," the duke said to Caroline. "If you haven't consummated the marriage, this sham can be annulled. Your husband once loved Louisa. He moped over her for months. She's far more suitable as a wife."

"Get out!" Tristan bellowed again. If his father didn't

leave, he'd send Caroline for Jon and the men from Swan's Nest. He'd have his father carted to Cheyenne and put on a train to New York. He may have forgiven the man, but that didn't mean he'd tolerate the duke hurting Caroline.

The duke's expression softened, deceptively so. Looking almost kind, he spoke to Caroline. "I suspect my son married you to offend me. You've been used."

"That's a lie," she retorted.

"It's true enough. As such, you're entitled to compensation. If you leave by dawn, I'll instruct Pennwright to arrange for an income for the rest of your life." He named an amount that would impress any woman, even a future duchess.

Caroline put her hands on her hips. "You're more pitiful than Tristan said!"

The duke's eyes narrowed. "You're a fool, Caroline."

"I love my husband. If that makes me a fool, so be it."

If the duke heard what Caroline said, he didn't show it. "You're not shrewd enough to be a duchess. Neither are you beautiful or wealthy, but you *are* entertaining. I'm sure the dowager will enjoy hearing about the scandalous American woman who married for money."

"Don't you dare—" Tristan clenched his teeth.

The duke chortled. "Gossip is entertaining, don't you think? Especially when the stories include, shall we say, a wife's marital inadequacy?"

Looking pleased, the duke headed for the door. As he turned the handle, he faced them. "I expect to be kept informed of your condition, Tristan. And I expect to keep Freddie close at hand."

He left without waiting for a reply, leaving Tristan seething with anger, burning up with fever and alone with his wife. The duke's knowledge of the illness made protecting Freddie even more urgent. The man would be watching the boy like a hawk. He might even try to leave with him. Looking at Caroline, he prayed for his Father in heaven to do what Tristan could not… He asked God to protect his son.

Caroline hated the thought of gossip, especially gossip of such a personal nature. How far would the duke go to make her a laughingstock? She hated being afraid, but his threats were real. She thought of the Bible command to honor one's father and mother. How did a son or daughter honor a man like the Duke of Willoughby? She had no idea, but she knew how to protect Freddie. Glaring at Tristan, she barked an order. "Don't you dare die!"

His eyes twinkled, a response she didn't expect. Neither did she expect him to give her a crisp salute. "Yes, ma'am."

If only the fever would take orders as easily. "Get back in bed. You need rest."

He didn't budge.

"Tristan!"

He stood staring at her, a smile spreading slowly across his face. Half wondering if he'd become delirious, she walked to his side with the intention of putting her hand on his forehead. As she lifted her arm, he took her hand and held it. "Nothing's changed," he said. "The fever's the same, but something else is quite different."

"What?" she asked.

He let go of her hand and grasped her arms instead, holding her gently in place as he looked into her eyes. "I won't kiss you while I'm feverish. Nor will I suggest we make love, but I seem to recall we declared our love for each other."

She blushed. "Yes, we did."

"Which means you no longer need to stay in the nursery. Stay with me, Caroline. We'll hope and pray together."

"I'll stay," she said. "But I have to be honest. Your father scares me. Someday you'll return to England. If he ruins my reputation with lies, you and the children will be affected."

"We won't be returning for years," he said quietly. "By then the rantings of an old man will be forgotten."

"Not by the Dowager Duchess of Somerville." She spoke the name with all the weight it would carry in England. "The nieces are just as pretentious. I've heard them gossiping. Years from now, people will talk. I know this is true because it happened with Charles."

"You're having doubts."

"I'm worried about you and the children. I know what it's like to be scorned. I can't stand the thought of Dora being embarrassed by her American mother."

"And *I* can't stand the thought of my father poisoning your mind." His voice rose with each word. She worried he'd waste his strength on being angry, so she stood on her toes and kissed his cheek. "We won't discuss it now."

"Then when?"

A tap on the door surprised them both. Caroline opened it but just a crack. She saw Bessie and let her inside. "He's feverish," she said to her sister. "What else can we do?"

Looking peeved, he glared at her. "I can speak for myself."

"I know that!"

Bessie looked from Caroline to Tristan and back to Caroline. "If he's well enough to bicker, that's a good sign."

"We're not bickering," they said in unison.

Ignoring them, Bessie felt Tristan's brow for fever.

"You're warm, but it's not particularly high. How's your stomach?"

"Fine." The malaria usually caused him to be nauseated. "I imagine I'll be sick later."

Bessie nodded. "It's to be expected. Stay in bed and drink as much water as you can. Take quinine in the morning but no more tonight. Mostly you need to rest so your body can fight the fever."

He wiped his hand through his hair. "Unfortunately, I've done this before."

"I'll check back in the morning." She left, closing the door without a click.

In the sudden quiet, Caroline faced him. Tristan spoke first. "Where were we?"

"We were arguing about your father."

"It's a waste of time."

"But necessary," she replied. "We'll talk when you're well. Maybe there's no reason to worry about what he says. The house party will be over in a week. It *is* going well, isn't it?"

"It's going splendidly." Sadness filled his eyes. "We're back at the beginning, aren't we? I need to survive the malaria, and you need to believe you can be a duchess."

"Yes."

"Come," he said holding out his hand. "We'll sit together by the fire."

"You should lie down."

"So should you."

She blushed.

He smiled. "Shall we?"

"Yes."

As husband and wife in name but not in body, they lay together fully clothed, talking and hoping and waiting to see if the fever would spike.

It didn't.

They slept.

In the morning Caroline awoke. Rising up on one elbow she looked at Tristan's face for signs of illness. His cheeks were still flushed but they weren't as ruddy, and his forehead had a sheen of perspiration…and spots… tiny blisters that looked just like chicken pox.

"Tristan!"

He roused sleepily. "What is it?"

"I have to see your chest!"

He looked utterly undone. If she hadn't been tied in knots with worry, she'd have laughed. "I think you have the chicken pox. When you had it as a child, did you get a lot of them?"

"No," he answered. "Just enough to itch."

"You can get them again if you have a mild case."

"It *was* mild." Fully awake, he checked his torso and started to laugh. "I'm covered with spots!"

He leapt to his feet and went to the mirror. Preening like a vain man, he looked at the rash on his brow, then turned to her. "I've got the pox, all right. And I've never been happier in my life."

She went to his side. "I'm happy, too."

"I'll be absent from the festivities for a few days, but be ready to dance with me on the last night." Even ailing, he had a commanding air. "By then you'll see the woman I see—the very beautiful *and* very poised duchess of Willoughby."

"I hope so."

"I *know* so."

She envied his confidence. She'd been ready to fight for him and she still would, but the duke was a formidable enemy. However, she believed in a formidable God. She'd do her best to stay strong, but under no circumstance would she saddle Tristan with an incompetent wife. Their future still depended on the house party and its success. She had to triumph or leave him. There was no middle ground for a future duchess.

It wasn't long before Caroline faced her next challenge. With Tristan's chair empty at the supper table, she had to tell a house full of guests they'd been exposed to the chicken pox. She also wanted to end whatever rumors the duke had contrived about Tristan dying from malaria. Before the first course was served, she asked for everyone's attention. Her guests dutifully turned in her direction.

"Some of you know Tristan is ill," she said, focusing on the duke. "I want to assure you it's not serious. He has the chicken pox."

"Oh, dear!" Louisa cried. "It's my fault. I had it when I arrived."

"Illness happens," Caroline said graciously. The disease had also affected three ranch hands. Tristan had probably caught it from one of them. "Frankly we're relieved it's not more serious. As some of you know, he contracted malaria in the West Indies. He's been fighting fevers for several months."

The duke slanted a glance at her. "Malaria is potentially fatal."

"It is," Bessie answered. "But Tristan has overcome the worst of it. As a nurse I've seen many reactions to the fevers. At this point, it's reasonable to assume it's a chronic problem, not a fatal one."

"I see." The man almost looked disappointed.

Whitmore broke in. "Malaria is a badge of honor in my book. The marquess contracted it serving his country." With the duke and the dowager present, Whitmore used Tristan's formal title.

"He has my admiration," Terrence Pierce added.

The guests chattered for a moment about the child-hood illness, expressing admiration for Tristan and relating their own stories. The awkward announcement was soon forgotten, and the conversation veered to other topics. To Caroline's dismay, the topics included monologues by the duke that held subtle criticism of her. More than once he gave her the look of a cat hunting a mouse. She managed to remain poised, in part because her friends were protecting her.

Josh and Adie deflected his taunts with kindness.

Matt and Pearl sang her praises.

Mary and Jonah distracted him with endless questions about England.

The Whitmore nieces, Mr. Pierce and Mr. Blackstone looked as tired of his monologues as Caroline, but they said nothing out of inborn respect. The dowager yawned rather deliberately, then gave Caroline a look that demanded she stop the man from dominating the table. Caroline wanted to comply, but she had no idea how to control the man and his runaway tongue. The evening droned on until dessert arrived. Predictably, the duke protested the cherry tarts.

"I don't care for cherry." Pushing the plate aside, he snapped his fingers for his valet. "Go to the kitchen and find something edible."

Caroline turned as red as the cherry filling. Tristan would have cut him off with a barb of his own, but she felt tongue-tied. Forcing herself to be strong, she spoke up. "We also have macaroons, your grace. Perhaps that would satisfy your palate?"

He looked close to gagging. "I want pudding!"

Caroline had no idea how to handle a grown man having a tantrum. It wasn't very dukelike in her opinion, nor was it polite. She had a good mind to tell him he'd eat what he was given, but the dowager interrupted.

"Willoughby, shut up!"

"Duchess!"

"You heard me." She waved her finger at him. "I'm sick of hearing about your palate! We're in America. You can't expect the same *quality*."

Did she mean the tarts or did she mean Caroline as Tristan's wife? Caroline had spoken to the woman only briefly and had been intimidated. With her piercing eyes, the dowager seemed to stare through the elegant gown to the inadequate woman who'd been the governess.

With the duchess's criticism ringing in the air, every face in the room turned to Caroline. Heat rushed to her cheeks, staining them with a telltale blush. At a loss, she looked at Louisa. Instead of speaking, Louisa gave her a look that said, *Speak up! Defend yourself!* Caroline tried to say something—anything—but nothing came out of her mouth.

She cleared her throat.

She smiled.

Finally she found her voice. "Things *are* different in America."

"They certainly are!" said Stuart Whitmore.

"Very," said Mr. Pierce.

"Astoundingly so," said one of the nieces.

Some of the guests lifted their forks and enjoyed the tarts. Others, including the duke and dowager, pushed the plates aside. It was awkward and embarrassing and Caroline hated herself for being so unsure. Every doubt she'd had about her ability to be a good wife to Tristan played through her mind. He said he loved her and had confidence in her, but she didn't have it in herself. She'd failed badly tonight, but she had time to redeem herself, if only she could find a way.

The meal ended with continued awkwardness. She went upstairs hoping to find comfort in Tristan's company, but he'd fallen asleep. She went to the nursery where she collapsed in her narrow bed, praying for the strength to do what was right for the man and children she loved, not just for now, but also for the future. She couldn't stand the thought of being an embarrassment to her family. She desperately wanted to redeem herself in front of the Whitmores, but she had no idea how to do it.

The next morning, she dressed and went downstairs to breakfast. Louisa, the dowager and the duke were already eating. Determined to prove herself, she sat at the table as if she belonged. The dowager and Louisa were talking about fox hunts in England, with the duke describing the plans he'd made for Friday's horse race. Louisa showed boundless enthusiasm, and so did the dowager. As a much younger woman, she'd won prizes.

Her silvery eyes went to Caroline and lingered. "Are you participating, Marchioness?"

The use of her title made Caroline go pale. It was a direct challenge, and the dessert debacle was still ringing in her ears. So was the comment about quality in America. Where she'd find the courage—the faith—to ride Grandma in a race, she didn't know. But the words were out before she could change her mind. "Yes, I'm riding," she said with false calm. "I'm looking forward to it."

Chapter Nineteen

Tristan had been ill with the chicken pox for five days, and he couldn't stand one more minute away from the house party. He had a mild case this time, too, and the fever had broken quickly. The blisters itched, but he'd experienced worse punishment from mosquito bites. He was tired of being ill and tired of being pampered, though he greatly enjoyed Caroline's tender care.

He'd also spent time with his children. The day after he'd fallen ill, poor Dora had erupted in spots. She was far sicker than he'd ever been with chicken pox, so he'd spent hours reading to her. Freddie had remained healthy, and that had been a problem. With Tristan confined, the boy spent hours with the duke. He'd become even more disrespectful to Caroline. Tristan had spoken to him, but Freddie needed more than a lecture. He needed to see for himself how a gentleman treated a lady.

Tristan intended to begin that lesson today at the horse race organized by the duke. The male riders included all the men except Reverend Blue and Jon. Along with Bessie, they were making plans for Saturday's marriage ceremony. Louisa and the Whitmore girls would also ride. Caroline had hinted at participating, but he'd told

her no. In his opinion she had nothing to prove. After
the race, Tristan hoped to be making arrangements with
Josh himself. He and Caroline were legally bound, but
it seemed fitting to take vows that reflected their deeper
commitment.

First, though, he wanted to run hard on Cairo and
win the race. As he approached the horse barn, he saw
Grandma saddled and waiting at the mounting block.
Next to the horse he saw Caroline in her split skirt. She
was feeding a carrot to Grandma and scratching the
horse's neck.

Tristan paced to her side. "*What* do you think you're
doing?"

"I'm riding today."

"But why?" He could see no benefit from her effort.
From everything she'd told him, the house party had been
a success. If she rode and fell, she'd be humiliated. Even
worse, she could get seriously hurt.

"I don't have a choice," she said to him.

"There's always a choice." They'd had this discussion
when she'd climbed on Cairo to cross the river. She'd
fallen that day. Today's ride would be even more difficult.

She kept scratching Grandma, looking casual except
for a knot in her brow. "Louisa rides and so do the nieces.
At breakfast a few days ago the dowager talked about riding in England and how much she enjoyed it. She gave me
a *very* deliberate look. If I don't ride, I'll appear weak."

"I don't care," Tristan said irritably. "I want you to
be yourself."

"And *I* want to be strong."

She faced him. "This is important to me, Tristan.
Please understand."

"I *do* understand," he said gently. On a whim, he

kissed her cheek. "You won't change your mind, will you?"

"No."

"Then we'll ride together."

"Don't you dare hang back with me! You and Cairo can win."

"I'd rather keep an eye on you."

Her mouth tightened with dismay. "You don't think I can finish the race."

If he told the truth, he'd damage her confidence. But neither could he offer false assurances. "It's rough terrain, Caroline. Far rougher than anything you've ridden. Yes, I'm worried about you. I love you, my dear."

She blushed. "I love you, too."

"I also believe in you." He kissed her forehead. "Do your best, and I'll do mine. I have to admit—besting my father would give me great pleasure."

"Me, too," she said smiling. She indicated the mounting block. "If you'll excuse me, I have a race to run."

Tristan helped her into the saddle, then went to get Cairo. He hoped the race went well because Caroline's confidence hung on the outcome.

Turning her back to Tristan, Caroline clicked to Grandma and rode to where Louisa and the Whitmore girls were waiting. Louisa had a horse Caroline knew to be fast. The nieces had selected gentler mounts. All three of them were sitting sidesaddle and looking relaxed. Next to Louisa, Caroline saw Stuart. Dressed in jodhpurs, he looked very English and very interested in Louisa. Mr. Pierce was riding a brown bay and Mr. Blackstone was mounted on a pinto. Slightly apart from the crowd, she saw Matt and Jonah on a couple of surefooted mustangs.

Even more removed from the riders, she saw the duke and Freddie on Arabians nearly as impressive as Cairo.

Louisa greeted Caroline as she approached. "Caroline! How wonderful of you to join us!"

"My pleasure," she said amiably.

When the duke gave her an arrogant look, Freddie followed suit. Soon Tristan would join them, and the group would go to the starting point a short distance from the corral. Once she'd decided to ride, Caroline had spoken with Jon. Yesterday he'd taken her over the route at an easy pace. With the exception of crossing a wide but shallow stream, it seemed within her ability. She didn't expect to win. She just had to prove she could hold her own. She didn't have to be first, but neither did she want to be last. She simply wanted to be adequate.

After the conversation with Caroline, Tristan didn't know what to do about the race. If he held back to keep an eye on her, she'd think he didn't believe in her. If he rode to win and she got in trouble, he'd be angry with himself. Climbing on Cairo, he decided to take the race a stride at a time. He'd make the decision on the run, literally.

As he neared the group of riders, he spotted Freddie and the duke on two of his fastest Arabians. Tristan had no doubt his father could handle the horse he'd chosen, but he'd have preferred Freddie to ride his usual gelding, a horse far more manageable than the Arabian mare. Not only would Tristan need to watch out for Caroline, but he also had to keep an eye on Freddie. In his current state of arrogance, the boy could easily go beyond his ability.

Tristan joined the riders, accepting greetings from everyone except Caroline and his father. They both ignored him, adding to the autumn chill threatening to replace the Indian summer. At least for today the sky would be clear, an important fact considering the route his father had selected for the race. The riders would circle the base of a hill, cross a wide stream strewn with boulders and return to The Barracks through a rolling meadow. The recent sunny weather meant the stream would be low and the rocks would be visible. Tristan knew the loop well, but the others would find the terrain challenging.

"Shall we proceed?" the duke said.

Murmuring agreement, the riders turned their horses and went down the trail at a walk. Tristan rode close to Caroline but said nothing. When they reached the meadow where the competition would begin, the riders formed a line. The duke raised his voice. "It seems to me we need a prize for winning and a consequence for losing."

"Here, here," said Stuart.

Jonah and Matt said nothing.

Louisa whispered something to the Whitmore girls and they all laughed. Almost sure to lose, Caroline remained stoic. Tristan couldn't put an end to his father's jabs at Caroline, but he could cover for her. In a jovial tone, he said, "There's to be music tonight. The winner dances with the woman of his choice."

Louisa answered with teasing tone of her own. "And if a lady wins?"

"Fair is fair," Tristan called. "She dances with the gentleman of her choice."

Louisa arched a brow at Stuart Whitmore, who gave her a bold look in return. At least for Louisa, the house party had been a success. She and Whitmore had become inseparable.

The duke raised his voice again. "And a consequence?"

Tristan looked pointedly at Caroline. "The last rider dances with me." He'd given her a reason to be last, and

he'd done it with humor. He hoped she'd play along with
him, but her jaw stayed tight. The men laughed and
agreed, certain they'd best all four of the women.

Tristan had contained the duke with humor, and the
man didn't like it. Looking peeved, he shouted again.
"Shall we begin the race?"

The riders formed a line across the meadow. With
one eye on Freddie, Tristan lined up next to Caroline.
The duke raised his arm high. "On the count of three...
One... Two... Three!"

The horses broke at a dead run. Tristan held back,
watching as Caroline took off on Grandma. When she
dug her heels into the mare's side, he had the terrible feeling she was riding to win, or at least riding not to be last.
He stayed with her as she rode with the pack across the
meadow. Louisa had the lead and Whitmore was chasing her. The nieces were close to Pierce, and Blackstone
seemed interested only in staying in the saddle. Freddie
and the duke were riding side by side, strategically holding back because their horses could pick up speed later.
Matt and J.T. were also hanging back, no doubt keeping
an eye on Caroline. Caroline had friends. She also had
an enemy in the duke.

When they reached the first turn, she risked a glance
at Tristan. "Go! I want you to win!"

The duke was closing the gap between them. Tristan
shouted back. "I'm staying with you."

"Then I'll ride harder!"

To his consternation, she pushed Grandma into a run.
They'd galloped before, but without pressure and in a
smooth meadow. She didn't have the skill to maintain
such a pace, but she was determined to try and equally
determined to force him to ride to win. If he left her,
she'd slow down.

"You win," he shouted. Reluctantly he dug in his heels and gave Cairo free rein. Stretching into a full run, the stallion shot past the nieces, then by Louisa and Whitmore. Tristan relished the speed, the wind, the beat of Cairo's hooves. As he rounded a wide turn, he saw the stream glistening in the sun. The water sparkled on the scattered rocks and made a ribbon of rustling light. Tristan slowed Cairo to a walk, crossed the stream with care and took off for The Barracks. It felt good to run, and it would feel even better to win.

With the other riders out of sight, he crossed the finish line with the intention of claiming his prize—a dance with Caroline, the woman of his choice.

Still riding hard, Caroline watched Tristan and Cairo disappear around a wide bend. The duke and Freddie were still behind her, and Matt and Jonah were lagging even farther behind. As she rounded the turn herself, she saw the stream that had to be crossed. She'd been expecting it, but the rippling water sent a wave of fear down her spine. She immediately commanded Grandma to slow her pace, but the curve ended in a downhill slope and the horse had more momentum than she'd realized.

Grandma's hooves chewed up the apron of sand, then hit the water with a splash. The horse stopped so fast Caroline nearly flew out of the saddle.

Behind her she heard the rumble of hoofbeats, then a shout to get out of the way. She urged Grandma forward, but the horse balked. One of the Arabians charged past her. It was either the duke or Freddie, she couldn't tell which. As she struggled to calm Grandma, the Arabian stumbled. The rider shot over its head and crashed into a boulder. The horse regained its balance and ran, leaving a body in a black coat in the water. The legs seemed short and the coat seemed too small for a grown man.

"Freddie!" She cried, half climbing and half falling off of Grandma.

As she staggered to the rider, she took in the length of the legs and size of the boots. They were too big to belong to the boy. She sloshed past a boulder and saw the duke's gray hair rippling in the current. Judging by the angle of his head, he'd broken his neck. And from his open eyes she knew he'd died instantly. To be sure, she knelt in the water and took his pulse. As expected, she felt nothing.

Behind her Freddie was calling for his grandfather. In a final act of respect for a human being, if not for a man who'd been a tyrant, she closed the duke's eyes and stood. Freddie ran up to her. "Is he— Is he—" The boy couldn't finish.

"I'm so sorry, Freddie. He's gone." Instinctively she put her arm around him, but he pulled back.

"He—he can't be!"

"His neck's broken."

"It's your fault! You stopped in the middle of the trail. *You* made him fall!"

Freddie ran across the stream, shouting for help and weeping at the same time. Caroline stood frozen in place with her skirt wet, her heart thudding and her boots sinking into the mud. Matt and Jonah arrived at a gallop, both sliding to the ground before the horses stopped. Matt came to her side and put his arms around her. Jonah went to the body, checked for a pulse, then shook his head. "I'll get a wagon."

He climbed on his horse and rode back the way they'd come, leaving her with Matt and the silent weight of guilt. Louisa came from the other direction at a gallop, followed by Whitmore and the others. Still holding her shoulders,

Matt spoke quietly. "I'm going to explain what happened. Will you be all right?"

She nodded yes, but her dreams had just been destroyed. For the rest of her life she'd be the American who killed the Duke of Willoughby with her incompetence. Even worse, Freddie blamed her for his grandfather's death. She'd never win the boy's affection, nor would she earn the respect of the Whitmores. Her future as Tristan's wife had died with the duke. She'd insist on an annulment.

Still mounted on Cairo, Tristan watched the finish line for signs of the other riders. A minute ticked into three, then five. His nerves prickled with worry then caught fire like dry brush. He was about to go back down the trail when he spotted Jonah Quinn approaching the barn at a gallop. When he reached Tristan, he reined his horse to stop. "It's your father. He's dead."

"Dead?"

"He fell. His neck's broken."

Tristan didn't doubt him. Quinn had seen as much death as he had. In even tones, the man told how he and Wiley had witnessed the accident from the top of the trail. He described Caroline's awkward stop, the duke passing her and Freddie's accusations. Quinn had hard edges, and he spoke with authority. "It wasn't Caroline's fault."

"Does *she* know that?"

"She should, but she's pretty shaken up."

Caroline needed him and so did Freddie. Turning Cairo, Tristan looked back at Jonah. "I'd be obliged if you'd arrange for a wagon."

"Yes, sir."

Tristan left at a gallop, covering the path he'd ridden minutes ago with Caroline. Approaching the stream, he saw a tableau that told the story he most dreaded. Caroline was standing apart from the crowd with only Matt Wiley for a friend. The others were on the opposite side of the stream, crowded together like a mob at a hanging. Louisa had an arm around Freddie, and Whitmore stood at her side. The nieces, Pierce and Blackstone were staring at Caroline as if she were a murderess.

Tristan rode down the hill at a funereal pace, his eyes on the body of the man who'd fathered him. The heaviness in his chest wasn't for what he'd lost but for what he'd never had. He looked next at Caroline, saw the resignation in her eyes and knew that once again his father had come between Tristan and a woman's love. Unless he was misreading Caroline's expression, he knew she'd ask for an annulment.

With every eye on him, he dismounted, walked to his wife and drew her into his arms. She stiffened but he held her anyway. "It wasn't your fault," he murmured.

"Yes, it was."

"Quinn and Wiley saw it. He did this to himself."

Shuddering, she slipped away from him. He let her go but only because he heard someone sloshing across the stream. He turned and saw Whitmore. The man lowered his chin in a sign of respect, then raised it. "Your grace, allow me to express my condolences."

Your grace...

It wouldn't be years before Tristan left for England. It would be days. And judging by Caroline's expression, persuading her to accompany him would be the fight of his life.

Chapter Twenty

Caroline wore black to the duke's funeral, but no one else did. The guests had come for a party, not mourning. Wanting to be respectful, she'd asked Evaline to remove the trim from one of her dresses and to dye the gown black. The dress reminded her of the conversation she still had to have with Tristan. Last night, she'd knocked on his bedroom door, intending to ask for the annulment. When he didn't answer, she went looking for him. She'd heard him in his study with Pennwright, talking about his father's holdings and his political responsibilities. He'd spoken with a new gravity, and she had decided to put off the confrontation. After the burial, she'd tell him she wanted to end their marriage.

First, though, she had to endure the funeral. The duke had died yesterday and was being buried without the pomp he would have wanted. Even the sky was cold to him. Gray clouds leaked rain, enough to dampen the earth but not enough to evoke a sense of tears. Josh spoke eloquently of eternity. By the time he finished, Caroline felt stronger. She didn't know if the duke had made peace with his Maker, but she hoped so.

Josh finished the service with a prayer. At the closing

"amen," Tristan dropped a handful of dirt on the coffin. As the breeze carried away the dust, a single clump hit with a final thud. Tristan stepped to the side of the grave to accept condolences. Caroline joined him and together they greeted the mourners. Tristan invited Freddie to stand with them, but the boy refused to be with Caroline. She offered to give him her place, but Tristan said no. She felt terrible. Of the guests in attendance, only Freddie wept.

He'd chosen to stay with Louisa and Stuart, and he was with them now, glaring at Caroline and fighting tears. He wasn't alone in his criticism of her. All day she'd heard whispers among the Whitmore crowd. The nieces had practically run from her.

The dowager duchess had offered sincere condolences to Tristan, but her remarks to Caroline had been oddly challenging. *You'll be remembered, Duchess Willoughby, for how you handle these next few days.*

Had it been a warning or encouragement? Caroline didn't know, and she no longer cared. She felt responsible for the duke's death. No matter what she said or did, she'd be blamed for this tragic day.

When the last guest departed from the gravesite, she turned to Tristan. "I'd like to speak with you in private, your grace."

Tristan disliked being called *your grace*. He especially disliked Caroline's tone when she said it. They'd done battle about names and titles before. In the beginning he'd wanted her to call him "major." Now he wanted to be called Tristan. Even better, he wanted to be called "darling," or "my love." The last thing he wanted from Caroline was the cold etiquette of a subject or a soldier.

"You know my name," he said. "Use it." It was an order, and he'd accept nothing less than obedience.

She sealed her lips.

"My name...say it."

"I don't want to say it." Her voice cracked. "I'd like to speak in private, perhaps in the barn—"

"All right." They'd arranged their marriage in the stable in Wheeler Springs. The barn at The Barracks was a fitting spot to return to the promises they'd made.

Side by side, they left the knoll that had become the family cemetery and walked to the barn where she'd found the courage to learn to ride. He wanted that brave woman to rise up against the cloud of the duke's death. Instead Caroline had the look of a waif. He didn't want their talk to be interrupted, so he took her to the tack room and closed the door. At the river crossing, he'd coaxed her onto Cairo with peppermint and patience. Today he had nothing to offer except his love.

He took her hands in his. "I love you, Caroline. I want you to come to England with me."

"I can't," she murmured.

"Why not?"

"I'll be forever known as the woman who caused your father's death. It will affect the children. It will affect *you*."

"I don't care, and neither should you. I'm now a ridiculously important man. The title humbles me, but it also gives me the privilege of being stubborn. It will take far more than a beautiful American wife to cause me embarrassment."

"I'm not beautiful."

"You are to me."

She shook her head. "I can't risk it, Tristan. If we

don't annul the marriage, you'll be criticized. I'll be a
pariah—"

He suddenly understood. "I'm not the one you're protecting, am I? You're protecting yourself."

"No!"

"Don't lie. It's unbecoming."

"I'm not lying!"

"But you are," he countered. "You're lying to yourself. You want to end our marriage because you're afraid.
You love me. You love Freddie and Dora. How can you
walk away from us?"

"Freddie hates me," she murmured.

"He's a troubled boy. He needs you more than ever.
And Dora—" He couldn't finish. The thought of his
daughter losing another mother sickened him.

She knotted her hands into fists, but there was nothing
to pummel except her own dreams. "You don't understand! I stayed with Charles and he was killed. I shouldn't
have married him in the first place. If I'd been stronger,
he'd still be alive."

Tristan couldn't see the logic. "Do you really think
my *life* is at stake? Even my dignity? I'm a duke. No one
will dare question me."

Sadness filled her eyes. "You said that to me before,
and it wasn't true."

"When?"

"You told me Cairo would obey you, and he bucked
me into the river. Jon ignores your orders. Evaline and
Noah overrule you. Even Dora has you wrapped around
her finger." With the mention of Dora, her voice softened
into a lullaby. "But that's all right because they love you.
The people in England will be looking for something to
criticize. No matter what you say, Tristan, the fact re-
mains. In England I'll be an embarrassment to you. The

children will be ashamed of me, especially Freddie. I came to bring healing to you and your children, not to cause a deeper rift."

"Freddie's a boy." His voice started to rise. "You can't let a confused child guide your decision."

"I have to think of his feelings."

He lowered his voice. "And Dora? What about her?"

A sob broke from her throat. "How does a mother choose when her children have different needs? I hate the thought of leaving her—"

"Then don't."

"She'll miss me, but she's young. She'll be all right. She *has* to be." She shook her head. "Maybe if we had more time—"

"We don't." He considered delaying the inevitable, but his first conversation with Pennwright eliminated that possibility. His father's secretary, now *his* secretary, had given Tristan the details on his father's activities. The sooner Tristan arrived in England, the sooner he could end his father's reign of terror over the people of Willoughby. For years the duke had taken advantage of the locals. Some were living in poverty. As much as Tristan wanted to stay in Wyoming until Caroline found her courage, he had a duty to fulfill. "I'm making arrangements to leave at the end of the week. Come with us."

She shook her head. "I can't."

"Then what will you do?" He couldn't leave without her. He simply couldn't. But neither could he stay in Wyoming when he had responsibilities in England. He thought of God balancing the needs of the entire world. It was an impossible task.

Blinking back tears, she straightened her spine. "I'm going back to Denver. I already spoke to Adie. She thinks

I should go with you to England, but she won't turn me away."

He wanted to shout at her, to quarrel and issue orders. Instead he clenched his jaw. "So it's decided.

"Yes."

He turned his back and paced to the door. "If you change your mind, you know where to find me."

"I do," she murmured. "But nothing will change."

With his temper flaring he left the tack room. He wanted to call her a coward. He settled for pacing back to the house alone. As the new duke of Willoughby, he had to meet with Pennwright. They had letters to write and arrangements to make. Unless Caroline found the courage to be his wife, the arrangements would include the annulment of their marriage.

He had tried to influence Caroline and failed. He hoped he'd have better luck with Freddie. The boy's behavior, especially his criticism of Caroline, had to be addressed immediately. Tristan would be patient with Freddie's grief, but he couldn't tolerate arrogance. He needed to speak to his son even more urgently than he needed to meet with Pennwright.

The wind pulled at his coat and whipped through the cottonwoods, causing the branches to rub and squeak. Just as he reached the house, the clouds let loose with a torrent of rain. Refreshments were being served to the guests—he wouldn't call them mourners—in the side parlor, a cozy room that should have been filled with tears and poignant memories. When he didn't see Freddie or Louisa, he went back to the entry hall. He heard voices in the front room, entered and saw them on the divan. Whitmore was seated across from them, listening as Louisa told Freddie about Willoughby Manor, preparing him for his new life.

She meant well, but Tristan had grave concerns about the boy's behavior. The seeds of arrogance had to be removed and replaced with seeds of honor, faith and concern for others. He entered the room quietly. When Louisa looked up, he said, "Would you excuse us, please?"

Whitmore stood and spoke for them both. "Yes, your grace."

Someday Tristan would be accustomed to hearing those words, but today he felt the cost of doing his duty. "Thank you."

Louisa said goodbye to Freddie, then left arm in arm with Whitmore.

Tristan sat across from his son and took in his formal appearance. Dressed in a tailored coat, the one stitched by the duke's valet, he looked like a miniature version of the duke. Only his eyes, red-rimmed and puffy, belonged to a child. Freddie was angry and hurt, and he wanted to blame someone. Tristan understood because he'd grieved his father's love for years. He'd been just like Freddie until he'd made peace with himself and God. Thanks to Caroline, he'd even made peace with the duke. The irony of what he had to say struck him as poignant.

"I know you're angry, Freddie."

The boy shot daggers at him.

"And I realize you blame Caroline for the accident." Tristan paused. When Freddie said nothing, he continued. "She's not responsible for what happened. Your grandfather was riding too fast. He made the decision to cross the stream without slowing down."

"But she was in the way! She made him fall."

"I don't agree," Tristan said reasonably. "But suppose she did. If by accident she made the worst mistake in the world, what do you think we should do?"

"I hate her!"

"Does that solve anything?" Tristan could have been talking to himself. Had resenting the duke done any good? None at all, but he saw a chance to do some good now. "Your grandfather and I didn't get along. In my opinion, he made mistakes. Some of them were as serious as the one you think Caroline made. Even so, I forgave him."

"I'll never forgive her." The boy shoved to his feet. "She's common and she's stupid!"

"Freddie!" Tristan would tolerate anger but not disrespect. "You owe Caroline an apology."

"No!"

The boy ran out of the room and up the stairs. Tristan stood but let him go. He could only hope that time would open Freddie's eyes to the truth. The alternative—that the anger would fester and grow—troubled him deeply. What did a father do with a stubborn child? He knew how an officer disciplined a soldier, but Freddie was troubled and grieving. Patience seemed to be in order, so Tristan returned to the parlor where the guests were waiting for him.

As he entered, he heard murmuring about the accident. The nieces were being particularly critical. So was Blackstone. The dowager sat by herself, listening to the gossip and fanning herself as if the air were stale. She saw Tristan and summoned him. "Your grace!"

"Yes, Dowager?"

"Where is your wife?"

"She's—" Tristan hesitated. Telling the dowager that Caroline was hiding in the barn would do not good at all. "She's indisposed.

"I see," the old woman said. "That's unfortunate."

She'd issued a warning of sorts. Unless Caroline faced the gossip now, the accident would become fodder for rumors for months to come. Tristan wanted to stop the criticism, but despite what he'd said to Caroline, even a duke couldn't control scandalous talk. The only person who could vindicate herself was Caroline. He'd planned to cancel the remainder of the house party, but now he wondered if he should insist she keep her obligations.

He addressed Dowager Somerville. "May I ask you a question?"

"Certainly."

"Would you be terribly scandalized if we resumed the house party as planned?"

She gave him the haughtiest look he'd ever seen. "Your wife is currently an object of scandal. What do *you* think you should do?"

Tristan had no doubt whatsoever. Caroline needed a chance to redeem herself, both in the eyes of their guests and in her own opinion. "Thank you, Dowager. If you'll excuse me, I have an announcement to make."

"Of course."

He cleared his throat for attention. "Ladies and gentlemen!"

The room silenced immediately. He could have been addressing soldiers instead of aristocrats.

Tristan lightened his tone. "You came to The Barracks for a party, not a funeral. As you know, we have plans for a wedding. I see no reason to deny Jon and Bessie a celebration. The ceremony will be held as planned, and there will be a reception with music and dancing. No one is to wear black." He paused to let the order sink in. "I'll pay my respects to my father in England. That was his home, and it's where our grief belongs."

He glanced from face to face, daring people to question him. No one said a word. He'd issued an order and it would be followed. He supposed being duke had some advantages, though the person who mattered most wasn't in the room. "Very well," he said. "The house party will continue as planned."

Two days from now, Jon and Bessie would take vows. The marriage would be celebrated with a meal and dancing, and Caroline would have a chance to shine. His wife would wear her finest gown and he'd dance with her. He could only hope it wouldn't be the first and only time.

Two hours after supper, Caroline was huddled on her bed, her knees pulled to her chest and her neck bent in defeat. Rain beat on the window in uneven rhythms, and the wind shook the house. The Indian summer had disappeared in a day, and winter loomed on the storm. She thought of the duke's fresh grave and how it would turn to mud. Mud took her back to the day she'd buried Charles. Good friends had refused to stand with her. Bessie alone had stayed at her side. Soon she'd lose Bessie. Her sister would become Mrs. Jonathan Tate, and Caroline would return to Swan's Nest.

A knock sounded on the storage room door. It had to be Tristan. She dreaded another quarrel, but she'd been expecting him. "Come in."

He walked into the room, stood at the foot of the bed and put his hands behind his back as if he were inspecting a soldier's barracks. "Has Evaline spoken to you?"

"Not since this morning." She'd talked to the housekeeper about assisting the Whitmores with their packing. She expected the exodus to begin tomorrow and she welcomed it.

"Then you're not aware of a change in plans," he said firmly. "The Whitmores aren't leaving."

"Why not?" Intimidated, she pulled her knees tighter to her chest. They'd always met on his territory. Tonight he'd invaded hers. "We can't possibly continue with the house party."

"We can, and we are."

"That's scandalous!"

"I don't particularly care." He seemed rather pleased, a reaction that unnerved her even more. "Our guests are staying for Jon and Bessie's wedding. As planned, we'll have a celebration. You will *not* wear black, is that understood?"

When she didn't answer, he went to her wardrobe, flung open the doors and pulled out a pink gown with a draped skirt and gold rosettes. She loved the fabric, mostly because it accentuated the pink tint in the diamond ring on her finger. Common sense told her to slip it off and give it to him, but her hands felt encased in stone.

Tristan held the gown to the side and gave it a shake. The satin whooshed and shimmered in the lamplight. "I like this one."

So did Caroline. She'd expected to wear it to the dance at the close of the house party, but the duke's death made the color inappropriate. "I couldn't possibly wear that gown, not now."

He hung it back in the wardrobe, the wide skirt on full display. "You *can* wear it and you will."

Without another word, he walked out of her room and into his, leaving the doors open with an invitation of sorts. Whether the invitation was to continue the argument or to reconcile, she didn't know.

She stared at the pink dress until her vision blurred into a dream of dancing in Tristan's arms. She thought of the dream game with the children. That night she'd believed their dreams could come true. With her heart pounding, she studied the satin folds. Wearing the gown would take courage…but courage didn't guarantee victory. She'd found the courage to cross a river on Cairo and she'd fallen. She'd dared to ride in a race, and she'd caused an accident. She'd put her fears aside and married Tristan, and now her heart was breaking.

She stared at the door to his room, aching to swallow her pride and go to him now. She wanted to believe he didn't care about gossip or her imperfections, but she knew their marriage would be a constant thorn. Even if she did everything right, Tristan would pay a price and so would she. So would the children.

"Help me, Lord," she murmured. "I don't know what to do."

When no answer came, she decided to go to him. Silently she rehearsed what she had to say. *I care for you, Tristan. But not enough to go with you to England.* She imagined taking off the ring. *This belongs to Dora.* The mention of the child sent tears to her eyes and she wondered if she could even speak. *Someday you'll marry again, and she'll have a mother.* And Tristan would have a wife. He'd be as happy as Jon, who had made Bessie's dreams come true long after she'd given them up.

Caroline had dreams, too. The ring on her finger suddenly felt tight, a reminder that many of her dreams had come true and that she'd lose everything unless she found the courage to stand up for herself.

She looked again at the dress, then at the open door to Tristan's room and she knew… She couldn't wear black to her sister's wedding. If the pretty gown caused ridicule, she'd know where she stood with the Whitmores and all of England. She'd know if she could cope with the pressures of being Tristan's duchess. For now, the ring would stay on her finger.

Chapter Twenty-One

Two days later, the guests gathered in the great room for Jon and Bessie's wedding. It was dusk, and a hundred candles were burning on the mantel and in candelabras throughout the room. Reverend Blue stood tall with a Bible already open. Jon stood at his side, his hands folded in a dignified pose. Tristan was next to Jon. He had the ring in his pocket and his eyes on the doorway where Caroline would enter before the bride. When the bridal march started, he'd know if she'd worn the pink dress.

To his dismay, the Whitmores had ignored his implied request to wear their colorful finery. The dowager had chosen a dark gray silk with black buttons, and the nieces were wearing navy-blue. Even Louisa had dressed in subtle colors, a mauve that bordered on gray. Tristan turned his gaze to the other side of the room. The women from Swan's Nest didn't own ball gowns. They were wearing what they'd brought, dresses that would have fit well in church. If Caroline wore the pink gown, she'd stand out like a tropical bird. He liked the idea, but he doubted she'd feel the same way.

The fiddler, an Irishman by birth, warmed up his bow with a scale, then played a melody that struck Tristan as ponderous. He supposed it fit the seriousness of the occasion, but he would have preferred something more triumphant for Caroline's entry. As the notes increased, he stared at the doorway.

He saw the hem of the gown first, then the rosettes and the pink draping and finally the bodice that fit her curves. In the gold light of the candles, the pink silk reminded him of the flamingos he'd seen in Africa. It shimmered between vibrant hues and pale ones, a mix of strength and fragility that also characterized his wife. In her hands he saw a posy made of ribbons and sprigs of pine. The evergreen made the dress even brighter.

Surrounded by women in muted colors, she stood out like a rose in the rain. He watched as her eyes scanned the room, taking in the drab dresses worn by the other women. Her chin stayed steady, but he saw panic in her eyes. He nodded his approval to encourage her, but she didn't smile back.

With every step she took, the dress reflected another candle and shimmered more brightly. Tristan scanned the faces on the Whitmore side of the room. When Caroline turned, she'd see the dowager's arched brow. The nieces both had a superior air. Pierce and Blackstone seemed bored, a reaction Caroline would interpret as disdain. Neither critical nor supportive, Louisa and Whitmore had the look of statues.

Caroline reached the end of the aisle, greeted Josh with a smile and turned. As she watched the audience, Tristan watched *her*. The instant she saw the critical stares, she flushed as pink as the dress. He willed her to stare back. Instead she focused on the doorway. The music switched to a more joyful tune and Bessie walked into the room. Caroline focused solely on her sister, smiling through a sheen of tears. Whether the tears came from happiness for Bessie or the loss of her own, Tristan didn't know. He knew only one thing… He wanted Caroline to triumph, and he wanted their marriage to be everything except inadequate. He loved her. He was proud of her and the night wouldn't end until he proved it.

The ceremony uniting Bessie and Jon couldn't have been more different from the vows Caroline had exchanged with Tristan. Josh spoke eloquently of commitment, the joy of sharing ordinary days and the blessings of faith, hope and love. She didn't dare look at Tristan. The instant she saw the Whitmores, she realized the bright dress had been a mistake.

She stayed brave through the ceremony.

She tolerated sly looks during dinner.

When the crowd moved into the great room, Adie, Mary and Pearl surrounded her. She tried to hide behind them, but Mary tugged her aside. "That dress is stunning," she said in a near hiss. "Stand tall and show it off."

"I can't," Caroline murmured.

"Yes, you can." Mary had no patience with shyness. A former actress, she enjoyed being the center of attention. Caroline preferred to bake pies in a cozy kitchen. Tristan had been wrong to ask her to wear the colorful dress. Judging by the dowager's scowl and the giggling from the nieces, she'd committed a faux pas as memorable as the riding accident. She wished she'd worn gray or blue or brown, anything but pink.

The fiddler played the first notes of a waltz. The banjo player and guitarist joined in. As Jon and Bessie enjoyed their first dance as man and wife, Caroline faked a smile. She couldn't think of anything more awful than dancing with Tristan, her pink dress swirling in a testament to her failure and her heart thudding with the knowledge she couldn't be his duchess.

When the waltz ended, Jon kissed Bessie for the joy of it. Matt and Pearl stayed seated, but the other couples from Swan's Nest paired up for dancing. The Whitmores resisted the entertainment. The dowager looked especially disgruntled, a sign Caroline had sunk into even deeper disgrace.

"May I have this dance?"

She turned and saw Tristan offering his hand. His eyes sparkled blue and his face radiated good health. Even if the fevers returned, he'd live. The realization filled her with bittersweet joy. His future was bright, but she couldn't share it. She looked down at his palm, his fingers long and inviting. She didn't want to be a spectacle, but neither would she give up the one time she would dance with her husband.

She accepted his hand. "I'd love to dance."

He guided her to the middle of the floor where they spun and whirled with the couples from Swan's Nest. Her heart felt light and so did her feet. Tristan guided her expertly, matching his stride to hers and turning her with ease. She felt giddy and almost brave. He tightened his grip on her waist, drawing her close and speaking into her ear. "You're beautiful, Caroline. You make me proud."

A lump rose in her throat. "You're being kind—"

"I'm telling the truth." His eyes burned into hers. "I love you. Come to England as my wife."

"I—I—can't."

"I don't care what people say." His hand tightened on her waist. They were spinning faster and faster. Suddenly the music sounded shrill and her feet turned to lead. The other couples had stopped dancing and were watching them. She missed a step and they faltered. Tristan held her up, giving her the balance she'd lost but not the confidence. When the fiddler ended the song with a flourish, they were left face-to-face in a circle of onlookers. Behind Tristan, she saw the Whitmores.

The dowager arched a brow.

The nieces giggled.

Mr. Blackstone sniffed and Mr. Pierce sipped his punch.

Whitmore whispered something in Louisa's ear. She whispered back, then gave Caroline a tentative smile.

Tristan turned his head and saw the same critical expressions. She murmured into his ear. "Now you know, I'll never be accepted."

Abruptly he faced her. Instead of glaring at the Whitmores, he glared at her. "We're going to dance again." He raised his arm to signal the fiddler, but Caroline stepped back. "I can't." When Tristan gave her a stern look, she fled from the room.

"Caroline!"

She reached the hall and headed for the stairs. She hadn't intended to make a scene. She just needed a minute to compose herself, but Tristan's call to her had drawn even more attention. She was halfway up the stairs when he strode into the hall and looked up.

"Caroline…"

She stopped in midstep and faced him. "Yes, your grace?"

"Do *not* call me that!"

"I won't," she said. "Not ever again. I want an annulment." She saw no reason to explain. He'd witnessed the stares and snide remarks. He'd come to her rescue, yet another sign of her weakness, but they both knew her humiliation wouldn't stop. Looking at him now, she felt more deficient than ever. She had nothing left—no pride, no hope. She had her faith for comfort, but she lacked the courage to live beyond her own abilities. The admission shamed her yet again.

Tristan broke the silence. "I'm leaving tomorrow. You'll need to say goodbye to Dora."

Tears welled in her eyes. "Of course."

He pivoted and went back to their guests, leaving her to decide for herself whether to return to the celebration or to go upstairs and begin packing for Denver. She chose to pack for Denver.

Tristan returned to the great room and made excuses for Caroline. He claimed she'd been taken ill. In truth she lacked the fortitude to stand up to a cantankerous old woman and two bratty girls. He had the wherewithal to put the dowager in her place, but he also had the grace to excuse her. He did both with a few words. If Caroline hadn't left, she might have impressed the woman. Instead she'd left in shame.

Tristan stayed until Jon and Bessie left. As he said goodnight to his guests, he told them he'd be leaving for England in the morning. He accepted both condolences and well wishes, then wandered to the veranda where he inhaled cold air. The sky dimmed as clouds covered the moon, then brightened again when they passed. In the distance he saw the garden and the cottonwoods, a reminder of his own family tree, the roots and the branches named Freddie and Dora. He wanted to be a good father. He wanted his children to have a mother, and he wanted that woman to be Caroline.

Tristan, too, was a branch, and tonight he saw himself as a child much like Freddie. Confused and grieving, the boy didn't understand what had happened or why. He only knew how he felt. Tristan had greater knowledge and had tried to comfort him, but Freddie rejected him. Tonight Tristan saw himself as Freddie and God as the father who wanted to provide comfort, hope and love to a child who didn't understand.

Humbled, he bowed his head and prayed aloud. "Father God, You love my family even more than I do. You understand Freddie and Dora, and You know what Caroline needs. Increase her faith. Remind her she's loved for exactly who she is. In Jesus' name, Amen."

He wanted to go to her and convince her of her worth, but she wouldn't listen to him. There was a time to coax and a time to exhort, a time to fight and a time to surrender. The time had come to accept Caroline's decision. His trunks were packed and ready to go. Evaline had seen to the children's things, and he'd arranged with Jon to oversee the ranch and tend to Cairo in his absence. Someday he'd return to this beautiful land, though he didn't know when.

Tomorrow he'd bid farewell to Noah and Evaline. Perhaps in the spring he'd send for them along with his horse. Looking at the sky, he considered his travel plans. The stagecoach left from Wheeler Springs, but another road ran direct from The Barracks to the bridge over the Frazier River. If Noah would drive them to Cheyenne, Tristan would save a day in travel. The annulment could be arranged in Cheyenne as easily as in Wheeler Springs. He'd also had to visit his banker. He'd never discussed an allowance with Caroline, but he intended to provide for her.

He didn't want to leave her, but with the decision made he grew restless. If he and the children left tonight, Dora might not cry, and Caroline wouldn't have to endure Freddie's hostile silence. As for himself, he had nothing else to say and he was sure Caroline had the same sense of finality. Leaving without a fight seemed kind, so he went back in the house in search of Noah. He found him sipping tea in the kitchen. The houseman greeted him with a nod. "Do you need me, Major?"

Tristan appreciated the old title. "I do. I want to leave tonight for Cheyenne." He told Noah about his plans and asked him to drive the carriage and return it to The Barracks.

Noah arched a brow. "I'll take you, sir. But it's late. Are you sure you want to leave tonight?"

"Yes."

Noah paused. "Is Mrs. Caroline accompanying you?"

"No, she isn't."

"I see." His brown eyes clouded. "I'm sorry, sir."

"As am I," Tristan said quietly. "It's a long trip. I appreciate your company."

"Yes, sir." Noah excused himself and left to tell Evaline of the plan.

Tristan went upstairs to write a note to Caroline. Maybe someday he'd come back to America. He'd find her and he'd persuade her to believe in herself. It had taken buckets of peppermint to win Cairo's trust. He didn't know what it would take to convince Caroline to turn their marriage into all it could be. He only knew that he'd failed.

Chapter Twenty-Two

Caroline stood in front of the mirror in her room looking at herself in the pink dress and wishing she'd followed her instincts and worn black. Defeated, she removed the pink diamond from her finger and set it by the lamp. Tomorrow she'd return it to Tristan. She changed from the ball gown into a calico, let down her hair and plaited it into a braid. Next she opened the trunk and filled it with her clothing, everything except the pink dress. She'd never wear it again.

When she finished packing, she put on her nightgown and slid into bed. She lay on her back for an hour with her eyes open and stinging with tears. Miserable, she gave up trying to sleep and went to the window. Staring into the dark, she took in the fallow garden, the cottonwoods and the hills where she'd raced Grandma. Tomorrow she'd say goodbye to Dora and Freddie. She didn't know which would hurt more—saying goodbye to the child who loved her or enduring the scorn of the one who didn't. She couldn't imagine Dora thinking she didn't love her, nor did she want Freddie to think she was leaving because of him. She'd made the decision on her own. As for what she'd say to Tristan, she prayed the words would come.

She didn't know how long she'd been at the window when someone knocked on the hall door. It was late. She didn't want to speak to anyone, not to Tristan and not to her friends. She opened the door with the intention of telling her visitor to leave. She expected Adie, Pearl and Mary, and that's who she saw, along with Louisa who had an odd smile. The four women were in their nightgowns and wrappers.

Adie grasped her arm and pulled her into the hallway. "You're coming with us."

"I'm tired," she said holding back.

"You can be tired later." Mary had a twinkle in her eye. "You have to see what's happening in the kitchen."

"Absolutely!" Louisa declared.

Pearl was in the back, smiling shyly.

Caroline didn't want to see anyone, but curiosity got the better of her. She followed her friends down the stairs to the brightly lit kitchen. When she stepped inside, her mouth gaped at the sight of the dowager duchess. The woman was wearing a purple satin wrapper, a mob cap and the meanest frown Caroline had ever seen. She was also wearing an apron and rolling pie dough. Armed with the rolling pin and a scowl, she'd have been intimidating except for one small problem. She had a streak of flour under her nose. It looked very much like a mustache.

Caroline suppressed a giggle. "Good evening, Dowager Somerville."

"Evening? It's not evening! It's the middle of the night and *you* should be in bed. What kind of home do you run, *Duchess* Willoughby!"

"I run a fine home, Dowager."

The woman snorted. "That's not what I see!"

"Why, I never—" Caroline bit her tongue, but she'd *had it* with the dowager's snobbery, the giggling nieces and the humiliation—and she had nothing left to lose. Furious, she put her hands on her hips. "For your information, Dowager Somerville, I run the kind of *home* where a cantankerous old woman can bake a pie in the middle of the night! I run the kind of *home* where children live their dreams and everyone is welcome regardless of titles or manners. I run the kind of *home* where love covers a person's mistakes. That includes you!"

The old woman raised the rolling pin like a scepter. "That's the way to talk, my girl! Give it to me! Give me all you've got!"

Caroline didn't think about what the woman had said. She only knew it felt good to be mad instead of defeated. She lifted a silver tray off the counter and shoved it in the woman's face. "*You* have a mustache!"

The dowager pointed the rolling pin at Caroline's chest. "And *you* have courage!"

"You bet I do!" Caroline wielded the silver plate like a shield.

Looking positively gleeful, the dowager brandished the rolling pin like a sword. "En garde, Duchess! Choose your weapon!"

Slowly, like the sun rising on a cloudy day, the absurdity sunk into Caroline's mind. Adie started to laugh, and Mary let out a hoot. Pearl was laughing so hard she had to hold her stomach, and Louisa let out a very unladylike guffaw. All four of them had tears of laughter streaming down their faces. Caroline turned back to the dowager.

Lowering the rolling pin, she smiled like a grandmother. "I knew you had it in you, Duchess. I just *knew* it! My maternal grandmother was an American. She gave my grandfather all his gray hair, but he loved her for it."

"You did this on purpose?" Caroline asked.

The old woman nodded. "Someone had to make you

see your abilities. Your husband tried, but we don't always trust the judgment of those who love us. They see us with blinders on, which is rather convenient. Sometimes it takes a stranger to test one's grit. And you, Duchess Willoughby, have grit!"

Caroline's eyes widened. "I believe I do."

"I'm sure of it," Adie said.

"Me, too," added Pearl.

"I quite agree," Louisa answered.

Mary grinned. "We did a good job, didn't we? I thought of the mustache."

The dowager's eyes twinkled. "I've wanted to make a flour mustache since I was a little girl." Looking positively impish, she dragged her finger through the flour and ran it under Caroline's nose. Laughing, Caroline gave a mustache to Adie, who shared the fun with Mary and Pearl. Pearl did the honors for Louisa, who still looked dignified with flour on her nose. The women laughed and hugged, wearing flour mustaches and feeling like the best friends they were.

The dowager drew back first. "I do hope to see you in England, my dear. We're a stuffy lot, but I'm sure you can cope."

Louisa hugged her. "She means it, Caroline. No matter what happens, I'll be your friend."

Tears of happiness pushed into her eyes, but then she thought of her quarrel with Tristan. "I'm afraid I owe my husband an apology."

"So make it," the dowager said.

"I will."

"Good," Adie replied. "I know you and Tristan took vows, but perhaps you'd like to renew them? I feel cheated not being at your wedding!"

"Me, too," echoed Mary and Pearl.

Caroline's eyes brimmed with happiness. "That would be wonderful, but first Tristan has to forgive me."

The dowager harrumphed. "He's already forgiven you. I saw how he looked at you in that *scandalous* pink dress. He was positively smitten."

Caroline hadn't even noticed. She'd been so concerned with the opinion of others that she'd missed her husband's admiration. Turning to the dowager, she hugged her again. "Thank you for everything."

"My pleasure," the dowager said sincerely.

The women blew out the lamps and retreated upstairs. Caroline hugged her friends goodnight, went to her room and slipped quietly through the closet to Tristan's suite. His room was dark and cold, a sign he hadn't bothered with a fire. She imagined him sleeping alone, chilled between the sheets. In the dark she inched forward, softly calling his name. "I'm so sorry, Tristan. Will you forgive me?"

Silence answered. Not a breath, not a stirring of the bedding, She inched forward, blind and lost in the dark, her hands reaching for the man she loved. "Tristan? Can you hear me? Please say you forgive me—"

She touched the corner of the mattress, then a blanket that had no wrinkles. With her heart pounding, she found a match and lit the lamp. The golden flare revealed the empty bed and a letter on the pillow. It was addressed to her.

My dearest Caroline,
It seemed wise to avoid more painful goodbyes, so I left with the children for Cheyenne. Rather than travel by stagecoach, Noah is taking us directly. He'll return in a week or so with the documents for the annulment. When we took vows, I promised to

*provide for you. Please accept the gift of an annual
allowance for the rest of your life.*

*If I could, I'd give you riches far greater than
money.*
With love,
Tristan

Caroline didn't want an allowance! She wanted her
husband. It was dark, but the sun would rise in an hour or
so. If she rode hard, she could catch up with Tristan and
the children. She had the courage to make the trip, but
she wasn't foolish enough to do it alone. She hurried to
her room, put on her riding habit and raced up the stairs
to the third floor. Any of the men could help her, so she
pounded on the first door she reached.

Jonah opened it with his typical caution. If he'd been
sleeping, it didn't show. Mary came up next to him. She
still had a spot of flour on her lip. "What's the matter?"
she asked.

"Tristan left with the children—"

"When?" Jonah asked.

"A few hours ago." She told them about the note and
the direct road to Cheyenne. "I'm going after them."

"You're not going alone." Jonah had his boots on before she could blink, and Mary was handing him a can-
vas duster.

"Let's go," he said as he punched into the sleeves.

Behind her another door opened. Matt came into the
hall. Josh came out of the third door. He'd been sound
asleep and it showed. Mary, Pearl and Adie crowded into
the hall with their husbands, murmuring and looking
worried.

Jonah took charge. "Get dressed, gentlemen. Tristan
left with the kids. We're taking Caroline to find him."

"Where'd he go?" Josh asked, yawning.

"Cheyenne," she answered. "And then to England. We have to hurry."

The men put on boots and jackets, kissed their wives and left the house with Caroline in the lead. Behind her they formed a shield of sorts, guarding her back as they paced to the barn in silence. She'd have ridden after Tristan alone if she'd had no other choice, but God had provided these good men to help her.

When they reached the horse barn, Matt and Jonah surveyed the stalls. In addition to Cairo and Grandma, the two Arabians were ready to ride. The other horses were out to pasture. They saddled the Arabians and led them to the yard. Figuring she'd ride Grandma, Josh approached Cairo. "Hi, fella."

The stallion snorted at him.

"He's not fond of me," Josh said drily. "I guess I'm staying."

Matt came up behind him. With a twinkle in his eyes, he jerked a thumb at the stall holding Biscuit. "You could ride that one, preacher."

Josh laughed and so did Caroline. It eased the tension, but only a bit. It didn't seem right for Josh to stay behind. Looking at the stallion, she thought of the peppermints she'd given him. He was the fastest horse in the barn. With Matt and Jonah on the Arabians, Grandma would be the slowest. She welcomed the men's protection, but she intended to reach Tristan first. She went to the tack room, fetched a handful of peppermint sticks and approached the stallion. "Let's see if Cairo will let me ride him."

"But why?" Josh asked.

"He's the fastest." A month ago his speed would have terrified her. Today she needed it. Murmuring to Cairo the way Tristan did, she fed him the treats. He knew her from the riding lessons and calmed immediately.

"You have the touch." Josh gave her a questioning look. "If you can handle Cairo, I'll ride Grandma."

"She beats the pony," Matt joked.

Caroline soothed Cairo while Josh saddled him. When he finished, she led the stallion to the mounting block and climbed on. To her relief, the horse gave her the respect he usually reserved for Tristan.

Matt and Jonah mounted the Arabians. Josh led Grandma out of the barn and swung into the saddle. With Caroline in the lead, the four of them headed for Cheyenne. Tristan had described Grandma as a rocking chair with legs. Cairo moved like a locomotive on a flat plain. Steady and powerful, he set a fast but sustainable pace. Caroline gripped the horse with her legs and moved with him. In the cold light of dawn, the woman and the horse went after the man they both loved.

Tristan, Noah and the children had been on the trail for two hours when the sun rose in the eastern sky, turning it the same shade of pink as Caroline's dress. Another hour passed, and then another.

Noah was perched on the driver's seat, humming quietly as he steered the carriage along the road that led to the Frazier River. Tristan was in the passenger compartment with Dora asleep in his lap and Freddie next to him. The boy had scooted to the side and hadn't budged. With hours of travel ahead of them, Tristan considered Freddie's silence and how best to break it. He knew all about leading horses to water and getting blood out of stones. He'd been as reluctant to speak to God as Freddie was to speak to him now. In the end, it was love that had broken through to him. If Tristan had learned nothing else, he'd learned that a father's love had no conditions. With Freddie in a pout, Tristan could show that kindness to his son.

"I think you'll like Willoughby," he said amiably. "It's different from Wyoming, and it's certainly different from the West Indies."

The boy kept staring out the window. "Grandfather said England is foggy."

"It is."

Tristan had kept his voice low, but Dora yawned and stretched awake. Last night, he'd asked Evaline to dress the child for travel. She'd roused, but only barely. Tristan had lifted her into his arms and carried her, feeling the weight as she slouched against his shoulder. She'd been asleep when they'd entered the carriage. Now, startled by her surroundings, she came fully alert. "Where are we?"

Tristan made his voice jovial, though he felt no pleasure. "We're going on a trip, my dear."

"A trip?"

He couldn't bear to tell her they were going to England without Caroline. He thought of the woman he loved, the dream game and Dora's desire to be a princess. He'd use whatever he could to lessen the emotional blow he had to deliver to his little girl. "We're going to England, Dora. You're going to live in a castle like a real princess."

"Where's Mama?"

He'd heard Dora use the endearment with Caroline, and it had charmed him. Now the words were a knife to his heart. "She's staying in America."

"But why?" Dora's voice rose to a shriek. Dissatisfied with Tristan's answers, she turned to Freddie. "I want to go home! I want Mama!"

Freddie's eyes widened with confusion, then dimmed with emotions Tristan couldn't discern. When the boy turned abruptly to the carriage window, Tristan dared to hope his son was feeling the sting of regret for how he'd treated Caroline, and how he'd indirectly hurt Dora by pushing Caroline away. The girl was weeping copious tears, muttering that she wanted to go home. Tristan soothed her as best he could, but Dora kept crying. Caroline would have known what to say. She had a mother's heart. If only she'd had the courage to come with them...

Dora cried herself into exhaustion. With his own heart in tatters, Tristan stared out the window.

"Father?"

Turning, he faced his son. Freddie's eyes had the sharp gleam of shattered crystal. He'd worn that expression for days after Molly died. Tristan put his own grief aside and spoke kindly. "What is it, son?"

"I've been thinking about something Grandfather said."

Tristan braced for trouble. "What was it?"

The boy looked at his sister, sleeping now, then he murmured. "He said I was more important than Dora."

Favoritism. It was the most diseased root of the Smythe family tree. What made one child valuable and another worthless? He thought of the saying about beauty being in the eye of the beholder. Perhaps that was true of paintings and possessions, but children were beautiful just as God created them. Freddie needed to understand that bloodlines didn't give a man worth. The boy was no better than anyone else. Ironically, Caroline needed to know she was no less worthy than the duke, the dowager or anyone else.

Tristan kept his voice matter-of-fact. "You and Dora are equals. There are no favorites in this family." Certainly not in Tristan's heart, or in God's heart.

Freddie looked troubled. "That's not what Grandfather said."

"What did he say?"

"He said I was his favorite because I'm like him."

Tristan held back his disgust, but just barely. He'd forgiven his father before, and he'd do it again. He'd do it until the poison had been purged from his family tree. "You resemble him, but you have your own mind and your own dreams—"

"I want to be a scientist."

"And you can be," Tristan agreed. "Someday you'll be the Duke of Willoughby. You'll have a title and responsibilities, but you'll still be a man just like Noah and Jon and your grandfather."

"A man like you?" Freddie said with admiration.

Tristan's chest swelled with pride. He couldn't hug Freddie without embarrassing him, so he patted Dora's back. He'd lost Caroline, but she'd given him back his children. He smiled at his son, a boy who had his eyes, Molly's nose, Caroline's wisdom and a mind of his own. "You'll be a better man than I am, son. I'm sure of it."

Freddie still looked troubled. "Grandfather said something else. He said Miss Caroline was common."

"Far from it," he replied. "She's one of the finest women I know."

Freddie was chewing on his lip, a sign of the burden he carried. Finally, he looked into Tristan's eyes. "He said she'd ruin our family tree with her American blood, but I like her. Even when I was mean, she was nice."

"Yes, she was."

"I was wrong about her causing Grandfather to fall. He was riding too fast." Freddie turned back to the window. "I'm sorry. I wish I could tell her."

So did Tristan. He considered turning the carriage around, but Caroline had made her decision independent of Freddie's resentment. "Perhaps you could write to her from Cheyenne."

"I'll do it," he said in a solemn tone. "Do you think she'll forgive me?"

"I'm sure of it." He gave Freddie a crisp nod, an acknowledgment of the boy's new maturity. "She loves you, son. So do I. Love and forgiveness go hand in hand."

"Maybe Aunt Caroline will change her mind," the boy said hopefully. "She could still come to England, couldn't she?"

"Yes, she could." Tristan would welcome her with open arms, but he doubted Caroline would reverse her decision.

They were nearing the Frazier River. The bridge had been repaired, so the crossing would be nothing like what Tristan had experienced with Caroline. Instead of feeling the water on his boots, he'd hear the wheels on the fresh planks. Now, though, he was hearing something different... He heard hoofbeats, several of them, and they were approaching fast. The Carver gang hadn't been apprehended, so he prepared for the worst.

"Get down!" he commanded Freddie.

The boy dropped to the floor of the carriage. Tristan set Dora next to him. She roused, but Freddie consoled her. Noah slowed the rig, turning it slightly for reasons Tristan didn't understand. As the wheels ground to a halt, he slid a pistol from under the seat and aimed at the closest rider...a rider on a black Arabian stallion...a rider wearing a split skirt...a rider with long brunette hair.

"Tristan!" Caroline shouted. "Wait!

Just as she'd once aimed a gun at him and lowered it, Tristan uncocked the pistol and removed it from the window. "Children, you can get up, but stay here."

He climbed out of the carriage, handed Noah the revolver and strode to the woman and the horse. In the distance he recognized Matt, Josh and Jonah. Seeing Caroline's safe arrival, they had stopped at a distance. She slid off Cairo and tumbled into his arms. "Don't leave. Please, don't go. I love you."

He loved her, too. But he had responsibilities. Was she asking him to stay, or did she want to go with him? He didn't know, and he couldn't hold her close until he understood. "What are you saying?"

She told him a crazy story about the dowager, a rolling pin and flour mustaches. When she finished, he was more confused than ever. He needed to sort through the facts. "So you're friendly with Dowager Somerville?"

"I am."

He hesitated, then asked the question that would set the course for the future. "Exactly where do you intend to continue that friendship, here or in England?"

"Oh!" Her eyes twinkled. "I didn't make that clear, did I, your grace?"

The title usually irked him, but she said it with a smile. He didn't dare smile in return. "No, you didn't."

"Then let me be direct." Stepping back, she held her head high and squared her shoulders. "If the Duke of Willoughby will accept my apology, I intend to accompany him to England. Not only will I be a mother to his children, I'll assume my duties as Caroline Bradley Smith, Duchess of Willoughby."

"I see." Tristan's dreams were coming true, but he was still a man and he wanted to be in charge. With a glint in his eyes, he arched his brows. "You *do* realize what such a position entails."

"I do, your grace."

"I expect you to follow orders."

Her hazel eyes sparkled with mischief. "And I expect the same of you. Is that agreeable?"

"It depends on the order." He cupped her chin.

"Kiss me," she murmured.

As far as orders went, he couldn't think of a better one. Her eyes drifted shut and so did his, then the carriage door slammed and startled them both. Looking up, he saw Dora running to them, her arms outstretched and her eyes on Caroline.

"Mama!" she cried.

Caroline scooped the girl onto her hip. Freddie trailed after his sister but with a firm stride. He traded a look with Tristan, then approached Caroline.

"I'm sorry, Aunt Caroline." He swallowed hard. "I was mean about Grandfather's accident. It wasn't your fault."

Her eyes misted. "Thank you, Freddie. That means a lot to me."

The boy looked at her with a new eagerness. "Are you coming with us to England?"

"That's up to your father, but I'd like it very much."

Tristan cleared his throat. "We were just discussing the possibility. Freddie, take your sister and wait with Noah."

"Yes, sir."

Caroline kissed Dora's forehead and set her on her feet. Freddie led the girl to the carriage, bending to the side to whisper something that made her giggle.

Tristan faced his wife. "Where were we?"

Her cheeks turned as pink as the fancy gown. "We were discussing orders," she said shyly.

"Ah, yes." He wasn't ready to end this moment. In essence, it was all the courtship they'd have. He wanted to enjoy watching her blush, so he gave her a private look she'd soon know well. "I believe it's my turn to issue an order."

"Yes, your grace." She put her hand on his chest, palm flat in a pledge of sorts.

The desire to tease her evaporated like a mist. He could only think about the love they'd almost lost and the future that awaited them. He put his hand over hers and pressed. "Promise that you'll never leave me."

"I promise." Her eyes misted. "I love you, Tristan. I can't imagine life without you."

He looked at her hand and saw that she'd removed the wedding ring he'd given her. Whether she'd taken it off in a fit of despair or removed it only for the ride, he didn't know and it didn't matter. They were starting anew and he wanted matching gold bands. "Marry me again," he said. "Let's say the words before God and mean them."

"Yes," she cried. *"Yes!"*

He pulled her into his arms, drawing her close as he matched his lips to hers. She was his wife, his duchess, the mother of his children and of the children to come. When he kissed her, it was far more than adequate. It was spectacular.

* * * * *

Rhonda Gibson lives in New Mexico with her husband, James. She has two children and three beautiful grandchildren. Reading is something she has enjoyed her whole life, and writing stemmed from that love. When she isn't writing or reading, she enjoys gardening, beading and playing with her dog, Sheba. You can visit her at rhondagibson.net. Rhonda hopes her writing will entertain, encourage and bring others closer to God.

Books by Rhonda Gibson

Love Inspired Historical

Saddles and Spurs

Visit the Author Profile page
at Harlequin.com for more titles.

THE TEXAN'S
TWIN BLESSINGS

Rhonda Gibson

Forget the former things; do not dwell on the past.
See, I am doing a new thing!
—*Isaiah* 43:18–19

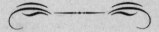

Tina James, thank you for always believing in my stories and trusting me to get them written on time. James Gibson, your love means more to me than you will ever know. Thank you for keeping the midnight oil burning so that I can find my way after a long night of writing. And as always, thank You, Heavenly Father, for giving me my heart's desires.

Chapter One

Granite, Texas
Late Spring 1887

Hot, aggravated and about at the end of his rope, William Barns stood on his grandmother's porch juggling his year-and-a-half-old nieces, Rose and Ruby. The little girls squalled louder.

"Eat!" Rose twisted sideways, her little voice pleading.

They were hungry, so was he, and as soon as his grandmother opened the door from the other side, she'd help feed them. Of that he had no doubt. He shifted the twins higher on his chest. Today they'd had milk and bread in their diets and little else.

The heat was getting to them and making the girls cranky; him, too, if he was honest about it. Colorado springtime and Texas springtime were very different in the way of weather, and the effects on him and the girls were going from poor to bad fast.

Why was his grandmother taking so long? If he remembered correctly, the house was not that big. He'd been a kid the last time he'd stood on this porch, and even then it had seemed small. William clinched his jaw in an effort not to get impatient with the girls and his grand-mother. Surely she'd heard him knocking.

The trip from Denver, Colorado, had been exhausting. Rose and Ruby demanded his undivided attention. He'd had no idea how much was required of his late sister, until she'd been killed and he'd taken over the twins' care. What a load she had carried and carried well.

His heart ached at the loss of his sister, Mary. If only he'd gone to the bank that day, instead of her. The throbbing in his ankle reminded him why he'd stayed with the napping twins while his sister had gone to town and faced down two bank robbers. If only he hadn't slipped on the frozen snow and broken his ankle after the last ice storm they'd had, he would have been the one at the bank.

Rose, apparently tired of the juggling, chose that moment to throw up sour milk all over his shirtsleeve. Ruby, spying her sister's distress, let out a wail that pierced his eardrums.

As the curdled milk scent reached his nostrils, he briefly wondered how his delicate, prim sister had managed to take care of his darling nieces with the ease that she had. They burped putrid liquids, and the diapers, well, he'd almost taken to wearing a clothespin on his nose while changing them.

Exhausted, Rose laid her head upon his shoulder and shuddered her unhappiness. Mirroring her sister's actions, Ruby did the same. Regardless of their disgusting smells and loud crying, William loved his nieces with all his heart.

"I'm sorry, baby girls. I know you're hot and tired, and sick of me pouring liquid into you." He kept his voice soothing and calm. "Just hang on a few more seconds. Grandma's on the way, and she'll have something good for us to eat."

His chest ached with the sorrow weighing down upon him. He felt as if the responsibilities of the girls might be more than he could take. Why did everything have to change?

Memories flooded his tired mind. On the fateful morning he'd lost his sister, his brother-in-law and town sheriff, Josiah, had been out of town but was to return later in the day. William later learned that Josiah had been lured away by fake information that the robbers were in the town next to theirs. He'd hurried off to help the sheriff there, and while he'd been gone the criminals had robbed their bank.

Three rough-looking men had arrived in town shortly after the bank opened. They'd entered the bank, threatening those inside if the teller didn't turn over the money. When they'd escaped in a blaze of gunfire, they left Mary lifeless and the bank teller wounded.

Witnesses had whispered that it had all happened so suddenly. The bank robbers had taken Mary's money and left her for dead. She had stumbled out of the bank, clutching the morning's mail to her wounded chest. It was when she fell in a heap of petticoats that everyone realized she'd been hit by the gunfire. His sister had died on the dirty street, leaving behind an angry, grieving husband and two beautiful, motherless little girls. And him.

A piercing cry sounded within his left ear, pulling William from the painful memory. "Ruby, please don't scream." He looked to the dark window on his left. Where was his grandmother? Why hadn't she answered? He turned and pounded on the door with his elbow.

Aggravation at the delay crept up his spine and into his already pounding head. The longer he stood there, the worse he felt. William refused to give in to the irritation at having to wait for his grandmother; one angry man in the family was enough.

The memories he'd been shoving away flooded in once more. Josiah had allowed his rage and grief over the murder of his wife to run so deep he'd practically forgotten his daughters. William had been left with no choice but to take over the care of the girls. Once his sister had been put to rest, Josiah had gone after the murderers with the promise to come back for the girls, but William wasn't holding his breath.

Even though Josiah was a good lawman, William worried about his brother-in-law's state of mind. Josiah blamed himself for his wife's death. He'd even made the statement he wasn't sure he was a fit father and that if he couldn't protect Mary, what made him think he could protect his girls? William had tried to talk to him, offer comfort, but in the end, Josiah had left a bitter and angry man.

After three months of waiting, William couldn't stand living in the same town that his sister had died in. He'd left word with Josiah's neighbor that he was moving to Granite, Texas, and that Rose and Ruby would be waiting there for Josiah when he'd finished his business with the bank robbers. He worried Josiah might never come for his daughters—the man had been so resentful—and Josiah had probably taken risks that could end his life, leaving the girls orphans.

Rose trembled, and one look at her white face reminded William that he needed to focus on her and her sister instead of rehashing what had happened or worrying about what might have happened to their father. Until he heard from Josiah, he was responsible for the little girls, and right now they needed real food and a place to rest. He reached for the door handle and found it locked. William sighed. She wasn't home.

"Excuse me."

He turned to the soft voice that had managed to be heard over the little girls' cries. A young woman stood behind him in the yard. Her red hair blazed under the sun, and light freckles crossed her nose as if she'd too often forgotten to wear her bonnet. Green eyes filled with sadness looked up at him. The freckles across her nose and cheeks gave her the appearance of being very young, but the depth of emotion in her eyes made him think she might be older than she looked. Realizing he was staring, William responded. "Yes?"

"My name is Emily Jane Rodgers. I'm Mrs. Barns's neighbor." She pointed to the house across the street, then turned to face him once more. "Mrs. Barns no longer lives here." Her sweet voice seemed to drip with warmth and deep sorrow.

William shifted the girls, who had quieted down at the sound of the female voice. "Nice to meet you, Miss Rodgers. I'm William Barns. Where has my grandmother moved?"

Renewed sorrow seemed to fill her pretty green eyes. "I have a key to the house. Let's go inside, so that I can explain." She brushed past him, and scents of cinnamon and sugar filled his nostrils.

The girls stared at the redheaded woman. Ruby stretched out a chubby hand to grasp a strand of her hair as she worked the key into the lock. Thankfully, the little girl couldn't reach Miss Rodgers, but her failed attempt had her leaning farther, straining against his arm till he thought he might drop her. He tightened his hold on Ruby, turning aside from the temptation.

Finally the woman opened the door and stepped within the cooler interior. William followed as questions regarding his grandmother bombarded his tired mind. They stood in the sitting room, where all the furniture was covered with fabric of various colors. His hopes sank in his chest as he realized that if his grandmother had moved, she would have taken her things with her. He used his boot to shut the door.

Miss Rodgers dropped the key into the pocket of her apron that hung about her small waist and then moved to the window. She pulled back the heavy curtain to allow sunshine into the room before she turned to face him. Dust particles swirled in the air around them. "I'm sorry I have to be the one to tell you this, but Mabel passed away last month from a cold that had moved into her chest." Sorrow filled her voice.

He gasped. A new sharp pain pricked his heart. A stinging dryness scalded the backs of his eyes. William looked about for a place to set the squirming twins, who wanted to get down and explore this new place. William realized he didn't dare put them in the layer of dust that covered the floor. He shifted their weight and held them close to his aching chest.

He'd lost his sister and now his grandmother. Who was next? One of the twins? His brother-in-law? He'd also lost his fiancée, Charlotte, thankfully not by death, but she'd been clear that having children or taking care of someone else's was not a part of her future with him. They'd parted ways since he wanted children and intended to protect and keep his nieces until their father's return.

The questions returned once more. How much more could he take? And how was he going to care for the girls by himself until his brother-in-law returned? This was not how he had pictured his life. Doubt rose in multiples. Why was the Lord testing him? Had he offended Him in some way? He loved the fellowship with his Lord and tried to honor and please Him above all others. But his load seemed to get heavier every day. As if the Lord had heard his thoughts, William's troubled spirit quieted, and he forced his lips to part in a curved, stiff smile at the woman staring solemnly back at him.

Emily Jane watched the emotions cross the handsome face of the man in front of her. William Barns wore a dark brown cowboy hat. Wavy black hair peeked out from under the brim and curled about his collar. It was his sapphire-blue eyes that held her attention; they told a story of their own. From the depth of sorrow staring back at her, Emily Jane read that this wasn't the first time death had recently broken his heart.

Without giving her actions much thought, she reached for one of the babies, who had resumed kicking and crying. "Here, let me take one of them." Poor little mites needed their mother. Emily Jane felt sure that Mr. Barns mourned her death as well as his grandmother's; why else would he show up alone with the two little girls?

He placed the little child into her outstretched arms. "Shhhh, it will be all right." Emily Jane rocked from side to side as she held the small one against her shoulder.

The child settled down and sniffled but no longer cried as if she were being tortured. Emily Jane looked to Mr. Barns and saw that he copied her actions. She offered him what she hoped was an encouraging smile. "Do you have fresh diapers for these sweet girls?" Emily Jane asked, as she continued to rock and pat the small back in her arms.

"Out in the wagon." He spun on his booted heels and limped away. "I'll be right back," Mr. Barns called over his shoulder.

"Go!" The little girl in her arms tugged in the direction that Mr. Barns had left. She cried in earnest when he and her sister continued out the door.

Emily Jane pulled the darling close and patted her back some more. "He'll be right back." Emily Jane looked about the room during his absence. In the short time Mabel Barns had been gone, the house had become quite dirty.

Would William Barns stay here now that he knew his grandmother had died? Or would he take his daughters and go to other family members for help with the children? She assumed the need for help with the girls had been what prompted him to visit his grandmother.

She refocused on the room as she jiggled the sobbing little girl in her arms. Dust covered every inch of the furniture, fireplace mantel and floors. If he stayed, it would take him a few hours to clean up the mess. Mabel had died a little over a month ago. Dusting was a daily job if you lived in Texas, especially Granite, a task Mabel had seemed to enjoy.

Emily Jane's throat closed. Fresh waves of sadness rolled over her as she mourned the loss of her friend. The child in her arms began to twitch and quiet down as if she sensed Emily Jane's sorrow.

"Let's get this wet diaper off of you, little one." Emily Jane walked to the sofa and pulled the dust-covered protective sheet off of it. To keep the sofa from getting wet, she took off her apron and laid it on the cushion. Then Emily Jane sat down and began to unpin the soiled cloth diaper.

She guessed that the child was about a year old, maybe a little older. Twins were often smaller than other children. Her black wavy hair matched the color of her father's, and brilliant blue eyes shone from her face. A frayed yellow ribbon had been tied in her hair. "You sure are a pretty little girl," Emily Jane said in a soft voice, happy the child was no longer screaming and crying. The tot looked like her handsome father.

Emily Jane shook her head to erase the memory of melancholy within his eyes. She didn't want to focus on William Barns's good looks, either. No, she wasn't interested in handsome men. She had a new life ahead of her. One of independence with no controlling husband or demanding children to steal her joy of baking.

The little girl looked up at Emily Jane and sucked her thumb while Emily Jane pulled the wet cloth from under her. As soon as she was free of the sodden diaper, she pulled her thumb from between her lips and said, "Shew wee."

Boot steps clacked against the wood floor. Then Mr. Barns handed her a leather pouch that resembled a saddlebag. "Shew wee is right." His warm voice brought a grin to the child's face. Emily experienced an unusual feeling in the pit of her stomach. What would it feel like to have someone's happiness within your power? She'd probably never know since she had chosen another direction for her life. One where she decided which path to take instead of a man doing it for her.

Emily Jane took the bag and found the clean diapers. As soon as she got the cloth pinned into place, she handed the first little girl over to Mr. Barns and took the second child.

"Thank you, miss, but you really don't have to do that." He moved as if to change places with her.

"I don't mind," Emily Jane answered as she proceeded to change the second child. The big man hobbled about the room. He touched the fireplace mantel and sighed. She wondered what had happened to his ankle but didn't think it was her place to ask. As soon as the second child was diapered, Emily Jane stood.

"Did Grandmother sell this house to you?" he asked. His voice broke, and he turned his face away.

Emily Jane shook her head. "No, a few days before her passing, she gave me a key and told me that if any of her kin should show up to let them in. I suppose she was worried you'd arrive after bank hours and wouldn't be able to get the extra key from the bank and so therefore wouldn't be able to get into the house."

Confusion furrowed the skin of his brow. "Does the bank own the house?"

"I'm not sure. All I know is what she told me. That Doc had done all he could for her and to give you the house key. Oh, and she also instructed me to tell you that you need to go to Mr. Fergus at the bank and tell him you are her kin. He has further information as to what is to become of this place." Emily Jane knew her words were rushed, but she hadn't expected a handsome man with two small children to be the "kin" that Mrs. Barns had predicted would come.

Mr. Barns frowned and voiced his thoughts. "How did Grandmother figure I was coming? There was no way she could have known. I didn't even know myself until a short time ago."

Emily Jane shrugged. "I'm not sure if she knew which of her grandchildren would arrive. She sent a letter off, but I don't know to whom. I assumed, since you are here, it was you."

He shook his head. "Maybe her letter was one of the letters that Mary dropped on the day she died. The wind blew several letters away, but in all the ruckus no one heeded them."

The soft words were spoken as if he were talking to himself. Emily Jane was pretty sure he wasn't speaking to her. His blue eyes were focused in the past as if he'd forgotten she and the little girls were in the room. But now she knew the little girls' mother's name and that she'd recently died.

Not willing to be ignored, both of the children began to whine and fret once more.

He seemed to snap out of the memories and return to them. His voice sounded tired and hopeless as he said, "They are hungry. I was hoping Grandmother would be able to feed them and help me get them ready for bed."

Emily Jane looked about the house. It wasn't fit for children, at least not without a good cleaning. She sighed as her motherly instincts took over. Being the oldest of twelve, Emily Jane was used to helping her mother by taking matters into her own hands, while her father took care of business. "Let's go over to my house, and I'll find them something to eat." She didn't wait for his answer, simply scooped the child off the couch and headed to the door.

She heard him follow and decided to have a quiet talk with herself regarding the Barns family. It was her Christian duty to help him get settled into their house. After that, William Barns and his girls were on their own. She didn't have time for children, and no matter how much he might need a wife, she did not need a husband. Emily Jane glanced back at him. William Barns was a handsome man; he'd find a woman to marry soon and it wouldn't be her.

The last thing Emily Jane wanted was to get married, especially to a man who already had two children. She didn't want children. After helping her parents with eleven brothers and sisters, Emily Jane had had enough of kids to last her a lifetime. Plus, she also didn't want a controlling man in her life. She'd had twenty-three years of her father controlling her and her mother. No, sir, Emily

Jane Rodgers wasn't going to allow a man to control her again. She had bigger plans for her life. Someday she'd open her own bakery and be able to support herself. She'd own her home and be able to buy new things instead of having to wear hand-me-downs, supplied by the local church ladies.

Emily Jane opened the door to the house that she shared with Anna Mae Leland. Anna Mae was the local schoolteacher. They'd met when they'd both answered Levi Westland's mail-order-bride advertisement. Well, Anna Mae had willingly answered it; she, on the other hand, had been forced to answer it by her father. He'd decided twelve children were too many to feed, and Emily Jane was the oldest and the one he could get rid of the easiest. It hurt that her father and mother had so easily sent her away, to a man she'd never met in a place she'd never been. How could a parent do that to a child, especially their firstborn? Emily Jane didn't plan to have children, but if she did, they would be loved unconditionally; that much she knew for sure.

The screen door shut behind him as Mr. Barns followed her inside the house. Emily Jane led him to the kitchen. She set the child she held on the braided rug beside the table, walked over to the cabinet and scooped up two empty pans and two large metal spoons. "Please, have a seat, Mr. Barns, and I'll have dinner ready in just a few moments." Emily Jane handed the little girl on the floor a spoon and placed one of the pans down in front of her. That would keep the child busy for a few minutes. She motioned for Mr. Barns to set his bundle of joy down beside her sister.

He did so with a sigh and a smile that said *thank you*.

Emily Jane nodded and then handed the second little girl the other spoon and pan. She'd have to stop thinking of them as little girls and ask what their names were. While he pulled out a kitchen chair, she turned to the stove.

Again, she had something to be thankful for. Emily Jane had already fried up chicken, made mashed potatoes and warmed up a jar of green beans just before she'd seen him and the girls arrive. She expected Anna Mae to arrive home from school any minute now.

And then what? He couldn't stay in the dusty house tonight, and he couldn't stay here.

She glanced at him over her shoulder. His deep blue gaze met hers. Emily Jane could get lost in the depths of his needs. She could...but she would not. She simply couldn't allow that to happen.

The girls banged happily on the pans. The noise filled the room and prevented the need for polite conversation. Emily Jane didn't want to enjoy the sound of children playing, but deep down she did. She also didn't want to be aware of the man sitting at her kitchen table. But she was. They reminded her of home and all that she'd lost when she'd answered Levi Westland's mail-order-bride ad all those months ago.

Would she be able to ignore the man and children in her kitchen? Had things just changed in her life? If so, how was she going to distance herself from the handsome man and his beautiful girls?

Chapter Two

"Thank you for the offer of supper. I'll be happy to pay you for what we eat." William laid his hat on the table and ran weary fingers through his hair.

The young woman, Miss Rodgers, turned from the stove with a platter of fried chicken. She set it down on the table. "That won't be necessary. I always make more than we can eat."

"We?" It hadn't dawned on him that Emily Jane Rodgers would have a husband and her own children to take care of. He'd been so absorbed in the loss of his grandmother and the dilemma of what to do with the girls that he'd not even considered the marital status of the woman before him.

She nodded. "Anna Mae and I."

Was Anna Mae her sister? His gaze moved to the sisters, who banged happily on the pans with the spoons she'd supplied. They were very close and affectionate with each other. He had heard that was the way with twins. Would they someday live together? He sighed tiredly. Right now, their future was as unclear as his own.

Miss Rodgers walked back to the stove for more food. She turned with a bowl of green beans and a plate of biscuits. His stomach rumbled with hunger. It had been a while since he'd had a good home-cooked meal. During the trip, he'd made sure the girls had food and milk but hadn't worried about his own stomach.

She gave him a knowing smile. He had no doubt in his mind that Miss Rodgers had heard his belly rumble. "Anna Mae Leland is the schoolteacher here. She should be home any moment." She placed the rest of the food on the table. Her gaze swept over the girls before she moved to the sideboard and pulled out plates and silverware.

"Are you sure she won't mind having company?"

"I'm sure. Anna Mae loves children, so these two will be a welcome sight to her." Miss Rodgers smiled at him again as she placed the plates on the table.

Her pearly white teeth flashed, but her eyes didn't hold the smile. Did she feel obligated to help him? Miss Rodgers seemed nice, but her gaze seemed dubious at best. Was it because they were alone in the house together?

He cleared his throat. "I need to go take care of the horse and wagon." He looked to where the girls played contentedly. Should he ask her to watch them while he unloaded the wagon and found housing for the horse? Or just assume she knew he needed her to do so.

They looked up at him with their mother's trusting eyes. Rose and Ruby were his responsibility. He'd take them. William stood and stepped toward the girls. Weariness rested upon him like the shroud of death that seemed to haunt his family at the moment.

"If you'd like, you can leave the girls with me."

Her soft voice held no regret at the suggestion, so William nodded. "Thank you. I won't be gone any longer than it takes to get the horse and supplies settled."

"Your grandmother kept her little mare in the lean-to in the back. It's small, only two stalls, but you are welcome to put your horse there also," she offered as she poured milk into two cups.

He nodded. "I'll look into putting him up at the livery tomorrow."

Just as William got to the door, Miss Rodgers called after him. "What are the girls' names?"

He turned to face her. "The one with the yellow ribbon is Rose and the other is Ruby. Those ribbons are the only way I can tell them apart, so please don't take them out of their hair." Shame filled William. What uncle, who had taken care of his nieces for as long as he had, couldn't recognize them without their silly bows? He hurried out the door before Emily Jane could ask him the question he'd just asked himself.

What must she think of him? Showing up with two little girls, dirty little ones at that, and not knowing that his grandmother had passed away? William crossed the dirt road. He moved to the back of the wagon and began pulling out the few belongings he'd brought. He told himself it really didn't matter what she thought. Emily Jane Rodgers had no say in what he did. Other than being their neighbor, she held no place in his or the girls' lives. And to be honest, he had too much on his plate to worry what some silly woman thought of him.

He had to admit, though, that she was very pretty and had been helpful. And so far silliness had not been part of her character, more a cautious, no-nonsense attitude toward his circumstances. She had known just what to do for the girls and had been willing to feed them. Was she just being neighborly? Or had she seen him as a single man with two children and a possible husband?

William shook his head. No matter how pretty or helpful Miss Rodgers was, he had no intention of becoming her husband. Or anybody's husband, for that matter. He picked up the closest box and realized being tired put very wayward thoughts into one's mind. Miss Rodgers was simply a nice woman. Very pretty and very nice. Nothing more. He hoped he was wrong that she might see him as a possible husband; he definitely wasn't looking for a wife.

He limped up the porch and entered the house. It was time to focus on himself and the girls. They needed a place to sleep tonight. William walked straight through the sitting room and into his grandmother's bedroom. Her bed rested against the center of the back wall. Other than the dust that covered everything, it looked much like it had five years ago when he'd last visited her. She had a small cabinet for clothes, a washbasin by the window and a small writing desk against the opposite wall. A side table sat on the other side of the bed and held a kerosene lantern and her Bible. He set the box of clothes down inside the doorway and then went to explore the rest of the house.

He followed a short hallway to the other side of the building where the kitchen and another bedroom rested. His grandmother had used the other bedroom for a sewing room as well as her guest room. Would the girls be too far away from him if he put them in this space?

William sighed as he went back out to the wagon. He lifted an oblong box from the bed that had served as Rose's cradle during their trip and carried it into the house and his grandmother's room. Then he went back for Ruby's. The girls would sleep in the room with him until they were old enough to be put in their own room. Plus, he'd need to clean only one room tonight.

On the way back outside, William noticed the bag that held the girls' diapers and drinking cups beside the sofa where Emily Jane had left it. He scooped it up and continued on to the horse and wagon.

It didn't take long to find the lean-to behind Emily Jane's house and take care of the animal. What had happened to his grandmother's horse? Miss Rodgers had said that she kept her here. William made a mental note to ask her about the little mare.

Taking a deep, unsteady breath, he hurried around the house, only to stop disconcerted at the door. Was he supposed to knock or go on in? He knocked.

Footsteps hurried across the floor. So far he hadn't heard the girls crying; that was a good sign, right? A rush of fragrances, sugar and cinnamon, hit him when she opened the door. He breathed deeply, enjoying the calming smells, making another mental note to cook something spicy at his grandmother's so the stale smell would leave.

"Mr. Barns, please, come on inside. You didn't need to knock. I expected you to return." She spun around on her heels and hurried back to the kitchen.

The slight bite in her voice had him hurrying after her. Had the girls misbehaved while he was gone? The diaper bag slapped against his side as he went to check on his nieces.

The scene that met him almost had him laughing out loud. Each girl sat in a chair by the table. Miss Rodgers had tied them to the chairs with what looked like aprons. Their faces were clean and their eyes sparkled as they gnawed on chunks of bread. They smiled up at him.

He eased into a chair beside Ruby. "I hope they weren't too much trouble."

Miss Rodgers sat across from him. "Oh, no, they were just hungry. Now that they're eating, they seem content and happy."

The front door opened and closed in the sitting room. A voice called out, "Emily Jane, I'm home."

This must be the Anna Mae that Miss Rodgers had mentioned.

"I'm in the kitchen," Miss Rodgers called back. She offered him a smile. "I'm sorry for the yelling, but if I don't answer she will think it strange."

He grinned back. "So the yelling back and forth is normal?"

"It's become a part of our routine." A slight blush filled her cheeks, and he wondered why.

"You would not believe my day." The woman called Anna Mae stopped abruptly, her gaze taking in the scene at the table.

Light brown hair, piled on the top of her head in a bun, and big brown eyes made Anna Mae Leland look plain next to Emily Jane. At least, that was William's first impression of her. She wore a simple gray dress, dusty brown shoes and a beige apron. He wondered if she dressed like that as a way to hide or become invisible to those around her.

"Oh, I'm sorry. I didn't realize we had company." Her brow crinkled, and then she looked at the two girls. A smile replaced the scowl. "Who are these darling ladies?" she cooed.

The little children smiled happily in return and kicked their legs back and forth. Who wouldn't smile at someone whose tone of voice had gone from normal to doting?

Miss Rodgers introduced them. "Anna Mae Leland, this is William Barns, Mabel's grandson, and his daughters, Rose and Ruby."

William stood and shook the hand Anna Mae extended toward him. His hand engulfed her smaller one.

"It's nice to meet you, Miss Leland, but I have to correct Miss Rodgers. Rose and Ruby are my nieces, not my daughters."

"Oh, I'm sorry. I assumed they were yours." Her voice drifted off as if caught in a high wind.

"Nothing to be sorry about, Miss Rodgers. It was an understandable mistake," William assured her, returning to his seat.

Both ladies were seated and, after a short grace, began filling the girls' plates with soft food. Mixed emotions threatened to overwhelm him. He didn't know whether to be relieved or offended at this liberty. He'd been the only caretaker of the girls since their mother had been killed. To suddenly relinquish that duty left him floundering, a bit as if he'd lost something precious. He shook his head. What on earth was wrong with him? This was what he'd needed his grandmother's help with. It was as simple as that.

William then filled his plate. As he sank his teeth into the first bite, he closed his eyes in pure pleasure. "Ummmmm," he all but groaned. He hadn't tasted fried chicken this good in... He didn't know how long. "You are a wonderful cook, Miss Rodgers," he praised.

"Thank you."

Miss Leland wiped Ruby's mouth and then said, "Wait until you taste dessert. Emily Jane is the best baker in these parts."

William watched Emily Jane finger a loose tendril of hair on her cheek as if embarrassed at her friend's praise.

"Thanks, Anna Mae." Her voice was smooth but insistent. "But we both know that isn't true. Violet is the real baker. I still have lots to learn from her before I can ever open my own bakery."

So she wanted to open her own bakery. Which to his way of thinking meant she wasn't lazy. Good for her.

His sister had been a hard worker with dreams of her own, also. Too bad her life had ended before she'd had a chance to realize them.

William listened to the women talk. His gaze moved to his nieces, who were making a mess of their dinners but were so happy he didn't have the heart to make them stop. He was surprised that neither Miss Rodgers nor Miss Leland asked him questions regarding the girls and the lack of their mother and father.

In the short time since he'd arrived in Granite, Texas, he'd learned that Anna Mae Leland was the schoolteacher who loved children and that Emily Jane Rodgers was a friend of his grandmother's and an aspiring baker. Yet, neither knew much about him, which to his way of thinking wasn't all bad.

The last thing he needed was for either of them to start looking at him as an eligible bachelor. Since Charlotte's rejection, he had no interest in women. His focus would be on the girls until their father returned. They were his sole concern now.

"Will you be staying long in Granite, Mr. Barns?" Miss Leland asked.

William rubbed his chin. "I guess that depends on what the banker says about the house and if I can find a job."

Miss Leland nodded as if she understood. "Well, you might talk to Mr. Moore over at the general store. His wife just had their first child, and I hear he's looking to hire someone."

Working at the general store wouldn't be so bad, at least until his money arrived at the bank. Selling the mercantile in Denver had made him a wealthy man, but until the money arrived he'd need to work. Not that he wouldn't work after the money came in. It wasn't in his nature to be lazy and watch others labor. "Thank you, Miss Leland. If all goes well at the bank tomorrow, I'll stop by the general store."

Rose and Ruby chose that moment to let everyone know they were done eating and ready to move to another activity. Their cries filled the house and had both women jumping to pick them up.

"I need to get these two down for the night." William reached for Rose.

Miss Rodgers caught his attention. "Where?"

"I'll take them to my grandmother's house. Her bedroom isn't that bad." He hoped she didn't think he was yelling at her. The girls' cries were so loud that he had to raise his voice to be heard.

She shook her head. "It's too dusty for them there."

Before he could respond, both women handed him a little girl.

"Try to comfort them. We'll be back in a little while. Between the two of us, we'll have the house livable in no time," Miss Leland instructed him as the two ladies walked out of the kitchen.

William hurried after them. The screaming children seemed unaware of the noise they were making. "I can't let you do that," he protested.

"It's no trouble at all," Miss Rodgers called over her shoulder as they left the house.

He continued after them, aware of several older women looking out their windows or standing on their porches. Instead of protesting further, William hurried across the road to his grandmother's house. *I'll be glad when I get control of my life once more,* he thought as the children howled and the women charged onward, on a mission to clean his grandmother's home. He hurried into the house behind them, then stopped abruptly and sneezed; not once, not twice, but three times in a row. Dust particles swirled so thick he could hardly see the ladies jerking covers off the furniture. Then the twins sneezed. "I think we'll just sit out on the porch awhile," he muttered to himself, since the ladies paid him absolutely no attention.

Emily Jane loved working at the bakery, but on mornings like this, she wished her hours weren't so early. Her new neighbors had kept her up most of the night with their cries for attention, and getting up at three in the morning had her even more tired than normal. A yawn filled her chest as she placed plates of pancakes in front of Mrs. Green and Miss Cornwell, two of her neighbors. She turned her head to release the yawn.

"Thank you," Mrs. Green said tiredly between huge yawns. "I didn't get a lick of sleep last night."

"I know," Miss Cornwell said, pouring honey over her pancakes. "Those babies cried almost the whole night. Disgraceful."

Emily Jane should have walked away, but instead she turned to face the women and said, "They weren't that bad."

"No? Didn't you hear them?" Mrs. Green asked, as her blue eyes searched Emily Jane's.

"Yes, I heard them, but they were in a strange new place and were overtired. I'm sure they'll settle down once they get used to their new home," she answered, wiping down the table beside them.

"So he's staying, then?" Miss Cornwell lifted the fork to her lips but waited for Emily Jane to answer.

"I don't know." Emily Jane didn't want the women assuming she knew more about William Barns's business than she should. Although she did wonder what he'd found out at the bank this morning.

The bell over the door jingled as three more ladies from her neighborhood entered the bakery, Mrs. Wells, Mrs. Harvey and Mrs. Orson. They hurried to where Mrs. Green and Miss Cornwell sat. Mrs. Harvey slipped into a chair at the table next to the other two women.

Mrs. Wells covered her mouth as a yawn overtook her. "Excuse me. I didn't get a wink of sleep last night with all that crying."

"We were just talking about that," Mrs. Green said, leaning forward in her seat.

Mrs. Orson shook her head. "I don't think anyone got any sleep last night. Mr. Orson paced the floor all night. It was very annoying. I'll be glad when that man takes his children and moves on."

Emily Jane decided to change the subject. "Ladies, what can I get you this morning?" she asked with a forced smile.

"Just coffee for me," Mrs. Orson answered.

Mrs. Harvey smiled up at her. "Do you have any of those fruit-filled pastries?"

Emily Jane returned her smile. Fruit-filled pastry was one of the new items she'd suggested that the bakery start serving. "Yes, ma'am, we have apple and peach this morning."

"I'd like to try the peach and a cup of your coffee."

"I'll have the same." Mrs. Wells dropped into the chair opposite her friends. Her bulky figure pressed against the table as she leaned forward to continue the conversation Emily Jane had interrupted. "Has anyone learned if they are staying? Mabel was a friend of mine, but even she would have understood our reluctance to having crying children in our quiet neighborhood."

Seldom did they ever agree upon anything, but it seemed lack of sleep had all five graying heads nodding in unison.

Emily Jane left them to their gossiping. Why did they have to be so mean? Rose and Ruby were children who had simply been overtired the night before. She placed the fruit pies on two small plates and poured two cups of coffee, then returned to the women's table.

"What are we going to do, if he stays here?" Mrs. Orson demanded.

She set the plates and steaming cups in front of the women. "I really don't think the girls will be that much trouble once they are settled." Emily Jane straightened her spine and resisted the urge to yawn again. "You know, talking about Mr. Barns and his children like this isn't very Christian-like, ladies."

Mrs. Green huffed. "Well, if you like Mr. Barns and his screaming children so much, why don't you marry the man and keep those kids quiet?"

Emily Jane stood there with her mouth hanging open. Were they serious? She…marry a man to keep his children quiet? She glanced about the table. The other four women nodded their heads in agreement.

"I am not the marrying kind, ladies. I have dreams of opening my own bakery someday, and those dreams do not include a man with two children." She offered each of them a smile, before hurrying to the kitchen and away from their speculative looks.

A little while later, Emily Jane entered the front door of her home. She carried the box of baking supplies to the kitchen table. After talking to her neighbors, her thoughts had clung to what they'd said. She admitted to herself that they were right in that Rose and Ruby had cried most of the night. It amazed her that the girls' voices had carried so clearly upon the still night air, keeping most everyone in the neighborhood awake. But the plain and simple fact of the matter was that she could do nothing about their unhappiness. She wondered briefly why that bothered her so much.

She emptied the box, placing each item on the kitchen table. Today she was going to try her hand at adding a new ingredient to her oatmeal raisin cookie recipe. One of the joys of her job was that Violet, the manager of the bakery, supplied the ingredients for her to bake up new recipes. In return, once the recipe was perfected, Emily Jane fixed it at the bakery. Customers seemed to love her new creations.

As she mixed the flour with the rest of the ingredients, Emily Jane's thoughts drifted to the women. She'd been surprised at their suggestion that she marry William Barns. Did they really think that if she married him, then the girls would settle down? How rude of them.

Emily Jane stirred the mixture hard and fast. There was no way she'd marry William Barns. She had no intention of marrying anyone and definitely not a man with children. The girls did remind Emily Jane of her own sisters, but that was no reason to get married to a complete stranger, not that he'd asked her. She shook her head. No, she wasn't getting married now or anytime soon; she had a dream of opening her own bakery someday, and that dream didn't include a family or a man who might be like her father and think he could control everything she did.

Chapter Three

William stood holding a niece on each hip. He stared at the group of five women, wondering if they had lost their minds. He could see one or even two of them being a little addled due to age, but all five?

"We're not asking you to move away, at least not right now. All we're asking is that you consider Miss Rodgers as a future bride. She could help you with the girls, and she really is a sweet little thing," Mrs. Harvey said as the others nodded their agreement.

When the women had stopped him on the sidewalk in front of the bank and introduced themselves as his neighbors, he'd been happy to meet them; but now they were butting in where they didn't belong, and he planned to put a stop to their meddling. "Look, ladies, I know you mean well, but I have no intentions of marrying Miss Rodgers or anyone else. Now if you will excuse me, I'm going home." William thought they'd move to the side and let him pass.

He thought wrong.

Mrs. Orson put both hands on her chubby hips and demanded, "Why not? Those girls need a mama. If they had a mama, she'd know how to keep them quiet so a body could rest at night like God intended. Miss Rodgers comes from a large family. She's perfect and knows how to take care of small children."

So that was it; they didn't care about Miss Rodgers. They just wanted him to keep the girls quiet. Rose sucked her thumb with her head on his shoulder. Ruby's chubby little hand played with the hair on the back of his neck. He returned his attention to the ladies. "You're right, but I'm not the man to get one for them. I'm sorry we disturbed your sleep last night. I'll try to keep them quieter."

"If you are going to stick around here, won't you need a wife to take care of the children while you work?" Miss Cornwell asked in a quiet voice.

The elderly woman did have a point. He'd need someone to help him take care of the girls but didn't think the woman had to be his wife. Surely he could pay someone to watch Ruby and Rose.

Thanks to his visit to the bank, William now knew that his grandmother's house belonged to him and his sister, Mary. A lump formed in his throat as he thought of Mary. Now that she was gone, William would make sure that the girls would own the other half of the house. He'd made arrangements for his money from the sale of the mercantile to be transferred from the bank in Denver to the Granite bank. Then he'd walked over to the general store and asked about the job Miss Leland had mentioned the night before.

Mr. Moore had eyed the girls and then agreed to give William the job. He'd asked William if he could work from ten in the morning until four in the afternoon, and William had agreed.

"You ladies wouldn't happen to know of any young ladies who would be willing to watch the girls while I work, would you?" He hoped the change of subject would sidetrack them enough to drop the idea of him marrying Miss Rodgers.

Mrs. Orson sighed. "You got a job?"

"Why, yes, ma'am, I did." He looked directly at the sour-faced woman.

She shook her head. "I see. The only lady I know of who is home during the day and able to keep up with two small children would be Miss Rodgers." Mrs. Orson looked to the other women for agreement. "Emily Jane gets home around eight thirty every morning. Isn't that right, ladies?"

The group nodded. He could see the spark of joy and scheming in their eyes. William couldn't believe he'd walked right into their plans for him and Emily Jane. Well, hiring the woman to watch the girls and marrying her to watch the girls were two very different things.

Rose began to fuss at standing in place too long. Ruby decided it was time to join her sister in the protest, and she too began whining and trying to push out of his arms.

"If you will excuse me, ladies, I need to get these wiggle worms home."

William took a step but stopped when Mrs. Green called to him.

"Mr. Barns, you will check with Emily Jane about watching the girls, won't you?" she inquired.

"She is really good with young children. After all, she has had lots of practice," Mrs. Harvey prompted.

They were an insistent bunch, he'd give them that. He grinned at Mrs. Harvey. "I'll ask her, and thank you for the recommendation." William hurried down the sidewalk toward home but could still hear them as he walked away.

"He really seems like a nice young man."

"I think he and Emily Jane would make a nice couple, don't you, Lois?"

"I do hope those girls settle down soon. I need my sleep," another grumbled.

"Well, after a woman gets her hands on them, I'm sure they will become little darlings, and Emily Jane is just the woman for the job," Mrs. Orson said in a no-nonsense tone.

Their voices faded as William hurried toward the house. As soon as he started walking again, the girls quieted down. They were already little darlings. He really didn't see that having a woman in their lives would change them that much.

Each girl laid her little head on his shoulder. It was a short walk to his grandmother's house, now his and the girls' new home. He reached for the doorknob and found a small cloth bag hanging on it.

William ignored it; even though his curiosity was stirred, his hands were full. He carried the girls inside for a morning nap. After changing their diapers, he put them in their cradles. Thankfully, they curled up and went to sleep almost immediately.

Tiptoeing from the bedroom, William sighed and closed the door. His gaze moved about the sitting room. Thanks to Miss Leland and Miss Rodgers, the house now looked and smelled fresh. Once they'd started cleaning the night before, they hadn't stopped until the whole house shone.

He remembered the bag on the front doorknob and went to retrieve it. The sweet scent of sugar and spice filled his nostrils. William pulled it open and saw two cookies inside. Had Emily Jane brought them over? Or perhaps another neighbor. Until he found out, William decided not to give them to the girls.

After the racket the girls had made last night, it wouldn't surprise him if one of the neighbors put a sleeping draft in the cookies. He grinned at the silliness of his thoughts. Still, he'd wait on giving them to the girls until he was sure they were safe.

He walked over to a big chair and sank into its cushions, laying the cookie-filled bag on the side table. A yawn stretched his mouth wide. Nap time for the girls was one of his favorite times of the day. Often at night, one or both of them would wake up fussy. When was the last time he'd gotten a full night's sleep? As his eyes drifted shut, William's thoughts went to Emily Jane Rodgers. Would she watch the children? If so, he silently prayed she could get the girls into a regular sleeping routine.

Emily Jane pulled a fresh batch of oatmeal raisin cookies from the oven. She never tired of the baking smells that filled the kitchen. This recipe was no exception. She'd played with the ingredients a bit and liked the results. *A pinch of this and a pinch of that* had been her mother's motto, but Emily Jane liked the results of being precise with her measurements. She wrote everything down as she went, and if the dessert turned out well, she could fix it over and over again without adjusting anything.

She put the cookies on a cooling rack and sat at the table to sip her coffee. All morning she'd been thinking about the neighbor ladies. How could they be so mean? Yes, children were noisy, yes, they cried, and, yes, the twins' voices did carry on the night breezes, but that was still no reason to wish them gone. A smile teased her lips as she thought about how they would have reacted if they'd lived near her family. Her five brothers and six sisters were far from quiet.

Living out in the middle of nowhere pretty much explained why she and her sisters Sarah and Elsie had never married. There were no boys nearby to marry. Anxiety spurted through her. Had twenty-two-year-old Sarah and twenty-one-year-old Elsie been forced to answer mail-order-bride ads, too? Emily Jane hoped not, but then again, if it worked out as well for them as it had for her, maybe it would be the best thing for her sisters.

She thought over her own experience as a mail-order bride. Thanks to her father's decision to lessen the mouths he had to feed, Emily Jane had answered an ad. She'd arrived in Granite, Texas, expecting to be courted by Levi Westland. His mother had written to Emily Jane and two other women telling them to come to Granite. She'd promised Emily Jane that if Levi didn't choose her as his bride, then she'd help her find a husband.

Emily Jane shook her head as memories flooded her mind. She hadn't wanted a husband then but wanted to be obedient to her father's wishes and had come to Granite. It had been a relief when Levi had chosen Millie Hamilton as his new wife.

After Levi and Millie's wedding, Bonnie Westland had offered to make good on her promise of a husband, but Emily Jane had assured her she was happy without one right now. Thankfully, Bonnie had understood but still assured Emily Jane that, should she change her mind, she'd be willing to help her find the perfect man. As if there were such a thing as a perfect man.

Emily Jane walked to the sink and placed her coffee cup in the hot soapy water. She hadn't written her family since she'd arrived in Granite. The last thing she wanted was for Pa to tell her to come home and start the husband hunt all over again.

Still, she often thought about her siblings. Her sense of loss was beyond tears. She missed their laughter; she missed her sisters whispering in bed at night so as not to wake their parents. She found herself listening sometimes for their voices. And the little ones—tears welled within her eyes—how she missed cuddling their bodies close, burying her nose in their necks and smelling the powdery softness. Her lips pressed shut, so no sound would burst out. It had been a long time since she'd felt such a strong urge to cry. She straightened her shoulders and dared the tears to fall. Yes, Ruby and Rose made her homesick to see her family again, but her time of grieving the loss of her siblings was over. She'd proved adept at handling herself without any help from others and couldn't afford to be distracted by homesickness.

Emily Jane placed the cooled cookies into the metal cookie bin and decided to work on a new batch. Cookies that were different, plus a new recipe would take her mind off family. She'd wanted to try her hand at making lemon cookies and had gotten the ingredients to try them.

A knock at the front door pulled her away from the bowl of flour. Emily Jane wiped her hands on her apron. She'd had more company in the past two days than she'd had in a month. A chuckle escaped her as she realized that that really wasn't much company, just Mr. Barns and his nieces. Very seldom did anyone come calling during the day.

She pulled the door open and found them standing on the porch as if just by thinking their names they'd appeared. "Hello, Mr. Barns. Please come in."

He stepped inside and inhaled. "Something sure smells good in here."

Emily Jane grinned at the two girls looking over their uncle's shoulder. "I just baked a batch of oatmeal raisin cookies. Would you like to try them?" Heat filled the room, making it warmer than it had been a few moments earlier, so Emily Jane left the front door open.

"If it wouldn't be too much trouble, we'd love to try them. Wouldn't we, girls?" He followed Emily Jane into the kitchen.

"No trouble at all. I've been experimenting, so you'll be the first to taste my new creation." She took Rose from him and set her on the floor.

He set Ruby down beside her sister and frowned. "Experimenting?" William placed the girls' bag on the floor at his feet.

Emily Jane saw the worry on his face and laughed. "Yes, experimenting. I do it all the time with cookies, cakes, bread and different kinds of pastries." She picked up a cookie and handed it to him.

She scooped two sugar cookies from a plate on the sideboard and handed one to each of the girls. "Here you go," Emily Jane said as their chubby little hands wrapped around the sweet treats.

Emily Jane watched William take a big bite and then close his eyes. "Well, what do you think?" The lines of concentration deepened along his brows. She waited for his reply, surprised at her feelings of uncertainty.

He swallowed and then opened eyes that brimmed with appreciation. "I think you can test your cookies out on me anytime. These are delicious." William popped the rest of the cookie into his mouth and looked to the sideboard, where more cookies rested on various plates.

"How about some coffee to go with a small plate of cookies?" Emily Jane moved to the coffeepot and poured him a generous cup.

"Both sound wonderful." He sat down at the table.

Emily Jane's gaze moved to the girls, who happily nibbled at their sugar cookies. She should have set them at the table but no matter; the crumbs could be swept up after they left.

"Did you leave a couple of cookies on my door this morning for the girls?" William asked.

She nodded. "I hope you don't mind."

"Not at all. I just wanted to make sure it was you before I let them have them." His grin brightened his face.

Emily Jane decided not to focus on his good looks and placed several cookies onto a dessert plate. She carried them to the table and set them in front of William. "So, what brings you over? Surely it wasn't the cookies I left for the girls." She sat down across from him.

"Straight to the point. I like that in a woman." He set his coffee cup down. "This morning I had a chat with the neighbor ladies."

She looked down at the angelic faces covered in cookie crumbs. *Oh, please, Lord, don't let him be here to ask me to marry him and take care of the girls.*

"And they suggested you might be interested in watching the girls while I work." He searched her face, his eyes curiously observing. She wondered briefly what he expected her face to reveal. Emily Jane had no idea. His voice was calm and steady and gave nothing away. "This morning Mr. Moore offered me a job working in his store from ten to four every day. He suggested I find someone to watch the girls and start work this afternoon. I sort of hoped you'd be able to watch them today."

She wanted to help him, she really did, but the thought of growing attached to the girls worried her. And how much time would they take from her experimental cooking?

"What hours did you say you would have to work?" Something in his eyes beseeched her to help.

"From ten to four."

She found herself nodding. "I'll help, but only until you can find someone else."

A sweet grin split his lips, revealing straight white teeth.

"That's all I'm asking. Thank you. I'll be back a few minutes after four to pick them up. Thank you again."

William hurried from the house as if he suspected she might change her mind at any moment.

As the door closed behind him, Emily Jane asked herself the hard questions. Had she done the right thing by agreeing to help him? Emily Jane knew it was the right thing to do, but was it the right thing for her? Was it possible she'd lose her heart to these darling little girls and William?

Chapter Four

Emily Jane didn't have time to think any more about the choice she'd made in watching the girls. Rose began to cry almost as soon as the door closed behind William. She scooped down and picked up the little girl. "Now what are you fussing about? He'll be back soon." She patted the little girl's back.

Thankfully, even with a wet diaper, Rose stopped her complaining and nestled close to Emily Jane. She looked down at Ruby and saw the little girl crawling toward the sitting room.

First thing she'd need to do was find a way to confine the twins to one area. Unlike their uncle, Emily Jane couldn't hold them both at once, at least not all the time, and strapping them to a chair all afternoon wasn't an option. "You two are lucky I have little brothers and sisters and know how to build a fun pen for you to play in."

She set Rose down and snatched up Ruby before she could crawl from the room. Someone knocked at the front door. "Now, who do you suppose that is?" Emily Jane asked Ruby, who wiggled in her arms, trying to get down.

"Who is it?" Emily Jane called.

"Elsie Matthews, dear."

Mrs. Matthews was a sweet woman who lived two houses down. In her late sixties, she was the least of the busybodies who lived in the neighborhood. "Come in, Mrs. Matthews. We're in the kitchen."

The door opened, and the older woman stepped inside. "I hope I'm not disturbing you."

Emily Jane motioned her in. "Not at all. I was just figuring out how I would manage these two this afternoon. Can you stay long?"

"Long enough. What can I help you with?" She pulled her shawl from around her slight shoulders and hung it on the nearest kitchen chair.

Rose crawled over to the older woman and pulled on her skirt. "Up," said the little girl, smiling.

Emily Jane watched as Mrs. Matthews scooped the child into her arms and tickled her belly. "So you were one of the wee folk making all that noise last night, weren't you?"

In reply, Rose giggled.

Emily Jane carried Ruby to the center of the kitchen and set her down again. "They both need baths. Would you mind keeping an eye on them for just a second while I step out back and get the washtub?"

"Be happy to, but are you going to drag in that big tub just to give these two a bath? Wouldn't it be easier to just wash them one at a time in the washbasin?" Mrs. Matthews placed Rose beside her sister.

Emily Jane laughed. "Yes, but the washtub will hold them both. I'm going to use it as a pen so that I can get some work done."

"That's an excellent idea." Mrs. Matthews's light auburn hair streaked with gray bobbed on the top of her head as she nodded her approval.

Emily Jane hurried to where their washtub sat by the

back door. Normally they did their laundry on Saturday, so the tub would be available for the girls to play in for a couple of days yet. William should have someone else lined up to watch the girls by then.

Rose and Ruby giggled and crawled after Emily Jane. Mrs. Matthews laughed. "Oh, no, you don't. You two have to stay and play with me for a few minutes." She knelt down, offering her apron strings for them to pull on.

Emily Jane lugged the big tub inside. It was wooden with metal rings around the top, middle and bottom of it, the perfect size to hold two little girls. Normally Anna Mae helped her carry it inside, but since she wasn't available and Mrs. Matthews had her hands full with the girls, Emily Jane tugged on it until she got it into the kitchen.

Mrs. Matthews hurried over. "Here, let me help you with that."

Together they set it against the wall by the back door. "I think you might need something soft inside for them to sit and play on."

"I'll go get a blanket, be right back." She hurried to her bedroom and grabbed a small nine-patch quilt from the foot of her bed. It was her reading quilt. She enjoyed curling up in it and reading her Bible before going to sleep each night.

When she returned to the kitchen, she saw that Mrs. Matthews stood holding Rose with Ruby sitting at her feet pulling at the buttons on her black shoes. "This should do it." Emily Jane spread the quilt out in the bottom of the tub and then reached for Ruby. Mrs. Matthews added Rose.

The girls grinned up at them. They really were sweet little things. Emily Jane went to the cupboard and pulled out spoons and pans for the girls to play with.

"Would you like a cup of tea?" Emily Jane asked.

Mrs. Matthews sat down in a chair at the table. "I'd love one. And while you are making it, I'll keep an eye on the girls. Maybe you could tell me how you ended up with these two this afternoon?"

Emily Jane nodded. "Mr. Barns, Mabel's grandson, started work this afternoon at the general store. Some of our neighbors suggested I'd be a good person to watch them." She poured water into a large pail for the girls' bath and also filled the teapot.

"Oh, I'm sure they did." Mrs. Matthews laughed. "They came over to the house this morning, complaining about the girls crying last night. You'd think they were all a hundred years old the way they gripe."

Trying to hide a smile, Emily Jane nodded. "Yes, they came by the bakery this morning, too."

"Meddling old hens." Mrs. Matthews's hazel eyes met hers. "I'm sure they had a lot to say."

Warmth filled Emily Jane's cheeks as she remembered them suggesting she marry William Barns and give the girls a mother. She shook her head at the memory. "Can you believe they suggested I marry him?"

"Why?" Mrs. Matthews tilted her head to the side and scrunched up her brow. "I mean, for goodness' sake, you just met the man."

Her expression was comical, and Emily Jane giggled. "To give his nieces a mother. They seem to think a mother would be able to stop them from crying at night."

"That's preposterous." Mrs. Matthews cooed down at the twins. Emily Jane gazed at the girls, who looked so much like William. *Where are their parents?* she wondered. *And why aren't they taking care of the girls?*

A few minutes after four that afternoon, William knocked on Emily Jane's front door. Weariness seeped through his bones like honey from a leaky jug. Working with Mr. Moore hadn't been hard. It was the sleepless night up with the girls. His energy level was zero and his nerves stretched tight.

She opened the door with a smile and stepped back to allow him inside. The aroma of fried ham drifted to William, reminding him he still needed to feed the girls. His stomach growled, so to cover his embarrassment, William said, "Something sure smells good in here."

"I'm glad you think so. We saved a plate for you." Emily Jane motioned for him to follow her.

He didn't need to be asked twice. William shut the door and did as she bade. His gaze took in the clean kitchen and the girls.

Surrounded by blankets, they were playing in a large washtub. Their hair and faces looked freshly washed, only neither wore their ribbons. Shock filled him. How was he going to tell them apart? "Miss Rodgers, what happened to the girls' hair ribbons?" He knew the question came out tight and sounding angry, but he couldn't stop the feelings of confusion and fear coursing through him.

Ruby and Rose squealed with happiness at the sound of his voice. They scrambled to pull themselves up on the side of the tub. He knelt and gave them both hugs. They smelled of soft, clean powder.

"Oh, they were horrible, so I threw them out." She pulled a covered plate from the back of the stove and turned to face him.

"I remember specifically telling you that those ribbons were the only way I could identify them. Did you forget?" As he looked into the identical faces, he felt robbed. Something important had been taken from him.

How was he going to know which girl was Rose and which one was Ruby?

She set the plate down on the table. "No, I remember. But since Rose has a birthmark behind her right knee, I didn't think you'd mind me throwing out the ribbons. They were pretty ragged, and I plan to replace them. I just haven't had time yet."

William picked up the little girl closest to him and looked at her leg. How had he missed the small brown mark that looked like an ant behind her knee? He should have seen it. Maybe the girls did need a woman's care. He kissed Rose on the cheek and then put her back into the tub. "No, that won't be necessary."

Ruby extended her arms, reaching for William to give her a cuddle and kiss, too. He obliged by picking her up and kissing her soft cheek. She giggled.

When William set her back down, he noticed two colorful cloth balls in the tub with them. Picking one up, he said, "These are pretty."

Emily Jane poured a glass of water and set it beside his plate. "Mrs. Matthews, another one of our neighbors, brought those by earlier for the girls. You should come eat this before it gets cold."

William gave the ball to Rose and stood. "I appreciate all you've done for the girls today."

"It wasn't much."

He laughed. "You gave them a bath. That's huge. I put off doing that until I can't stand the smell anymore. They are a handful at bath time." William sat down and lifted the cover from his plate of fried ham, mashed potatoes and green beans.

Her gentle laugh had his gaze moving to her face. "Well, that explains a lot."

William laughed with her and then offered a quick

grace before forking a chunk of ham and chomping into it. "You know, if you keep feeding us, I'm going to have to pay for my meals here, too."

Rose chose that moment to fuss. She was tired of being in the tub. Emily Jane walked over and picked her up. "Shhhh, little one, Anna Mae has a headache. We don't want to wake her, do we?" She leaned the little girl against her shoulder and rubbed her back.

"I'm awake," Anna Mae said as she entered the room. She smiled at William and the girls on her way to the coffeepot. "I think my headache has about run its course." She poured a cup of the fragrant liquid.

Emily Jane smiled. "I'm glad."

Anna Mae returned to the table and sat down. "How was your first day at work, Mr. Barns?" She took a sip and studied him over the rim of her cup.

William sat up a little straighter in his chair. He cleared his throat before saying, "I believe it went well. Wilson says I'm a natural."

Anna Mae nodded. "I'm sure you are. Isn't today the day that supplies arrive from Austin?" she asked, still keeping her gaze locked on him.

"Yes, ma'am. It is."

Anna Mae grinned across at him. "Please, there are no ma'ams here. Call me Miss Anna Mae, and you may address Emily Jane as Miss Emily Jane. I believe that is formal enough for around town and here at home. Don't you, Emily Jane?"

"That will be fine."

William nodded his agreement. He could tell by the stiffness in her voice that Emily Jane wasn't pleased with him calling her by her given name but that she'd complied out of politeness.

"Now that that is settled, would you mind telling us

what arrived from Austin today?" Anna Mae asked, setting her cup down.

Ruby had been left out of the conversation long enough. She squealed, letting them know she too wanted out of the tub.

William rose to get her.

Anna Mae waved him back into his seat. "I'll get her. Please, continue eating and tell us all about your day."

William did as Anna Mae requested. He found the schoolteacher to be a delight. She seemed truly interested in his everyday goings-on, and Ruby cuddled close to her as if they were meant to be together. Of the two ladies, Anna Mae might be a better choice for the girls as a new mother. Even so, he didn't feel the same attraction toward her as he did with Emily Jane. That line of thinking was dangerous. William focused on his food.

He finished his meal as quickly as possible and then stood to leave. "Thank you for dinner and taking care of the girls today, Miss Emily Jane." William picked up the girls' bag. "Tomorrow Mr. Moore and I are going to put up a poster announcing that I need someone to watch the girls. Do you mind taking care of them one more day?" While he talked, William dug around in the blankets in the tub.

Emily Jane handed Rose to Anna Mae and then picked up his dirty dishes. "That will be fine." She stopped and watched him for a moment. "What are you looking for?"

He straightened and said, "The girls' stuffed animals."

She carried the plate, silverware and cup to the dish tub. "They are still in your bag." Emily Jane poured more hot water over the dishes.

William turned with a frown on his face. "Then how did you get them to take their afternoon nap? They can't sleep without their toys."

Emily Jane turned with a sweet smile. "They didn't take an afternoon nap."

As if to confirm her words, Rose yawned. Ruby followed suit. The little girl snuggled closer to Anna Mae.

"No nap?" William couldn't believe it. Over the past few weeks, he'd taken to putting the girls down for an hour or more every morning and again in the afternoon so that he could get some much-needed rest, too.

She shook her head. "No nap."

"Why not?" William asked.

Anna Mae answered. "So that they will sleep tonight." She stood and handed a very sleepy Ruby to William and Rose over to Emily Jane.

"And they didn't fuss?" he asked as Ruby cuddled up against his shoulder.

Emily Jane wiped her free hand off on her apron. "No, they were too busy playing with Mrs. Matthews and sampling cookies. Tomorrow we'll start with a short nap in the afternoon and then see how well they sleep. But for tonight you should have no trouble whatsoever getting them to sleep the night through." She smiled at Rose, who stared back at her with big blue eyes.

Baffled at how easily Emily Jane seemed to have taken care of his nieces, William patted Ruby on the back. He did like the idea of them sleeping all night.

Anna Mae shook her head. "My head is beginning to ache again. Emily Jane will help you get home."

"That isn't necessary." William walked to Emily Jane with the idea of taking Rose into his free arm.

Rose curled up against Emily Jane's chest. "Nonsense. It won't take me a minute to walk over and lay her down." Emily Jane's face softened as the little girl closed her eyes and stuck her thumb into her mouth.

He nodded. "All right." William followed her as she

led the way across the kitchen, through the sitting room and outside. Her light blue skirt swished against the wooden porch steps as she descended.

"It's a lovely evening." Her soft voice floated back to him much like the fireflies that buzzed about the yard.

A cool breeze brushed across his cheeks, bringing with it the ever-present scents of cinnamon and sugar. He inhaled. "It sure is."

They walked side by side to his house. *His house.* Six months ago, William wouldn't have thought he'd be in Granite, Texas. Sorrow hit him full in the chest. If he'd known six months ago that both his sister and his grandmother would be gone, he'd have spent more time with them and less time trying to build a business.

"So far, spring is my favorite season in Texas." Emily Jane pulled him from his sad thoughts.

He slipped around her and opened the door. "I take it you aren't from around here?" William stepped back so that she could slip past him.

"No, I grew up in Kansas." She walked back to the bedroom and laid Rose down in one of the cradles.

William placed Ruby into the other. Both girls curled up and closed their eyes. He was amazed at how quickly they went down.

William asked, "When was the last time they were changed?" William hated asking such a delicate question, but the thought of them, their bedding and their toys being wet in the morning didn't appeal to him. He'd rather change them now and not have to deal with the mess later.

A dimple in her right cheek winked up at him as she grinned. "Right before you arrived. They should stay dry for the rest of the night. I doubled their diapers just in case they fell asleep before you got them home." She walked toward the bedroom door.

Why hadn't he thought of doing that at night? Emily Jane truly was a woman who knew how to take care of children. He followed her from the room and then gently shut the door behind them.

Emily Jane continued toward the front door. She stepped out on the porch. "I'll see you tomorrow."

"Thank you again." William leaned against the door-jamb and watched her hurry back to her house. She really was a pretty little thing, red hair, green eyes and that cute dimple that had made its appearance tonight. Given enough time, would Miss Emily Jane change her mind and be interested in taking on a more permanent position watching his nieces?

Chapter Five

The next morning as he entered The Bakery, William marveled at the fact that both girls had slept through the night. He carried them to the nearest table and sat down. Aware of several sets of eyes upon them, he sighed. People were forever staring at him and the twins. He wasn't sure if it was because it was uncommon to see a man with two little girls alone or if it was because the girls were twins.

"Good morning. You must be William Barns." William looked up into the face of a smiling woman. "My name is Violet Atwood. What can I get for you and these two darlings this morning?" Violet's hazel eyes studied him with a curious intensity.

Had Emily Jane mentioned him and the girls? Was that how Violet Atwood knew of them? Or had others been talking about him? His thoughts went to the group of ladies who'd spoken to him the day before. Now there definitely was the possibility that they had mentioned them.

He realized that Miss Atwood was waiting to take his order. William cleared his throat before saying, "Good morning. I'd like a cup of coffee for myself and a slice of bread for the girls. Nothing too sweet." William didn't mention that the cookies he'd given them for breakfast already had them squirmier than two playful puppies. He looked down at his nieces.

Rose was attempting to grab Ruby. Ruby pulled against his arm to get at the salt and pepper shakers on the table. It was all he could do to hold on to the two wiggling girls. He sighed.

"Be right back with your order."

He nodded and tightened his grip on the children. His gaze followed Violet Atwood about the room. Her graying brown hair had been piled up onto the top of her head. Miss Atwood wore a brown day dress with a white apron that covered her ample stomach. William wasn't sure about her age but was impressed with the way she zipped about the tables, refilling coffee cups and then hurrying back to the front of the bakery, where he could see her laying out slices of bread on a plate and pouring his cup of coffee.

She seemed to be the only one working in the small establishment. Had Emily Jane already finished for the day? He'd hoped to see her this morning.

Ruby knocked the salt over, and Rose kicked her feet with joy at the sight. The two girls giggled, bringing more attention from the other diners. William righted the salt-shaker and pushed a little farther away from the table.

"I imagine those two keep you pretty busy." Violet set the plate of bread and coffee on the opposite side of the table out of Rose and Ruby's reach. "I have just what you need to be able to eat and drink in comfort. Be right back."

William didn't have time to comment as she whirled around and headed through a small side door that he'd assumed earlier led to the kitchen. Both Rose and Ruby were pulling against his arm to get to the plate of bread.

He wished he had some form of harness to put on the little girls. William both dreaded and welcomed the day they'd be able to walk and sit in a chair on their own.

The sound of wood bumping against wood drew his attention back to the side door. He could see Violet wrestling with something and then heard Emily Jane's soft voice. "Here, let me help you with that, Violet." Emily Jane came through the door and held it open for the older woman.

"Oh, thank you, Emily Jane. I don't know what I'd do without you."

Emily Jane's teasing laughter and words floated to him. "Learn to prop the door open before trying to force a high chair through it?"

Violet giggled like a schoolgirl. "I suppose so. Now, get out of my way so that I can get this to our customers."

Emily Jane turned around. Her big green eyes settled on William and the little girls. He wondered if she'd be upset that he'd brought them to her place of work; after all, she'd seen quite a bit of them since they'd arrived.

A smile brought the dimple in her cheek out of hiding as she followed Violet to their table. "Good morning, Mr. Barns." Emily Jane reached for Rose, who at the moment was pulling on the tablecloth, inching the bread and coffee closer with each tug.

He handed his niece over. "Good morning to you, too." William turned his attention to the high chair. It stood about thirty-five inches tall with a dark varnish over red with stenciled white flowers on the wide headrest. "I wish I had brought one of those from Mary's house. It sure would have made things easier at home."

Violet finished making sure it was secure and motioned for Emily Jane to place the little girl inside. "You can always stop by Levi Westland's furniture store and see if he has any more available. He made this one special for the bakery." She ran her hand over the pinewood.

"That's a splendid idea." William grinned up at her. Rose banged her small hands against the wooden tray in front of her. Ruby tried to do the same to the table but William moved her to his other side, farther away from her target.

"Emily Jane, are you going over to the general store on your way home today?" Violet asked as she placed a bit of bread into Rose's hand. She handed the other half to Ruby.

Emily Jane nodded. "Want me to pick up something for you?"

While Ruby's hands were full of bread, William reached for his coffee. Maybe now was the time to go to the general store, too. He needed to replenish his grandmother's cupboards, and if Emily Jane was going and had any suggestions on what he'd need, he'd welcome them.

"Well, if it's not too much trouble. We could use more coffee." Violet patted Rose on the head.

"No trouble at all." Emily Jane smiled at her boss.

William jumped into the conversation. "Well, speaking of trouble, I'm not sure what to pick up to replenish Grams's cupboards. Would you mind if the girls and I tagged along with you?" He sipped his coffee and watched her over the rim of his cup.

For a brief moment, Emily Jane looked as if she were going to refuse his request. Her gaze moved from him to the girls. He suspected it was the way the girls were gobbling their bread, as if they'd not eaten all morning, that persuaded her to agree. "I'll be happy to help you find what you need." She turned toward the kitchen, untying her apron strings as she left the table. "Let me finish up in the kitchen. I'll only be a few minutes."

"Take your time." William smiled into his cup. So far the day was turning out quite nicely. The girls had slept in; he'd managed to have a cup of coffee, and now Miss Emily Jane was going with them to the general store. She'd know what he'd need for the house and the girls. His mood turned a bit somber as the familiar feelings of insecurity attacked him. There was so much he didn't know about the care and future of little girls. Which, if he were truthful, was why he'd ended up at The Bakery today anyway. He'd forgotten to replenish the cupboards. Anyone else would have remembered that babies needed to be fed as soon as they arose in the mornings, but, no, he hadn't even thought of it.

And their clothes. He continued the self-incriminating examination. Who would change a baby's diaper without getting the needed items first? He'd changed Ruby this morning and forgotten the clean diaper. He shifted nervously in his seat, assailed by a terrible sense of helplessness. He ate a slice of the bread and finished his coffee.

"I'm sorry. That took a little longer than I'd anticipated." Emily Jane breezed back in as swiftly as she had left. Her gaze moved to the girls. "Are we ready to go?" she asked, smiling at the girls.

"We're ready." William stood. The soft scent of cinnamon teased his nose as Emily Jane bent over and lifted Rose from the chair. "I thought you had escaped out the back door so you wouldn't have to be troubled by us today," he teased.

"I'm sorry," she said, her voice soft and clear. "I couldn't leave till I cleaned up the mess I made. Violet works the crowd alone when I'm gone, and the added work would not have been fair."

Her face was full of strength, shining with a steadfast and serene peace. He realized that he felt hope when he was around her. Things didn't look so bleak. She laughed softly at Rose's gaze of happiness when she kissed her on the neck, eliciting soft giggles from the child. Suddenly the morning seemed to be going splendidly.

William turned toward the door without waiting for her to follow. He felt totally bewildered by his behavior. First he was sad at the loss of his family, then happy at having Emily Jane enter his life, then uncertain how to deal with the girls and his slight attraction to Emily Jane. What on earth had caused this tumble of confused thoughts and feelings?

Not since he was a kid had a woman caused so many conflicting emotions. And he'd just met this one. Maybe he was turning into a ninny. A setting hen. It had to be because he'd been taking care of babies. That had to be it. Everyone turned to mush around them. He clenched his jaw and imposed an iron control over his thoughts. Enough. He needed a little time away from Emily Jane to remind himself that she had no power to change him. She did not hold the key to his happiness, nor his thought process. And contrary to what the little old ladies in this town thought, he was not going to marry her only to have his heart broken when she decided that taking care of Rose and Ruby was too much work.

Chapter Six

Emily Jane enjoyed the walk to the store. Rose giggled as they strolled. The twin pointed at a little boy and his dog as they ran across the street. Ruby giggled along with her while William strode in silence. She couldn't help but wonder if he regretted inviting her along. His brows were pulled into an affronted frown, and a muscle flicked in his jaw. She didn't know him well enough, so she couldn't decide if he was angry or contemplating some deep subject.

The bell jingled overhead as he held the door open for her. She stepped inside the store and waited for a few seconds to give her eyes a moment to adjust. The wonderful scents of spices and leather filled her senses.

Carolyn Moore stood behind the counter. "Emily Jane, how good to see you." She walked over to where they stood. "Who is this cute little girl?" Carolyn asked, touching Rose's arm.

Rose tucked her thumb in her mouth and laid her head on Emily Jane's shoulder. She pressed her body as close to Emily Jane's as she could. For a brief moment, protectiveness rose in Emily Jane. She realized how foolish that was, considering the store owner was a good friend and would never hurt the child.

"This is Miss Rose." Emily Jane smiled at them both.

Carolyn laughed. "It's nice to meet you, Miss Rose." She turned her attention to William and the child he carried. "And who might this be?"

When William didn't answer but stood with his mouth twisted in a wry smile at Carolyn's teasing, Emily Jane answered. "That is Miss Ruby." Carolyn knew who both girls were, of course, but knew the method of pretend surprise would make the girls feel more comfortable. She was an old hand at winning children over.

"Well, hello, Miss Ruby." Carolyn laughed. "My, aren't we all being so formal today?" She waved her hand in front of her face much like Emily Jane assumed a woman of wealth would wave a fan.

Carolyn's laughter was contagious, and soon Emily Jane's, Ruby's and Rose's giggles joined in. William stared at them all as if they'd lost their minds. Emily Jane couldn't help but laugh harder, looking into his bemused face.

Mr. Carlson, Carolyn's elderly father, called from the back of the store. "Women sure are a funny breed. William, come on back here and let the women get their cackling done." He busily set up a checkerboard that was his constant companion.

"I'd love to, Phillip, but I need to get some shopping done before I return to work here in a bit," William called back to him.

Emily Jane enjoyed the way his voice rose to answer the other man. It was loud enough to be heard but not booming like her father's. So far there wasn't much she'd found dislikable about the man. From his beautiful blue eyes to his full lips. He carried himself with a commanding air of self-confidence, and yet there were times when he appeared so vulnerable.

Reining in her wayward thoughts, Emily Jane pulled her gaze from his handsome face and looked to Carolyn. Being caught staring at William caused heat to travel into Emily Jane's cheeks. She quickly blurted out, "Violet asked me to pick up some coffee for her, too."

The other woman grinned and nodded. "I'll have Amos run it over. He's been pestering us for a job this morning. We use him as needed to run deliveries for us, so he'll be happy for the work. I told him to come back in a bit, so he should return soon."

Emily Jane dug into her purse and pulled out a coin. "Would you make sure he gets this for helping me out?" She handed the money over with a smile and prayer that Carolyn would forget whatever thoughts she had about her and Mr. Barns. Amos and his mother could use the extra coinage, and Emily Jane was always happy to find a way to assist them. "Also, tell him to stop by the house when he gets done."

Carolyn looked at her with a quizzical expression. "We're paying him, Emily Jane."

Relief washed over Emily Jane that Carolyn seemed to be distracted now. "I know, but I want to make sure he knows he's appreciated." And that was the truth. Amos worked hard to help his ma out, and he was growing into a fine young man. For that Emily Jane was grateful.

An understanding glance passed between them before Carolyn tucked the money into her apron pocket and turned her attention to William. "Now, do you need any help with your shopping, Mr. Barns? I know you know where everything is, but with these two sweeties, I'm not sure you will be able to gather up what you came for. If you'd like, I could take your list and gather your supplies for you."

William shook his head. "No, thank you. I'm sure there are more things I'll need that I forgot to put on the list. Luckily, Miss Emily Jane has agreed to help me with the girls, so I should be able to manage for now."

Emily Jane nodded. "I'm going to pick up a few spices, too." She noticed a small wagon sitting beside the door. It had tall railings on each side and the back. Emily Jane pointed at it. "Carolyn, may we use that wagon?"

"Oh, yes. Of course."

She carried Rose to the wagon and set her inside. "Look, Rose. Want to ride?"

The little girl giggled and kicked her small legs. Emily Jane picked up the long handle and pulled Rose to William and Ruby.

"What a great idea." He put Ruby down beside her sister. The two girls laughed and banged against the wagon's sides. He dug inside the bag he had flung over his shoulder and gave both the girls their stuffed animals.

"Those should keep them busy while we get our shopping done." William made his way to the sugar and flour barrels. He pulled a sack from the pile and began filling it with sugar.

She heard him humming as he scooped the white granules into the bag. Emily Jane looked back at the girls, who seemed content to slap at each other with their toys and giggle. Experience with her siblings told her the girls wouldn't be content long. She hurried to help William complete his shopping so that she could get on with her own.

For the next thirty minutes, Emily Jane and William piled merchandise on the front counter while the children played in the wagon. She helped him pick out canned goods that the girls could eat, as well as breakfast foods such as eggs and salt pork.

Emily Jane looked at the mountain of supplies and decided that his basic shopping was complete. William had moved to the men's department, which consisted of ready-made shirts, pants and boots.

Happy to have his shopping done, she turned her attention to the fabric and ribbons. Emily Jane chose yellow and green ribbons to replace the girls' bows. Impulsively, she added matching yellow and green fabric. The girls needed new dresses, and since she was good friends with Susanna Marsh, the local dressmaker, Emily Jane decided to add those to William's pile.

Next, Emily Jane walked to the wall of spices. She needed baking soda, baking powder, cinnamon and ginger to resupply her baking cabinet at home. Thankfully, Levi Westland, the owner of The Bakery, had agreed to let her have a running tab at the general store so that she could practice making various sweet breads, tarts, pies, cakes and cookies for the eatery or she would not have been able to afford all the wonderful seasonings.

Someday she'd have her own bakery. It would be as big as The Bakery and would have round tables with blue-checkered tablecloths. She'd pay extra for a large glass window so that people passing by could see inside. And she'd also find a way for the smell of her freshly baked goods to vent outside and entice passersby to come inside.

The recipes she created each day and passed on to The Bakery were hers, and someday she'd be making them in her own store. She'd need to move from Granite, so that she wouldn't be in competition with Mr. Westland and Violet. Moving was not something she looked forward to doing. Emily Jane frowned, as she wondered once again where she would go.

A loud crash and the sound of splashing liquid snatched her from her daydreams. Twin cries erupted, and a strong vinegar odor permeated the small store, alerting everyone that the children were loose and wreaking havoc on their surroundings. Emily Jane followed her nose and reached the scene of the accident first. Pickle juice spread slowly across the floor. Candy and glass also splayed around the scene. The expressions on the twins' faces made Emily Jane want to double over in laughter, but the seriousness and cost of pulling the pickle barrel over and knocking it against the counter, causing the candy jar to break, could be more of a reason to join the crying girls. She rushed to their side.

Where was everyone else? Her gaze flashed to the front counter. Carolyn hurried through the door that led to their quarters behind the store. Mr. Carlson looked as if he'd just been startled from a nap, and William stood beside the boots, his mouth opened in a quick intake of breath. Surprise and dread had siphoned the blood from his face, and he appeared frozen in his steps.

Rose and Ruby screamed louder as their dresses and undergarments absorbed the liquid. Rose kept lifting one foot as if offended that the sticky juice covered it. Emily Jane lifted Ruby from the mess but held her out from her body, which infuriated the little one, and she curled her legs up trying to wrap them around Emily Jane's waist. Finally she could hold it no longer. Undiluted laughter floated up from her throat and burst from her lips in a great peal.

For a brief moment he'd allowed himself to relax. William had thought the girls were secure in the wagon, and he'd be able to shop without having to worry about them. He'd been wrong. What a nightmare. He should have known better.

He righted the pickle barrel, struggling to maintain an even, conciliatory tone to comfort the girls. "Shhhh." The noise did not cease. He looked Rose over to make sure she wasn't cut or hurt. The candy jar had broken into four pieces, none of which were close to the girls. He sighed as he picked up Rose and held her out in front of him like a sack of onions. He and Emily Jane looked like twin statues; but laughter danced in her eyes, and her lips curled into an irresistible grin. She looked quite lovely, and he found the thought vaguely disturbing.

More disturbing, though, was the racket the babies made; then Emily Jane surprised them all. Her nose crinkled, her lips puckered, and she blew through her lips, making a whistling sound that caused both Ruby and Rose to stop crying. Twin sets of blue eyes lifted to study her face. Their expressions stilled in wonder.

Carolyn ran to them. "Are they all right?" she asked.

"They are fine. Just wet," Emily Jane answered with a grin. "Aren't you, darling?" She wiggled the girl as if gently shaking the moisture from her dress.

"Mrs. Moore, I am so sorry," William began.

She stopped him by laying her hand on his arm. "It's not your fault or the girls'. It's mine. I knew I should have moved that barrel and placed it closer to the wall this morning." She laughed and dropped her hand. "But instead I was going to wait and have you do it this afternoon." Carolyn motioned for him to hand her Rose.

William did as she indicated and handed the wiggly girl over. He picked up the barrel. "Where would you like me to put it?" If the barrel had been full, the girls could never have tipped it over. His job was to fill it every evening; only yesterday they hadn't received new pickles to fill it with. When full, it would have been hard for even him to move.

"Over by the counter." She placed Rose into the wagon. "Bring the other baby over here, too, Emily Jane." Carolyn pointed to the wagon, and Emily Jane waddled to it, the baby extended awkwardly in front of her. Mr. Carlson came from the back room carrying a mop and a handful of rags. "Here, William, take these and wipe the bottom of the barrel before putting it down." He handed William the rags, then went to where the pickle juice covered the floor.

"Thank you, Phillip. I'm so sorry for the mess. Just give me a minute, and I'll come mop up the juice." William wiped the bottom of the barrel and then hurried to where Phillip sloshed the pickle juice around with the mop.

Emily Jane stood beside the wagon. She held their stuffed animals and danced a pretend waltz with them, entertaining Rose and Ruby and keeping the peace. Every time one of the twins reached for the stuffed animals, Emily Jane exaggerated a dip or swayed even faster. Rose began to sway with her, apparently hearing the same silent music. William stared at the scene and admired Emily Jane's intuition. She was a natural. Then why did he sometimes get the feeling she didn't like children?

Carolyn brought him a bucket to wring the juice from the mop. "It's amazing how fast little ones can make a mess." She gently removed the mop from his hands. "Here, I'll clean this up. Why don't you take the girls home and get them out of those wet dresses? I'll have Amos deliver your supplies when he comes in."

Emily Jane reached to take one of the girls from the wagon.

"I really am sorry," William apologized again.

"Emily Jane, leave those babies where they are. You can use the wagon to take them home and not have to soil your own clothes." She turned to William. "Don't give it another thought. Accidents happen. I'm just glad the little ones weren't hurt."

He nodded. "Thank you. I'll be back in a couple of hours." William took the wagon handle and pulled it through the door Emily Jane held open.

"I need to go pay for my things," she said when he had passed the threshold.

William nodded. Her voice sounded tight. He hesitated, blinking with bafflement. Hadn't she just appeared happy, dancing around the girls? But if he could garner a guess, he'd say she wasn't happy now. "I'm sorry we ruined your morning."

"Nonsense. Let me go pay for my things, and I'll help you get the girls cleaned up." Emily Jane shut the door behind her as she reentered the store.

He pulled the girls toward home. The older they got, the harder it was to take care of them. Emily Jane had tried to sound cheerful when she'd offered to help clean up the girls, but he could tell the incident had upset her.

Maybe she felt he'd taken advantage of her kindness. Maybe he had.

William's thoughts were full and troubled as he looked back at the little girls. They were happy to be riding in the wagon, and their big eyes darted from left to right, taking in their surroundings, completely unaware of the trouble they'd just caused. He sighed.

As soon as he could find someone else to watch them, he'd put some distance between himself and Miss Rodgers. He wanted to remain friends with her but feared the girls' antics would only make her feel used, and William didn't want that.

He had only a little over an hour, and the girls needed a bath and fresh clothes. Thankfully, he'd rinsed out their other two dresses the day before and they were cleaner than what they wore now. There was no time to warm up bathwater for them, so the girls would have to do with a quick wipe down with a wet cloth.

"Mr. Barns! Wait!" Emily Jane called.

William pulled the wagon to a stop and paused for her. When she caught up to him, Emily Jane said, "I thought you would wait for me."

"Oh, I figured you'd had enough of us by now. And I have to get these two pickles home and cleaned up before I bring them over to your house." He offered her a smile.

Emily Jane looked at the two girls. "That's why I stopped you. I always have hot water on the back of the stove."

Her sweet smile gave him hope that with her help, he'd learn how to take better care of the girls. A hope that died almost as swiftly as it had arrived. He should have been watching the girls at the store. What if Emily Jane helped him clean the girls now and then decided they were more work than she'd anticipated? What would he do then? Who would watch them?

The wheels of the wagon crunched on the dirt and rocks as he fell into step beside her. "Well, thank you. I know we've taken up most of your day, and I hadn't meant for that to happen."

His voice washed over her like a soothing balm. What was it about this man that made her want to help him? Was it his warm, caring voice, his brilliant blue eyes or the fact that he held an injured air about him? Emily Jane transferred her gaze to him. "You're welcome." She held the door open to the house and watched as he lifted the wagon onto the front porch. The muscles in his arms bulged, revealing the outward strength he possessed.

"I'm going to have to get me one of these," he said, stepping onto the porch and then pulling the wagon past her into the sitting room.

Emily Jane laughed. "I'm sure Mr. Westland will have one or maybe can make you one." She brushed around him and the girls and walked to the kitchen.

The wagon squeaked along behind her. "I hope so, but it looks like it will be this afternoon before I can get by there."

"I'll go get fresh towels and soap. Go ahead and take the girls to the kitchen." She hurried to her bedroom to gather what she'd need to get the girls clean again.

When she entered the kitchen once more, William and the girls waited patiently. Emily Jane knew the tots were getting sleepy and hoped the bath would revive them enough to eat lunch. She'd put them down for a nap later. She set the soap and towels down beside the sink, pulled an oversize tub from under the cabinet and began filling it with hot and cold water. Thankfully, the bucket of water she'd had heating on the stove wasn't too hot.

As she lathered the washcloth with the bar of soap, William pulled the little girls' dresses off. Emily Jane straightened and reached for the first child. "Let's give whoever you have ready a good scrubbing."

William handed over a smelly little girl. She kicked her legs, revealing the birthmark behind her right knee. "Here you go. She's all yours."

"Come along, Rose. Let's get this pickle smell off you." Emily Jane set the little girl into the water. The sweet smell of lavender-scented water filled the air.

Rose giggled and splashed.

"Where should I put these?" William asked, holding

up Rose's and Ruby's dresses and diapers. He crinkled his nose at the strong vinegar scent that floated from the garments.

"There is a washbasin just outside the back door. Drop them in it." While William took care of the soiled clothes, Emily Jane quickly began cleaning the little girl's face, arms and legs. She washed Rose's hair and then wrapped her up in a fluffy towel.

William reentered the room, and Emily Jane handed him Rose and picked up Ruby. She quickly dunked her into the warm water and proceeded to bathe her.

"You are very fast. I figured this would take a while." He held Rose close to his chest and inhaled the lavender fragrance of the soap.

Rose tittered and kicked her little feet within the soft towel.

"I've had lots of practice," Emily Jane answered as she poured water over Ruby's head, rinsing the soap from her hair. "Normally, I'd let them play in the water for a few minutes, but this tub is very small and the water will cool fast. I don't want them catching a cold." She picked up another towel and scooped Ruby from the water.

"Mrs. Orson mentioned you come from a large family."

So the neighbors had been talking about her. Emily Jane wasn't surprised. She was curious about what they'd said. "What else did Mrs. Orson have to say?" With the used washcloth, Emily Jane wiped pickle juice off the boards in the wagon, then gently lowered Ruby into it, still wrapped in the towel. She flinched at the sharpness in her voice.

Emily Jane motioned for him to do the same with Rose but kept her eyes trained questioningly on his face. He shrugged. "Not much, just that they thought you would make a good mother for the girls." William took the wagon handle and pulled it toward the door.

Shocked that Mrs. Orson and her friends would be so bold, Emily Jane shook her head. "I am not getting married."

The events of the entire day taunted her and reinforced her feelings on the matter. She didn't want to get married, did not want children. Today she'd forgotten the girls for just five minutes and look what had happened. Children needed constant supervision and care. What if they'd fallen and hit their heads? Or found something more dangerous to get into. The way she figured it, he needed to know that she didn't plan on marriage to anyone. What must he think? Then a shocking notion hit her full force. Had he heard the rumors about her and the other mail-order brides?

Chapter Seven

William heard the conviction in her voice and wondered what had ruined her thoughts of marriage. Wasn't it every little girl's dream to get married? He listened to her footsteps follow him across the house and out the front door. He could be mistaken, but it seemed they dragged a little, as if she were being coerced to come along.

His fiancée, Charlotte, had wanted marriage but not children. William realized now in hindsight that he should have asked Charlotte why she didn't want children. Instead he'd been hurt that she'd broken off the engagement so easily. Of course, Charlotte hadn't loved him; she'd just liked the idea of having an easy life as the wife of a businessman.

He'd been lucky to find out Charlotte's true feelings about raising a family before they'd gotten married. He wanted children, but now wasn't the time to dwell on it. His focus at the moment was the raising and care of his nieces, not on getting a wife and having more children.

He lifted the wagon from the porch and set it on the ground, then drearily headed for home. The girls needed fresh diapers and dresses before he could go to work. His brain was in tumult. He needed to be alone to settle his thoughts. A man couldn't work with things all muddled up in his head.

"You don't have to come with us, Miss Emily Jane. I'm able to dress the girls on my own. I've been doing it for months now." William wished he hadn't added the last sentence. It sounded cold and bitter, most likely due to the stresses of the past few months and this morning's pickle disaster.

He noticed that she walked a few more steps before stopping. He looked back at where she stood and saw that she clenched her hands in front of her. "I'm sorry, Mr. Barns."

He paused, blank, for a moment too startled by her words to comment. Was he destined to be in a permanently confused state of mind when dealing with women?

"What are you sorry for?"

He noticed a faint blush steal into her cheeks. Her shoulders lifted as she drew a deep breath. "I snapped at you a few moments ago, and I shouldn't have." She unclenched her fingers, then twisted them in the folds of her apron.

Before he could speak, she held up her hand.

"Please, let me finish. I am not going to get married. Yes, I came here as a mail-order bride. That is true. But now that I don't have to fulfill that promise of marriage, I have other dreams. Dreams that don't include a husband and children at this time." She took a deep breath, and her eyes searched his. "Dreams that a husband would never allow."

A window curtain fluttered in the house next door. William caught a glimpse of Mrs. Green peeking out at them. He motioned for Emily Jane to follow him back to his house. "Come inside and we can discuss it further." He walked toward his house and hoped she'd follow. Emily Jane Rodgers wasn't the only one who didn't want to get married, and he needed to tell her so.

He pulled the wagon to his front porch and lifted it up. He scooped a girl under each arm, carrying them like sacks of potatoes. They giggled, and he regretted the action immediately. For serious conversation, he needed them sleepy and pliable; not wide-awake and playful. He entered the house and, with his foot against the door, held it open for Emily Jane. Mrs. Green's curtain fluttered again. William sighed and left the door open, praying it would prevent further gossip and save Emily Jane's reputation.

She walked forward, running her hand over Rose's damp hair as she passed. He smelled cinnamon and apples. She took Rose from his arms and tickled her belly. Rose buried her face against Emily Jane's shoulder and wrapped her little arms around her neck. Emily Jane hugged her close, kissing the side of her head.

"I hope you get someone to watch them soon. Doing so will help the neighbors forget about you and me marrying." She sat in the rocking chair and unwrapped Rose, using the towel to further dry her hair. She motioned for him to stand Ruby in front of her.

Their baby chatter filled William's ears as he hurried to the bedroom to gather fresh diapers and dresses. There was absolutely no doubt in his mind now that, like Charlotte, Emily Jane did not want to take care of his nieces. And just what kind of dreams could a woman have that didn't include a husband and children?

He returned to the living room and scooped Ruby into his arms. While he dressed her, William talked. "I'm not ready to stand up in front of a preacher with you, either." He offered what he hoped was a friendly smile, but it felt more like a grimace to him. "Like you, marriage isn't something I can consider until these little girls' daddy returns for them." He ran his fingers through Ruby's dark curls. He looked over her head to find a probing query in Emily Jane's eyes. He quirked an eyebrow questioningly.

She looked away. "Doesn't it bother you that the neighbors want us to get married?"

William shook his head. He placed a freshly dressed Ruby onto the sofa beside him, then took a wiggly Rose from her. "No. They mean well." He paused. "Well, they mean well for themselves. All they want is for these girls to sleep all night so they can sleep. Can't blame them for that. I'd like for them to do that, too." He pulled a little blue dress with white flowers on it over Rose's head. Maybe if he kept his hands busy, he wouldn't want to kiss the pretty lady who looked so confused and vulnerable right now.

Emily Jane's expression stilled and grew serious. "And after their pa returns, will you be racing to the altar with some lucky woman?"

He felt his jaw tense. She didn't want him for herself, didn't want the twins, but felt she had the right to question his plans? The funny thing was, he found himself eager to answer.

"No. I think I'll take my time in choosing a bride." He raised his head and looked her in the eyes. "I was engaged a few months ago, but when my fiancée learned that I was taking on the girls, she canceled the wedding. Seems she didn't want or need children in her life." William's eyes searched her face, probing, trying to read her thoughts. For reasons he couldn't quite yet fathom, he needed to know if Emily Jane felt the same way as Charlotte.

Compassion filled her features. She sat forward and looked at him intently. "I'm sorry to hear that, Mr. Barns." She seemed to consider the situation thoughtfully.

Her head bent, and she studied her hands. Nervously, she stroked the arms of the chair, finally offering a little shrug. "But I guess it was better you found out before you got married."

He nodded. She was right, but it didn't take away the sting of rejection that still lingered close to his heart. "What about you? What is this dream you mentioned?" William shifted sideways and handed each girl their stuffed animals. Both girls rocked, bouncing themselves off the back of the couch.

Folding her hands in a pose of tranquillity, Emily Jane answered, her posture defying her appearance of calmness. Her eyes danced with excitement, and her body movements held a restless energy. "I want to open my own bakery," she blurted out.

He exhaled a long sigh of relief. So that was all it was. "And you can't do that with a husband and kids?"

Emily Jane answered in a firm voice. "No."

"Why not? Carolyn Moore helps her husband run the general store, and they have a child. Couldn't your husband help you?"

She laughed cynically. She looked at him as if he were out of his mind. "I can't imagine a man willing to help a woman out with her business. Carolyn helps Wilson Moore with his business, not the other way around. And she's still expected to take care of the baby, the house and Mr. Moore."

Rose threw her stuffed animal in his direction. William caught it and handed it back to her. "I see your point, but if the right man comes along, he might be willing to work alongside his wife."

"*Might* is a big word, Mr. Barns. Taking care of children always falls to the wife. No, I'm happy with the idea of not getting married and not having children." Emily

Jane stood. "We should probably get these girls over to my house, so you can get to work." She picked up the stuffed animals and the scattered blocks he'd left on the floor earlier that morning and put them in the bag that William had brought into the sitting room.

William loaded the girls back in the wagon. As he pulled them across the street, he considered all that Emily Jane had said. She seemed very sure of her decisions, and that bothered William. She had tarred all men with the same brush. He wondered why. It had been his experience that people responded certain ways because of things that happened to them. Either in the distant past or present. He looked down at her as she walked beside him on the dirt street. She carried herself confidently, her hair ruffled slightly by the breeze. Had someone in her past made her think that a husband wouldn't share her dreams? Wouldn't desire to be a helpmate?

If he were to marry her, William knew that he'd support her in the pursuit of her dream. But he wasn't going to marry her. He wasn't going to marry anyone. Emily had said herself that she didn't want children. Were all women more concerned with becoming independent? If so, did they all want to give up motherhood? Or had he tarred all women with the same brush?

Later that day Emily Jane told Anna Mae about her discussion with William. She shook her head in disbelief at Anna Mae's reaction. Disappointment rang from her friend's voice like a church bell over the valley.

"Please, say you didn't tell him you weren't interested in marriage or having children," Anna Mae moaned. "That isn't something you tell a man, Emily Jane." Anna Mae was starting to sound like her mother.

"Why not?"

"It just isn't done."

Emily Jane placed both hands on her hips. "Why? Because he's a man?"

"That's part of it." Anna Mae stood and handed Ruby the stuffed toy the little girl had thrown over the edge of the pen Emily Jane had created for the twins moments earlier.

"What's the other part?" Emily Jane turned back to the stove and poured fried potatoes from the skillet onto a platter. Then she prepared to turn the steaks one last time, waiting for Anna Mae's answer.

"Well, men talk to each other. What if Mr. Barns goes around telling everyone that you aren't the marrying kind? Where will you be when you are ready to get married?" Anna Mae walked to the door and took a deep breath.

"He's not going to go telling all the single men that I don't want to get married. Not that there are that many single men here. And even if he does, I don't care. It will save me from having to tell them." She flipped the meat over. "Besides, I don't see you trying to find a man to get married to."

Anna Mae turned from the doorway. "You know good and well that I can't even think about getting married until I'm finished teaching. It's in my contract with the school-board members. Besides, right now teaching is all that I'm interested in. Not men." She picked up Ruby and cuddled her close.

Emily Jane focused on putting the meat onto a platter. Having the children and William around had been fun, but now she wanted to focus on her baked goods. Tonight, after supper and after William and the girls went home, she intended to try a new crepe recipe.

It did not escape her notice that if she were married,

her intentions would be out of the question. She'd have children to put to bed and darning to do on their clothes once they were asleep. Not to mention taking care of her husband. How many evenings had she sat and sewn Father's and her siblings' clothes? Too many. And the worst part was, it was expected.

Anna Mae put Ruby back inside the pen and picked up Rose. She lavished on Rose the same love she'd shared with her twin moments before. Emily Jane wondered what thoughts swirled around in her friend's head. Did Anna Mae regret signing a two-year contract to teach in Granite? She didn't really know that much about her friend other than she had also answered Levi's advertisement for a mail-order bride. She knew, too, without a doubt, that Anna Mae loved to teach and that for the most part she kept to herself when she wasn't at the school.

"I'll go gather the girls' dresses and diapers off the line. I'm sure they are dry by now." Anna Mae set Rose beside her sister, who promptly hit her with a stuffed animal. The two girls giggled and chattered away as if they understood one another, yet neither spoke more than one or two words clearly.

"Thank you." She knew from experience that Anna Mae would be outside for a while. Anna Mae enjoyed walking under the shade trees in the backyard and did so quite often. "Dinner will be ready as soon as Mr. Barns arrives," Emily Jane called after her friend.

"I won't be long." The back door shut with a soft bang.

Ruby pulled up and looked over the side of the pen. Her blue eyes searched the back of the room. Emily Jane assumed the little girl was looking for Anna Mae. Anna Mae had a way with children that Emily Jane envied.

Both Rose and Ruby seemed fascinated with Emily Jane's red hair, but neither acted as attached to her as

Ruby did to Anna Mae. Over the past couple of days, the little girl had bonded with the schoolteacher.

Emily Jane wondered if Anna Mae reminded Ruby of her mother. She couldn't help but be curious about the girls' father. What was he like? And why wasn't he here taking care of the girls instead of William? And what had happened to their mother? But more important, why did she care? Emily Jane couldn't answer the last question. She just knew that she did care, and that in itself was dangerous.

On his way home from work, William couldn't shake his thoughts of Emily Jane. Her pretty green eyes had clouded over with hurt when she'd talked about not getting married or having children. Did she secretly want both worlds? The one where she'd have her own business and the one where she'd be married and have beautiful redheaded babies?

He started up the front porch steps, then paused. He tilted his head, intently listening for what had caught his attention. He heard it again. "Mr. Barns." Anna Mae stepped around the side of the porch, a finger to her lips. She motioned for him to follow her.

She'd caught him off guard, and that made him irritable. Didn't she or Emily Jane worry about their reputations? He walked to where she stood but refused to go around to the side of the house. He looked over his shoulder and saw Miss Cornwell on her front porch watching them intently. William returned his attention to Anna Mae. "What can I do for you, Miss Anna Mae?"

"Shhh," she whispered loudly. He barely refrained from laughing. "For starters, you can keep your voice down. I don't want Emily Jane to hear us." She tucked a strand of brown hair behind a shell-shaped ear.

He decided to enjoy this secret meeting and whispered back, "Okay, what can I do for you?"

She must have seen the humor in his expression because she chuckled softly and then answered, "Nothing. I just wanted to talk to you about Emily Jane, and I don't want her to hear us."

Not sure what to say to that, William waited for her to continue.

"She told me about your conversation."

William cocked an eyebrow at her. He didn't know which conversation Anna Mae referred to but couldn't imagine it was the one about marriage. Still, if it wasn't that one, then why be so secretive?

"Emily Jane told me she explained to you that she didn't want to get married and didn't want children. I think you should know why she said that." Anna Mae looked up at him with big brown eyes. "Emily Jane comes from a very large family and she's the oldest. All her life she's taken care of younger brothers and sisters. I'm sure that Emily Jane is afraid she will become attached to you and the girls, and she's trying to force you away. Please, bear with her. She's just trying to find her way right now. Her father was hard, even to the extent of making her come here as a mail-order bride, so marriage isn't something she's seeking right now. But, please, Mr. Barns, don't tell anyone else of your conversation. I feel sure she'll want a husband and children someday."

William didn't know what to say. What did she think? That he was going to run out and let all the eligible bachelors in Granite, Texas, know that Miss Emily Jane Rodgers didn't want to get married? Seriously, what kind of men had these two women been dealing with? He shook his head. "Of course not."

She visibly relaxed and sighed at the same time. "You have no idea what this means to Emily Jane."

Why did he get the feeling Anna Mae was the one afraid of losing out on marriage and children? Was she trying to protect her friend from what she feared would happen to her? So many questions had troubled his mind today that William's head began to pound.

She stood before him with her hands clasped over her apron. "Thank you."

"Miss Anna Mae, I think you should know that I'm not looking for a wife or a mother for the girls." William watched her face. Anna Mae seemed to have that same look that the neighbor women had presented. She didn't believe a word he'd just said.

When she didn't reply to his statement, William pressed on. "If that is all you needed, I should go inside and get the girls."

Anna Mae smiled. "Emily Jane fixed steak and potatoes. You are in for a real treat tonight. She really is an excellent cook." She turned to go back around the house.

"Miss Anna Mae," he whispered after her.

She stopped and looked back at him. "Yes?"

"Aren't you coming inside?" He motioned to the front door.

Anna Mae hurried back to him. "Oh, no, not that way. I'm going to grab the girls' clothes off the line and come through the back door. Remember, don't mention our conversation to Emily Jane." She turned and walked away again before he could respond.

William retraced his steps to the front door. He waved to Miss Cornwell to let her know he was aware of her curiosity. She lifted her hand in return, then stomped into her house.

Women, at least the women in Granite, struck him as

an odd bunch. They were nosy, secretive and stubborn. He started to knock on the door, then paused as something Anna Mae had said struck him as odd.

So, Emily Jane's father had forced her to answer the mail-order-bride ad. Why would a man do that to his daughter? Was he the reason she was against marriage? The throbbing in his head grew. William raised his hand once more and knocked on the door.

He fought the feeling of protection that welled up in him thinking that Emily Jane had been forced to answer an ad to marry a man she'd never met. Who did that to their daughter? Did her father realize the emotional damage he'd inflicted on her? William couldn't wrap his mind around any possible reasoning the man might have had. He shook his head. Why was he wasting time on something that was none of his business and he couldn't fix even if it were? He reminded himself that his sole responsibility was to Rose and Ruby. He couldn't allow himself to dwell on Emily Jane and her feelings.

Chapter Eight

Emily Jane met William at the door with a child on each hip. "I hate to rush you away, Mr. Barns, but I have extra baking to do tonight, so I've packed your dinner and the girls' dinner for you to take home." Her stomach muscles tightened at the startled look on his face. Would he be angry that she was sending them away?

Guilt hit Emily Jane like a baker kneading dough. After Anna Mae had left to get the clothes, Emily Jane had decided she couldn't stand the idea of having another meal with William and the girls. She needed to put distance between them. She couldn't change her feelings this far into realizing her dreams, and she didn't plan to do anything that might make her have feelings for William or the twins. Being in repeated close proximity might cause that to happen. At least, her heart seemed to warn her it could be a possibility.

"Uh, thank you." William reached for Ruby.

Once the child was on his hip, Emily Jane handed him the girls' bag. "I'll carry Rose and the food basket over for you."

William nodded. As they crossed the street, he said, "Look, Miss Emily Jane, if fixing dinner for us is too much, you don't have to do it. I'm sure I can take care of the girls' meals." He opened the door to his house and set Ruby and the bag inside the door before reaching for Rose.

Emily Jane sighed. "Fixing the meal is no trouble, Mr. Barns. I just need to work and thought this would be easier on both of us." She backed away, unable to break some invisible bond his warm blue eyes seemed to hold over her.

"Well, thank you for taking care of the girls today. I..."

Emily Jane didn't let him finish. She turned to leave before he could ask her to help with the children tomorrow. Closing that door of opportunity firmly, she waved goodbye over her shoulder and hurried across the street, calling out, "You're welcome. Good night."

She burst into her house with the finesse of a raging bull. Her heart beat loudly in her chest. She panted like an overheated puppy. What was wrong with her? She placed an unsteady hand against her heart to calm its wild pounding. Since when did she run from men and little children?

"Well, that was interesting." Anna Mae stood observing from the kitchen doorway.

"What?" Emily Jane knew she failed miserably at acting casual. She pushed her hair out of her eyes and walked toward her roommate and friend.

Anna Mae moved aside and allowed her to pass. "Watching you rush him out of here like the house was on fire." She paused, giving her next question more weight. "Why did you do that?"

Should she give Anna Mae the same excuse she'd given William? It wasn't a lie. She did have work to do. Emily Jane hurried to set the table, avoiding Anna Mae's gaze. "I don't want to get attached to them, Anna Mae. And you know why?"

"Because you are afraid to fall in love and have a family? Afraid it will mess up your plans of owning your own bakery?" Anna Mae set two glasses on the table and filled them with cold milk she'd pulled from the root cellar.

"No, I'm not afraid to fall in love and have a family. I'm choosing not to fall in love and have a family. There is a difference. And if I don't fall in love and have a family, then I don't have to be afraid of never owning my bakery." Emily Jane slid into her chair and waited while Anna Mae said a quick prayer over their evening meal.

Anna Mae began to eat in silence. Her quietness made Emily Jane pick at her food and wiggle about in her seat. She hated when Anna Mae used her schoolteacher approach against her.

It wasn't just about falling in love and having a family. It was also about having a man like her father in her life who took away all possibilities of being independent. Emily Jane pressed on, explaining further. "Really, Anna Mae, I don't need a man in my life right now." She'd begun to sound like a little girl again; Emily Jane hated that sound.

"I didn't say you did. What I am saying is that that man needs help with those little girls, and for some reason the good Lord has put you in his path." She gave Emily Jane the "don't interrupt" look before continuing. "Mr. Barns told me himself that he is not looking for a wife. So, relax." She laid her fork down. "All he's asking from you is that you help with the girls."

Emily Jane wondered how much the good Lord had to do with it and how much the neighbors had to do with it. She sighed and took a sip of milk. If Mr. Barns had told

Anna Mae he wasn't interested in marriage, well, then, maybe he wasn't. She sure hoped that was the case. Either way, it was time to change the subject. "How was school today?"

"All right, I guess. Mr. Sorrow came by and said that Matt wouldn't be attending any longer. He has a field to help take care of." She picked up her plate and carried it to the slop bucket. "You would think he'd be more interested in Matt's education. The boy doesn't want to be a dirt farmer like his father."

Anna Mae continued to discuss her students. Emily Jane listened, thankful that the schoolteacher's mind had been diverted from her and the Barns family. While Anna Mae talked, they worked together to straighten the kitchen.

Once the kitchen was clean, Emily Jane changed her mind about making the crepes and gathered ingredients to bake a batch of sticky buns. Making the buns always made her feel better, and right now she needed to feel better. About herself. Regret troubled her mightily for sending William and the girls away.

"I think I'll go read for a while," Anna Mae said.

Emily Jane nodded as she mixed the ingredients for the batter. It would take about an hour and a half for the dough to rise. Her mind, already on the prospect of making a fresh batch of yum yum cookies, wandered back to her reaction to William and the girls. Was she being silly? All he'd ever asked her to do was watch the girls. Why, he'd never even flirted with her. Why on earth did she keep thinking he wanted to marry her?

Emily Jane covered the top of the dough with a cloth and then mixed ingredients for the yum yum cookies. She beat the whites of two eggs to a stiff froth, then gradually added a cup of sugar, a heaping cupful of desiccated coconut and two heaping teaspoons of arrowroot. As she worked, Emily Jane knew she'd need to apologize to William for her rude behavior. She buttered a large baking pan and dropped teaspoons of dough about an inch apart onto the pan. When the pan was full she dusted her hands together and slid the cookies into the oven.

While they baked, she vigorously cleaned the kitchen again, driven by some need to work out her problems with manual labor. She tried to reason out why she'd behaved the way she had. Why did she feel threatened every time she thought of marriage and having a family?

Emily Jane sighed. She didn't want to marry a man who would dictate her every move. Her father was that sort of man. When he'd overheard her and her mother talking one evening over a plate of sticky buns about Emily Jane's dream of owning a bakery, he'd laughed and told her that no self-respecting husband would allow his woman to work outside the home. Shortly after that, Pa had tossed a newspaper in front of her and told her it was time she found a husband. It had hurt when he'd continued to tell her that he had enough mouths to feed and she'd need to make her own way now.

Emily Jane wiped down the table. It had hurt so much more when her sweet mother had stood beside her husband and pointed at Levi Westland's mail-order-bride ad, telling her Mr. Westland would probably make her a fine husband. Her parents had more or less abandoned her after that. In the days that had followed, they'd spoken very little to her; had even given her chores to her younger sisters, making Emily Jane feel unwanted and unnecessary. Just thinking of that time shattered her insides and jabbed at her confidence. At the end of two weeks she'd known it would not improve if she stayed. She'd answered the ad and received a letter from Mrs.

Westland. Levi's mother had promised if Emily Jane would come to Granite, Texas, she'd make sure Emily Jane found a good husband. She'd left the day after the letter arrived, and her family had not contacted her since.

Thankfully, though, Levi Westland had chosen Millie Hamilton for his bride, leaving Emily Jane free to pursue her dream of owning her own business and giving her freedom from marriage. She glanced at the kitchen clock and then checked on her cookies. Pulling them from the oven, Emily Jane wished her mother were there to share them. The old saying must be true. A child never stopped desiring the love of a mother, even when that mother cut your heart to shreds.

She sought to erect a wall between herself and the emotions rioting through her. She quickly put the cookies on a cooling rack and placed more on the pan to bake. Well, she'd chosen the wrong recipe tonight. Yum yum cookies were her mother's favorite. How could she help but think of her? Had her mother taken over the cooking at home?

At a young age her mother had given the three oldest daughters permanent chores. Emily Jane cooked and baked, Sarah did the laundry and Elsie taught the little ones to read and write. The two oldest boys worked the fields with their pa. Ma probably took care of the cooking now, if she wasn't expecting again. The baby, Nellie, was two, so it was about time for Ma to have another child. The last two pregnancies had left Ma so weak she couldn't do much of anything but sit in her chair and sew.

Tears pricked the backs of Emily Jane's eyes and slipped from the corners. She'd suffered a great loss. She missed her family. She dashed tears away with the back of her hand and grabbed a plate. There was no time for weeping over her lost family. She plucked warm cookies from the cooling rack and put them on the plate. It wasn't William and the girls' fault that her family had abandoned her, and it was time she apologized for her rude behavior to them. She headed to the door, silently praying that William wasn't a man who would make her beg for his forgiveness.

William sat on his porch relaxing. The squeak, squeak of the rocker lulled him to a peacefulness that had been lacking the past couple of months. After dinner, Rose and Ruby had gone to bed with no muss or fuss, the house was fairly clean, and the evening breeze felt cool on his smooth, freshly shaven face. This was the good life, as far as he was concerned. What more could a man want than a full stomach, a happy family and a rocking chair for evenings just like this one? His gaze moved to the house across the street. He sighed.

A woman moved about the kitchen, the lamplight casting long, eerie shadows. A few minutes later he watched a light come on in one of the back rooms. William assumed Anna Mae lit the lamp in the back of the house since he could still see movement in the kitchen, and he'd learned already that the kitchen was Emily Jane's domain.

His full stomach proved she was a fine cook. He'd really overdone his share of eating tonight. The steak had been done to perfection, the potatoes were tender, and she'd added a pudding that had teased his sweet tooth to distraction.

William's thoughts returned to the red-haired, freckled woman across the street. What would she be like if she ever lowered her guard around him? He yawned. He'd probably never know, especially if someone else stepped forward to take care of the girls.

Right before he'd left work, he and Wilson had hung

two posters outside the general store. William thought back to the words on the paper. *Help Wanted: Someone to watch twin girls, age one. Contact Mr. William Barns inside.*

Would anyone answer his ad? And if they did, would he be able to trust them with Rose and Ruby? He ran a palm over his tired eyes. The girls were a handful. William worried an older woman would quit as soon as she started. He hoped a young woman would answer his cry for help.

He looked up and was surprised to see Emily Jane crossing the dark road. What was she doing out this late in the evening? Had she come for her basket? William thought about standing when she arrived at the bottom of the steps but was too weary to do so. "Good evening, Miss Emily Jane."

Emily Jane jumped but managed to catch the plate she carried before it hit the ground. William realized that his chair sat back in the shadows and she probably hadn't seen him. "I'm sorry I startled you."

"No, it's all right. I'm the one who came to say I'm sorry." She stepped up on the porch and leaned against one of the railings.

William used his boot and set the rocking chair into motion. "What do you have to be sorry about? Dinner was excellent and the girls were happy when I picked them up. A man can't ask for much more than that."

Emily Jane stood with her back to the moonlight. A halo of silver encircled her head. William couldn't see her face very well in the shadows and wondered if the moonlight would bring out the freckles across her nose.

She cleared her throat as if nervous or preparing to say something difficult. "I shouldn't have rushed you and the girls away this evening. That was very rude of me, and I apologize." Emily Jane bowed her head and fiddled with her apron.

William noted the sound of submission in Emily Jane's voice and for reasons unknown to him didn't like it one bit, nor the slumped stance she'd taken. He preferred the woman who looked him in the eyes and spoke her mind. The little redhead should be expressing herself in a confident way, not like a whooped puppy cowing behind her master.

He stood and walked over to her. Placing a hand under her chin, William raised her head so that he could see into the depths of her eyes. Just as he expected, defiance and shame warred for dominance. They were there in her eyes for him to see.

In a soft voice he offered, "You do not owe me an apology, Emily Jane." For a brief moment, he wondered if Anna Mae had made her feel bad about her treatment of him and the girls this evening. He shook off the thought. Still holding her head up so that he could look her in the face, William continued. "You said you had work to do. That was good enough for me." He caressed her cheek with his thumb, then gently released her chin.

Surprise and relief crossed her face. She opened her mouth to say something and just as swiftly snapped it shut. She seemed confused that he'd given her permission to be herself.

William sank back down in the rocking chair. "Would you like to sit for a spell?" he invited, pointing to a second rocker.

Emily Jane held out the plate for him to take before sitting down. "I hope you like yum yum cookies," she said when he took the plate, "because that's all I have for a peace offering." Emily Jane tucked her skirt under her legs and then set the chair to rocking.

"I like all cookies." William lifted the towel that covered the confections and pulled one out. He balanced the plate on his knee and then took a big bite from the sweet treat. The rich flavors teased his taste buds, and he closed his eyes and made a noise in the back of his throat. "Ummm, ummmm."

Emily Jane smiled. "Sounds like you enjoy eating my cookies."

"It is a very good yum yum. I'm not sure there will be any left to share with the girls in the morning." He popped the last of his cookie in his mouth and reached for another.

She shook her head, causing him a moment's pause in praising her more for her cooking. Why did women tell you with their eyes that they loved the attention you gave them but with their mouth and actions say something entirely different?

"You really should start making them eggs and bread for breakfast. They are eating way too many sweets."

"Can I help it if they are like their uncle William and love your cookies?" He finished off the second treat with a flourish.

"Yes. You are the adult." Emily Jane realized what she'd said and slapped a hand over her mouth.

He took one look at her face and burst out laughing. "There is the woman I like to see. You're right. I need to fix them healthier meals."

"Oh, Mr. Barns, I am so sorry. I spoke out of turn." Emily Jane stood.

William reached out and grabbed her hand. "Please, don't leave." Her wrist felt warm in his hand. He could feel her pulse as her heart pumped.

Emily Jane turned and looked back at him. In the shadowy darkness his blue eyes beseeched her to stay.

She realized it was time that they had a talk. For as long as she watched the girls, they would, of necessity, be spending time together. Emily Jane wanted to make sure he understood her reasons for not wanting marriage and children. She sat back down.

"I put up an advertisement today." He set his rocker into motion once more. "As soon as a suitable person applies, you will be free from taking care of the girls."

His voice sounded dejected, almost hurt that she didn't want to keep the girls. Emily Jane wanted to reach out to him, to explain, but where did she start? She'd never even sat on a porch with a man, much less spoken intimately with one. And to her way of thinking, speaking about marriage to a man, either for or against it, was certainly intimate. Her head was puzzled by the new thoughts. Why had it worried her so much that he might be upset at her rudeness earlier in rushing him from the house? She'd used a firm tone many times with men to get them out of The Bakery or to spur her dad or uncles into gathering wood for the stove. Pensively, she looked into the darkness. She had to admit, though, it had bothered her greatly.

A firefly blinked in the front yard, interrupting her musings. She watched several others join it. The insects always brought her comfort. She sighed. "Mr. Barns, it's not that I want to be free of the girls. They are actually very sweet."

"Is it because you have work to do that you don't want to continue watching them?" he asked.

"No, it's more like I grew up with lots of little brothers and sisters and, for the past few months, have enjoyed not having to take care of them. I know the neighbor ladies suggested you marry me, and just today they suggested again that I should offer to marry you, too. But I am not ready for marriage or having children. For the first time in my life, I feel free." Emily Jane looked in his direction.

William stared out across the yard, watching the fireflies, too. Did he ever think about the days before he took over the care of the twins? Was he missing his freedom now?

"Will you ever want to get married and have children of your own?" he asked, his head turned to look at her, and his eyes held Emily Jane's.

The deep sea-blue pulled her in, leaving her feeling breathless and warm at the same time. "I don't know. I've been taking care of children since I was five years old. Surely God has other plans for my life besides being a mother and a wife."

A soft chuckle drifted toward her. "Some women believe that being a mother and wife is what God plans for them to do."

Emily Jane nodded, her eyes searching his face, trying to probe into his thoughts. "Yes, but God has different plans for different people. Wouldn't you say so?"

"I would. Marriage isn't for everyone." He released her gaze and looked out over the yard again.

She detected a hint of sadness in his voice and something stirred within her. She knew about his fiancée but couldn't help wondering if the right woman came along, would William offer his heart to her.

He tucked his hand under the cloth and pulled out another cookie.

Was he eating for comfort? Or simply giving his hands something to do? He'd said Charlotte, his fiancée, had left because of the girls. To make him feel better, Emily Jane said, "You know, you aren't going to have the girls forever. Surely their father will come get them, and then you'll be free to find a woman who wants children and can get married."

"True, but like you, Charlotte had other plans for her life and they didn't include having my children. Who's to say that the next woman I want to marry doesn't feel the same way? No, I think I'll just keep my heart to myself for the time being." He looked at her and winked. "Less chance of it getting broken that way."

William tried to make light of the conversation, but she saw in his eyes that he felt rejected and unloved. Emily Jane said the first thing that came to her mind. "She must not have loved you." Immediately she realized she'd spoken aloud. "I'm sorry. That was rude."

William turned and looked at her again. "No, you spoke the truth. I didn't love her as much as I thought I did, either."

"No?"

He shook his head. "If I had loved her as much as I should have, I'd have asked her to reconsider and convinced her I didn't need to have my own children. Instead, I let her go. But I still dream of a wife who loves me and wants to have my children. A dream that I fear is hopeless."

Hadn't he said moments earlier that he didn't want to get married? "But I thought you weren't in any hurry to get married."

William laughed. "I'm not. After my sister died, I promised myself I'd take care of her daughters, so first, I have to make sure that Rose and Ruby lack for nothing and are kept safe until their father comes for them. Secondly, before I offer marriage again, I will make sure that I love the woman enough to give up everything for her."

Would he ever find a woman that he loved that much?

Emily Jane stared into his handsome face. Was there really that type of love in the world?

Emily Jane admired William. He knew what he wanted and was willing to wait for just the right person. And now she knew he wasn't interested in marrying her—how could he be? She'd just told him she didn't want children. Emily Jane relaxed.

"You know, the girls really aren't that much trouble. If you'd like, I could continue watching them for you while you are at work. I'm sure their father will be along soon to get them." She leaned back in her chair and gave it a gentle push with her feet.

He did the same. The sound of the rockers creaking on the porch filled the cool evening air. "I don't know, Miss Emily Jane. You have work to do."

Did he want her to beg to watch the girls? If so, it wasn't going to happen. She tucked a wayward strand of hair behind her ear. "Well, it's your choice. Hiring someone new means the girls will have to get used to someone else, and you will have to take extra time carrying them over to whoever watches them. Plus, I'm sure that the one that answers your ad will want payment, where I am happy just to watch them. Like I said, though, the choice is yours." She tried to hide her playful grin.

"Well, since you put it that way, I'll give in and let you take care of them." William couldn't control the laughter that sprang from his throat.

It came out clear, strong and warm. Emily Jane rested a hand against her stomach that fluttered like the fireflies' wings in the yard. There was no doubt in her mind that all the ladies in Granite would be contending for his attentions soon.

Why did that thought leave a bitter taste in her mouth?

Chapter Nine

"Does this mean we can be friends as well as neighbors?" William asked, hoping that the playful, sweet Emily Jane would stick around awhile. Now that she knew he wasn't interested in marriage, maybe she would become friendlier and less stiff around him.

She stood. "Yes, I'd like that. And from now on, you and the girls will eat dinner at our house." Emily Jane smiled at him, then walked to the steps.

William followed her. He stood on the top step. "Thanks for the cookies. I think we should call them peace-offering cookies, don't you?"

Her sweet laughter floated on the breeze to him. "I like that. I think that's the name I'll give Violet tomorrow for the menu. Good night."

"Good night." He watched her until she stepped inside her house with a final wave.

As he turned to go inside, William wished Emily Jane wanted marriage and children. She'd make some man a perfect wife.

But not him.

What he hadn't told Emily Jane was that he couldn't see marriage in his future. Unlike Emily Jane, most women hid the fact that they didn't want a family. He wanted children, and now that Charlotte had proved how easy it was to deceive him about their true feelings of having children, William didn't trust himself to find a woman who was honest and open like Emily Jane had been tonight.

He took the cookies to the kitchen and looked about. It didn't feel homey like Emily Jane and Anna Mae's. His grandmother hadn't been a woman to put up lacy curtains or keep frilly towels lying about. William sighed. He missed his grandmother and sister. Loneliness crept into his chest as he realized he would never have the homeyness of a woman's touch in his house again. He rubbed his chest in an effort to ease the dull ache that seemed to have taken up residence there.

After a restless night, William rose the next morning with a headache and two little girls crying for dry diapers and full tummies. He wondered how mothers did all that they did in a day. When was he going to have time to do laundry, fix meals and make sure the girls were happy?

The rest of his morning was hectic, and by the time he knocked on Emily Jane's door, his nerves were shot. Rose and Ruby seemed happy, but William wasn't sure how much longer he could continue at this pace.

Emily Jane answered the door. Her smile turned into a frown when she saw his haggard looks. "Rough night?" she asked.

He offered her what he hoped was a charming smile. "More like a rough morning." William kissed Rose on the cheek before handing her to Emily Jane.

"Do you have time for a cup of coffee?" she asked, stepping back so that he could enter with Ruby.

William sighed. A cup of coffee sounded wonderful.

Between changing the girls' diapers, fixing breakfast for them and cleaning them up after eating, he hadn't had time to make coffee, too. He rubbed the stubble on his chin. "A cup of coffee would be nice, but it will have to be a fast one."

"Fast cups of coffee are my specialty." The sweet smile sent a fresh appreciation through him for the woman standing beside him. "Come on, girls. Let's fix Uncle William a cup of coffee before he keels over."

His name on her lips sounded like music to William's ears. It was the first time she'd used it, and he wanted to hear it again and again. William shoved the silly thought aside. Lack of sleep made a man loopy in the brain.

Emily Jane hadn't expected him to show up unshaven and rumpled. Were two little girls just too much for him? If so, how had he managed before he'd gotten to Granite? Of course, now that she thought about it, he'd been out of sorts that day, too.

She placed Rose in the pen she'd created, handed her one of the cloth balls and then hurried to get a coffee mug and pour William a cup. "This should perk you up," she said, handing him the coffee.

"Thank you." He continued to hold Ruby as he took a drink.

Emily Jane reached for the little girl. Ruby came into her arms and snuggled against her neck. She hugged the little girl close before placing her in the pen with her sister.

Of the two girls, Rose seemed the most affectionate. She smiled the easiest and laughed more often than her twin. Emily Jane patted Ruby on the head. Later she'd get the little girl out and give her an extra cuddle, too.

William sat down at the table and sighed. "This is

really good coffee, Miss Emily Jane. One of these days you'll have to show me how you make it. Mine never turns out this smooth."

She laughed. If you weren't careful when making coffee, you could end up with coffee grounds in your cup; she had a feeling William drank a lot of grounds. "Are you hungry? I'm sure I can put together a plate of bacon and biscuits."

"No, thanks. I took your advice and made the girls a pan of scrambled eggs and buttered bread. They don't eat as much as I thought, so I had lots of eggs for breakfast this morning." He drank from his cup as if he was still washing down the eggs and bread.

Emily Jane turned to pick up Ruby from the pen. Ruby squirmed in her arms, pushing against her shoulder. Emily Jane hid her smile. The poor man had stuffed himself with eggs and bread this morning. No wonder he was tired. "I see."

He drank the rest of the liquid in his cup. "Thanks for the coffee. I better get to the general store." William stood to leave. "I hope you don't mind we are a little early. I wanted to run by the furniture store and see if Mr. Westland has any more wagons for sale."

Emily Jane held Ruby's hands as she tried to walk across the kitchen. Unlike Rose, who liked to cuddle, Ruby wanted down to explore. If Emily Jane guessed correctly, Ruby would be the first to walk. She wasn't as timid about falling, and she didn't cry as quickly as her sister. She laughed. "I don't mind at all. I hope he has an extra wagon." She swung Ruby up into her arms. "We're going to have a good day today, aren't we, Ruby?"

Ruby pushed against her shoulder in protest, wanting back down, but Emily Jane's back couldn't take the bending over any longer. She returned her to the pen.

William grinned at the two girls. "They really are sweet little things, aren't they?"

Emily Jane looked at them. "Yes, they are. But, like all children, they have minds of their own and often their thoughts do not align with ours." She offered him a smile. "I wish I could tell you the older they get, the easier it will be, but that's not entirely the truth."

He laughed. "Good to know." William bent down and kissed each of the girls on the head. "Be good for Miss Emily Jane. I'll be back after work, hopefully with a bright new wagon. Bye-bye." He stood and wiggled his fingers at them.

"Bye-bye," the girls echoed, but it sounded more like *bite, bite*. They tried wiggling their fingers like him and ended up poking them in their mouths in cute embarrassment.

William chuckled aloud. "Thank you for watching them. They seem very happy to be here."

Emily Jane hated to admit it but said, "I enjoy having them." And it was the truth. She missed her little sisters, and taking care of Rose and Ruby seemed to ease the loss a bit.

Once he was out the door, Emily Jane went into her bedroom and quickly sorted her dirty clothes. Then she moved into Anna Mae's room and did the same. If she hurried, she'd be able to get them washed and on the line to dry before she'd need to start supper.

"Hey, girls, want to help Emily Jane wash today?" she asked, dropping the laundry beside the front door.

"Go!" Both Rose and Ruby called out at the same time.

Emily Jane walked back to them. "Yes, you get to go. We need to visit Mrs. Matthews for a few minutes." She scooped up the girls, one in each arm, and then carried them out the door and across the street to the other lady's house.

She knocked with her elbow.

A few moments later, Mrs. Matthews answered. "Come in, child, and bring those little darlings with you."

"I really don't have the time to stay but was wondering if maybe you could help me with the girls for a few minutes."

"Sure, Emily Jane. What do you need me to do?" She stepped out onto the porch and took Rose from Emily Jane's arms.

"Do you mind if I leave them with you for just a few moments while I run over to Mr. Barns's house and borrow Mabel's washtub? The girls are using mine for a pen, and I'd really like to get some laundry done today." Emily Jane blew a stray lock of hair off her forehead.

Mrs. Matthews closed the door and started down the porch steps. "Of course I don't mind. But I'd rather just go to your place to watch them, if you don't mind. I can put them back in their pen and watch them play with those balls I made them." She continued on across the street, not waiting for Emily Jane to answer.

As she followed the older woman, Emily Jane felt a laugh building in her tummy. Mrs. Matthews didn't want the twins to destroy her perfectly cleaned home. Who could blame her?

Emily Jane trotted after the older woman. "Thank you. I promise I'll get the tub and be back as fast as I can." She hurried up the steps ahead of her neighbor and held the door open.

"Don't give it a second thought and don't rush." She passed Emily Jane as she walked inside. "This is what friends do. We help each other." Mrs. Matthews headed for the kitchen, where she deposited Rose into the pen.

Ruby wasn't going to be left behind and called, "Down!" She pushed against Emily Jane's shoulder.

"Hold on, you little darling." Emily Jane eased Ruby into the washtub with her sister. "There, now. You two can play for a few minutes."

Mrs. Matthews made her way to the coffeepot and clear jar full of cookies. "Do you mind if I make myself a snack?" she asked, pouring a cup of the coffee and reaching for the cookies at the same time.

"Help yourself. I'll be right back."

"Thanks. I can't ever resist your cookies."

Emily Jane laughed. "Have as many as you want. I'm off to get the other washtub." As she left the kitchen, she heard the girls yell, "Eat!"

Mrs. Matthews's laughter followed Emily Jane out the door. Emily Jane welcomed the soft breeze that brushed the hair off her forehead as she made her way to William's house. She circled around to the back, where Mabel had always left her washtub on the back porch.

She didn't think William would mind her using it. She hurried to the washtub. Just as she reached for it, she heard a high-pitched whimpering that sent a shiver down her back.

Chapter Ten

Emily Jane crept cautiously toward the washtub sitting on the back porch of William's house. The cries grew louder as she approached. She peered behind the tub, and twin blue-black eyes stared back at her. Emily Jane recognized the little pups as baby foxes. They huddled behind the tub shivering. "Oh, you precious babies." Matted tearstains marred their beautiful dark faces. Their fur had splotches of red within the facial mask and along their bodies. How long had they been crying? And where was their mother? "Where's your mommy?" She cooed and rubbed the tops of their heads. They tried to lick her hands, their tails wagging up a frenzy, feet scratching the sides of the bucket as they tried to climb out.

She searched about for their mother, not seeing her. She looked down upon them and realized they were too young to be on their own. Their fur still had the markings of a five-or six-week-old puppy, but soon everyone would recognize they were fox pups. Her father, and probably most of the men in town, would say to drown them, but that wasn't Emily Jane's way. She gently picked them up and set them inside the tub.

The fox pups whimpered as Emily Jane dragged the

washtub across the street. She continued on around to the back of the house, where the well stood. Thankfully, it was sheltered under a large elm tree. Summer was quickly coming upon them, if the heat from the sun today was any indication.

Emily Jane wiped a few beads of sweat from her brow. She reached in and stroked the little foxes' soft heads. A light breeze blew, cooling her brow and reminding her that she had work to do. She stood. The fox pups and the girls shouldn't be too hot while she scrubbed the bed-clothes.

The tub wasn't as heavy as hers, but, still, tugging it about had winded her. Emily Jane placed her hands on her hips as she stared down at the babies. What was she going to do with the fox pups while she did the wash? Her gaze moved about the yard. Then to the small lean-to that housed William's horse.

A soft snicker greeted her as she entered the shed. "Hello, little lady." Emily Jane reached out her hand, palm forward, toward the mare.

The horse bumped Emily Jane's hand with her velvety nose. She blew gently on Emily Jane's palm.

Emily Jane rubbed her nose and laughed. "You sure are a friendly girl. Are you lonesome out here by your-self?"

Head bobbing was Emily Jane's answer. "I'll try to come out more often, then," she promised, looking about the lean-to.

Her gaze landed on a small wooden crate against the far wall. "That might work." Emily Jane walked the short distance and picked it up. She turned it over to make sure the bottom was secure. "Yes, this will do nicely." As she got ready to leave, Emily Jane stopped long enough to pat the horse once more before returning to the well.

Mrs. Matthews stood on the back porch. "What do you have there?" she asked, wiping her hands on her apron.

"A crate to put pups in."

"Pups? What kind of pups?" Mrs. Matthews stepped off the porch.

"The kind that need care. They are too young to be on their own," Emily Jane answered, scooping the first fox cub from the washtub and placing it into the wooden crate.

Mrs. Matthews gasped. "Emily Jane, that is not a puppy! That's a fox cub." She placed her hand over her heart as if she'd just had the shock of her life.

Emily Jane would have laughed, but knew instinctively she was about to fight her first battle to keep the baby foxes. "I know, but they are still babies and have no mama to take care of them."

"You mean to keep them?" the older woman asked as Emily Jane picked up the second fox pup and put it with the first. She hurriedly used her apron to wipe out the bottom of the washtub.

Emily Jane noted that both fox pups were girls. "Yes." Feeling mischievous, she added, "Unless you want them."

"Oh, no. Once the men find out you're keeping fox cubs, there's going to be a town meeting. Take my word for it."

"Town meeting? You're kidding, right?"

Mrs. Matthews shook her head, her eyes saddened as she looked down on the little fox pups. "No, the farmers around here don't take kindly to foxes." She made a tsking noise with her tongue and teeth before turning to reenter the house. "I'll go check on the girls."

Emily Jane hurried after her. "I don't see what the big deal is over a couple of fox pups." She understood the men feared the foxes would get into their henhouses, but they were in town, not out on the farm.

Rose and Ruby stood, holding the side of their washtub. They squealed with joy as the women entered the kitchen. "Up!" the little girls chorused.

"In a minute," Emily Jane answered. She hurried to the clothes that were by the front door and carried them to the back door. Then she returned to pick up Ruby.

"What are you doing now?" Mrs. Matthews asked.

Seeing the perplexed look on the older woman's face, Emily Jane answered, "I'm going to put the girls in the lighter washtub and do the wash in ours. That way when I'm all done, I'll be able to get the girls back into the house without having to disturb you." She smiled so that Mrs. Matthews wouldn't think she was ungrateful for her aid.

"Here, let me help." She scooped up Rose and the toys.

Emily Jane grabbed the quilt that cushioned the bottom of the metal tub. She followed Mrs. Matthews back outside. The older woman stopped beside the tub and waited for her. Rose looked like a kitten trying to crawl over Mrs. Matthews's shoulder.

As fast as she could, Emily Jane spread the blanket over the bottom of William's washtub and set Ruby inside. "There you go. You girls have a new place to play."

Mrs. Matthews set Rose down beside her sister. "Are these two ever still?" she asked, placing both hands on her hips and watching as the girls tried to pull up to the side of the tub.

"They must be when they sleep." She laughed.

"Come on. I'll help you carry that other tub out here and then I think I'm going to go get a bite to eat and take a nap." She didn't give Emily Jane time to react, simply headed back to the house.

"You two be good. We'll be right back." Emily Jane hurried up the back porch and followed her friend inside.

Together they managed to get the tub outside and in the shade of the tree. The sound of fox pups whining could be heard on the soft breeze. Rose and Ruby stood on tiptoe, trying to see over the edge of the tub. They had curious looks on their tiny faces, eager to learn what made the noise. Mrs. Matthews frowned in the direction of the wooden box.

Emily Jane sighed. "I'm not going to keep them forever, Mrs. Matthews, just until they are old enough to fend for themselves." The fur babies were hungry. She didn't want to take time out of her afternoon to feed them, but what else could she do?

"That's good to know, dear." She looked at the girls. "I suppose I'll head home now, unless there is something else I can do for you, Emily Jane?" The expression on her face said she was tired and hopeful that Emily Jane was finished with her.

Emily Jane smiled at her friend. "No, you have been more than a help to me today. Thank you."

Mrs. Matthews nodded. "If you need me, I'm just down the road."

Emily Jane waved goodbye and then turned to her wards. How had she, a woman who didn't want to keep children, ended up with four? Two real children and two furry ones? She guessed she should count her blessings. Only one pair had to be diapered. She chuckled out loud. What would William think of the fox cubs? Would he too expect her to get rid of them?

William liked Levi Westland. The man was fair in his prices and seemed to have a big heart for the local business. Thankfully, he still had a wagon for sale, which

William was more than happy to buy. He dug deep in his pocket and paid for the wagon and two high chairs.

"If Amos comes by, I'll have him take the chairs over to your place," Levi said, pocketing the money.

"Don't go to any trouble. I'll go by the house and hitch up the wagon." William looked about the store. If he was going to hitch up the wagon anyway, he might as well see if there was anything else he needed.

The store held lots of rocking chairs, kitchen chairs, tables of all shapes and sizes and several chests. His gaze moved to the wall where several wooden pictures hung. They resembled puzzles, only stained and framed.

"If it's all the same to you, I'd like to offer Amos the job." Levi began to sweep at the clean floor.

William remembered that the young boy also helped out at the store, running errands. Wilson Moore had explained that what money the boy made he gave to his mama to buy supplies and food. Amos had brothers and sisters, and the family needed his money. To William's way of thinking, that spoke highly of the boy. He nodded. "Sounds just fine to me."

"Thank you. I'm sure his ma will appreciate the extra money."

He couldn't pull his gaze from one of the pictures. It drew him back time and again. It was a big elk with different shades of colored wood accenting the muscles along its neck and legs. "What's the story behind the pictures?" William walked closer to the wall and reached up to touch the smooth wood. "Do you special-order them?"

"No, they are created right here in Granite." Pride filled Levi's voice. "My wife is the artist behind each one. I simply take her drawings and cut the wood into the pieces she's drawn. Once they are glued into place, she puts the finishing touches to them."

William moved from one to the other. There was a cat, dog, raccoon, hummingbird and mountain lion. The mountain lion's eyes seemed to bore into William's. "They seem so real."

"Yeah." Levi walked up beside him and looked at the mountain lion. "That one is a little too real for my taste, but it is one of our bestsellers." Levi returned to his sweeping.

The dark mountain eyes pulled at William. He had to agree with Levi; it was a little too real for his taste, also. "Well, I guess I should be going. I'm sure Miss Emily Jane has had enough of the girls to last her for a while."

Levi nodded. "I heard she was taking care of your kids while you worked." He leaned the broom back against the wall.

William laughed. "Well, you heard it partially right."

Levi raised an eyebrow and crossed his arms over his chest. "How so?"

"They aren't my girls. I'm their uncle." William walked toward the door. He was sure Levi had further questions but was too polite to ask.

Just as he started to leave, Levi asked, "Has anyone invited you to Sunday services?"

William shook his head. It would be nice to attend. He hadn't heard a good preaching since his sister's death. Taking the girls alone had been too big of a job. As soon as one settled down, the other would raise a ruckus. Since he spent more time outside the service than inside, he'd just stayed at home. But he missed the fellowship. Would Emily Jane be willing to attend with him?

"We meet at nine on Sunday mornings. This Sunday we're having a picnic to welcome summer. You're welcome to sit with my wife, Millie, and me." Levi uncrossed his arms and picked up a dust rag.

"I just might take you up on the offer. Thank you."

He reached for the doorknob.

"Good."

William opened the door, picturing himself, Emily Jane and the girls walking up to the church on the hill. It felt good to consider going to services again. But he didn't even know if Emily Jane attended church, and if she did, would she want to spend the day with him?

Levi called after him, "Tell Emily Jane Millie and I said hello."

William nodded and then closed the door behind him. How long would it be before Millie decided to visit Emily Jane? How long before the whole town wanted to know his story? Would Emily Jane tell them? Or steer them in his direction?

He realized she didn't have a lot that she could tell. All Emily Jane knew was that his sister had died and his brother-in-law would be coming for the girls. At least, he hoped Josiah would be coming for them.

For the first time since his arrival, William focused on his future plans. If Josiah didn't return for the girls— and the only way his brother-in-law would abandon Ruby and Rose was if he were killed—then they were his responsibility for life.

Did he want to stay here in Granite? His gaze moved about the town. Levi's furniture store was on a side street; if he looked to his right, he could see Beckett's hardware store, the stables and, a little farther up the hill, the school. When he turned to the right, he could see several open lots.

William walked toward Main Street. He passed the bank on his left and a doctor's office on his right. To the left of the bank stood the saloon and once again open town lots. Granite, Texas, had the potential to grow into a much larger town.

He crossed the street and passed the eatery before coming to the general store. William had a few minutes before he had to be at work, so he decided to continue looking over the town. The sweet scent of feed and fertilizer drifted from the feed store as he passed it.

Circling to his right, William looked up the hill and saw the whitewashed church with a tall steeple and bell on the top. What would it be like to attend that church every Sunday? If he stayed, he'd soon find out. A small house sat next to it; he assumed it was the preacher's home. Half a mile from the church sat the sawmill.

He continued on, admiring the other businesses as he went. His thoughts went back to Levi Westland. According to Wilson, Levi owned three of the businesses in town, including the furniture store, Beth's Boardinghouse and The Bakery, where Emily Jane worked.

Levi had made sure to give jobs to the widows in town so they would be taken care of. Didn't the Bible plainly say that we should take care of them? William silently said the prayer. *Lord, if it be Your will for me to remain an unmarried man and help others, I'm willing to follow where You lead.*

He circled back to Main Street once more. As he passed the blacksmith shop, the livery, the jail and finally the eatery, William felt a peace overcome him. God hadn't confirmed that he'd remain unmarried, but He hadn't tossed a scripture back at him that man was not meant to be alone.

William heard the sound of laughter when he arrived at Emily Jane's house. It was coming from the backyard, so he circled around to see what was going on. Emily

Jane, the girls and two puppies were playing under the big elm tree beside the well. The pups leaped about the girls, and Emily Jane laughed as the girls squealed their joy.

"Can I join in? This looks like fun."

Emily Jane turned to him with a big smile on her face and dancing in her eyes. The girls stopped their playing and looked to him. Both little girls flashed big smiles at him, also, revealing two tiny teeth in each of their mouths.

The puppies continued to frolic about the little girls, which immediately took the girls' focus off of him. Rose fell sideways with laughter. Ruby grabbed at the nearest puppy's tail.

"The more the merrier," Emily Jane said, turning her attention back to the playing children.

William continued toward them. Where had the puppies come from? He started to ask and then realized that these were no ordinary pups but fox pups. "Emily Jane, where did you get these fox pups?"

She grinned at him. "At the fox-pup store?" she teased.

Didn't she realize the seriousness of the situation? What if their mother showed up? "I'm serious."

Emily Jane squared her shoulders. "I found them behind your house. They were alone, frightened and hungry. So I brought them back here."

Something in her eyes put him on the defensive. "What about their mother? Did you consider her when you brought the pups over here to play with my girls?" He didn't wait for her answer. William scooped up Rose and then Ruby. He carried them like a sack of potatoes into the house.

The smell of beef stew teased his hungry stomach. Rose and Ruby wiggled and began to cry. It was obvious that they were not happy at having to leave their new furry friends. William set them down on the floor and ran his fingers through his hair. The little girls immediately took off crawling toward the back door.

Once more he scooped them up and then sat down at the kitchen table. His heart pounded in his chest at the thought that the mother fox could have returned at any time and attacked Rose, Ruby or even Emily Jane. What had she been thinking?

Emily Jane followed a few minutes later, tugging on the washtub that she'd used for the girls' pen. Her eyes dared him to say something. She took Rose from him and put the girl into the tub. Then she did the same with Ruby.

Planting both hands on her hips, Emily Jane turned to him and answered his earlier question. Fire flashed from her eyes. "Yes, I did think about the fox pups' mother. I don't think she is alive, or she would have been with her pups. They were hungry and ate as if they hadn't eaten in a day. They were also very thirsty. I've kept an eye out for their mother all day, and she never came." She took a deep breath and then continued. "If you think for one minute that I would put these girls in harm's way, you have another think coming, William Barns."

Chapter Eleven

Emily Jane stared down at the man sitting at her kitchen table. Calm blue eyes looked up at her. There was no anger in their depths, only understanding. What did he have to be understanding about? Hadn't he just accused her of not caring about the girls' welfare with his actions? Or had she misread his motivation for picking up the girls and taking them into the house?

"I don't think you meant to harm the girls, Emily Jane. But I also don't think you thought your actions through. A mother fox isn't something to trifle with." He folded his hands in his lap and looked back at her.

She sat down in the chair opposite him. "Look, I know that the mother fox isn't around. I would never have let the girls play with the fox pups if I thought she was."

"I know that. I simply reacted. I'm sorry." He continued to hold her gaze.

"I'm sorry, too."

The girls stood holding on to the rim of the tub looking at the adults. Emily Jane would never hurt Rose or Ruby. William was right; if the mother fox had returned, the little girls might have been injured.

Emily Jane turned her attention back to him. "I won't let them play together anymore."

William's smile warmed her heart. "I didn't say they couldn't play together, but I would like to wait a few days and make sure their mother isn't going to return before they do."

"Aren't you going to tell me to put them back where I got them from?"

He laughed. "Would you do it?"

A smile tugged at her lips. "Nope."

The front door opened, and Anna Mae called out that she was home. Emily Jane answered her call and then stood up. "I best get supper on the table." She walked to the basin and washed her hands.

"What do you think Anna Mae will say about your fox pups?" William whispered across the room.

Emily Jane did her best Anna Mae schoolteacher imitation. She put one hand on her hip and shook the other one at him. "If you think those nasty fox cubs are coming in this house, you better think again." Then she giggled.

"What fox cubs?" Anna Mae demanded from the doorway.

William's rich laughter washed over Emily Jane like warm summer rain over the tulips. She wanted to bask in the sound of it. By not telling her she'd have to get rid of the fox pups, William Barns had endeared himself to her just a little bit.

The next morning, the bell jingled over William's head as he entered the general store. His boots sounded loud on the wood floor. It wasn't a large store, but it did have most of what the town needed. Unlike his store in Denver. His store had grown as his business had grown.

Carolyn looked up from where she stood behind the

counter. Dark circles under her eyes told the tale of a sleepless night. "Good morning." She stifled a yawn.

"Good morning. Little Wilson having trouble sleeping?" William asked as he walked behind the counter and pulled a green apron from a hook underneath it.

She offered him a weak smile. "Afraid so. My little fella had a tummy ache last night."

William tied his apron on. "Is he sleeping now?"

Carolyn nodded and yawned again.

"Why don't you try to take a nap, too? The store is quiet, and I can always call up the stairs if I need to." He picked up a dust rag and headed to the canned-goods shelf.

"You don't mind?" she asked, pulling her own apron off and stuffing it under the counter.

William smiled at her. In the past few months he'd had his share of sleepless nights due to babies wanting to doze in the day and be up at night. "Not at all."

"All right, then. Wilson and Pa are over at the Crawford ranch. They should be back shortly. Thanks, William." She yawned again, gave a weak wave and opened the door behind the counter that led to their living quarters.

The store seemed quiet once she'd gone. William walked about studying the shelves. They didn't seem very full. Was it because people had made a lot of purchases? Or were the Moores having financial problems that prevented them from restocking the shelves? How could he find out without hurting their pride? A man didn't meddle in another man's affairs. He'd make it a matter of prayer, and the Lord would work it out. He had no doubt of that.

He dusted the cans and shelves while his mind worked. He had his own life to figure out. He needed direction.

A plan. He liked knowing a bit about his future, and he wasn't afraid of hard work. In fact, he welcomed it. There was nothing more satisfying than accomplishing something and seeing a job well done. So, what was he going to do? That was the question uppermost in his mind at the moment. If the Moores were in financial trouble, would they allow him to help them out? His mercantile had sold for a nice sum of money. Maybe Wilson would be interested in a partnership. If not, should he consider starting another business here in Granite?

Excitement coursed through him. It felt good to consider his options. For months now, he'd lived from moment to moment, without time or strength to think or plan ahead. The twins took every minute of his time, and he fell into bed exhausted each night. But now, with Emily Jane's help, he had time to think on things, and that was important to him.

For the first time in a while, William found himself totally alone in his thoughts. He had needed this time for himself. A broom rested next to the end of the shelf he was dusting. William picked it up and headed to the front with it. He'd sweep the boardwalk and think there.

He opened the door and stepped out into the warm sunshine. The posters he'd put up a couple of days before hung in the breeze. William reached up and pulled one down. Emily Jane had agreed to watch the girls until Josiah returned, so he no longer needed the posters.

Crumpling the papers, William stuck both into his apron pocket. The broom swished the dirt about as he continued to sweep. The sun warmed his neck and shoulders.

"Good morning, Mr. Barns," a young voice called as Amos ran up the sidewalk.

"Good morning, Amos. What's the rush?"

"I was stopping by to see if you all had any deliveries for me."

"Not this morning," William answered, resting on his broom.

"All right. Thanks." Amos stuck his hands in his pockets and continued down the boardwalk. His shoulders drooped, and his boots kicked at small pebbles as he left.

The first thing William decided to do was give Amos a more permanent job, once he decided on a business to open in Granite. He looked to the broom in his hand. "Hey, Amos!" he called after the boy.

Amos turned and returned to him. "What can I do for you, Mr. Barns?"

"Well, I was hoping you would finish sweeping up here for me. I just remembered I do have an order in the store that will need to be delivered." William handed his broom to the nodding boy.

"Be glad to. Thank you, sir." Amos grinned as he swept at the boards.

William reentered the store. The bell jingled over his head. He began gathering up cleaning supplies. His place needed a good cleaning. He'd send the stuff to Emily Jane with a note asking her to keep them at her place until he got off work. The smile grew on his face as he wrote out the order. Amos would earn a little money this morning, and he'd have a cleaner home tomorrow morning.

Emily Jane sat on her front porch with a bowl of dried beans in her lap. She brushed the hair from her forehead and smiled. The laundry was done. The babies were all fed, clean and napping. The warm scent of bread baking coming through the open window gave her a sense of great accomplishment.

She picked a rock from the beans and tossed it into

the yard. Her gaze moved to the little wooden box at her feet where the two fox cubs slept. Would the men in town truly be upset if they discovered she kept baby foxes? If they were anything like her pa, they would be.

Mrs. Green's dog barked. Emily Jane looked up to see Amos coming down the street carrying a large box. He seemed to be heading to her house. She frowned. She hadn't bought anything from the general store that needed to be delivered.

"Good morning, Miss Rodgers. Mr. Barns asked me to drop this box off at your house and said he'd pick it up when he comes to get the girls." Amos set the box on the porch.

"Oh, I see. Well, thank you, Amos, for bringing it over. Would you like a cookie or two?" She gave him a smile, knowing he'd jump at the chance to have fresh cookies.

He nodded. "Thank you."

"Good. I'll be right out with the cookies." Picking up the bowl of beans, she continued on inside. First, she checked on the girls. They were curled together like a couple of sleeping puppies. Each had thrust a thumb into her mouth. The desire to reach down and wipe the soft curls from their foreheads overwhelmed her. Resting the bowl of beans on her hip, Emily Jane gave in to the urge and did just that.

Rose smiled in her sleep; Ruby scowled. So much alike and yet, so different. She ran a finger across Ruby's soft brow, easing the frown away.

Careful not to wake them, Emily Jane went to check on her bread. She set the beans down on the table beside the cooling loaves. She'd made two extra for William and the girls, knowing he wasn't much of a cook. Or at least, he didn't seem to be.

Taking a dipper of cold water from the bucket, Emily

Jane made a glass for herself and one for Amos. She sipped at the cool liquid, then put several cookies into a cloth for Amos and his family to eat later. Then she chose two more for Amos to munch on now. Emily Jane put everything onto a tray and carried it all back outside.

"Here, let me help you with that." Amos hurried up the steps and took the tray from her.

Emily Jane turned and shut the door behind her so as not to wake the girls with their conversation. "I decided your family might like a few cookies, too. I hope you don't mind taking them home to your mother." She smiled at Amos and returned to her chair.

"Oh, thank you. I'm sure the kids will love them." He sat down on the porch step. "I can't stay long. I'm hoping Mr. Westland has a delivery or two for me to do today." He handed her her glass of water and stuffed a whole cookie into his mouth.

Emily Jane hid her grin behind her glass. Amos was a good boy, and she liked his mother, too. When he'd finished his snack and ambled back down the road, she glanced into the box that he'd set down earlier. A turkey feather duster, sponges, sulfur soap, borax and a washboard rested inside.

It was obvious that William had plans of deep cleaning his new house.

Emily Jane rose and returned to the kitchen. She rinsed the beans several times. She could always tell when cooked beans hadn't been washed really well. They had a dirt taste to them. Tonight she'd set them to soak and tomorrow they'd be ready to cook. A small hunk of salt pork added to them and a cake of corn bread would make a great meal. She couldn't wait till the people with gardens started bringing in fresh vegetables to sell. Sliced cucumber, tomatoes and baby onions would taste so good.

With the beans setting on the table, she headed back to the sitting room to check on the girls. They still slept peacefully, but it would soon be time to wake them. Until then, Emily Jane tiptoed past them and hurried out the back door. She checked the ends of the sheets for dryness, then pulled them from the clothesline.

She carried them to each bedroom and dumped the correct set on the beds. First she made up Anna Mae's, then her own.

Straightening from smoothing the bedsheet, she smiled intentionally. Perhaps tomorrow she'd check on the little girls' beds and wash their sheets, as well. In fact, it wouldn't hurt to check on them now.

Emily Jane tiptoed back through the sitting room, out the front door. She picked up William's box and crossed the street. Would he be upset if she used the products he'd ordered to clean his house?

Chapter Twelve

The house looked amazing. William had noticed the child's wagon on his front porch when he'd arrived home. Now he saw the two high chairs and the box with cleaning supplies in the kitchen. Both indicators that Amos had visited, but who had cleaned his house? Maybe Emily Jane would know.

A few minutes later, he knocked on Emily Jane's door before entering. William wiped his feet on the rug as he waited for her response.

"Come on in. We're in the kitchen," Emily Jane called from the back of the house.

As soon as he entered the kitchen, she asked, "How was your day?"

"Pretty good. Levi had the chairs and wagon I wanted. I was wondering if you'd like a set of high chairs over here, too." He walked over to the girls and kissed each of them on their soft curls.

Rose smiled up at him. Joy radiated from her little face. Ruby studied him with a slight grin. He could tell she was happy to see him, too, but as always, she seemed more guarded in her expression of happiness. He'd be glad when the twins could talk more. It would be interesting to see what each of them was thinking.

"That depends. How long do you think it will be before their father comes for them?" She placed a platter of pork on the table.

William sat down and sighed. "I have no idea."

"I'd hate for you to spend money on extra chairs and then he returns and not need them." She set a bowl of green beans and a plate of biscuits on the table and then turned to get cups and the coffeepot.

"If he comes and decides to stay, he will want them, too. Do you need help with anything?" William asked as she brought the coffee to the table.

Emily Jane stopped and looked at him as if he'd grown horns on his head. Slowly a smile spread across her face, and the dimple in her cheek winked at him. "No, but thank you for offering."

When she smiled and that dimple presented itself, William felt his heart's rhythm pick up a beat. *Get ahold of yourself,* he silently ordered. *A woman's smile shouldn't have this effect on you.* "Do you know if anyone besides Amos went into my house today?" he asked to take his mind off her cute smile.

A guilty expression crossed her face. "I went over for a little while this afternoon."

He fought to keep from grinning at her. "And cleaned my house?"

She nodded, wringing her hands in her apron. "I hope you don't mind."

He couldn't contain his enjoyment at her guilty expression a moment longer and laughed. Once he'd gotten control of himself, William answered, "No, I don't mind, but if you keep doing things for us I'm going to have to pay you."

A slow grin spread across her face. "You three keep making messes like that, and you won't be able to afford me."

This time he didn't try to get control of his laughter. Her sense of humor pleased him to no end. After several long moments, he gasped. "Then I guess we'll have to learn how to clean up after ourselves, won't we, girls?"

The twins grinned happily. Feelings of warmth spread through William. Being with Emily Jane and the twins felt homey and right. He pushed the thought away and welcomed the sound of Anna Mae's voice when she came in and called, "I'm home!"

"We're in the kitchen, Anna Mae," Emily Jane answered.

The schoolteacher entered the room with a smile. Like William, she went straight to the girls and gave them each a kiss on the cheek. "How are my pretty girls tonight?"

Ruby immediately started reaching for the young teacher. "Up!" she said with a big smile on her face. Her black curls bounced in time with her jumps.

William shook his head in wonder. "You know, Miss Anna Mae, I think you are the only person that Ruby is ever that happy to see." It did his heart good to see his niece respond to Anna Mae like that. He'd begun to worry about her. After her mother's death, Ruby had become quieter than normal and seldom smiled. But her happiness at seeing the young schoolteacher gave him hope that she'd revert to her old self soon.

Anna Mae laughed and untied the little girl from her chair. "I'm happy to see her, too." She hugged Ruby close, then turned to Emily Jane. "What can I do to help?"

Emily Jane grinned. "Just wash up. Everything is ready and on the table now."

Anna Mae gave Ruby one last squeeze and then returned her to the chair. It took a moment to get her tied back in, but as soon as Ruby was secure she said, "I'll be right back," then headed to the washbasin on the back porch.

"Go!" Ruby called after her.

William reached over and patted Ruby on the head. "She'll be right back."

Ruby frowned at him. Ruby babbled something to her sister that was gibberish but that Rose must have understood because she mimicked the sound. Both girls smiled and looked toward the door that Anna Mae had just left through.

"She really loves Anna Mae," Emily Jane said, setting glasses of milk onto the table.

Before William could answer, Anna Mae returned and slid into her seat beside Ruby. "See, that didn't take long," she said to the little girls.

Emily Jane pushed Ruby's plate to Anna Mae and Rose's to William. He accepted the plate, knowing the twins would make a mess with the food before prayer time if she'd put them in front of the girls.

"Eat!" Rose yelled, banging her hands on the table.

A wide grin broke out over Ruby's face, and she did the same.

William shook his head at the girls. He kept his features firm as he said, "No, you know we say prayers first."

Both girls bowed their heads and waited. Thinking it was cute the way they responded, he looked to the two women to see their reactions. Emily Jane and Anna Mae had mimicked the girls and bowed their heads, as well.

He lowered his head and quickly said grace, all while fighting the chuckle that wanted to burst forth. What was it about having dinner with Emily Jane, Anna Mae and the girls that filled him with joy? Were they starting to feel like his family?

Before he said the final "amen," William reminded himself not to get too close to either of the young women. He wasn't ready for a wife or love. His only concern was for the two babies sitting at the table. They were his responsibility. There was no time for love or thoughts of love.

"Amen." All four of the females at the table echoed his final word.

William and Anna Mae pushed the girls' plates before them. Anna Mae reached for the potatoes and William the pork. As they filled their plates, Anna Mae said, "Emily Jane, I see you still have the fox puppies." Caution filled Anna Mae's voice as she said, "Emily Jane, you know you can't keep them, right?"

"Wrong. I can and will keep them." Emily Jane reached for the pork as if what she'd just said wasn't a big deal.

"They are so little. How are you going to feed them?" Anna Mae pressed.

Emily Jane finished chewing and laid her fork down. "Just like I did this afternoon. I'll feed them broth and finely chopped meat until they are old enough to eat more."

"The men are going to have a fit." Anna Mae sighed loudly.

"Maybe, but I really don't see where it's any of their business what I do in my own home." Emily Jane straightened in her chair and looked at William.

If she thought for one minute he was going to cross horns with her, then Emily Jane had another think coming. There was no way he was going to argue over two fox cubs. He spooned potatoes into his mouth and turned his attention to Rose, avoiding eye contact with Emily Jane.

"Well, they are still young," Anna Mae commented.

Emily Jane's voice softened. "Yes, and even if I wanted to return them to the woods, they wouldn't be able to fend for themselves. So I've decided to keep them, at least until they are old enough to take care of themselves."

William wiped at the potatoes in Rose's hair. "Don't handle them too much. You want them to be able to adjust to the wild when you release them."

"I won't. Only enough to feed them. I'll also keep them out of sight of the men in town. Hopefully, they won't find out about them, and there won't be any trouble over the little mites."

Her voice sounded sad. William didn't know if it was because she'd have to give up the fox pups or if it was because she had wanted to cuddle them. Something told him that Emily Jane would try not to handle the fox pups too much but would fail.

Anna Mae changed the subject by telling them about her day. It seemed the schoolboys were up to more mischief than usual. They'd locked one of the girls in the outhouse the entire lunch period. Then later in the afternoon, they'd also thought to dunk one of the girls' pigtails in the inkwell only to end up with ink all over their faces. The little girl they'd chosen was quicker and had thrown the contents of the inkwell at them. She had both Emily Jane and William laughing.

Life here in Granite was interesting, to say the least. During his short time here, he'd met Emily Jane and Anna Mae, who were both turning out to be fun friends.

What more could a man ask for? The unbidden answer came to him swiftly. *A warm home and a wife to share it with.* Would he ever have that? Could he ever trust a woman enough to share his home? His life? Even his heart?

Emily Jane walked down to Levi's store. The smell of wood and oil greeted her nose as she entered. Since William and the girls had arrived, she hadn't done any shopping other than grocery shopping at the general store.

"Well, hello, Miss Rodgers. What brings you in here this fine day?" Levi stood off to the side, oiling down what looked like hinges.

"Hello, Mr. Westland. Anna Mae's birthday is coming up, and I wanted to see if you have a wooden box or something else that I can get her." She walked over to a small table that held several boxes.

"Feel free to look around."

"Thanks." Emily Jane picked up each box and admired the artwork on them. They were pretty; she wanted something special for her best friend, but what?

She continued around the room. The animal pictures on the wall fascinated her. Emily Jane stopped in front of an elk. He looked so lifelike that she couldn't help but stare at him. One glance at the price tag told her she couldn't afford it without putting a big dent in her savings.

"Millie outdid herself on him," Levi said, coming to stand beside her.

Emily Jane nodded. "I'm sure some lucky man will be thrilled with him." She smiled over at Levi.

The bell over the door sounded. Emily and Levi turned to see who had entered. William Barns smiled at them. "Hi, Levi. I stopped by to see if you were able to finish the girls' pull ponies."

Levi nodded. "They're in the back. I'll go get them."

Emily Jane wondered where the girls were. "Pull ponies?" she asked instead.

William walked over to her. "Yep, they are little ponies that the girls can pull across the floor."

She frowned, unable to picture what he was talking about.

"You'll see in a moment." He smiled.

Unable to contain the question any longer, Emily Jane blurted out, "Where are the girls?"

"Anna Mae asked if she could take them over to Miss Marsh's dress shop with her." He shook his head. "She thinks the girls need to be around the ladies."

Emily Jane hid her grin. Anna Mae had mentioned the girls needed new dresses for church. "Maybe I'll go over there, too. I need to be with the ladies more, too."

He frowned.

She laughed.

"Here you go, William." Levi walked over to them and handed William the little wooden horses. One was painted white, the other black. A long light rope had been tied to each of their necks and little wooden balls were attached to their hooves.

He held them out for her to see. "See? Pull ponies."

The door jingled again. Levi turned to help his new customer.

"I see." Emily Jane shook her head. Rose and Ruby were going to be very spoiled little girls if everyone continued to shower them with gifts. Yet Rose and Ruby were sweet girls and motherless.

William studied her face. "Too much?"

"Not at all. They will love them."

"Would you like to get a cup of coffee with me?" William asked.

She hesitated.

"I'll even throw in a piece of pie."

Emily Jane grinned. "Pecan?"

"I'm sure Beth has pecan. Let me pay for these and we'll be on our way."

She picked up a small hand mirror. Butterflies had been painted on the handle. A perfect gift for Anna Mae. As she followed him, Emily Jane asked herself, *What am I doing?* She answered her silent question. *Spending time with a friend—that is all.* Still, she worried that they might become more than friends. Would that really be so bad?

Chapter Thirteen

Sunday morning, William plopped the girls into the wagon and hurried toward church. He hadn't asked Emily Jane for her help. He couldn't bring himself to do so, since she already watched them during the week. They'd enjoyed an hour over coffee and pie, but William couldn't see himself imposing on Emily Jane. She'd shared her ideas of coming up with more pie and pastry dishes. Creating recipes and building a recipe book for her bakery seemed to be where all her dreams lay. Taking care of the girls really was an inconvenience to her. Not that she'd say so, but he'd seen the way her eyes had brightened and her voice had sung with dreams of being independent. He sighed.

William looked over his shoulder at Rose and Ruby. They both giggled as he jogged along the path to church. The little ribbons waved as the light breeze pushed their hair out of their faces. They were his responsibility, not Emily Jane's or anyone else's. He loved them and didn't mind taking care of them.

As he hurried to the church, he questioned his sanity in attending the service. How would he keep two little girls quiet? William knelt down beside the wagon and smoothed the black curls on each little head. Rose grabbed his hand and pressed it against her soft cheek. Love wrapped around his heart like a warm blanket. As long as there was breath in his body he would never let anyone hurt them. He would be their protector, their hero. Guiding them, correcting them, loving them would always be his main purpose.

Therein lay the crux of the matter. The most important thing he could teach them would be the salvation story, that Jesus loved them and gave His life for them. And just like he needed help with their physical care, he needed backup with their spiritual care. Therefore, they needed to be in church, and that trumped worrying about how quiet or not they were in the service. As long as their papa was gone, it was his job to make sure they learned whatever they could of church at their age. But, oh, how he wished he'd thought to prepare snacks and a few toys. His determination faltered a few minutes. Then he gritted his teeth, gathered them up into his arms and carried them inside.

Everyone stood with a hymnal in their hands, voices raised in song. William looked about for a place to sit. The little church was packed. Again the desire to return home hit him hard.

Motion caught his eye, and he glanced toward the middle of the pews. Anna Mae signaled for him to join her and Emily Jane. She gave Emily Jane a little shove and whispered something in her ear.

Emily Jane looked his way, and the most beautiful welcoming smile graced her face. With a will of their own, his legs carried him and the girls toward her.

Anna Mae stepped out into the aisle to let him in, and Emily Jane scooted farther into the pew. As soon as he was between them, Anna Mae stepped back into the pew, sandwiching him and the girls in the middle.

Ruby leaned over his arm, stretched toward Anna Mae, and Rose did likewise, reaching for Emily Jane.

Both women took the little girls and offered him more smiles. A hymnbook was thrust into his now-empty hands. Emily Jane's sweet voice rose in song as the congregation sang "In the Sweet By and By." He loved the sound of her dulcet voice lifted in praise.

Rose and Ruby sang out in babyish babble, bringing a smile to his face. His sister would have been proud of her little girls. Their tiny eyes sparkled as they clapped their hands and sang unto the Lord. William exhaled a long sigh of contentment. He'd made the right choice. It felt good.

The final "amen" resounded, and Emily Jane gathered up her purse and Bible. William and the girls had distracted her so much from the service that she couldn't say what the sermon had been about if her life depended on it. If she were truthful, though, with herself, William had been the primary distraction.

Every time she'd inhaled the rich warm fragrance that was the essence of William, her heart had been set aflutter. When he'd arrived, his hair had still been damp. Now the ends curled around his ears and neck looking as soft as the girls'. Her fingers itched to touch him.

Had she lost her mind? Sniffed too many raw spices? What was wrong with her? Where had those thoughts come from, and in church, too! Emily Jane hoisted Rose up higher on her hip as she walked toward the preacher, who waited by the door to greet them.

"It's nice to see you this morning, Miss Rodgers."

She shook the minister's hand. "Thank you. It's nice to be here."

"I see you have a little visitor with you." He reached out and shook Rose's chubby little hand.

Emily Jane smiled at the shy look on Rose's face. "Yes, this little darling is Rose."

"It's nice to meet you, Rose." He turned to William, who held Ruby. "And you must be the little girls' father."

William answered with a tight smile. "No, sir. I am their uncle, William Barns." The two men shook hands.

"I'm glad you could make it this morning, Mr. Barns. I hope you will return."

William nodded. "I'm looking forward to it. That was a mighty fine message. I enjoyed it."

Emily Jane continued out the door. It was good that he had been able to focus on the sermon even if she hadn't. She saw the little wagon sitting beside the porch and carried Rose to it.

Storm clouds blocked the sun that had shone so beautifully earlier in the morning. She sighed and knelt down beside the wagon. "Rose, it looks like I may not be able to plant my herb garden this afternoon."

Rose pulled herself to the side of the wagon and reached for Emily Jane. "Up," she said.

"Sorry, little one. I have to head home as soon as your uncle William gets out here in case I get the chance to get those seeds in the ground." She pried little hands from the front of her dress and kissed them to soothe the building protest.

"Hello, Emily Jane."

Mrs. Wells and Mrs. Harvey stood beside the wagon looking down on her. She straightened and smoothed out invisible wrinkles in her skirt. "Good morning, ladies.

Did you enjoy this morning's sermon?" Where was William? He should have been out already.

"Yes, we did," Mrs. Harvey answered.

"Up," Rose demanded again, latching on to the material of Emily Jane's dress.

"Would you be interested in baking a cake for the women's spring festival this year?" Mrs. Harvey asked.

"Spring festival?"

Mrs. Harvey's eyes grew big. "Oh, that's right. You weren't here last year when we had it. It's the social event of the year."

Mrs. Wells snorted. "Really, Sylvia. That is laying it on a little thick, don't you think?"

"Not at all. As soon as the crops are in the ground, we celebrate with a small fair and a barn dance. It's an all-day event. And the best part is that it's mainly for us women."

Mrs. Wells nodded. "That part is true. The fall festival is for the whole family, but the spring one is for us ladies."

Sylvia Harvey sighed. "Anyway, as I was saying, would you be interested in baking the cake?"

Emily Jane looked from one woman to the other. She wanted to help out but not if it meant hurting someone else's feelings. Violet came to mind. Had she made last year's cake?

"I wouldn't ask but Violet recommended you. She said it's a tedious job that you would enjoy." Mrs. Harvey rushed on. "You see, we ladies want it to be bigger than last year and much prettier."

William chose that moment to walk up. "Good morning, ladies. If you will excuse me, I'll take Rose and be on my way." He hurriedly put Ruby in the wagon with her sister and made his escape.

Disappointment seeped into Emily Jane as she watched him hasten away. Not even a goodbye to her. She sighed.

Hadn't she just said she wanted to hurry home and plant her seeds? So why was she feeling as if her best friend had just dismissed her without a backward glance?

William called back over his shoulder to her. "Thanks, Emily Jane, for watching Rose for me. We'll see you tomorrow morning."

"Emily Jane?"

She kept all expression from her voice as she focused once again on Mrs. Harvey. "When would you need the cake?"

"Next Saturday. We'll pay you for it."

Emily Jane forced a smile. "Can I pray about it today and let you know tomorrow?"

Mrs. Wells waved her hands as if to shoo Emily Jane away. "Oh, sure, sure. Now that that is settled, let's go have lunch. I'm starving."

At first Emily Jane thought they were inviting her to join them, but the two women turned and walked away, leaving her standing, looking after them. Alone and feeling as if she'd just lost her best friend, Emily Jane started home.

Anna Mae was having lunch with one of her students' families. It was one of the small things the community did for Anna Mae. Each week the schoolteacher had lunch with one of her students and helped the family in any way they needed. Anna Mae had been called on to do everything from helping with schoolwork to tending the children while the parents went for a walk in the woods.

Emily Jane normally went home and baked, but today she didn't feel like baking. She had almost made it to her house when the clouds opened and rain began to pelt her. To her astonishment, tears joined the moisture from the sky on her face. What was wrong with her? She enjoyed Sunday afternoons alone. So, why did she feel so left out today?

* * *

Thunder boomed, and the force of it shook the house. Rose and Ruby buried their faces in William's shoulder. Rain pounded the tin roof over his head as he rubbed their backs. "It's just thunder and rain." He comforted them in a soft voice.

William remembered his mother telling him a story from the Bible when storms came. He hugged the girls close. "Rose, Ruby, my mother used to tell me a story about a man named Jesus, and how He wasn't afraid of thunder and rain. Would you like to hear the story?"

They snuggled close. With thumbs in their mouths, Rose and Ruby looked up at him expectantly. Fear filled their young eyes, but William thought he could see trust there, too.

"All right." He cleared his throat and began. "Jesus told people stories called parables that taught them lessons. Kind of like the preacher at church did this morning. Then He decided to take a boat ride with His disciples to the other side of the sea. Well, on the way, He grew sleepy." William grinned down at both the little girls. He wasn't sure if they understood the Bible story, but their small faces were less tense from the storm. "Probably from telling stories." Rose wiggled closer to him. "Anyway, Jesus went to sleep on a pillow." William tried to round his eyes and pretend he was scared. "Well, a big storm came. It was so big that the waves from the sea filled the boat up with water. The disciples got so scared, do you know what they did?"

Both girls shook their heads, and Rose fiddled with the buttons on his shirt.

Whether they truly understood him or not was unimportant to William. He continued. "They woke Jesus up." William nodded. "They woke Him up and asked Him if

He cared that they were about to die. Do you know what Jesus did next?"

Again the girls shook their little heads.

William hugged them more tightly and continued. "Well, He stood up and scolded the wind, and then He said, 'Peace, be still.' And the wind stopped blowing and the sea calmed down."

Ruby pulled her thumb out of her mouth with a pop. She sat up and looked over at Rose. They exchanged toothless grins.

Like in his Bible story, all was calm about the house. The thunder had stopped, the rain no longer pounded the tin roof, and there was no wind.

The front door burst open, and Emily Jane came running into the house. She stopped long enough to slam the door behind her but screamed, "Get to the hallway!" Without giving him a chance to respond, she grabbed Ruby and ran toward the hall.

William's heart lurched in his chest. He scooped up Rose and followed Emily Jane. "Why are you so upset? The storm has passed."

"No, it hasn't." She thrust Ruby into his free arm and hurried into his bedroom.

What did she mean? Everything was still. Had the woman lost her mind? He focused on the bedroom doorway, while holding his trembling nieces in his arms.

And then he heard it. It sounded much like a locomotive coming down the tracks fast. He remembered the sound. A tornado would soon be bearing down on them, if it wasn't already. Instinctively, William sank to the floor and covered Rose and Ruby with his body.

Emily Jane pulled and tugged the mattress from his bed over them all. "Help me use this to cover us," she ordered, panting from her excursion and fear.

The girls started to cry. William knew they were un-aware of the tornado that bore down on them. All they knew was that the adults' faces had turned as white as sheets and that their friend Emily Jane was scared.

William cringed as lumber and tin splintered apart. Nothing had ever prepared him for the horrible sound. Sheer, black fright swept through him. He grabbed the mattress and shoved Emily Jane and the girls under it. He knew there wasn't enough room for him, so he used his body and arms to wrap them safely within the mattress.

Panic twisted icy fingers around his throat. He had difficulty breathing. Would he remain safe till the storm cleared? Would the girls? And what about Emily Jane? He winged a prayer heavenward, even as he tried to keep his body from shaking. *Lord, please save us and Emily Jane. She risked her life to warn me. Please, keep her and the girls safe.*

Chapter Fourteen

In horrified shock, William watched the corner of the roof lift, then slam back down. The force of the wind raised it again and peeled it back a bit farther, then again slammed it back down. Each time it lifted, things in the house flew around, crashing against the walls and floor. Rain and dirt covered his head and shoulders. The wind sucked at him. With his body covering the mattress, he braced his legs and wedged his shoulders against the hall wall. The roar of the angry cyclone sent a chill up his spine. He could no longer hear the girls' cries, and he fought with all his might to hold the mattress over them.

As suddenly as the tornado had hit, it left. Rain flooded through the gaps in the roof. Emily Jane pushed at the mattress, reminding him that he still had her and the girls covered.

He shifted around and, with his arms and feet, pushed the mattress off them. "Are you all right?"

The girls crawled across the floor and Emily Jane's lap to get to him, their cries tearing at his heart. Their little faces were as white as goose feathers. Fear rounded their eyes. All they wanted was him, and William reached for them, thankful they were alive.

Emily Jane nodded as she helped the girls over her body, sitting up in the process. "You should have come under the mattress," she scolded. "You could have been killed." Tears washed down her beautiful face.

William heaved her and the girls into his embrace. All three of them wept into his shoulders. He looked up into the sky and thanked the Lord for their safety.

After several long moments, Emily Jane pulled out of his hold. Rain mingled with her tears. "I'm sorry. I didn't mean to fall apart like that." She looked around the room, unaware she still clung to his shirt.

He answered as calmly as he could and hoped his words offered reassurance. "That's all right. My shirt was wet already."

The dimple in her cheek wobbled out. "Good. I wouldn't want to ruin your best Sunday shirt." Neither of them missed the shakiness still in her voice.

The girls seemed to realize the immediate danger had passed and finally quieted down. Rose turned to Emily Jane. "Up." She held her arms out, waiting for Emily Jane to do as she requested.

Emily Jane took the baby and held her close. Ruby laid her wet head on William's shoulder. Her sobs were quiet but still flowing.

"How did you know?" he asked Emily Jane as he stood up with Ruby.

She took the hand he offered but proved unsteady on her feet, so he clasped her close to his side. "I have been here all spring. This is Texas, and you learn real quickly the signs of a tornado."

William nodded. She was right; he should have recognized the signs, but it had been years since he'd been anywhere near a tornado. If she hadn't come, what would have happened to him and the little girls? He shivered at the thought.

"Thank you." With her hand clasped firmly in his, she followed as he led the way back into the sitting room, stepping carefully around broken glass and overturned furniture.

The couch that he and the girls had been on when she'd rushed inside now lay crushed under the chimney. "I think you saved our lives," William said, solemnly.

"It wasn't me, William. It was God." Emily Jane reclaimed her hand and opened the door and looked outside. She gasped. "Oh, dear Lord, no." Her wail scared the girls, and the crying started back up.

He hurried to her side, and what he saw turned his own legs to mush. Her house had been destroyed. Nothing remained standing. Rubble now lay where her house had once been. He asked the question carefully, dreading the answer. "Emily Jane? Was Anna Mae at home when you came over here?" *God, please, don't let her have been home. Please.*

Everything was gone. Emily Jane swallowed the lump in her throat and answered William. "She's supposed to be at one of her students' homes."

"Thank the Lord."

A crash sounded behind them. Emily Jane turned in time to see the back wall of his home fall. They were in danger. The whole house could come tumbling down around them.

William must have had the same thought, because he grabbed her hand and pulled her out the door. Other people were fleeing what used to be their homes, as well. They turned to look at the house that was still standing, even though it had only three walls.

Emily Jane glanced away from the scary sight. Mrs. Matthews stood in the road. She looked as befuddled as Emily Jane felt. Her gray hair had come unpinned on one side, and her dress was torn at the shoulder. Emily Jane hurried to her side. "Are you all right, Mrs. Matthews? You're bleeding. We should get you to the doctor."

The older woman smoothed her hair back with a shaky left hand. "I believe so." Her shoulder hung at an odd angle, and blood slowly seeped through the sleeve of her dress.

Mrs. Green joined them. "It looks like it hit every house in our neighborhood," she cried, holding on to a small picture frame.

A rumbling started, and everyone turned in the direction it came from. Emily Jane gasped as William's house collapsed upon itself. Only minutes before they'd been standing inside; now it was just a pile of rubble like her own house.

His shoulders slumped, and a whoosh of air exited his lungs. "Thank You, Lord, that we weren't inside."

Ruby patted her uncle's cheek. She stuck her thumb back in her mouth and looked to her sister, Rose. The two little girls seemed as calm as their uncle.

How could he pray so calmly? Like her, he was now homeless. What were they going to do? Where were they going to go? Tears flowed down her face. She couldn't have controlled them if her life had depended on it.

William turned to look at her and Rose. "Houses can be rebuilt." He cupped her face in one large hand and wiped a tear with his thumb. "I'll help you rebuild yours."

"Emily Jane!"

She turned to see Anna Mae running toward her. Panic and fear distorted the other woman's features. Had she seen the house yet?

Her best friend grabbed her and Rose and hugged them close. "Are you all right?"

Emily Jane clung to her. "I'm fine. But I think Mrs. Matthews should see a doctor."

Anna Mae released her and held her at arm's length. Anna Mae ran her eyes over Emily Jane, checking for any sign of harm. Satisfied she was fine, Anna Mae turned her attention to Mrs. Matthews.

"Emily Jane is correct. We need to get you to the doctor."

Mrs. Matthews shook her head. "No, there will be others that need him much more than myself."

Anna Mae nodded. "That may be so, but we'll let him decide who needs treatment first and who can wait." She took the older woman by her left arm and walked away, weaving in and out of the crowd gathered in the street.

Why wasn't she more like Anna Mae? Emily Jane felt helpless at the destruction about them. She turned to look at the space where her house had stood. Crushed like flatbread.

Bread. Her recipe book. Emily Jane thrust Rose into someone's arms and ran to the house. She stumbled over the rubble that had been her sitting room, into what was left of the kitchen area. Even the stove was gone.

Wood and nails tore into her hands as she desperately dug to find her recipe book. Emily Jane ignored the pain. Every recipe she'd ever created was in it. Her great-grandmother's recipes were within the pages of the two-inch-thick volume. Tears streamed down her face in a flash flood. Why hadn't she left it at The Bakery? Her mother had given it to her the day she'd left home.

A strong arm pulled at her. "Emily Jane, you are tearing your hands up. Stop."

"I have to find my recipes!" Emily Jane sounded like

a wild woman, an out-of-control woman, but she didn't care. Her life's work was buried somewhere in the wreckage.

"If you won't stop, I'll help you look." He began tossing boards, broken dishes and all other forms of shards to the side.

Everything was broken or torn. Fire burned in her hands. Emily Jane looked down at her fingers and found them bleeding. She'd been unaware of the pain until now. She looked at William, who continued working at her side. What was she doing? Emily Jane placed a hand on his forearm. "Stop. You're going to hurt yourself."

"No more than you. Look at your hands. I know this is all a shock to you, but the book can be replaced."

His compassion and care for her broke through all her defenses. Great sobs tore through her chest. It was gone. Her most prized possession was gone, but she wouldn't allow anyone to hurt themselves over the recipes. "I'll stop, too." She hiccuped.

He pulled her into his embrace. "Cry it out." William rubbed her back as he held her close. Emily Jane didn't care what others thought; she did as he said and wept till the hurt and despair lessened.

An hour later, the rain still came down in a slow shower. People were digging through the rubble of their homes. Some looked lost and forlorn; others seemed to be on a mission to find something personal, just as Emily Jane had been earlier.

She felt Rose wind her small fingers in her hair. "Eat," the little girl demanded, placing her other hand on Emily Jane's cheek and pulling her around to face her. "Eat," she said again.

"I'm afraid you are going to have to wait a little while,

sweet girl," Emily Jane answered. She turned to William. "What should we do now?"

He looked about them at the elderly women and a few men who were now homeless. As they waited to hear his reply, the people shuffled toward him. It seemed the tornado had taken out their whole community.

William sighed. "We rebuild."

Mr. Orson stepped up beside him. "Yes, we rebuild. It's what we've done in the past. It's what we will do now. Well said, young man." He pounded William on the back.

Mrs. Orson looked to her husband and huffed. "And while we are rebuilding, where do you expect us to live?"

Emily Jane made a decision and prayed the school council would agree with it. "We can stay at the schoolhouse and maybe the church."

William nodded.

"Are they still standing?" Mrs. Green asked. Her red hat sat sideways on her head and had definitely seen much better days.

"Yes, they are. And you are more than welcome to stay at the church for as long as it takes to rebuild."

Emily Jane looked to the preacher. When had he arrived? It didn't matter; all that mattered was that he'd answered and said the church would house folks.

More and more townspeople joined them. Each person's face reflected the devastation about them. Would they all band together?

Miss Cornwell shook her head. "It takes money to rebuild." A tear ran down her face. "And I don't have it."

Susanna Marsh came to stand beside Emily Jane. She placed an arm around her shoulders. The smell of roses almost overpowered Emily Jane as she leaned close and whispered, "Where is Anna Mae?"

"With Mrs. Matthews. She took her to the doctor," Emily Jane whispered back.

Susanna began wrapping Emily Jane's hands in a soft cloth. The blood had stopped flowing earlier, but Susanna seemed to feel she needed to cover the wounds. As she worked, the people around them carried on conversations about what they were going to do.

A school council member came forward. "I am making it official. We'll use the school to house folks. With spring planting under way, the school was going to close soon anyway. I'm sure Miss Leland will be happy to help anyone she can."

Susanna asked in a quiet voice, "Will you be staying at the school with Anna Mae?"

Emily Jane nodded. "If there is room."

"You are welcome to stay with me—both of you are."

It blessed Emily Jane's heart that Susanna would open her home to her and Anna Mae. Susanna once saw them as competition for Levi Westland's bride position, but now she was showing that she was a true friend. She hugged Susanna tightly for a moment. "Thank you, but for now, I think we will be needed to help these folks."

Susanna looked about the crowd of elderly faces and nodded. Then she released Emily Jane and walked over to Miss Cornwell. Susanna slipped her arm around the older woman's shoulders and held her tight. Miss Cornwell hugged herself about the waist and cried softly.

Miss Cornwell was the town spinster. She'd never married. No one knew why. They just knew that she hadn't. Had she ever regretted not marrying? Emily Jane thought, someday, she might ask her.

Susanna spoke into the older woman's ear, much as she had into Emily Jane's moments earlier.

"What do you think she's saying to her?" William asked in a low voice.

Emily Jane gave him a watery smile. "Susanna is probably offering her a place to stay."

Miss Cornwell nodded.

Susanna turned to the crowd. "Ladies, please come over to the Sewing Room, when you can. I have dresses that I want to give you all." Then she led Miss Cornwell away from the crowd.

Tears and rain ran down the women's faces. Susanna had a heart of gold, something she was revealing to many who didn't know her and to those who thought they knew her but didn't. Susanna's gift of dresses wasn't a cheap present, and even though she hadn't meant it to, it had bought her many friendships.

"Those who want to stay at the church, please, follow me," the preacher called as he turned and walked toward the church.

The school councilman said almost the same thing, only he turned toward the schoolhouse. Emily Jane stared after each man.

For the second time in the past year, Emily Jane was homeless. She had no family, no spouse and no one to care what became of her. For a moment she thought about wallowing in self-pity but then realized that her thoughts weren't entirely true. Emily Jane had friends, and her friends needed her.

Rose chose that moment to repeat, "Eat."

Ruby's little voice joined Rose's. "Eat."

"Let's head over to the general store. I'm sure I can get Wilson to open it for me." William started walking.

Emily Jane followed. Thankfully, the rain now came down in a fine mist instead of the earlier downpour. Rose laid her head on Emily Jane's shoulder. "Eat?"

She patted the little girl's back. "In a few minutes."

William banged on the store door. Within a few moments, a light approached the entry. Mr. Moore opened the door.

"William, what are you all doing out in the storm?"

He motioned for them to enter.

Emily Jane inhaled the comforting fragrances. Water dripped on the wooden floors, and she inhaled sharply. "Oh, we're getting the floor wet."

"Never mind the floor. What are you doing out in this storm?" Wilson Moore demanded for the second time.

"A tornado hit our street. All the homes are gone."

A gasp sounded behind the counter. Emily Jane turned to find Carolyn Moore standing there bouncing her little boy against her shoulder. "Is everyone all right?" she asked.

William answered. "As far as we know. Mrs. Matthews went to the doctor with a hurt shoulder. She's the only one that I know of that was hurt."

Carolyn looked to Emily Jane.

Emily Jane nodded her agreement.

"That's disturbing news, William. We heard the strong winds, and then the rain came in torrents, but we had no clue it stirred up a tornado. What can we do to help?" Wilson asked, glancing about his store.

"Eat," Ruby said, rising off of William's shoulder and reaching for an apple.

Carolyn hurried around the counter. "Oh, you poor baby." She touched Ruby's damp locks. "Emily Jane, bring the babies upstairs, and we'll get some food in their bellies. Wilson, you give William whatever he needs."

At his nod, Carolyn led the way to her living quarters. "I've just put away chicken, mashed potatoes and corn bread. We'll get these girls fed in no time. You must be devastated. Is your home repairable?"

Emily Jane hugged the girls close. "No, all the houses were flattened or close to being flattened. Mine and William's are piles of rubble." She felt tears run down her face. Not only for herself but for her friends and neighbors. What was going to happen to them all? How would William care for the girls now?

William watched as Emily Jane followed Mrs. Moore. Did she know what a blessing she was to others? The way she'd hurried to his rescue when the storm had hit, the way she'd rushed to assure the elders in her neighborhood that they had a place to stay until their homes could be rebuilt, and the way she'd taken Rose and Ruby under her wing to protect and provide for them was something Charlotte would never have done.

Charlotte had been beautiful on the outside but not loving and kind. Emily Jane was both beautiful on the inside and the outside. It was too bad she didn't want children or a husband. William mentally shook himself. He wasn't ready to become a husband and decided to keep all thoughts like those at bay. He and Emily Jane were friends, and that was all they would ever be. Besides, even if he were thinking such thoughts, right now he had nothing to offer her.

Once the women were out of the room, Wilson asked, "What can we do to help?"

William took a deep breath. "You might not like what I'm going to suggest."

"Let's hear it, and then I'll let you know if I like it or not." Wilson crossed his arms and waited.

"Do you mind if we sit and talk? I've had kind of

a stressful afternoon," he said, prolonging the moment when he'd tell Wilson what he had in mind.

Immediately Wilson nodded and headed to the back of the store. He motioned for William to sit at the table where the older gentlemen enjoyed playing checkers. As soon as William was seated, he sat, too. "Now that I'm sitting down, what did you have in mind?" he asked with a half grin, his expression one of total seriousness.

William ran his hands through his wet hair. "As you know, most of the people who live on my street are elderly and have very little money. Those homes were all most of them had."

Wilson nodded. "Yes, it's very sad."

"They are staying either at the school or the church. There is no food, no clothes and no bedding at either place," William continued, searching Wilson's face.

"I can help with some of that but not all." He motioned about the store. "I'm sure you noticed this is a small store, and recently I've been struggling to keep it stocked."

William nodded. It was just as he'd suspected. "What would you say if I offered to become a business partner?"

Wilson's eyes grew big as he pulled away from the table. "I thought we were talking about helping our community."

"We are." William crossed his arms over his chest. "Those people are the reason I'm bringing it up now instead of later. Let's put our cards on the table. I'll start. I owned a big mercantile in Denver. But when my sister—Rose and Ruby's mother—died, I couldn't stand living there any longer. So I sold my business and came here. I'd planned on starting a new business as soon as my money arrived from the Denver bank to this bank. Now with the people needing help and you needing help, I thought I'd ask."

Wilson sputtered and started to protest.

William held up his hand to silence the rant that was sure to come. "You just said yourself that you're having trouble keeping the shelves stocked."

Defeated, Wilson looked down at the table. He traced a splintered edge with his callused finger. "That's true, but I didn't plan on selling."

"And I'm not planning on buying."

That caught Wilson's attention, and he looked up. "Then what exactly are you proposing?"

William dropped his arms and leaned forward. "I'm proposing a partnership. A silent partnership."

"Why silent?"

He studied Wilson's face. Now was the moment of truth. "Does it really matter why?" William asked.

Wilson nodded. "It does to me. If you are doing something illegal or underhanded, I won't be a part of it. Even if it means losing this store."

William nodded. "I'm a single man, trying to raise my nieces. I don't want the town to know my financial business. There are fathers with daughters who would do anything to marry a wealthy man. I want a woman to marry me for me, not for how much money I have." He didn't bother telling Wilson he had no intentions of marrying; that was business he hadn't shared with anyone other than Emily Jane.

"That's understandable. So, tell me, how would this partnership work?"

William spent the next hour working out a deal with Wilson that left them both satisfied with the arrangement. Once finished, he walked the few aisles of the store, gathering supplies from each shelf, things the now-homeless people would need in the coming days. As he thought carefully about the items required, the loss the people had suffered overwhelmed his mind and made him choose more carefully. God had blessed him abundantly, and it pleased him to no end to be able to help others. The scriptures were correct when they said, *"It is more blessed to give than to receive."*

He had just finished boxing and loading the supplies when Emily Jane returned with Rose and Ruby. Both little girls wore dry dresses and had the satisfied look of two babies with full tummies. Emily Jane, also, appeared drier than when she'd left.

Carolyn arrived right on her heels with a small wicker basket. "I hope you're hungry. I've made you and Emily Jane several ham-and-cheese sandwiches for later and added a couple of bottles of milk for the girls."

"Thank you. That is very kind." William took a drowsy Ruby from Emily Jane. He nuzzled his cheek against hers, and she cuddled closer into his shoulder. Had they been at home in the rocking chair, she would have been asleep in a few minutes.

Carolyn handed him the basket. "Nonsense. It's the least I can do, considering." Her flushed cheeks indicated that he'd embarrassed her.

He offered her a smile and then turned to Emily Jane. "Have you decided where you will be staying?"

"The school, I guess. I believe that's where Anna Mae will be, and I plan to help her as much as possible."

William nodded. "I hate to ask, but do you mind keeping the girls with you a little bit longer while I distribute these supplies to the church?" He indicated the wagon full of food and blankets.

Emily Jane hugged Rose closer and reached for Ruby. "I'll be happy to take them with me." But Ruby was having none of it. She strained against Emily Jane's arms, reaching for William.

Ruby whined in a tired little voice. "Me go," she demanded.

He grinned and caved. "I tell you what—I'll take Ruby, and you hang on to Rose." William held his arms out, and Ruby all but jumped into them. His heart soared with love and thankfulness that they were okay. He held her tight against his heart.

Emily Jane nodded and turned to Carolyn once more. "Thank you again, for everything."

Carolyn hugged her. "If you need anything else, please, come see me. I'll help with the girls, too, while you two figure out what the future holds for you."

Her words stayed with William long after he'd left the Moores. What did the future hold for them? How could he help his new hometown? Would Emily Jane continue caring for the girls? So many unanswered questions plagued him as he made his way to the church.

Chapter Fifteen

The townspeople of Granite, Texas, came together in a phenomenal way to help the tornado victims. Last night they'd supplied blankets, pillows, and the women had brought in food for their evening meal. A fresh supply of drinking water and a roof over their heads had felt pretty good by the time they settled down for the night. Emily Jane prayed they didn't get sick from being in the constant drizzle the day before, but there had been no help for it. Everyone had tried to locate their personal belongings, which meant digging through the rubble of what remained.

The sun had yet to show itself when Emily Jane awoke. Her back muscles ached from sleeping on the floor with Rose cuddled up next to her all night. She eased her arm out from under the sleeping toddler, carefully stood and stretched the kinks from her body.

She looked down at her dress and found it wrinkled and soiled in places. As much as she hated to do it, Emily Jane knew she'd have to take Susanna up on her offer of a new dress. But, for now, the one she wore would have to do since she hadn't found any of her clothing in the rubble the night before. It was as if the twister had sucked up all that was valuable and left a pile of matches as payment.

Yesterday, in the final fading light with a soft drizzle drenching her dress and hair, Emily Jane had found her fox pups. Thankfully, they had survived. They were wet and cold, but huddled in their wooden box several feet away from the house. It was as if something or someone had simply picked them up and set them away from the damage. She'd wept, tears mingling with the rain, thankful the Lord had seen fit to allow them to live. Then she'd moved them to the lean-to, the only building on the block that hadn't been struck. William's mare had greeted her with a nervous whinny.

Emily Jane's tears hadn't been just for the pups but for everyone that the twister had touched. Sorrow for their loss but praise that God had spared their lives warred with each other in her heart. They may have lost their homes, but they all had their lives, and that was a blessing in itself.

Now in the gray light of dawn, sadness threatened to overwhelm her as she looked about the room. *Lord, these people are too old to start all over again. Please, be with them in the upcoming days as they realize what all they have lost.*

Thankfully, Anna Mae had agreed to watch over Rose while she worked. The baby slept peacefully as Emily Jane eased her over onto Anna Mae's blankets. Anna Mae looked up sleepily, then pulled Rose to her side before shutting her eyes once more.

Emily Jane stepped over the ladies who slept closest to her and quietly shut the schoolhouse door behind her. Thankfully, she had a job to go to and some money in the bank. Still, she couldn't help but long for her recipe book.

She hurried down the hill and toward the ruins that

once were her home. Though she no longer had a house to care for, she did have animals that would be hungry this morning.

The debris that filled the small dirt street spoke volumes of the destruction that had taken place the day before. Struggling to keep the tears at bay, she focused on the Lord and the fact that He had kept them all alive and most of them safe.

Mrs. Matthews's shoulder had been dislocated when she was slung against her house walls, but other than that, mostly she'd suffered only cuts and bruises. The doctor had popped the shoulder back into place and put her arm in a sling. He'd also stitched up the cut on her arm and given her orders to take it easy for a few days.

A washtub sat in the middle of the road. Bits of clothing were strung across the wood and tin that used to be someone's house. After work, Emily Jane intended to look again for her dresses, since surely they hadn't all been blown away. When she got to where her house had been, she hurried to the lean-to. Scooping up what hay was left, she fed the horse and then checked on the fox pups.

In just the few days she'd had them, they had grown, and their coats were starting to turn the rich red colors that marked them as a fox. They began to whimper when they saw her. Emily Jane knew they were hungry but had nothing to give them. She picked them up and gave each a cuddle before setting them at her feet.

They followed her to the well, where she dropped the water bucket inside. She heard it splash and then drew it up. Water sloshed over the edges as she hoisted it over the rock ledge. Emily Jane cupped the water into her hands and held it down for the fox pups to lap up.

As the sweet babies drank, she wondered how long it

would be before the men in town realized she was keeping fox cubs. That didn't really matter, since it was about time to release them into the wild. She'd ask William for help when she saw him next.

The sun crept up over the hill, casting red, pink and orange rays across the morning skies. After the continued rain all night, the sunshine was a welcome blessing. She tossed the remainder of the water from her hands and dried her wet palms on her apron. Emily Jane untied the bucket from the rope and then scooped the fox pups up in one arm.

Carrying them back to their box, she cooed, "I know you are hungry, and I promise to bring you something to eat in a few hours." She placed them gently into the box. "Until then, you two behave yourselves." Emily Jane filled the horse's bucket with water.

A few minutes later, she entered The Bakery through the back door. Violet Atwood turned with a frown. "What are you doing here, Emily Jane?"

"I work here." She pulled off the dirty white apron she'd been wearing and grabbed a nice clean one off the hook beside the door.

Violet made a tsking noise. "Yes, but with you losing your house yesterday, I didn't expect you to come in today."

Emily Jane walked to the washbasin and grabbed the bar of soap. She scrubbed her hands and arms until it felt as if her flesh might wash off. The cuts from the day before screamed out as the soap cleansed them.

"Where else would I be? Sitting in the schoolhouse? I don't want to just sit idle." Emily Jane wiped her hands dry. What she didn't say was that she didn't want to dwell on her future. What kind of future was it anyway? She had no place to live, and the money she'd saved up for her bakery would now have to be used to move into a new home. Her recipe book was probably long lost; even if she found it, the rain had probably ruined it. A single tear escaped and ran down her cheek. She swiped at it angrily. What was the matter with her? She was alive. Yet she wanted to be a baby and cry over a lost recipe book. *Shame on you, Emily Jane,* she scolded herself.

The house she and Anna Mae lived in didn't belong to them. So, for Anna Mae and herself it wasn't a matter of rebuilding; they would just have to find another home. Anna Mae could travel between her students' homes. Emily Jane didn't have that luxury. Not that staying with other families was much of a treat.

Emily Jane turned to face Violet. "Please, just let me work."

Violet came over and hugged her. "Of course. You are always welcome here. I just thought…"

"I know and I appreciate your thoughtfulness, but I need to work." Emily Jane began to gather ingredients to make a large batch of cinnamon buns. They were her specialty and her comfort.

"I'm glad you're here." Violet put the coffee on and began working alongside her. "I don't suppose you were able to save your recipe book."

She groaned aloud, unable to squash her grief a moment longer. The tears that she'd fought earlier rolled in huge rivulets down her cheeks. "Not yet. After work I intend to go through the rubble of the house and see what can be salvaged. I'm praying I'll find it undamaged, but with the rain and the wind, I'm not holding my breath."

"Oh, Emily Jane. I'm so terribly sorry. I know how much your grandmother's recipe book meant to you." Violet slipped an arm around Emily Jane's shoulders and squeezed her tightly for a moment. "I feel so helpless. I wish there was something I could do."

"Letting me work helps me get my mind off of things, so I appreciate it. You're helping me more than you know." For a moment they both became lost in their own thoughts.

Emily Jane knew that, like everything else, the book could be replaced. It would take time, but she could do it. Time? What would time bring for her?

As she kneaded the dough, Emily Jane thought about her future. What was she going to do? As they always did, her thoughts went to William and the girls. She knew her feelings for them were more than friendship, but she refused to call it love. She wasn't ready to give up her independence. Falling in love with William would lead to her wanting to be with him and giving up her dream of being independent and owning her own bakery. No, she was not in love with William. Maybe it was time to move to another town before she did start thinking in terms of love. Could she leave them? Her heart broke at the thought.

A week after the tornado, William left the bank feeling better than he had earlier that morning. The banker had accepted his plan and stipulations. His money had arrived several days before, and he, now with the aid of the banker, could help the elders of Granite, Texas, start rebuilding.

Over the past week, everyone had worked nonstop cleaning up the wreckage the tornado had left behind. It had soon become apparent that even though most of them owned their lots, none of them had the funds to rebuild. William knew he did, and he'd thought up a way to help everyone so that they could care for each other and have a roof over their heads while doing so. This afternoon, the plan would be revealed to the homeless citizens of Granite.

As they often did, his thoughts moved to Emily Jane. After the first night, she and Anna Mae had moved into Beth's Boardinghouse. They pooled their funds and rented a room together. But each evening the two ladies returned to the school to help with the evening meals. William found himself impressed with each young lady. They could have remained at the boardinghouse each evening, reading, quilting, sewing or just relaxing, but chose instead to help those less fortunate. That took character, Christian character, and he knew the Lord would bless them for their efforts.

Emily Jane offered to take the girls again, but with so many of the elder ladies wanting something to do with their time and offering to watch the girls while he worked, he'd assured her they were well taken care of. William hadn't realized that having the ladies care for the twins would limit his time spent with Emily Jane. Oh, how he missed her. He had made a huge mistake but had no plans to right the situation.

He told himself it was for the best. On the day of the tornado, William had wanted nothing more than to take her hurts away. A part of his heart had melted, and he found himself in deep waters. Totally new territory for him. The emotions created an uneasiness in him, making him feel insecure. He simply couldn't have that. He needed a clear head. In the first place, the odds were stacked against them. Emily Jane didn't want children and he did. Secondly, he hadn't heard a word from his brother-in-law. William feared Josiah was dead. Why else would he leave the girls for so long? So, that meant whoever William married would start off with a ready-made family. Not many young ladies were up for that.

He worked his way up the street toward the church. Thanks to the banker, who had agreed to make the announcement, William's plan would be revealed. However, the town would only hear that an unnamed beneficiary had offered a substantial sum of money to build a large building. Sixteen rooms to be exact, for those who couldn't afford to rebuild and didn't mind living in one home with other people. It would be much like a boardinghouse, but they wouldn't have to pay rent.

William was no builder, but he'd drawn out the house plan. Each person or couple would have two rooms to call their own. He expected most to have a bedroom and a sitting room, but that was entirely up to them. A large kitchen would be situated at the back of the house, and a great room would be in the center for dining and visitors.

When he entered the church, William slipped into one of the back pews. Mrs. Green and Mrs. Harvey held his sleeping nieces a few benches in front of him. Mr. and Mrs. Orson occupied the same pew as he did.

Mr. Orson leaned over. "Cutting it close, aren't you, young man?" he asked, with a twinkle in his eye.

"Had to work," William replied. It was the truth. He'd put in his hours at the store with the Moores. He'd stocked shelves with the merchandise that they'd ordered a few days before. It felt good to help others. He liked working. Nothing made a man feel better than a good, hard day's work.

"I think our friendly banker has been studying his books again and found another way to make a profit. Why else would he call this meeting?"

Before William could answer, Mrs. Orson hissed, "You two quiet down. Here he comes."

Everyone craned their necks to see what the banker would have to say. William watched as Amos and another young man walked up to the platform. Each young boy held a corner of William's drawing between them.

"Thank you all for coming," the banker said loudly. "I'm sure you're all wondering why I called this meeting."

Mrs. Orson huffed. "Why else would we be here?" she whispered loudly.

"Well, a few days ago I had a gentleman come into my office who was very concerned about your well-being." He paused as the crowd began to murmur.

"Who is this man?" Mrs. Wells demanded.

The banker raised his hand. "He's asked me to keep his identity a secret."

Again the small congregation began to mutter among themselves. William wondered if Mr. Anderson was ever going to tell the people why they were here. He stood up and walked toward the platform.

Once he stood by the banker, the crowd quieted down. "Ladies and gentlemen, give Mr. Anderson a chance to finish. I, for one, want to know what this is about." William searched the small sea of faces until he found Emily Jane.

She sat with Anna Mae, Susanna Marsh and Miss Cornwell. Her sad eyes held his for several moments. He made eye contact with each person.

"I believe you can continue now, Mr. Anderson." William sat down in the front pew.

"As I was saying, the bank has been given a large amount of money to help you rebuild your homes." The room remained silent, so the banker continued. "Your benefactor has a suggestion on how to use the money but wants you to know that it is only a suggestion. If you do not want to build according to his plan, you each will be allotted equal amounts of the money."

Whispers broke out about the church once more.

"I know this is a bit of a shock, but if you will look this way—" He pointed to the drawing the two boys held on the platform. "This is a plan for a rather large house. In it are sixteen rooms." Mr. Anderson indicated eight rooms on each side of a big box. "Those are the rooms. Now, what he thought was that the six people and Mr. and Mrs. Orson who lost their homes could live in two rooms each."

"All together?" Miss Cornwell asked.

He nodded. "Yes, but, please, let me finish before you ask questions or make any rash decisions."

She nodded. "Please, continue."

"This room—" he pointed to the box at the back of the house "—is the kitchen. And this room—" he pointed to the room in the front "—is the great room. It could be used as a dining room and a sitting room."

William waited. He couldn't see their faces. What were they thinking? That he was insane. The silence continued. Were they in shock?

He stood once more and faced them. "What do you think?"

They all began talking at once. William held up his hand. "Please, one at a time."

Mrs. Orson raised her hand and shook it in the air. Her lips were thinner than normal. Whatever she had to say might as well be said first. "Mrs. Orson, do you have a question?" William asked.

"Yes, I do. Will you be living in this big house?" She pointed at the drawing.

"No, ma'am. As much as I like this idea, I'm afraid

the girls would be too noisy to live in a community home like this one." He offered her a smile.

"Then where will you live?" There was genuine concern in her voice.

"I plan on rebuilding my grandmother's house," he answered, wondering where she was going with this line of questioning.

She nodded. "So those precious children will be close by, so that we can still watch them for you while you work?"

He couldn't contain the big grin that split his lips. A couple of weeks ago this woman and her friends had complained about his nieces. Now she wanted them close by so that she could take care of them. God had a way of working things out. "Yes, ma'am."

Miss Cornwell raised her hand. "Where will the house be?"

"Well, since you all own your lots, we were thinking of putting the house right in the middle of your land," the banker answered. "This house will be very large. Each room in this house has been designed to be very spacious. It will take up most of the street."

Mrs. Green raised her hand. "Who will own the house?"

"Your secret benefactor. But he can never make you move out because it will be on your land," Mr. Anderson answered. "I'll see to it that this is done legally, and you will never have to worry about losing your home by the hands of the bank or any man."

The questions continued for the next hour. William was thankful that Mr. Anderson had anticipated all their concerns.

He was surprised when Emily Jane raised her hand.

The banker responded. "Yes, Miss Rodgers."

"Mr. Anderson, who are the eight people who will

receive this house?" Her voice sounded small and lost to William's ears. He hadn't spent a lot of time with her since the tornado had blown both their homes away. Looking at her now, he saw the dark circles under her eyes and the fatigue in the droop of her shoulders.

Mr. Anderson pulled a paper from his front pocket and began to read the list of names. "Mrs. Lois Green, Miss Gertie Cornwell, Mrs. Mary Wells, Mrs. Sylvia Harvey, Miss Emily Jane Rodgers, Miss Anna Mae Leland and Mr. and Mrs. Orson."

Mr. Orson spoke up. "That is only seven. You said there are eight rooms."

"That is correct. Your benefactor had also anticipated Mr. Barns moving in, but as you've just heard, he has no intentions of doing so. The eighth set of rooms is for your families when they come to visit," Mr. Anderson explained, and he folded the paper with the names on it and put it into his pocket. "This is an all-or-none deal, folks."

The room began to hum again.

William stood once more. "Since this is a decision that only the eight people on Mr. Anderson's list have to make, I suggest that the rest of us return to our own business and allow them the chance to decide in private what they want to do." He started walking toward the door. As he passed Emily Jane's pew, he looked into her troubled eyes.

What would her decision be? Would she be willing to live in the same house with seven other people? If truth be told, he'd done this for her. Had this eased her mind any? Or would she continue to fret about her future?

Chapter Sixteen

Almost two hours later, Emily Jane left the church with the realization that she would have a real home soon. The eight people had agreed to let their benefactor build them a house. There had been a discussion as to who in the community could afford to be so generous. It was decided that the benefactor was probably none other than Levi Westland.

His family owned the largest cattle ranch in the area, and Levi himself owned at least three of the town businesses. He was known for helping the orphans and the widows. Once that conclusion had been made, the elders had agreed that they were safe in allowing the house to be built on their lands.

She'd seen hope in their eyes for the first time in days. Mr. Anderson had assured them that building supplies would be ordered from the sawmill that evening and that their new homes should be completed by the end of summer, if they could get the locals to help with the building.

"Emily Jane!"

She stopped and looked behind her. Mrs. Harvey hurried toward her.

"The ladies and I were talking this morning and we

wondered if you would still consider baking the cake for the spring festival. Only this year it's going to be the summer festival." She held her sides and panted as she waited for Emily Jane to answer.

"I'd have to ask Mr. Westland if I can use The Bakery kitchen to make it. But if he says yes, I'll be happy to make the cake." It was nice that the women still wanted to have the celebration.

Mrs. Harvey smiled. "No need to ask him. You can bake it in our big kitchen that the men will be building for us."

Emily Jane shook her head. "I'm not sure the house will be completed in time. Didn't Mr. Anderson say it would probably be the end of the summer before it would be complete?"

"Well, yes, but I really think the men can get it up faster. We women could help during the weekdays, and they could work on it on Saturdays." Mrs. Harvey seemed confident, and Emily Jane didn't want to discourage her, so she kept her thoughts to herself.

With a house that size, it would take more than a few months to build. For one thing, the men would not be able to work on it every weekend. They had businesses and farms to run. And, even with the best of intentions, the women were up in age, and after a few days they would have aches and pains in places they'd forgotten they possessed. No, she wouldn't share all of that with Mrs. Harvey. Emily Jane doubted a house that size could be completed by the end of summer, but only time would tell.

"I'll be happy to make the cake, Mrs. Harvey."

Those were the words the woman really wanted to hear. Emily Jane was rewarded with a huge smile. "Thank you." Mrs. Harvey turned away. "I need to go, but I'll talk to you soon."

Emily Jane didn't want to go back to the boarding-house just yet. The Nelsons, the owners of the house she and Anna Mae had shared, had decided to sell the lot and lean-to, so it was time to do something with the fox pups. They were now about eight weeks old, and it was obvious that they weren't just puppies. They no longer stayed in the box, so she'd shut them up in the lean-to; but now they'd have to be released.

She pulled the door open, expecting to be welcomed by wiggly fox pups. Instead, the giggles of little girls tilted up the corners of her own mouth. For sure there hadn't been much lately to laugh about. What a lovely sound. Emily Jane stepped inside and allowed her eyes to adjust to the darker interior of the building.

"Emily, would you hold the door open for me?"

The way William said only her first name made the blood course through her veins like an awakened river. It didn't come out harsh-sounding as her name often did when people used both Emily and Jane. Her hand fluttered against the door's jagged edge. "Sure." She stepped back as he passed with his mare in tow.

The fox pups raced out after him, and Rose and Ruby crawled rapidly behind the foxes. The little girls squealed with joy as the pups bounded to them, licking their faces and knocking them over.

William's warm laughter drew her focus back to him. "I think the girls have found lifelong friends to play with."

"That would be nice, but Mrs. Nelson told me this morning that they're selling the lot and lean-to, so it looks like I will have to take them to the woods and release them." Sorrow touched her heart. Coming each morning to take care of the fox pups had added meaning to her days. Now, well, like everything else, she was about to lose them. Tears pricked the backs of her eyes. Emily Jane refused to release them.

"Mr. Nelson gave me the same news. I'm moving Bess to the livery. She should have been there all along anyway." William stroked the mare's nose while watching the little girls play with the foxes. "Would you like us to go with you to release them?"

Emily Jane shook her head. "No, I'll do it." She didn't want to do it alone but also didn't want William and the girls to see her cry. Which she was sure would happen when she had to let them go.

"Do you have to do it right now?" He looked into her green eyes as if searching for the answer to his question there. "Would it hurt to wait a few days?"

Her breath caught in her throat at the intensity of his gaze. "I suppose not. Why?"

"Well, while I was visiting with Mr. Nelson this morning, he told me about a small farm on the north end of town that recently went on sale. Saturday, if you have the time, I'd like for you to go with me to look at it."

Emily Jane watched the girls cuddle the fox pups close to them. What would a few more nights in the lean-to hurt?

"The girls will be coming, too. We could make a day of it." His deep blue eyes beseeched her to say yes.

It would be nice to get out of town. "What time did you plan on going?" she asked.

"I thought we could go as soon as you finish work."

She grinned at him. "I'll go under two conditions."

"And what would those conditions be?" Playful suspicion filled his voice.

Emily Jane deliberately stalled. She looked at the little girls, who crawled after the fox pups in what used to be the backyard of her home. They were cute together. If only they had a place to keep them.

He cleared his throat.

She couldn't contain the teasing grin that tore at her face. He'd suffered long enough. "One, that you allow me to pack a picnic, and two, that when it comes time to let the fox pups go, you won't laugh if I cry."

William dropped the mare's lead rope and walked over to her. He slipped his arm around her shoulders and gently pulled her to his side. "I promise to eat all your picnic lunch, and I never laugh when a woman cries."

It felt good standing in the shelter of his arm. Emily Jane enjoyed the sensation for a few more moments before pulling away from him. It wouldn't be proper for anyone to see them standing so close. She scooped up a running pup and then collected the other one. "Let me put the foxes away, and then I'll help you take the mare to the livery." For some reason she didn't fully understand, Emily Jane wasn't ready to leave his presence just yet.

As she entered the small shed, Ruby's and Rose's cries filled her ears. They were another reason the fox pups had to go back into the wild. The little girls were becoming attached, but like her, right now, they were homeless and had no place for wild pets.

As she set the fox pups into the last stall and shut the door, Emily had a horrible thought. With William thinking about buying a farm out in the country, how often would he and the girls be in town? Once a week? Sundays only? Or maybe Saturdays to get supplies? She would see them only once a week. Suddenly all pleasure left her. How had her life become such a battle? Sadness and loss were her daily companions. And now she might have another huge loss to adjust to. Emily Jane didn't want to admit that she would miss William as much as the girls, but her heart whispered, *"You know you will."*

William immediately missed not having Emily Jane pressed next to his side. What had possessed him to hug her close like that anyway? Was it the sadness in her eyes? Or was it something else?

He picked up a sobbing Rose and put her in the wagon and then did the same with Ruby while Emily Jane put the fox pups back into the lean-to. "You can play with them again tomorrow." William pulled the girls back to the little mare and picked up her lead rope. He looked back at them to see that they had discovered their stuffed animals and were now happily playing.

Emily Jane walked toward him. Her shoulders were slumped. So many changes had happened in her life the past couple of weeks. When she came even with him he asked, "What was the final decision up at the church?"

Her dimple flashed as she looked up at him. "They are going to build one big house."

How did she do that? Go from being sad to smiling with the beauty of a child? She had to be hurting over the fox pups, but Emily Jane hid it well. She took the handle of the wagon from him. "I'll pull them."

William walked beside her. As they walked to the livery, the girls chattered away behind them, not making one lick of sense.

"I'm glad you were able to save the wagon," Emily Jane said.

"Yes, I lost the high chairs, but Levi has offered to make me another set at the cost of the lumber. Did you know the sawmill was one of the first businesses in Granite?"

She nodded. "Yes, and we are glad to have it. Not only

does it help Levi's business, but it also helps other people make sheds and lean-tos behind their houses."

They walked in silence for a few moments. Then she asked, "Do you think the big house will be finished by the end of summer?"

William didn't want to hurt her, but he had to be truthful. "I don't see how. It will take a lot of men to work on it, and most of them don't have time, especially at this time of year."

"That's what I thought, too. I really wish Mr. Anderson hadn't built everyone's hopes up so high."

It was William's turn to nod. "I'm sure he meant well." Still, he had to ask himself why the banker would make such an empty promise.

"Tell me about this farm we are going to look at Saturday," Emily Jane said, changing the subject.

"There's not much to tell. All Mr. Nelson said was that it belongs to an older couple who are thinking about moving back East. It has a house, a barn and a nice garden spot." He looked back, checking on the girls. "It would provide a roof over the girls' heads."

Sadness filled her eyes once more. Had his comment reminded her that for now she was homeless? William hated that he'd possibly hurt her in some way. "Emily, is there anything I can do to help you?" William reached out and took her free hand in his as they walked. It wasn't much comfort, but for the time being it was all he could offer.

She didn't pull her hand from his, but she heaved a big sigh. "Thank you, but I'll be all right. Once I replace a few personal belongings, I can start saving money for my bakery again." Her voice rang with determination, but he watched the play of emotions cross her features. Fear of the unknown, sadness and uncertainty flickered a moment. Then she gave him a half smile and released his hand. "Well, you are here, and everyone is in one piece, so I think I'll head back to the boardinghouse."

"Thank you for walking with us. I'm looking forward to Saturday," William said, not ready to let her go just yet.

"Me, too. I'll see you then."

With a heavy heart, William watched her walk away. How he wished he could get the house built faster, but to do so he'd need a lot of help. There were plenty of men in Austin who would love to work on the house, but hiring them would cost lots of money. Even with his inheritance, William knew he couldn't hire all that were needed.

Levi Westland stood within the livery doors. "Nice to see you again, William," he said, patting a big white stallion.

"Afternoon, Levi."

Levi knelt beside the girls' wagon. "I'll keep an eye on these two while you take care of your business with Mr. Hart."

Rose pulled herself up to the side of the wagon and gave Levi a big grin. It always amazed William how quickly Rose took to others, and Ruby, on the other hand, had to warm up to them. "Thank you. I won't be but a second."

Levi lifted the girls out of the wagon and sat down beside the door with them. He pulled out one of their toys and began to play with them. Assured they would be all right with Levi, William went in search of Mr. Hart.

It didn't take long to settle on a boarding price for his mare, and then William hurried back to Levi and the girls. The girls were curled up in his lap sucking their thumbs as he told them a story. Rose and Ruby loved hearing stories, and Levi was telling them about Jonah and the whale.

William waited until the story was complete and then took Ruby from Levi's arms. "Who knew you were such a good storyteller?" he teased.

Levi grinned. "It's easy to tell a story that you've read many times from the Bible." He pushed himself off the ground, bringing Rose with him. She yawned and snuggled more deeply into his shoulder. "Then again, judging from that big yawn, I might have bored them." A deep chuckle shook his shoulders.

Ruby grinned up at William. "Eat?" she asked.

"Sure, sweetie. Let's go see what they are serving tonight at the schoolhouse."

"Mind if I walk with you?"

"Not at all." William picked up the wagon handle and looked inquisitively at Levi. "Is there something you want to talk to me about? Or were you headed that way anyway?"

Levi fell into step with him. "Both."

"Talk away. I'm all ears."

"It seems someone donated the money to build the new big house, and I've been given credit for doing so." Levi shifted Rose on his hip.

Was Levi asking him if he'd donated the money? Or was he simply sharing information? William decided to wait him out and see what he'd say next. "That's very interesting."

"I thought it might interest you."

William ignored the other man's searching eyes. He didn't want anyone but the banker to know that he was the benefactor. "Why is that?"

Levi rubbed his chin. "You may not know this, but I grew up on a ranch not far from this town. I know every person that lives here and can't think of a one that can afford to pay for such a large home. Now, you, on the other hand, are new here, and I don't know what your financial situation is, and really it's none of my business. But I do know that my family isn't responsible for this blessing."

William smiled. "Well, if you are looking for me to say I did supply the blessing, it isn't going to happen. I guess we will just have to let sleeping dogs lie, as they say."

Levi slapped him on the back. "Agreed. That's what I'm saying, too. When asked, I'll just continue to say that the benefactor wanted it to be secret."

At that moment, William recognized a new friend in Levi. Levi knew that he was the benefactor but also planned to keep his secret. How many others would guess that it was him who had donated the money? Did it really matter? The scripture came to mind: *but when thou doest alms, let not thy left hand know what thy right hand doeth.* William would keep the secret and let them continue guessing.

"You know, it's going to take a lot of men to build a house that big." Levi glanced at him again. "I'm thinking another secret benefactor might be needed. Do you suppose the one who supplied the house will mind if someone else supplies the manpower to get it built?"

William chuckled. "I'm sure he wouldn't."

Levi slapped him on the back again. "That's exactly what the banker said, too."

William silently thanked the Lord above for the good people of Granite. Now Emily Jane would have a home sooner than they'd both expected. He felt a warmth enter his heart. He knew his feelings for Emily Jane were growing, but he also knew she was dead set on having her bakery without a husband and kids. And that was a huge obstacle to get around.

I you like to borrow one of my gowns? I have a

of roses to go well with it . . . well, that shade of blue

looks much better. I have a silk crêpe-lace underskirt

match the blue in your dress.

if you're going to be gone and then I'll quickly unlock

the door and let them go. . . . the minute you're gone

Now if you don't—

Chapter Seventeen

Saturday morning, Emily Jane's tummy wouldn't stop fluttering. Was she coming down with a stomach ailment? Or was it the simple excitement of doing something different with her day? She added another deviled ham sandwich to the picnic basket, then a small bag of sugar cookies; lastly, she put a bowl of the deviled ham in the basket and added a spoon so that she could feed it to the girls.

Walking to the foyer, where she'd decided to meet William and the girls, she tried to decide if there was anything she'd forgotten. She placed the basket on the small settee and sat down beside it.

Beth came down the stairs. She looked as pretty as a picture. Not a wrinkle in her dress or a hair out of place. "Good morning, Emily Jane. Where are you off to?" Beth set a box on the floor beside the couch.

She didn't want to answer Beth but didn't see a way out. "Mr. Barns has asked me to accompany him and the girls into the country." Emily Jane thought about adding that she would be watching the girls and releasing her fox cubs back into the wild but realized less information might be better than too much.

"Would you like to borrow one of my hats? That sun is going to darken your freckles." Beth sat down beside her on the settee. "I have a big floppy one that would match the blue in your dress."

"Thank you for the offer, Beth, but I've never worn a hat." Emily Jane looked at Beth's white skin. There were no flaws on her face.

Shock filled Beth's voice as she asked. "Why ever not?"

Only prideful women wear hats—Emily Jane's father's voice filled her thoughts. "My parents didn't approve of them."

A mischievous look crossed the other young woman's face. "Your parents aren't here now, are they?"

"Well, no."

"I'll be right back. The hat will save your skin, and no harm will be done. Your parents will never know. Besides, you are a grown woman." Beth hurried up the stairs.

Emily Jane shook her head with a smile. Beth had been kind to her since she'd moved in and only meant well. So, if wearing a hat would put a new smile on her face, Emily Jane would wear it.

Beth arrived with a pretty floppy hat in her hand. "See? It matches your dress perfectly."

"So it does." Emily Jane took the offered hat and placed it on her head. She stood up and walked to the looking glass that hung beside the door. It really was a pretty hat.

Today Emily Jane wore one of the two dresses that Susanna had insisted she take. It was a pretty blue with white buttons that ran down the front. The light blue hat had a white ribbon around the rim. If people didn't look too closely, they would think she was pretty.

"Thank you, Beth. It is very beautiful."

The other woman beamed. "I knew it would look wonderful on you."

Emily Jane sat back down. "What are you doing today?"

Beth picked up the box she'd set down earlier. "I'm going to take this dress to Martha, a friend of mine who has been sick. Unfortunately, she's lost a lot of weight, so I'm hoping this dress will fit her." A sadness entered Beth's eyes. "She's so young."

"If it's all right with you, I'd like to pray for her. God is the great physician, and I know He can heal her." Emily Jane smiled. She truly believed what she'd just told Beth.

"Thank you. I'd like that, and I know Martha will appreciate the added prayers."

The two women joined hands; Emily Jane bowed her head and began to pray. "Thank You, Lord, for loving us and watching over us. Beth and I both love You very much, and as Your children we come before You. You said if any of my children need anything all they have to do is ask. Well, Father, we are asking You to reach down and touch Beth's friend Martha. She has been sick a long time, Lord, and we know You can heal her. We ask for her healing in Jesus's name. Amen."

Emily Jane released her hands. "If there is anything I can do to help you or Martha, please, tell me."

A soft smile touched Beth's face. "You already have. Your praying with me has made me feel better. Thank you." She picked up her box, then opened the door.

"You're welcome," Emily Jane answered, happy that she'd been able to pray with her friend.

Beth walked out just as William pulled his horse and wagon in front of the house.

Emily Jane picked up her picnic basket and followed Beth outside. The warm morning breeze lifted the hat. She grabbed at it with her free hand.

William jumped down from the wagon. Beth waved at him as she passed. He nodded at her.

Emily Jane walked to the wagon. The tummy butterflies returned in full force. Rose and Ruby sat in their little box in the back of the wagon. They squealed and reached for Emily Jane.

"I hope I haven't kept you waiting," William said, taking the basket and giving her a hand up onto the wagon.

"Not at all. I needed to visit a little while with Beth anyway." She sat down and arranged her skirts. Then Emily Jane turned and kissed each twin.

They giggled and tried to get her hat.

William pulled himself up beside her. As he took the reins, he asked, "New hat?"

"Beth loaned it to me."

He smiled over at her. "It's very pretty on you."

A compliment? She felt a little uneasy. His sapphire eyes looked straight ahead as he gently slapped the reins over Bess's back.

A soft laugh drifted from his side of the wagon seat. "We're friends, Emily Jane. No need to get all nervous about a compliment."

How had he known? She cut her eyes under the hat to look at his profile. Was it possible that over the past few weeks they'd grown so close that they knew what each other was thinking? If so, that was dangerous. Maybe after today, she should put some distance between herself and William. People who could read each other's minds and expressions, from her experience, seemed to be in love. She wasn't ready for love. Yes, distance after today would be the best solution for them both.

* * *

William stopped at the lean-to that housed the fox pups and helped Emily Jane down.

"I'll be right back." She disappeared quickly into the small building.

He hated that she had to give up her fox pups. But it was for the best. So far the men hadn't been aware of them. If they had found out, William was sure they would have demanded she kill them. He thought about getting her a puppy to replace the fox pups. Would she want a replacement?

Emily Jane returned with the wooden box that had housed the fox pups when she'd first gotten them. They'd grown and were even now peeking over the top. Red tongues licked at her fingers and hands as she carried them to the wagon.

"Why don't we put one in with the girls and you hold the other one?" William asked, taking the box and helping her back into the wagon.

"We can try. I'm not sure if it's safe for the fox pup or the girls." She took the box back from him and set it on the wagon floor.

Rose and Ruby kicked their legs and squealed when they saw their furry friends.

"You play nice with the baby," Emily Jane said as she put the fox pup in the box with them. At least it was tall enough that even if the fox could get away from the girls, it couldn't get out of the box. She cuddled the second one to her as she watched the girls and pup.

The wagon shifted under William's weight as he pulled himself back up. He studied the girls trying to pet the fox and laughed as they attempted to avoid its quick tongue. "See? I think they will be all right. It's not that far out to the Guthrie place."

"You're probably right. But I think I'll keep a close eye on them, just the same." Emily Jane stroked the little fox's head that she held in her hands.

To distract her, he asked, "What do we have in that basket?" He glanced over his shoulder at the girls once more before flicking the reins and setting the wagon into motion.

"Just sandwiches, pickles and applesauce for the girls."

Disappointment filled his voice. "No cookies?"

As he hoped, she laughed. "Of course there are cookies."

"Sugar?"

"Your favorite?" Emily Jane asked, already knowing that he favored the sugar above all the rest.

"And the girls'," he agreed, nodding.

Once more she laughed. He loved the sound of her merriment. Emily Jane was unlike any woman he'd ever met. She was joy and sunshine, even when she was sad. Over the past few days, he'd come to realize just how much he liked her. William told himself he wasn't falling in love with the little redhead, but he was having a hard time convincing himself it wasn't true.

They were on the edge of town when a group of men in wagons of all sizes came rumbling down the road toward them. The wheels dug deep into the dirt, causing big ruts in the otherwise smooth road. William pulled to the side to let them pass. Emily Jane noticed all kinds of carpentry tools in the wagons as well as tents. One wagon was loaded down with bricks; the two big oxen that pulled it brayed as they slowly passed.

"What are they doing here?" He could hear the hopeful wonder in her voice.

William shook his head. "Maybe they are passing through."

Her voice sounded doubtful. "Perhaps."

Did Emily Jane sense that he knew more than he was saying? William decided not to look at her but to focus on the group of men as they passed.

A woman driving a covered wagon stopped next to them. "Where can I find the general store?" She was a heavy woman with a thick accent.

"Just continue on Main Street, and it's on your left," William answered. Then he asked a question of his own. "Where are you all headed?"

She laughed heartily. "Granite. We've all been hired to do a big job here. I'm the cook for this outfit and need supplies."

"What kind of big job?" Emily Jane asked. William knew instinctively what she was thinking.

"We're building the Elm Street house. It's a biggun, too. Something like sixteen bedrooms." She slapped the reins across the horses' backs and started them moving again. "Thank you for the information, folks. Be seeing you around."

As soon as the wagons had all passed, William pulled back onto the road. "It looks like the house might be finished by the end of the summer after all." He grinned across at Emily Jane. He felt as if a weight had been lifted from his shoulders.

"I'm glad. I have been concerned that the hopes of the others would all be crushed if we had to go into winter and they were still living in the school and church." Emily Jane looked back at the girls, who were all smiles.

William looked to his right. Mr. Nelson had said a small road to the right would take him straight to the Guthrie farm.

Emily Jane turned on the seat and played with the girls and fox pups. He'd picked up a few wooden blocks from

Levi, and Emily Jane was showing them how to stack them up and knock them over. "There were a lot of men in those wagons." Her voice sounded concerned.

"Yes, there were. It means the house will get built much faster." He saw the small road and turned.

"Where do you think they will all sleep? And what about food supplies?" She handed Ruby a block, then turned to look at him with those clear green eyes.

"Well, they seemed to have lots of tents, so I imagine they will use those and the wagon beds. As for food, the cook was on her way to the general store for supplies, and if I don't miss my guess, they will also do some hunting to supply their meat." It was sweet that Emily Jane was concerned for the builders' well-being. Every day his respect and feelings for her grew, whether he wanted to admit it or not. He shook his head. If he didn't miss his guess, he was a doomed man.

Chapter Eighteen

William pulled up in front of the small farm that seemed to appear out of nowhere. He set the brake on the wagon and then hopped down.

Rose clung to the side of the box. "Up," she said, reaching for William.

He pulled the little girl out of the wagon and into his arms, then turned to help Emily Jane down.

Emily Jane scooped up Ruby. The little girl reached out and touched the rim of Emily Jane's hat. "Pittie."

"Thank you. I think you look very pretty today, too." Emily Jane hugged the little girl close before handing her down to William. She climbed out of the wagon and then took Ruby back.

A man came out of the barn, followed by a woman about his age. "Good morning," the man called.

William stepped in front of Emily Jane and Ruby. He offered the couple a smile and tipped his hat to them. "Good morning. Is this the Guthrie farm?"

The older gentleman nodded.

His wife walked around him with a big grin on her face. "James, this must be the Barns family. Mr. Nelson told you they might be coming out to look the place over, remember?"

The man rolled his eyes. "Of course I remember, Esther. How could I forget? You've been talking about it all morning."

"So I have." She walked up to William and Rose. "I'm Esther and this is James."

William smiled. They were an interesting couple. Mrs. Guthrie looked as if she wanted him to hand Rose over but was too polite to ask. "I'm William, this is Rose, and Emily Jane is holding Ruby." He realized that they thought Emily Jane and the girls were his family. Since he didn't know the Guthries, William decided not to correct them. He would before they left but not yet.

"It's nice to meet you all. If you will excuse me, I need to go check on my bread. James, bring them up to the house when you're finished. I'd like to visit for a spell."

Mr. Guthrie nodded at his wife. Then he said, "The farm's not big. If you will follow me, I'll show you around." He reached under his big floppy brown hat and scratched his head.

William did as he asked. Their first stop was the barn. It was average size, held hay on one side and had three horse stalls on the other. Out the side door was a small fenced-in area for the horses to walk around in. A swayed-back horse stood in the yard, drinking from a watering trough.

"That's Spot. She's getting on in years, like Esther and me," he said by way of introduction to the horse.

William nodded, unsure what to add to that bit of information. He looked over his shoulder and saw Emily Jane looking at the little mare with pity in her eyes. It was obvious she thought the old gal should be turned out to pasture.

James Guthrie led them out a side gate made of oak branches and wire. "Behind the barn is the woodpile. I'm sure you could move it closer to the house, if you are so inclined. Personally, I use it as an escape from being cooped up all winter." He practically whispered the last part so that Emily Jane wouldn't overhear.

William watched her bury her face in Ruby's shoulder. If she was trying to hide her smile, she'd failed miserably. Her dancing eyes gave her away. "I'll keep that in mind," he said, turning back to the old man.

"We have a small orchard over this way." He started down a grassy hill that led to a cluster of fruit trees.

"What kind of fruit do you raise?" Emily Jane asked, sounding interested.

James looked over his shoulder. "We have fig and apple. Folks said the apples wouldn't do very well, but the missus and I have beautiful fruit every summer." Pride filled his voice.

"Oh, William, just think of the hot apple pies in the winter." Emily Jane's eyes were large and awe filled.

The old man laughed. "My Esther has a fig pie that brings folks to eat from miles around. I'll bet she'll share the recipe with you, Mrs. Barns."

Emily Jane opened her mouth, and William assumed she was going to object to being called Mrs. Barns. He shook his head at her, silently asking her not to say anything. It worked, because she closed her mouth and then smiled at the older gentleman. "That would be very nice of her. I'll be sure and ask when we get back to the house."

When James continued down the small incline, Emily Jane looked at him with a frown. He mouthed, "Please, trust me on this."

She nodded and followed behind him.

As he listened to the man describe every inch of the farm, William's mind flew with other thoughts. Mr. Guthrie had assumed they were married. It would be nice to have Emily Jane as a part of his family. She was kind, loving and honest. Why not ask her to marry him? If he was to buy the farm, the girls would need a constant caregiver, not just a part-time one. Emily Jane cared about the girls; it was evident in the way she spoke to them, touched them and even disciplined them. It would be convenient to have her with them all the time.

He wasn't doing it for love; no, his heart couldn't take being broken, and that was what happened when you loved someone. A person lost all objectivity. Even lost their own identity and became wrapped up in the other's life. No, it was all for the girls that they should marry. Supply a stable home. Who knew if their father would ever return? It certainly wasn't looking as if that would happen.

What was he thinking? Emily Jane followed the older gentleman to the orchard. She could see the unripened fruit hanging from the limbs and inhaled, hoping to catch a hint of their sweet fragrance. The Guthries didn't seem like a dangerous couple, and yet, she had the feeling William didn't trust them. Or was it that he hoped for a lower price on the farm, if the older couple thought they were married?

"Eat!" Ruby called, smelling the sweet fruit.

The old man laughed. "Makes me hungry, too, little one."

"We'll eat in a little while," Emily Jane told her.

"Eat!" Rose called from behind her.

"Later," William answered her.

The two girls began to pout and fuss. Emily Jane

set Ruby down and held her hand while she walked her around. Distracted, Ruby quit fussing but not Rose.

William set her on his shoulders and held her hands while he walked among the trees, admiring the fruit that hung heavily from the branches. "You have a nice crop this year."

"We've had this amount for the past two years. Last year, the missus sold several baskets of both apples and figs to Mr. Moore at the general store." He crossed his arms and beamed with pride. "Come harvest time, someone's gonna be busy for sure."

After visiting the orchard, they all headed back to the house. Mr. Guthrie showed them the well beside the house and Mrs. Guthrie's vegetable-and-herb garden. A small chicken coop sat behind the house, and a cow bawled for their attention in a lean-to beside the outhouse.

Emily Jane was tired of being out in the sun and wanted to see the inside of the house. Not that it would ever be hers, but she'd come this far; now she was simply curious. She looked to the house several times, trying to get William to take the hint and ask to see inside.

She'd about given up when Mr. Guthrie said, "I believe your missus would like a gander at the house."

William looked at Emily Jane, and she felt her cheeks grow hot at having been caught by the old man. He grinned and then said, "Lead the way, Mr. Guthrie."

He didn't have to ask twice. "Be honest with ya. I'd like a cold glass of milk myself." Mr. Guthrie opened the door and waited for Emily Jane to pass.

She stepped into a small mudroom and grinned. This house reminded her a lot of home. Her parents' house had a mudroom, and if she wasn't mistaken, the door before her led into the kitchen.

The older woman stuck her graying head through the

entry. "Come on inside. I have hot bread and butter waiting for you and those sweet girls."

"Oh, Mrs. Guthrie, you shouldn't have. I packed us a nice picnic lunch."

"Now, don't you go fretting none, Mrs. Barns. I promise it won't spoil their lunches."

Emily Jane followed her into a nice airy kitchen. She didn't feel right, letting the couple believe that she and William were married. "Please, call me Emily Jane." The table had been set with a platter of bread and a saucer of butter. Four plates sat about each side of the square table.

"Are you sure I can't offer you and the mister some lunch, Emily Jane? It really is no bother."

William answered before Emily Jane could. "No, ma'am. As nice as that sounds, we have another errand to run before it gets too late."

"I sure could use a nice cup of cold milk," Mr. Guthrie hinted to his wife.

She ignored him and asked, "Mr. Barns, I'd like to hold that little one, if you don't mind." Her eyes beseeched both Emily Jane and William for permission.

He smiled. "Rose is the friendly twin. I'm sure she won't mind." William handed the baby over.

"Well, looks like if a man wants cold milk, he has to get it himself," James gruffed. "Come on, Mr. Barns. I'll show you how to have some of the coldest milk this side of Austin." He turned and stomped back out of the kitchen.

William glanced at Emily, shrugged and then followed. The amused look on his face said he liked the Guthries. She just hoped he told them the truth about their relationship.

"What did he mean she's the friendliest? Aren't they the same?"

Emily turned her attention back to Mrs. Guthrie. "No, Rose is never shy around strangers, but Ruby here takes a while to warm up to folks." She hugged Ruby to her.

"Well, I've never been around twins, so had no idea."

Rose reached up and touched Mrs. Guthrie's wrinkled cheek. She smiled and then gave her an openmouthed kiss on that same cheek.

Mrs. Guthrie laughed. "Kids always did like me. We had six of them. But two of them died, and the rest moved away." Sadness filled her eyes. She stared out the window.

After several long moments, Rose hugged the old woman, bringing her back to the present.

She looked at Emily Jane and gasped. "Where are my manners? Please, sit down and give these babies some bread and butter."

"Thank you." Emily Jane sat. The girls were getting heavier. They'd soon be walking on their own, but for now carrying them left her arms tired.

"You have lovely children. How old are they? One?"

Emily Jane hated not telling her the complete truth. "Yes, they are one."

"When are their birthdays?" She buttered a slice of bread, then tore off a piece of it and handed it to Rose, who had already started trying to get her hands on it.

"I don't know."

"Oh?" Curiosity sounded in the older woman's voice.

"William had the girls when we met." Well, that was the truth.

"Oh, newlyweds." She nodded as if that was what she thought. "You know, being young, in love and starting a new life together is some of the best years of your life. And this farm is just what you need to raise these pretty girls." She tickled Rose's belly.

"Mrs. Guthrie?"

"Please, call me Esther. All my friends do." She seemed unaware that Emily Jane was feeling more and more uncomfortable with their deception.

Mr. Guthrie's voice stopped Emily Jane from telling Esther the truth. "Well, looks like we got ourselves a buyer, Esther." He walked to the table, set a jug of milk on it and then laid his hand on his wife's shoulder.

William walked to the table and stopped next to Emily Jane's chair. "Hold on a minute, James."

The older man's face crumpled. Esther sighed.

Emily Jane looked up at William. He stared down into her face. Then he said, "Before we agree that we're buying this place, we need to be honest with you."

James stood up straighter. "What do you mean?"

William stood a little taller. He should have told them sooner. "I can't buy your farm until I tell you that Emily Jane and I are not married."

"I see." A stern expression came across the older man's features. "And why did you let us assume you were?" he asked.

William looked down at Emily Jane. "Well, sir. It wasn't until after we arrived that I realized I should have come out here on my own. I let you believe we were married because I was trying to protect Emily Jane's reputation."

Emily Jane gasped. He looked at her and knew she hadn't considered how it would appear to others, coming together to look at the farm with no intentions of marrying.

"But to lie about it is even worse. So, I'd still like to buy your farm but will understand if you don't want to sell it to a single man."

For the first time Esther spoke. "Who do these beautiful little girls belong to?"

"They are my nieces. My sister was killed a few months ago, and I'm taking care of them until my brother-in-law comes to claim them." William put his hand on Emily Jane's shoulder. "Emily Jane has been helping me with the girls."

"And did the tornado truly take your home in town?" Mr. Guthrie asked.

Emily Jane stared at the tablecloth. "Yes, sir. It took both our homes." She answered without looking up. "I have to ask your forgiveness also."

Mr. Guthrie sighed. "Little lady, there is nothing to ask forgiveness for. If I had been in your young man's shoes, to save my Esther's reputation, I would have done the same." He looked to William. "Thank you for coming forward with honesty. I'll sell this place to an honest man, single or married."

Esther nodded her head in agreement.

William wasn't sure if they simply wanted to sell the farm or if they truly liked him and Emily Jane. Did it really matter? He didn't think so. Mr. Guthrie said he understood and was still willing to sell him the farm. "Thank you. I'll talk to the bank first thing Monday morning."

The two men shook hands, and Mrs. Guthrie grinned ear to ear. "I'm glad you and the girls will be living here, Mr. Barns. This farm was a nice place to raise our family. I'm sure you will enjoy it, too."

He nodded. Mr. Guthrie had said the same thing as he'd drawn the jug of cold milk out of the well. And William had to agree, the farm really would be a nice, quiet place to raise a family.

William glanced at Emily Jane, who was busy helping the girls with their snack. What would it be like to live here with her? Raise a farmyard full of kids, work the orchard and come home every night to a hot meal and a smiling Emily.

Get those thoughts out of your mind, William Barns. One, Emily didn't want a farmyard full of children, and two, until Josiah came for the girls, Rose and Ruby were the only children he should be thinking about.

Still, it wouldn't hurt to ask Emily Jane to marry him and help him take care of the girls. If he did, what would she say? There was only one way to find out.

Chapter Nineteen

An hour later, William helped Emily Jane back into the wagon. Mr. and Mrs. Guthrie passed the little girls up to them. "Thank you again," William said as he sat down.

Emily Jane checked on the fox pups. They stuck their little noses out of the box. The little girls squealed at the sight.

"What have you got there?" Mr. Guthrie asked, coming around to look into the box.

She straightened her spine, afraid the old man would want to kill them. "Two baby foxes."

He reached in and patted their heads. "What are you going to do with them?" His even tone told Emily Jane that the man was refraining from saying what he really thought. Her father often got that tone when he disapproved of something.

William answered, "We're going to take them up the road a bit and turn them loose."

Mrs. Guthrie stood off to the side, wringing her hands in her apron, a worried expression on her face.

"That's not a good idea." Mr. Guthrie looked up at Emily Jane.

"Why's that?" William asked.

Emily Jane knew what his answer would be. He'd say they would just be a nuisance to the farmers in the area. But she was surprised when the old man said, "They won't make it."

Emily Jane's stance of defiance changed to concern. "Why not?" Her voice quivered.

Mr. Guthrie looked at his wife. "The missus adopted a set of baby foxes a few years back, and they were just too friendly with folks. Ended up getting shot by the neighbor."

William patted Emily Jane's back. "We'll take them deep into the woods."

She knew he was trying to comfort her, but her mind raced at the horrible things that could happen to the babies. Her babies. She didn't want to desert them in the woods. Emily Jane stooped down and put Rose into the big box and then picked up one of the fox pups. Rose immediately grabbed the other one.

Sadness filled Mrs. Guthrie's voice. "They'll just follow you back. We tried that, too."

Panic filled Emily Jane. "Oh, William. If they follow us back, the men will kill them." How could she have been so stupid? She'd doomed the poor fox pups to certain death by keeping them.

"I know, but we don't have any place to keep them," William reminded her.

"You could leave them with me," Mrs. Guthrie said, quickly.

"Now, Esther. We are selling this place, remember? And we can't take them with us." Mr. Guthrie dropped an arm around his wife's shoulders.

Emily looked to William. If he bought the farm, would he be able to keep the fox pups? Her eyes searched his. She didn't want to come right out and ask him to keep the pups, but she didn't want to leave them in the woods where they would die.

"Mr. Guthrie, would it be too big of an inconvenience for your wife to keep an eye on them for a few days?" William continued to look deeply into Emily Jane's eyes.

He was going to do this for her. Her papa would never have bowed to such a simple request, and yet this man seemed to care about her and the fox pups. With difficulty, Emily Jane pulled her gaze from his. She feared he could see to her very soul. If he did, then he'd know that, with every kind action he showed her, her heart melted just a little more toward him.

The older woman clapped her hands. "I thought you'd never ask. Of course I'll take care of these darling babies."

Emily Jane quickly grabbed up the box she'd brought the fox pups in and handed it to her. "Oh, thank you." With one last stroke of its reddening fur, she handed the pup she held to Mr. Guthrie to place into the box. Then she proceeded to ease the other one out of Rose's grasp.

Rose fussed and tried to get the pup back. When Emily Jane passed it down to Mr. Guthrie, Rose let out a scream that caused the birds in a nearby tree to take flight.

Emily Jane picked up the little girl. "Rose, we have to leave the foxes here. Mrs. Guthrie will take good care of them, and in a few days you can come back and see them."

As if she understood, the little girl rested her head on Emily Jane's shoulder. She stuck her thumb in her mouth and watched as Mr. Guthrie put the fox pup in the box with her sister. Not for the first time, Emily Jane realized that the fox pups were twin girls, like Rose and Ruby.

"Thank you, Mr. and Mrs. Guthrie. We appreciate all

that you are doing, and I'm looking forward to seeing you, Mr. Guthrie, at the bank on Monday."

The old man looked up with a smile. "I'll be there when the doors open."

William's handsome face broke into a wide grin. He looked about the farmyard with a satisfied expression. His gaze turned to the farmhouse. Emily Jane thought she knew his thoughts. He was thinking about the large kitchen with the table in it for eating. And the fact that it had three bedrooms would give him and the girls lots of room. He looked down at her and grinned. "I'm glad Mr. Nelson told me about this place. It's perfect."

Something in his eyes made her want to stay here with him, make a home for the girls and just be content to spend her days baking and cooking for a family. Emily Jane thought about her parents in that moment. Her mother had probably thought the same way when they'd first married, but look at her now. No, what William's eyes offered was a fantasy.

Her gaze moved to the Guthries. They stood side by side. His arm was around Esther's shoulders, and he looked down at his wife. Love radiated from his face. He only had eyes for Esther. Had he even absorbed what William had said? Or was his heart too full of love for his wife to hear anything?

What would it be like to have a man so devoted to you that he only had eyes for you? Seeing the older couple together made her question her earlier thoughts about her parents. Were they still in love like that? Was her father simply burdened with raising such a large family?

If so, Emily Jane didn't want a large family. She glanced back at William, who had taken his seat at the reins and had reached for the wagon brake. He was a handsome man who seemed to have a big heart.

Lord, I don't want to fight Your will for my life. My heart is set on owning and running my own bakery. Not on marriage and having children. Please, help me to be able to put distance between William and the girls. I know I can't have both, and right now I'm not ready for love and a family.

William glanced over at Emily Jane. They'd been riding for about ten minutes from the Guthrie farm, and she'd already gotten the girls to lie down and take a nap. She faced forward as the wagon rambled on, but she remained silent. What was she thinking?

"I can hear the river from here. Would you like to stop there and have our lunch?" he asked to break the silence.

Emily Jane nodded. "The Guthries turned out to be really nice people, didn't they?"

"They sure did. I'm glad we came out here today." He'd seen the way she'd studied them right before they left and hoped she'd voice some of those thoughts now.

"Me, too." Emily Jane glanced back at the sleeping girls and smiled. "I think Rose and Ruby liked them, too."

He turned the wagon onto a rutted path. The little mare picked up the pace at the smell of water. "Those little girls like everyone."

Emily Jane chuckled. "True." She glanced his way, and his heart skipped a beat. The hat on her head seemed out of place, and yet it gave her a more grown-up look. He loved it when they felt the same about things. He wasn't very experienced in matters of the heart, but when they agreed, it bonded them a little bit more each time. He had to admit that something in her manner soothed him.

A grove of trees came into view. William turned the little mare toward it. They would be close enough to the river to enjoy the sound and sweetness of its waters but far enough away that the little ones wouldn't fall in when they woke up and started exploring.

"Should we wake the girls?" Emily Jane asked when he set the brake.

William looked back at their sweet faces. "No, let's let them nap."

She nodded and leaned over the seat to grab the picnic basket. William jumped out of the wagon and turned to help her down.

Emily Jane handed him the basket. She glanced once more at the little girls, then placed her small hand in his. William felt a small jolt of electricity pass between them. They both pulled back and then laughed. "That was some shock," she said, replacing her hand in his so that he could help her down.

Once on the ground, William released her and walked to the tree he thought would offer them plenty of shade for their meal. "How does this look?"

Emily Jane joined him. "Perfect." She looked up into the tree branches and grinned.

"This big oak would make a great tree for a swing," William said, his gaze following hers.

"In Kansas we lived on the plains. I have to admit I like these trees much better than no trees." Emily Jane turned her pure green gaze upon him. "We never had trees like this when I was a kid. And definitely no swing."

He opened the basket and found a lightweight blanket on top of the food. As he spread it out, he said, "I miss the aspen trees in Colorado, but these oaks are really nice, too."

She waited until he was finished spreading out the blanket and then sat down. "Even if we had had trees, I wouldn't have had time to swing in a tree."

William studied her serious face. "Too many brothers and sisters to watch?" he guessed.

Emily Jane nodded. "And too many chores to do." Sadness filled her voice and face.

Wanting to cheer her up, William nodded. "I'll be right back. There's something in the wagon I've been meaning to give you." He felt Emily Jane's curiosity peak as her gaze followed him back to the wagon.

Careful to keep it concealed, he carried his surprise back to her under a small towel. William hoped it would bring a smile to her face. He held the towel-wrapped gift out to her.

"You shouldn't be buying me gifts," she said, warily eyeing the package as if it might bite her.

He smiled. "I didn't buy it." William pushed it toward her again.

Emily Jane tentatively took it. "A book?" She looked up at him in confusion.

He laughed. "Unwrap it and find out." William held his breath as she slowly began to remove the towel.

A squeal tore from her throat as the last layer of fabric came off. "My recipe book! However did you find it?" She hugged it to her chest in delight, then lovingly caressed the front cover.

William sank down onto the blanket beside her. "I think it was a God thing. I was going through the rubble of your house and saw a bucket that didn't look damaged. Thinking I could salvage it, I picked it up and your book was resting underneath."

She opened it up and saw the water marks around the edges of the pages. "I never thought I'd see it again."

"I'm sorry about the water damage, but I think most of the recipes are still good." He lay back and then turned on his side, propping his head up and watching her as she examined each page.

"Oh, William, you have no idea how much this means to me." Her green eyes glistened with unshed tears.

"I'm glad you like it."

"I love it."

"Enough to marry me?"

Chapter Twenty

Emily Jane looked over at him with a smile. Surely he joked? But he wasn't smiling. William had to be teasing. He hadn't just seriously asked her to marry him. Had he? Emily Jane studied his handsome features. His eyes searched her face.

"No, stop kidding around," she answered, now feeling very uncomfortable.

"I'm not kidding. I've been thinking about it all day. If I move out here in the country, I'll need someone to watch the girls, and I don't expect you to drive out here every day."

She sat up straighter. "Do you hear yourself?"

"Yes, I do. Think about it. I'll make sure that you are taken care of. You'll make sure the girls are taken care of and you will be able to cook up those recipes to your heart's content." He motioned at the book within her lap.

Emily Jane pushed up from the blanket. "No, I will not marry you."

William looked as if he'd been slapped. "Why not?"

"I've told you, I want my own bakery. I want the freedom of running it."

Confusion laced his handsome face. "I didn't say you

couldn't have your own bakery. Maybe we can work something out."

How? How could she have her bakery and live out of town, take care of a husband and two children?

One of the twins woke up and began to cry. Even now, they couldn't discuss her reasons for not wanting to get married because the children needed tending.

The two little girls pulled themselves up and looked over the wagon bed at them. Emily Jane walked to them. "I'm ready to return to town, William. We can eat on the way."

"Very well." He sighed heavily.

She put her recipe book on the bench and then pulled herself up. When he arrived at the wagon, William handed her the picnic basket. Confusion continued to fill his features. How could he not understand her reaction?

They rode to town in silence. She fed the girls small bites of the deviled ham she'd prepared earlier, and William ate his sandwiches.

"Emily, can't we please talk about this?"

It was her turn to sigh. She glanced in his direction. How did she explain to him that she cared about him and the girls without building his hopes of marriage?

"Look, I know you are angry, but I meant no harm to you. We could be a family without..." His face reddened, and the words were stuck in his throat.

"I'm not angry, William. I understand what you are offering, but you don't understand. I have dreams of my own. I've told you, I want to buy my own bakery. I care about you and the girls." She paused to take a deep breath. "More than I should, but that doesn't mean I want to marry you. I still want to be a part of yours and the girls' lives but not through marriage and not because I'm in love with you."

"Are you?"

She looked at him in confusion. "Am I what?"

"In love with me?" Was that hope in his voice?

Emily Jane shook off the question. "No, I care about you but, like we agreed on before, only as a friend."

He turned his attention to the narrow road. "I'm buying the farm, Emily. I can't bring the girls in to you every day, and I don't expect you to come out there." His voice held a hint of sorrow that she couldn't ignore.

"I don't know what the answer is, William." Emily Jane thought of him marrying someone besides her. And the thought of him offering anyone the same marriage of convenience as he'd just offered her sent sharp pains into her heart, almost bringing her to tears. She didn't want to lose William and the girls, but she couldn't have it both ways.

The sun was beginning to fade as they pulled up in front of Beth's Boardinghouse. A horse and wagon stood in front of the walkway. Emily Jane felt the dull sense of foreboding. Only one person owned a rig like that pulled by that certain gelding. Her father had arrived.

William mentally beat himself up. He'd gone about asking Emily to marry him the wrong way. He hadn't wanted to spook her with words of love or caring. Love might have been a little too strong for the emotions that he felt for her anyway. But, still, he'd made it sound like a business arrangement, and now that he looked back on their conversation, he realized he was the only one who would have benefited from his proposal. She must think him the most conceited person she'd ever met.

"Oh no, oh no, oh no." Her whispered cry carried to him as he pulled up in front of Beth's Boardinghouse.

He set the brake and then turned to see what distressed

her so. She seemed to be focused on a gelding and wagon in front of them. "What's wrong?"

"My father is here."

Fear laced her voice. Her face had gone white, and the freckles on her nose seemed bolder. Protective feelings mounted up in William. "Can I help?" he asked, not sure what her answer would be.

She shook her head hard, and then as if she remembered she was wearing the hat, Emily Jane gasped and ripped it from her head. "Why is he here?" she whispered, covering her mouth with her free hand.

"Maybe we should go find out." William had never seen anyone react to their parent the way Emily Jane reacted to hers. "What are you afraid of?" he asked.

Emily Jane's green eyes swam in tears. "He's going to make me go home. I'm not married like I'm supposed to be." For a second she seemed lost in her own tormenting thoughts. Her eyes grew wide, and a lone tear slipped out one corner. "Oh, William, I can't go back there. I can't."

He took her by the shoulders and turned her to face him. "Emily, you don't have to. You are a grown woman, and you've been on your own for a while now."

She shook her head back and forth. "No, I'll have to go back. I can't defy my papa. I can't."

William's heart went out to her. "He wants you to get married?"

The tear made a slow trek down her cheek. "Then we can tell him that I asked you to marry me. It's the truth." With his thumb he caressed the tear away.

She went very still. "You did, didn't you?" She spaced the words evenly as if testing them for authenticity.

He nodded and offered what he hoped was an encouraging smile. "I did. And if we need to say we're engaged,

we can always call off the wedding after he goes home."
William paused.

Emily Jane wiped the moisture from her face. She
took a deep breath.

"You going to be all right?" He watched as she understood that he really did care about her.

The realization seemed to help her to regain control
of her fearful emotions. She straightened her shoulders.
"Yes, thank you."

William climbed down from the wagon and then
helped her down. He handed Emily Jane her recipe book
and then reached for Rose. The little girl giggled and
hugged Emily Jane's neck as he passed her over.

Ruby held out her arms. "Up," she said, reaching for
him.

He pulled the girl from the wagon bed and hugged
her close. William brushed a gentle kiss across her forehead. The twins may not be his children by birth, but
they brought overwhelming joy to his life. He could not
imagine ever hurting them or causing them fear. How
could any man do that to his daughter? Emily Jane should
be thrilled to see her papa, not fearful. His lips pressed
shut, so no sound would burst out, but he had no intention
of letting her father browbeat her into doing something
she didn't want to do. William wasn't looking forward
to meeting her father but purposed in his heart right then
to stand firm beside her for as long as she needed him.

A few moments later, they entered the foyer. Beth
Winters hurried to meet them. "Emily Jane, I am so sorry.
Your father is here, and I thought he knew that you hadn't
married Levi, and I'm afraid I told him." She stopped
and nervously dusted her hands over her apron. "And
I'm afraid he's angry."

Emily Jane stood taller. "It's all right, Beth. Papa is always angry about something. Where is he now?"

Beth pointed toward the dining room. "I seated him as far away from the door as possible. I wanted you to have time to compose yourself before having to see him." She reached out and gave Emily Jane a hug about the shoulders. "I really am sorry."

William was proud of Emily. He knew how scared she was, but she didn't show it now. His eyes locked on to hers. For a brief moment she allowed him to see her insecurity. Just as quickly she concealed it and smiled at Beth.

"Thank you for letting me know he is here, Beth. I'll go see him now." Emily Jane handed her recipe book to Beth. "Would you mind putting this in my room for me?"

"Not at all." Beth took the book.

William watched in appreciation as Emily Jane swallowed hard, lifted her chin and walked with unhurried purpose to the dining room. Unsure if he should follow or not, William hung back.

Beth whispered, "Don't leave her alone with that man, William. He's mean."

"He's her father, Beth. At some point I'll have to leave her alone with him," he whispered back.

She gave his shoulder a shove. "Well, now isn't that moment. Get in there."

William followed Emily Jane. She still held Rose, so if her father wondered why he was there, he could always say he had to claim his niece. Her skirts swayed slightly as she walked casually toward her father's table.

Emily Jane stopped beside his chair. "Hello, Papa. What brings you to Granite?" Her voice sounded calm, but her hand shook against Rose's back.

"Can't a father come visit his married daughter?" He wiped his mouth with a linen cloth off the table.

She nodded. "He could, but as you already know, I'm not married."

"Yes, I found that out from a stranger. Why didn't you write your mother and me and tell us you are still unwed?" His gaze connected with William's, who now stood behind Emily Jane. He picked up his coffee and returned his look to his daughter.

William stepped up beside Emily Jane. He hoped his presence would give her the assurance that she wasn't alone.

Emily Jane looked at him. "Well, Papa, I really didn't think you cared one way or the other. Several months ago you sent me off to marry a complete stranger."

He sat forward in his chair. "Girl, you're sassing me."

She shook her head. "No, sir. I'm telling the truth."

William's heart went out to Emily Jane. He could tell that for the first time in her life she was facing her past hurts. He prayed that her father would see her for the woman she'd become during his absence, instead of the young girl he'd sent away.

She was pushing her father's temper with her answer, and Emily Jane knew it. But she was an adult now, and though she still respected him, it wasn't in the same way she had as a child. He looked older than he had when she'd last seen her.

Her father studied her. "We'll talk about your behavior later. Who is this young man that seems to be hovering around you like a buzzard?"

It would be better for all involved not to take offense to his reference to William. "Papa, this is William Barns and these sweet little girls are Rose and Ruby. Mr. Barns's nieces." She forced a smile as she made the introductions.

William reached across the table and shook her father's hand. "It's nice to meet you, Mr. Rodgers."

"Emily Jane, I'm sure this young man would like to be on his way. Why don't you give him back that baby and have a seat?" He cut the meat on his plate with decisive force.

Before she could answer, William pulled out a chair and sat down. "I appreciate your concern, sir, but if you don't mind I'd like to get to know my future father-in-law better." He put Ruby on his knee and pulled out the chair beside him for Emily Jane to sit in.

Her father leaned back in his chair and crossed his arms. "Well, that is something I hadn't heard about, yet."

"That's because he just asked me this afternoon." Emily Jane took her seat and immediately had to move a water glass out of Rose's grasp.

"So when is the big date?"

Emily Jane looked to William. "We haven't set one yet, Papa. He's just asked me." She prayed her father would be happy with their engagement and go back to the Kansas farm he'd left. With it being planting season, she was surprised to see him here. What was so important that he'd come?

He nodded. "I see. Well, I'll just stick around until the knot is tied. Can't have you losing another husband."

More shaken at his words than she dared to admit, Emily Jane protested. "But, Papa, it will be months from now. And don't you have a farm to plant?"

The older gentleman dropped his napkin to the table and stood. "Nonsense, girl. All you need is a preacher and witnesses. The boys and your mama can take care of the farm for a few more days."

Once more her gaze moved to William. He sat observing them closely. What must he be thinking? Perhaps this was what he'd wanted all along. A flicker of apprehension coursed through her. Was she jumping out of the frying pan into the fire? Her mind worked overtime, torn by conflicting emotions. What did she want? Was she brave enough to stand up to her father? Could she tell him she'd changed her mind? Or the truth that she'd already refused William's offer of marriage?

"Well, since you don't seem to have any further objections, I suggest you get busy making arrangements. I'll be leaving soon." He threw the cloth napkin on the table and stood to leave.

Emily Jane called out, "Papa."

A smug look came across his face. She'd seen it many times when he'd caught one of her brothers in a lie. He enjoyed taking them to the woodshed and helping them to remember why they should never lie to him. "Yes, daughter?"

"Where are you staying?"

The grin left his face. "Got the last room at the hotel this afternoon. Can't really afford it, but since you don't have a home for me to stay in, I'll have to make do." He started to leave, then turned to face them again. "I'll see you in the morning. We have much to discuss."

Emily Jane nodded. She didn't like the way he said "we have much to discuss." Those words usually meant bad news for her. He'd said them the night he and Mother had told her she was answering Levi Westland's mail-order-bride advertisement. She couldn't bear to look at William, so she traced Rose's little hand. It didn't escape her notice for one moment that her fingers shook uncontrollably.

Beth hurried to their table. "Can I get you all dinner?" she asked.

William nodded. "Yes, Emily and I have a lot to talk

about, so we might as well feed the girls at the same time."

Emily Jane wasn't sure she liked William telling Beth or anyone else they had things to talk about. She wasn't sure what her father had in mind but knew that whatever it was, it meant bad news for her. She sighed. Could this day get much worse?

Chapter Twenty-One

Emily Jane admired Beth Winters. Beth ran Beth's Boardinghouse and had once confided in Emily Jane that doing so had always been her dream. She had also said that she was saving her money to buy the boarding-house from Levi Westland. Beth's future and that of her son's would soon be even more secure.

Beth and Amelia Blackwater carried over two high chairs for the girls. Amelia was new in town and had been looking for employment. Two days ago, Beth had rented Amelia the last available room in the boardinghouse.

Emily Jane realized that Amelia was wearing a kitchen apron. Had Beth hired her? The smile Amelia gave her confirmed that the girl was pleased with herself.

Things seemed to be falling into place for everyone but her. If only her father hadn't shown up. Emily Jane didn't know what to do. Her dream of owning a bakery was evaporating before her like early morning mist on the river's waters.

"Levi thought our customers might enjoy having these," Beth said as she set them up next to the table. "They are sure coming in handy today."

She took Rose from Emily Jane and put her into one

of the chairs. Amelia did the same with Ruby and then returned to the kitchen.

Emily Jane listened as William ordered the girls mashed potatoes, peas and creamed chicken. How far would she go to avoid going home with her father? Would she marry William?

Rose and Ruby looked at each other; their sweet grins touched her heart. What if their father never came back? If she married William, even in name only, and their father didn't come back, that would make her their adopted mother.

William reached across and laid his hand over hers. "What do you want to do now?" he asked in a soft voice.

She wanted to cry but now wasn't the time. "I don't know. I never thought he'd want to stay for the wedding."

"I know you don't really want to get married. Do you want to tell him we had a fight and the wedding is off?"

If they did that, her father would insist she go back to Kansas. Back to taking care of her brothers and sisters. Back to cooking plain meals. And there was no way she'd ever get her own bakery. If she married William, she'd be moving out to the farm, raising two little girls, instead of eleven, and she'd never own her own bakery. A pounding began in Emily Jane's head. "Not yet. Maybe if I pray and sleep on it, I'll come up with something."

Amelia arrived with William's and the little girls' food. She set a plate of meat loaf, mashed potatoes and peas in front of Emily Jane. "I didn't order this." Even if she had, she couldn't eat a bite. Her stomach rolled at the thought.

"I ordered it for you," William said, pulling Rose's and Ruby's plates out of their reach. "Girls, you know we pray first."

Emily Jane bowed her head and listened to the short

prayer William offered up for their meals. All the time, her mind raced. What was she going to do? No matter what she chose to do, her dream of owning a bakery was long gone.

While he prayed for their meals, William silently tacked on prayers for Emily Jane. His heart ached for her. She really was between a rock and a hard place.

As soon as he said, "Amen," Emily Jane pushed her plate back and picked up the glass of water. "Thank you for ordering for me, William, but I'm really not hungry." She set the glass back down without taking a drink then reached over and fed Ruby a bite of her mashed potatoes.

William spooned potatoes into Rose's mouth and then took a bite himself. He didn't want to push Emily Jane either way. But he didn't want to lose her, either.

"Papa is going to expect us to talk to the preacher tomorrow," she said in a soft, sad voice.

"Is your father a churchgoing man?" William continued to help Rose get her food into her mouth.

"Yes, back home he makes sure that our family fills up the first two pews. You'll see tomorrow. Papa will be on the front row waiting for me to join him." She offered Ruby a drink.

"Since you are marrying me, shouldn't you be sitting with me and the girls?" Had he overstepped his bounds? William held his breath while he waited for her answer.

He was pleased to see a smile creep across her lips. "Yes, I should."

William shared the grin with her. "Well, I never get there early because of the girls. I don't know why tomorrow should be any different. I'll pick you up, and you can ride in the wagon with us."

Emily Jane's brow furrowed. "I don't know. Papa is

a stranger here. Maybe I should get up early, go to the hotel and then sit with him during the service. He said we had more to discuss."

William nodded. He wasn't going to try to talk her out of sitting beside her parent. Emily Jane knew what was best for herself. He just hoped she wouldn't change her mind and leave him. William didn't want to go so far as to say he'd fallen in love with Emily Jane, but he would miss her if she left town. Something tugged in his heart. He refused to even consider that he had deeper feelings for Emily Jane than just friendship.

They continued the meal in silence, each of them deep within their own thoughts. Rose and Ruby laughed, played and smacked their lips as they ate.

Once the girls were finished, Amelia arrived at their table with a damp cloth to clean the potatoes from the girls' faces. Emily took it and washed first Rose's face and then Ruby's.

Was Emily Jane aware that she'd taken over the care of the girls even when he was present and could have washed their faces? Tenderness covered her expression as she talked softly to the girls and brushed food from their dresses. She kissed them each on the cheek and giggled when they returned her affections.

William stood. "Are you ready to head back to the school?" he asked, picking Rose up.

The little girls both kicked their legs. Emily Jane lifted Ruby and carried her out to William's wagon while he paid for their dinner. He'd never dreamed this morning that he'd be engaged this evening, but he was. What would tomorrow bring?

It was all William could do to get the girls dressed and himself to the church before the service actually started.

They'd always been close to late before, but today he had to get there early. There was no way he would let Emily Jane down.

Out of respect, she'd decided to sit with her father. And William had promised to be beside her. If they were engaged, it was expected.

He'd prayed most of the night about what he and Emily Jane were doing. Deep in his heart, William felt peace. She might not be aware of it or want to admit it, but they were going to be married. So, telling her father they were was the truth.

William stopped just inside the church door. It took only a moment to locate Emily Jane and her father sitting in the front row. As he made his way down the aisle, William marveled that Emily Jane's father was a churchgoing man but seemed so hard on his daughter. He still couldn't understand what kind of man would send his daughter off to marry a complete stranger.

Emily Jane's relieved eyes rose to meet him. She held her hands out to Rose, who immediately reached for her. "Good morning."

Her smile touched that soft spot in his heart. "Good morning." Their hands brushed as he handed Rose to her. Her eyes widened, and she quickly looked away. William grinned, knowing she'd felt that spark between them, too.

He took his seat. Her father leaned forward and nodded, then leaned back in his seat. There was no time for further interaction with anyone else. The preacher started the service.

When the final "amen" was said, Mr. Rodgers stood. "You have a good man of God here," he said, picking up his hat and slapping it against his blue-jean-clad leg. "I think he'll perform a good wedding ceremony."

Emily Jane nodded and also stood. "William and I

intend to talk to him about our wedding as soon as everyone heads home."

William continued to hold Ruby in his lap. He nodded his agreement with Emily Jane. Not sure what to say, he decided to let father and daughter visit. The rest of the congregation made their way to the back of the church.

"Since we didn't have enough time to visit this morning, I think I'll just wait here with you," her father said, sitting back down. "We can catch up until the preacher gets done, and then you two can carry on with your business."

Emily Jane sat down. "How is Mama?" She sounded like a little girl.

His features softened, and he touched her shoulder. "She is well. Been worried about you."

"I'm sorry about that, Papa." Emily Jane hugged Rose to her. "I couldn't come home."

He put his head in his hands. "I know. We thought we were doing the right thing."

Emily Jane touched the top of her father's head. "Papa, I've got a good life here. I'm fine. Tell Mama I'm doing well."

Her father raised his head. "How can you say you have a good life here and are doing well? You are homeless and work in a bakery. From what I can see, you haven't any money, and other than saying you are getting married to this man, I see no change in you. None."

"I love my job and have friends here," Emily Jane answered, lowering her head. "How did you want me to change?" she asked, hurt easing through her voice.

He sighed. "I wanted to see you in a nice home, pretty clothes and at least one baby on the way by now. Instead I found you like this." His voice sounded bitter.

William couldn't be quiet any longer. "Mr. Rodgers,

your daughter is one of the sweetest women I've ever met. She had a home before the tornado came. She's respected in this community. I'm blessed that she's agreed to marry me."

Her father stood once more. "Well, then perhaps after your wedding I can go home and tell her mother that her eldest daughter has turned into a woman she can be proud of."

William stood, too. "Emily Jane is already a daughter to be proud of."

Mr. Rodgers smiled. "Glad to hear you feel that way, son." He glanced over his shoulder. "Well, here comes the preacher. I'm heading back to the hotel for some lunch. Feel free to join me, when you get done."

William watched him shake the preacher's hand and then continue out of the church. One moment Emily Jane's father seemed to be a caring, loving father and then, within a blink of the eye, a man who seemed to enjoy making her feel small. He reached over and took her hand. "Are you feeling all right?"

Emily Jane looked up at him. "Yes. Papa means well."

He wasn't so sure of that, but William was wise enough to keep his opinion to himself. "Good. Are you sure you want to go through with this?"

She nodded. "When I told Papa that I have a good life here, that I love my job and that I have friends here, that was the truth. I'll be a good wife to you, and for as long as they need me, I'll take care of the girls."

"And I promise, I'll never ask more from you than what you are willing to give." William smiled at her. If they lived to be a hundred years old, he intended to make Emily Jane happy and never make her feel insignificant.

"I'm sorry to keep you two waiting. It seems everyone wanted to talk today." The preacher sat down on the platform. "What can I do for you today?"

Emily Jane looked to William to answer.

He rubbed the back of her hand with his thumb, enjoying the softness. "We would like to get married," William blurted out.

"Today?"

Emily Jane pulled her hand from his and massaged it with her other one. "No, not today but within the week."

"I see. May I ask why you are in such a hurry?" he asked, looking from one face to the other.

Again Emily Jane answered. "My father is in town for a few days, and I'd like him to be at my wedding."

"Did you have a day in mind?" the preacher asked.

William waited. When Emily Jane didn't answer, he turned to her. "Would Wednesday afternoon be a good time?"

She nodded.

The preacher tapped the top of his Bible. "Are you both sure this is what you want? Marriage is a lifelong commitment, not something to be taken lightly."

William answered, "I'm ready." His confidence spiraled upward. For once in his life, he felt sure of himself and his rightful place in the universe.

"Me, too." Her clear green eyes locked on to his. To his interested amazement, a spark of some indefinable emotion glowed with tenderness, and, could it be love? Powerful relief filled him. Then it was like watching a veil cover her face as her lids lowered and hid her thoughts from him. But not before he saw the expression of reproach and defeat cross her features. She sighed and then gave a resigned shrug.

Emily Jane looked defeated. She had given up. Surrendered. What did it all mean? A warning voice whispered in his head. Charlotte hadn't cared about him, either. Would time prove the same with Emily Jane? Was it too much to expect love and admiration from the woman he married?

Chapter Twenty-Two

Emily Jane couldn't believe it was her wedding day. So many people had graciously come forward with gifts for both her and William. There was one, though, that she had exclaimed over with intense pleasure. Susanna Marsh definitely knew how to make a bride happy.

Susanna had worked night and day to finish her gift for Emily Jane. A wedding dress cut and sewn from her own special design. It had taken Emily Jane's breath away. And now Emily Jane stood in front of the mirror draped in the many folds of material. The shimmering light green fabric twirled about her, making her feel like a princess from one of Anna Mae's storybooks.

"Here is a sixpence to put in your left shoe," Anna Mae said, holding out the coin.

Emily Jane frowned but took the money. "And why am I putting this in my shoe?"

"It represents wealth and financial security." Susanna giggled as she straightened out the hem of Emily Jane's dress.

"What about the rest of the poem? Did you get something old, something new, something borrowed and something blue?" Millie Westland asked.

Millie was a newlywed herself. She'd married Levi back in the fall. They were expecting their first child in a couple of months.

"No. I didn't know I was supposed to have all that stuff," Emily Jane answered, wishing the hummingbirds in her tummy would settle down.

"You can't get married without them," Anna Mae said, agreeing with Millie.

"Well, I think I can take care of the something borrowed," Millie said, taking a pretty comb from her own hair and handing it to Emily Jane. The little diamond studs reflected the light.

Were those real diamonds? "I can't accept this, Millie. It looks expensive." Emily Jane tried to hand it back to her.

Millie laughed, and her big tummy jiggled. "You are only borrowing it, Emily Jane." She tucked her hands over her belly. "I won't take it back until after the ceremony."

Emily Jane turned it over and over in her hand. It really was beautiful.

"Your wedding dress can be the something new." Susanna stepped back and looked at her. "You look beautiful."

Emily Jane felt her cheeks grow hot. "Thank you."

"She still needs something old and something blue," Millie said, easing down into a chair.

Anna Mae sat Emily Jane down on a stool in front of a mirror. "Here, let me put the comb in for you." She began combing Emily Jane's hair. "Your hair is so pretty. I wish mine was red instead of this mousy brown."

Before Emily Jane could answer, Amelia breezed through the door, her cheeks red, her breath coming in soft gasps. "Whew, I thought I wouldn't make it in time. I ran all the way from the restaurant." Her mouth formed a perfect O. "Emily Jane, you are so beautiful."

"What's that you've got, Amelia?" Susanna reached out to touch the flowers Amelia carried.

"I made this bouquet for you, Emily Jane. If you don't want to carry it, I will not be offended at all." She colored fiercely and scuffed the toe of her shoe against the floor. Emily Jane could not believe a woman as lovely as Amelia lacked confidence. She rushed to assure Amelia how touched she was by the gesture.

"They're beautiful, Amelia. I love them. I hadn't even thought of a bouquet." Bluebonnets mingled with baby's breath and green ivy. A white-and-green ribbon formed a delicate bow, and amazingly the green ribbon drew the green shimmers out of her dress. She reached for them, but Amelia held them out of her reach.

"Umm, there's something else. I took the liberty of going into your room. I hope you don't mind." She offered them a small, shy smile. She turned the bouquet over, and the base of the arrangement was Emily Jane's cookbook.

Emily Jane bit her lip to stifle her cry of joy. The exclamations of her friends echoed her feelings exactly. She flung her arms around Amelia, happiness bubbling in her heart. "Thank you, thank you. It's perfect."

"Stop that right now." The smile on her face belied the threat in Susanna's voice. "You'll put wrinkles in your dress before you ever walk down the aisle."

"Well," Anna Mae said matter-of-factly, "that takes care of the something old, the book, and something blue, the flowers."

"Now that I have everything from the poem, what is the point of having them?" Emily Jane asked, looking at the faces of her friends. "I mean what's the purpose?"

Susanna smiled. "They are supposed to bring you luck."

Luck. Emily Jane didn't think she needed luck.

Over the past three days, she'd begged God to get

her out of this mess, but He'd remained silent. She cared about William but still resented the idea of giving up her dream for marriage and children. Since the Lord had not intervened, Emily Jane resigned herself to the fact that having a bakery must not be the will of God and that she would make William the best wife that she could be.

She hadn't seen much of him. On Monday he'd gone to the bank and bought the farm. The Guthries had come to town with a single wagonload of the things they wanted to take with them back East and left town almost immediately after the sale was completed.

William and her father had stayed away while Emily Jane and her friends planned the wedding and the reception. Beth Winters had insisted on baking the wedding cake. Carolyn Moore decorated the church pews with streamers and flowers. Millie Westland had hired a group of musicians to play during the reception. It was going to be a wedding party that would be talked about for months to come. At least, that was what Millie had said. The kindness of her friends and the local townspeople filled her heart with joy. She exhaled a long sigh of contentment.

"Ladies, it's time to go," Levi Westland called through the door.

Millie giggled. "Come on, ladies." She opened the door to her husband.

Levi nodded his head at the women as they came out of Emily Jane's room. "There are two wagons out front to take everyone to the church," he said, smiling down at his pretty little wife.

Emily Jane's hand shook as she closed the door to her room. Her heart hammered as she walked down the boardinghouse stairs. Her knees trembled. The girls chattered all the way to the church, but Emily Jane remained silent, fingering the ribbons on the bouquet. She took deep breaths until she was strong enough to raise her head.

Was William as nervous as she? Was he having second thoughts? Did he feel as ill equipped as she did at undertaking the task before them today? One thing was for certain. They both walked into it with their eyes wide-open.

The church looked like something from a fairy-tale book. Green ribbons hung along the bench edges. Tiny blue-and-white flowers were interwoven within the ribbons. The church smelled of pine and honeysuckle. But none of this compared to Emily Jane.

She seemed to glide down the center aisle on her father's arm. The green gown she wore brought out the color in her beautiful eyes. Her red hair had been piled on top of her head, and ringlets framed her face. A comb pulled back one side, giving her a glamorous look. How had he missed how beautiful she truly was? Carried away by his own response, he failed at first to notice the heart-rending tenderness of her gaze. Everything took on a clean brightness, and his pulse quickened in giddy happiness. And then she stood in front of him.

He stepped forward, and Mr. Rodgers placed her small hand within his. Her mere touch made him want to vow eternal love for her. He held her hand throughout the ceremony, gently caressing the back of it with his thumb. William repeated his vows, unaware of them because his true focus was on the lady at his side.

At the preacher's instruction, he slipped a simple gold band onto her left ring finger. It wasn't enough. She deserved so much more. A knot tightened his throat as she repeated her vows with a gentle softness in her voice.

He could barely stand still as Emily Jane studied his

face unhurriedly, feature by feature, as if analyzing his reaction to every nuance of the ceremony. William felt as if they were the only two people in the world, wrapped in a silken cocoon of closeness. He'd had no idea that getting married would feel this way.

"You may kiss the bride," the preacher said in a loud voice.

William released her hands and gently cupped her face.

Their first kiss. Her long lashes closed over her eyes. Lowering his mouth, he took his first taste of her sweet lips. Raising his mouth from hers, he stared into her eyes. Why had he waited so long to kiss her? She tasted so much better than his beloved sugar cookies.

To his surprise, Emily Jane had returned his kiss. Her mouth moved shyly under his before she pulled away. He squeezed her hand, encouraging her, letting her know he loved her participation. A pink flush covered her cheeks, bringing out the freckles.

Without reservation, William ran his thumb over her mouth and then leaned his forehead on hers. They were husband and wife. Emily Jane had stolen his heart at their first meeting. Why hadn't he been aware of it all this time?

The minister patted him on the shoulder, then whispered close to his ear. "Face the congregation so that I can present you."

William reluctantly did as asked but used the occasion to wrap her briefly in his arms.

"I present you with Mr. and Mrs. William Barns."

The wagon bumped along the road to the farm. His gaze slid across the bench to where his wife sat. She'd changed into a light blue day dress, but her hair still remained up off her neck and shoulders, revealing freckles there, as well. Why that pleased him he couldn't tell, but his smile broadened in approval.

She'd been quiet for the past fifteen minutes. Was she as overwhelmed as he felt? Emily Jane shyly glanced his way, and once more that charming, soft pink flush filled her cheeks.

"I still can't believe we're married," he said to break the silence.

"Me, either." She fiddled with the fabric in her lap. "I hope you don't regret marrying me."

He reached out, touching her elbow. "Why would I?"

She wiggled around on the seat so that she faced him. "You might meet a woman that you fall in love with."

William grinned. "I might have already found that woman."

She exploded. "Then why in the world did you marry me?" Tears spilled from her eyes. "You should have told me."

He guided the mare to the side of the road and set the brake. There were those tears again. William tried to take her hands in his, but she pulled them away. Her eyes accused him of wrongdoings. "I did tell you."

Emily Jane shook her head. The curls about her face caressed her cheeks. "No, you didn't. I would never have married you if I had known."

"That's what I was afraid of," William confessed. He had never liked to see a woman cry, but in this case it sealed in his mind a certainty that Emily Jane had feelings for him. Why else would the thought of him loving another cause such a reaction? He felt his confidence grow.

She sniffled. "I don't understand. Why marry me when you could marry someone you loved?" The freckles across her forehead bunched up in a frown.

William sighed. He ought to own up sooner rather

than later, or matters could get completely out of hand in a hurry. However, this wasn't how he'd planned on telling her. He'd wanted to do so over dinner, but here they sat. He gentled his voice and said with quiet emphasis, "Emily Jane, I did marry the person I love."

Confusion and understanding warred together in her beautiful expressions. "You love me?" she whispered.

William brushed back the hair at her temple. Just touching her sent a surge of joy through him. She was his. They'd gotten married, and he'd just told her he loved her. He nodded. "I do. I think I have since the moment I met you but was too stubborn to allow my head to hear what my heart was already saying."

More tears filled her eyes. "Oh, William. I love you, too. But…"

He rested a finger across her lips. "All I need to hear is that you love me. I know how you feel about having children, and I've decided I'm happy raising Rose and Ruby. And when Josiah comes for them, we can still be happy without children."

She removed his finger from her lips and offered him a small smile. "What if I change my mind and want to have children?"

"Then we will have children." Was she trying to tell him that if he wanted children she'd change her mind and have them? Or was she simply letting him know that she wasn't dead set against having children? It didn't matter. He loved her no matter what.

"William Barns!" The shout startled them both.

Emily Jane looked over her shoulder to see who had called his name. A big man riding a roan-colored horse barreled down on them. His shoulder-length brown hair flew behind him like a waving flag under his dark black hat.

"Who is that man?" She turned to find that William had jumped down from the wagon and seemed to be taking a fighting stance.

The big man jumped from the horse, not giving it time to stop. He raced to William and grabbed him in a bear hug. The horse spun around and pranced back.

Emily Jane looked about the wagon for a weapon. She searched under the seat and found the shotgun. Just as her hand clasped the barrel, she realized they were laughing and slapping each other on the back.

"Josiah, I didn't recognize you with that long hair and beard. I think you took twenty years off my life just now. But, boy, am I glad to see you! I thought you might be dead!" William said excitedly.

Emily Jane sank to the wagon seat. Her legs shook like cold jelly. She placed a hand over her heart and watched the two men. Her brothers acted that way when they hadn't seen each other in a few days.

William looked up at her with a huge grin. "Emily, I'd like you to meet Josiah, Rose and Ruby's father. Josiah, this is Emily Jane Barns, my wife."

If she hadn't still been shaken up, Emily Jane might have laughed at the shocked expression on Josiah's face. He looked from her to William and back again.

In a gravelly voice, Josiah said, "Nice to meet you, Mrs. Barns."

"Please, we're family. Call me Emily Jane." She smiled down at him. Now that she knew who he was, she could see Rose and Ruby in his features. Mainly his cheekbones. Josiah had the same high cheekbones as the twins. Their black curls must have come from their mother, William's sister.

"Speaking of family, where are my girls?" He turned to William.

William slapped him on the back. "They are in town with Anna Mae Leland. The town schoolteacher. Why don't you come out to the house with us, and I'll catch you up?" William climbed back up into the wagon with Emily Jane.

Josiah nodded and swung back up into the saddle. He moved so fast, Emily Jane wasn't sure when his feet left the ground. She listened as he and William called back and forth to each other, neither seemingly able to wait for the overdue conversation till they got to the house.

"I'm sure glad to see you. Like I said earlier, I thought you were dead." William looked up at Josiah, riding as close to the wagon as he could get.

"I'm sorry about that. It took longer than I'd anticipated to catch my prisoners." Josiah's gaze moved to Emily Jane.

She smiled at him but didn't comment. It was obvious he wondered how much she knew about him and his reason for being separated from the girls.

"How are my girls doing?" he asked, patting the roan.

William shrugged. "I think they are good. I'm sure they've missed you."

"They are such babies, William. I'm not sure they know how to miss anyone." His sad eyes looked down on them. It was clear that Josiah missed his wife.

With a shake of his head, William answered, "I think you will be surprised."

They arrived at the farm. Emily Jane waited for William to help her down. She wasn't sure if they were going to have a houseguest or not.

"I'll put the horse and wagon away and be right in," William said, giving her a kiss on the cheek.

She felt a blush splash across her face and nodded. Emily Jane took the bag he handed her and hurried to the house. Once inside she looked about. This was her new home.

Standing in the sitting room doorway, she looked to the left where the Guthries had left their dining table and chairs. She knew from her last visit that the kitchen was through the next door to her left of the dining room. A stairway led to the two bedrooms on the second floor.

Taking a deep breath, Emily Jane climbed the stairs. The room on the right was obviously William's. A large bed, armoire and dresser filled the space. She crossed to the window and looked down into the front yard.

William and Josiah stood beside the barn. He'd released the little mare into the corral, and the two men rested their arms on the top fence rail, visiting. William turned and looked at the house. His head came up, and he gazed straight at the bedroom window. Could he see her? Or had he just sensed her watching them?

Emily Jane backed away from the window. Now that Josiah had returned, how much would things change? Would he need someone to watch the girls for him and ask her? Or would he take the girls and return to Denver? Her heart ached at the thought of the girls leaving.

She walked over to the bed and sank into the mattress. Did this mean that she could stay in town and work at the bakery? Would she be content to live on the farm and work in town? Her mind raced a mile a minute with questions and uncertainties that only her husband could answer for her. Her husband. My, but she did like the sound of that.

keep reminding of a man on a 51... a... as...
explained the chair, and he... began to drift
back to Emily and... and then... them. Will... to
wait to give Emily her wedding present.

Chapter Twenty-Three

William stood in the bedroom doorway watching his new wife sleep. Her red hair spread out over the pillow, and sooty black lashes rested against her freckled skin. He'd never seen a more beautiful woman.

He'd spent the night talking to Josiah and learning that his brother-in-law had pursued the bank robbers all the way to Mexico. They had given Josiah a merry chase, and he'd felt obliged to share all the obstacles the chase had entailed. After he'd caught them, it had taken another two months to get a trial date for the men. Then another to locate William and the girls.

Josiah had fallen asleep downstairs on the settee. William now stood watching Emily Jane sleep.

He tiptoed to the window and pulled the rocker beside it. The sun peeked over the horizon in the east. William watched as shades of pinks, oranges and fiery reds filled the morning sky. His gaze moved back to the bed.

Emily Jane smiled in her sleep. Did that mean she was happy? Or was she dreaming of the bakery that she no longer thought was within her grasp?

He sat down and waited for her to wake up. Until she knew just how much he loved her, William intended to keep his promise of a marriage of convenience. A yawn expanded his chest, and his eyes began to drift shut. He'd rest a few minutes and then wake her; William couldn't wait to give Emily her wedding present.

The hot sun and a cramped neck woke him. The bed was empty. Emily Jane had spread the quilt back over it and was nowhere to be seen.

William pushed out of the chair with a groan. He moved to his wardrobe and pulled out a fresh shirt. A glance at his feet reminded him he'd slept with his boots on.

Her sweet laughter drifted up the stairs. William followed the sound and found his lovely wife sharing a cup of coffee and eggs with his brother-in-law. An unfamiliar twinge ripped across his chest.

When she saw him enter the room, Emily stood and came to his side. She tiptoed to give him a kiss on the cheek and whispered, "Thanks for letting me sleep."

He couldn't resist and turned his face quickly and captured her lips with his. Her lips were warm and moist. His mood turned suddenly buoyant.

A hearty laugh surrounded them.

Emily Jane jerked away from him. "I'll get your coffee and eggs."

William released her and glared at his brother-in-law, who had spoiled the kiss. "Thank you."

"I thought you were going to sleep the day away." Josiah leaned back in his chair and sipped at his coffee.

He walked to the table and sat down. Emily Jane handed him a steaming cup. William smiled his thanks to her, then turned his attention back to Josiah. "Well, someone kept me up all night."

Emily Jane gasped.

He continued: "With tales of chasing bank robbers

and the woes of finding a good judge." William grinned at his brother-in-law, who seemed not to have noticed Emily's gasp.

Josiah dropped his chair to the floor. "Guilty as charged." He set the cup on the table and stood. "Now that you are up, I'd like to head back to town and get my girls."

William took the plate of eggs from Emily. "And go where with them?"

Emily Jane put a hand on his shoulder. She tilted her head and waited for Josiah to answer.

"I'm not sure. I can always go back to Denver." Even as he said it, William knew that wasn't his plan. Like him, Josiah would always associate the city as the place where Mary had died.

"You and the girls are welcome to stay out here with us," Emily Jane offered. She squeezed William's shoulder, and he looked up at her.

She had to be the most generous person he'd ever met. He reached up and laid his hand over hers.

"Thank you, Emily Jane. But are you sure you want two little girls underfoot night and day?"

William held his breath as he waited to hear what she would say. She'd offered their home, but had she really thought about what she'd said? And once he'd given her his wedding present, would she regret her offer?

This was just the opportunity she'd been waiting for. The little girls needed a woman in their lives. And truth be told, Emily Jane loved them.

She'd worried about Rose and Ruby while the men had slept. What was Josiah going to do with them? He was a single man who probably hadn't taken care of them a full day of their lives.

Emily Jane smiled at Josiah. He'd confided in her that he wasn't sure what he was going to do now that he'd caught the bank robbers that had killed his wife. He'd resigned as sheriff when he'd returned to Denver and come in search of his girls.

"I'm sure. Besides, you two will be here to help with them."

She picked up Josiah's plate and carried it to the washbasin. While William and Josiah had slept, she'd familiarized herself with her new kitchen. Mrs. Guthrie had left almost all the dishes, pots and pans and utensils that she would need to cook and bake.

Now that she knew the girls would be living with her, Emily Jane almost felt like this was home. The night before she'd confided in William that she loved him. She'd realized while they were talking about children that having her own child would be nothing like raising siblings. A small smile touched her lips at the thought.

"She seems pretty sure to me," William said.

Emily Jane felt his gaze upon her. She nodded at him.

"Well, if you are both sure. I promise to try not to overstay our welcome." He picked up his black hat and placed it on his head. "I'll go take care of the horses while you finish up your breakfast. Then I'm heading to town to get my girls."

William swallowed a big bite of scrambled eggs. "Give us a few minutes and we'll ride in with you."

Josiah chuckled. "I was hoping you'd say that. I've no idea where this Mrs. Leland lives."

"Miss Leland," Emily Jane corrected him absently. Why were she and William returning to town? Maybe he felt they needed supplies.

Whatever the reason, she was glad. Papa had said he'd be leaving right after lunch, and Emily Jane wanted to say goodbye to him. He was a hard man at times, but she knew he only wanted what was best for her and she loved him.

The door closed behind Josiah, and Emily Jane turned to her new husband. "Yesterday, I didn't have a chance to give you my wedding present. Would it be all right with you if I give it to you now?"

"You didn't have to get me a present." William smiled, pleased.

She offered him a returning grin. "Maybe not, but I wanted to." Emily Jane hurried to the bedroom and pulled out the package she'd stashed under the bed. Then she walked back to him, praying he'd like her gift. It had cost almost all the money she'd saved for her bakery, but now that she was no longer going to pursue that dream, Emily Jane had bought the gift for William.

"That is a big package," William said, standing to take it from her.

Emily Jane slipped into the closest kitchen chair and watched as he pulled the pretty blue, green and white ribbons from the butcher paper that held her gift. She watched his face and was happy to see the joy that leaped into his eyes as he pulled the present out.

William turned the picture of the elk in his hands. "How did you know?" he asked in wonder. Pleased, he touched the smooth wood and admired the many colors that accented the piece.

She giggled. "I asked Levi if there was something in his store you might like."

The smile slipped from his face. "Emily Jane, this is too much." He laid the elk on the table.

"No, it isn't." Tears filled her eyes as she thought of the love he'd proclaimed, and just knowing that he'd been willing to let her continue to work at the bakery was more than enough reason for her to use the money to buy the gift for him.

"Honey, that was the money you were saving for your bakery. Why would you spend it on a piece of painted wood?" His eyes questioned hers.

Emily Jane saw the emotions warring within their depths. Was he happy or sad? She couldn't be sure. She realized that now that Josiah had returned, she and William could try to make her dream of owning a bakery come true. But even though she really wanted to have the bakery, now that William was in her life, that dream didn't seem as important as it had before. He now gave her life meaning, and she wanted to enjoy every moment of their time together.

Emily Jane realized she'd been silent for too long. Doubt now filled his face. She stood and walked to him. "I love you, William, so very much it hurts in here." She clasped both hands over her heart. "I wanted to give you something that I knew you loved. The bakery was a dream but you are real, and I want to spend my days being with you."

Tears filled his eyes. William pulled her to him, and she relaxed against him as his arms tightened about her small body. She could feel his breath against her cheek and hear his heart beat in her ears. How good the Lord had been to her to give her this man. She smiled. This was where she truly belonged.

"Oh, excuse me." Josiah began to back out of the door he'd just barged into.

Emily Jane pulled out of her husband's arms. "We're ready," she called to Josiah. She looked up into her handsome husband's face. They had their whole lives before them.

He slid his hand down her arm and clasped her hands

in his. "Yes, we are." William held her hand as they followed Josiah to the wagon.

He lifted her up and then said, "Thank you for my gift. I'll cherish it always."

Emily Jane sat on the seat beside her new husband as they rode toward town. Her life had changed over the past few months. She had changed. Emily Jane tossed her head back and enjoyed the warm sun on her face and the feeling of being loved.

It didn't take them long to reenter Granite. Their first stop was the boardinghouse, so that Josiah could get the girls. Anna Mae was in the dining room feeding them lunch when they arrived.

Rose and Ruby saw their father at the same time. Both girls began chanting. "Da! Da!" They tried to fling themselves from their high chairs to get to him.

Emily Jane watched, her heart in her throat as he pulled them from their chairs and buried his face in their little necks. The girls grabbed his head and gave him openmouthed kisses on his cheeks, his ears and all other places where they could reach.

They refused to let him go, so great was their joy at seeing their papa. Josiah's tear-smothered voice whispered their names over and over as he examined their fingers, their little heads and legs. He seemed to be committing them to memory. Emily Jane swallowed hard and bit back tears.

When Josiah gained control of his emotions again, she introduced him to Anna Mae, who appeared tongue-tied. What in the world? One thing Anna Mae had never been without was words. She could talk the rings off a rattler. She watched with interest as the schoolteacher excused herself to get the girls' things from her room. "I'd like to go say goodbye to Papa," Emily Jane said to William.

He nodded. "Josiah, do you want to wait here for us to come back?"

Josiah looked confused. "I figured I'd just take the girls back out to your place."

William smiled. "Yes, but you'll need our wagon to get them there. I'm not sure even you could hold on to two squirming girls and keep that roan of yours in check at the same time."

A cloud of red raced up his neck and into his face. "I suppose you're right. I'm out of practice and didn't think that through," Josiah admitted. He continued to hold on to his girls; they stroked his hair and face with their tiny hands. "We'll be fine waiting here."

"We'll be back shortly." William took Emily Jane's arm and turned her toward the door. "I've also got a wedding gift I want to give you before we head home."

Home. It had been a long time since Emily had a home. She smiled at him. "I am so happy, I don't need a present."

"And your happiness is all I need," William answered. "But you will like this present or I'll eat my hat."

Emily Jane chuckled as they stepped out into the sunlight. He continued to hold her arm as they ambled down the walkway. Tiny currents of electricity seemed to pulsate where his fingers connected with her arm. He steered her past their horse and wagon.

"I thought we'd walk, if that's all right." William slid his hand down her arm and then clasped her fingers in his.

How could she refuse? Emily Jane's heart pounded in her chest as they approached the hotel where her father stayed. Thanks to his arrival, she'd married William and realized that he was nothing like her father.

Mr. Rodgers was just coming out of the hotel when

they arrived. Emily Jane released William's hand and hurried to hug her father. "Papa, I just wanted you to know that I'm so glad you came."

"I am, too." He held her away from him. "I know you think your mother and I were being cruel when we set you from our home, but, daughter, you must know that it broke our hearts to do so."

Emily Jane started to say she understood, even though she really didn't, when he raised his hand and stopped her from speaking.

"We wanted you to have a better life than what we could supply. I'm sorry if we hurt you." His green eyes glistened in the noonday sun.

Were those tears in his eyes? She rushed back into his embrace. "I love you, Papa."

He wrapped his strong arms around her. "I love you, too, EJ."

Emily Jane pressed her head against his chest and listened to his strong heartbeat. He hadn't called her EJ in a very long time. She remembered sitting on his lap as a little girl and listening to his heartbeat. Back then, he'd called her EJ. Then more children had been born, and Emily Jane and her father had grown apart. She thanked the Lord for giving her this time with him again.

She stepped out of his embrace. "You and Mama will come see us again, won't you?"

"Lord willing." He picked up his ragged bag and walked to his wagon and horse.

Emily Jane hadn't thought about it before now but wondered if her father would have left without saying goodbye if she hadn't shown up when she had.

As if to answer her question he said, "I planned on stopping by your place on my way out. I guess you saved me a trip." He put his bag in the bed of the wagon and then looked to William. "Take care of my little girl."

William stepped up and shook her father's hand. "I will do my best, sir."

"See that you do." He pulled himself up on the wagon.

The wagon held supplies and a bedroll. Emily Jane said a silent prayer for her father's safety on the way home. It was a long trip, and he wasn't getting any younger. She wished now that he'd brought one or two of her brothers with him to keep him company on the return trip.

Her papa reached down one more time and took Emily's hands in his. "Your mother and I love you very much and are proud of you, EJ." He released her hands and smiled. "We'll see you soon."

"'Bye, Papa. I love you." Emily Jane felt tears run down her face as he drove away.

William pulled her against his side. "We can go visit them whenever you want." He kissed the top of her head.

Emily Jane accepted his comfort until her father turned the corner and drove out of sight. Then she wiped her face free of moisture. "Thank you." She sniffed and forced a smile on her face. "Now, did you mention a wedding present?"

"Indeed I did. Come with me." William grabbed her hand and walked to The Bakery. He used a key, opened the door and then pulled her inside with a smile.

Why on earth would William give her a cookie or cake as a wedding gift? He knew she could make her own.

Bringing her here was confusing. She'd quit her job to move out on the farm with him. What was he thinking? When he continued to grin but not say anything, Emily Jane confessed, "I don't understand."

"What do you want more than anything?" he asked.

Emily Jane still didn't comprehend. She had no desire to hurt his feelings, but the truth came out before she could think of a way to soften it. "Not a cookie," she said.

He laughed. "I don't know. The owner of this place makes the best sugar cookies I've ever tasted. You sure you don't want a sugar cookie?"

Thankfully, the place was empty of customers at the time, or like her, they would probably think the man had lost his mind. She tilted her head and looked up at him. "You do know that I was the one who made the sugar cookies when I worked here, right?"

He nodded. "And as the new owner, you can still make them." The grin on his face grew even larger.

"New owner?"

William grabbed her around the waist and swung her about like a small child. "This is my gift to you, The Bakery." He laughed as he looked up into her face. "It's all yours. You are the proud owner of your own bakery."

Emily Jane merely stared at him, tongue-tied. Through the roaring din in her ears, she breathed one word. "Mine?" William had bought her The Bakery. She took a quick breath of utter astonishment.

He pulled her over to one of the tables and sat her down. His face had gone from excited and happy to concern. "Emily Jane, I thought you'd be happy."

Emily Jane found her voice. A cry broke from her lips. "Happy! 'Happy' doesn't begin to describe what I feel right now." She jumped up and walked to the counter. "When did you do this? Why did you do this?" She ran her hand lovingly over the smooth, cool surface. Her heart sang with delight.

"On Monday, when I bought the farm for Josiah and the girls."

She halted. Shocked. "What did you say? For Josiah and the girls? I thought you wanted the farm."

William laughed. "I'm no farmer. At first I'd thought the farm would be a good place for us to take care of the girls, but the truth of the matter is I'm a businessman."

Emily Jane knew he'd owned a store in Denver, so she nodded her agreement. She hadn't been able to picture him farming but hadn't had the heart to say so.

He took her hands in his and led her to the nearest table, where he pulled out a chair for her to sit down in. Once seated he said, "A few weeks ago, I became a silent partner of the general store. Levi and I have been discussing a couple of other businesses that I might like to invest in later. I probably should have told you earlier, but I wanted you to love me for me and not for my wealth."

Emily Jane didn't say anything; it was apparent William needed to talk.

"I realize now that that was wrong thinking. You are nothing like Charlotte. You have shown me nothing but love and kindness. You helped me realize that I can freely give my heart to you and never fear you will crush it." He knelt down in front of her. "I hope you don't mind that I gave the ranch to Josiah." There was a question in his statement.

"Of course I don't mind, but where are we going to live?" she asked, still feeling at odds with the world and everything in it. Her life felt topsy-turvy. If that was such a thing.

"Here."

"Here?"

He shook his head and chuckled. "You really are confused, aren't you?"

"It would seem so." She stood and walked to the large window that overlooked the street. How many times had she wished for a bakery like this one?

"Have you ever been upstairs?" William asked, taking her hand in his.

She shook her head no. Emily Jane had always assumed that Violet lived up there but had never visited her.

"Come on." He pulled her through the kitchen and up the back stairs. Another key unlocked the door.

"I thought Violet lived up here." Emily Jane entered the living space. It was wide-open. A couch with a small table in front of it sat on the left-hand side of the room; farther back was an open doorway where she could see a bed and dresser. To her right was an open kitchen area. She realized that it was directly over the kitchen in the bakery below.

"No, she moved out about a month ago. Levi said that she's moved into a small house a couple of streets over."

Emily Jane looked at him. Was it true? This was all hers? The Bakery? The living area above it? Everything? She had to know. "So we really can live here?"

He took her hands in his. "This is your Bakery. This is your home."

Emily Jane closed her eyes. Her arms circled her husband in a close embrace. God had brought a man into her life who loved her and was willing to help her live her dreams.

"Thank you for the bakery and believing in my dreams. I was so afraid you would be like my father and try to control me. Instead you have proved once again that you support my dreams and that you care enough about me to give me the freedom I need."

His heartbeat filled her ears, and she smiled. William Barns loved her. His heart beat for her. She couldn't believe how blessed she was.

She leaned back and looked up into his face. Brilliant blue eyes stared into hers. Emily Jane reached up and cupped his face in her hands. "Thank you so much. I love you more than words can ever express." Then she pulled his lips down to hers.

She gloried in the plan God had designed for her life. With certainty she knew that this man who held her tightly would love her for the rest of her life.

Epilogue

Emily Jane Barns couldn't wipe the grin from her face. The cake she'd baked for the summer festival was spectacular. She'd been working on the design for over a month. She stood back and admired her handiwork. It was four tiers tall and as round as a wagon wheel. The icing was done in red, white and blue. Stars decorated the top.

As was common nowadays, her thoughts turned to her husband. They'd been married three months now, and her husband had been busy building the town. William had recently opened a small restaurant and had also hired their first newspaperman, Mr. Sweeney, who now produced a weekly newspaper in Granite, Texas. He'd also given Amos his first real job as an assistant to Mr. Sweeney.

Emily Jane couldn't stop the smile from spreading across her face. Her husband was well respected by everyone, and Emily Jane couldn't be prouder of him.

She'd been busy herself. Taking care of the girls and running the bakery had taken most of her time and energy. But she'd loved every moment. She touched her stomach and grinned.

"That is a beautiful cake," Susanna said, coming to stand beside her. "When do we get to sample it?"

Emily Jane laughed at her friend. "Not for a couple more hours. According to Mrs. Harvey, the cutting of the cake takes place shortly after our picnic lunches."

Susanna frowned. "Who made her boss?"

"No idea, but I wouldn't cross her if I were you." She grinned at the dressmaker. "Isn't she one of your best customers?"

In defiance, Susanna dipped her finger in the icing at the bottom of the cake and licked the sweetness off. "No, but her best friend, Mrs. Anderson, is."

Emily Jane grinned. Mrs. Anderson was the bank president's wife and the richest woman in town, if you didn't count the Westland women.

"Where is that handsome husband of yours?" Susanna asked, changing the subject.

Emily Jane knew William was somewhere on the fairgrounds but where exactly, she wasn't sure. She looked about. "He's here somewhere."

"Have you told him about the baby yet?" Susanna whispered.

Emily Jane felt her jaw drop. "How did you know?" she hissed.

Susanna laughed. "I'm the one that does your dress measurements, remember? I couldn't help but notice your waist is a little thicker."

Emily Jane looked down. Was she showing already?

Susanna hugged her about the shoulders. "Don't worry. It barely shows."

Was she going to be like her mother and blossom with child immediately? Emily Jane wondered what her mother would think when she told her she would soon be a grandmother. She smiled.

Next month, they would be going to Kansas. Just her and William. Violet would continue running the bakery, and William was lining up helpers even now to make sure the restaurant continued running smoothly in his absence.

"I can't wait until the other ladies find out. Can you imagine all the baby quilts and clothes you'll be getting?"

"Shhhh, I haven't told William yet, and I don't want him to find out from you." Emily Jane shook her finger in her friend's face. "Hear me?"

"Yep, but it's gonna cost you one banana nut bread loaf to keep me quiet," she teased.

"I'll give you two not to tell anyone, not even Anna Mae. I want to be the one to tell him." Emily Jane smoothed the fabric over her tummy and grinned.

"Deal. Isn't that him over by our new sheriff?"

Emily Jane's gaze followed Susanna's pointing finger. William was standing beside Josiah. Josiah had proved he wasn't much of a farmer either and had recently taken the job of sheriff. They were on the edge of the woods where a horseshoe game was in progress not too far from them. Rose and Ruby played on a colorful blanket at their feet.

"Yes, it is. If you will excuse me, I have some important news to tell my husband."

Susanna's laugh followed her across the field. Emily Jane saw several of her old neighbors and smiled. Their home had been built, and now they lived as one family. She was happy for them and Anna Mae, who lived with them. Emily Jane saw her friend and waved to her.

As if he sensed her approach, William turned and smiled at her. His beautiful eyes held hers, and she prayed that their baby would have his wavy black hair and sparkling blue eyes.

She started to walk toward him when another bout of morning sickness assaulted her. Why now? Why so late in the morning? She didn't want to be sick now, but there was no stopping the nausea that engulfed her.

Emily Jane clutched her queasy stomach. Sweat broke out on her face, and she doubled over, sure that the contents of her stomach would soon be on the ground.

Susanna hurried to her side. "Are you all right?" she asked, motioning for William to come over.

She nodded. "I'm just sick to my stomach."

William hurried to her side. "Emily?" His eyes searched hers.

"I'm all right. Just feeling sick to my stomach." She tried to stand upright, but again a wave of queasiness enveloped her like a black cloak.

"Maybe we should take you to see the doctor." William's voice shook with concern.

Susanna thrust a glass of water into her hand and a piece of dry bread. "She probably just needs to sit down. The excitement of the day or this heat could be the problem."

"Thank you, Susanna." Emily nibbled at the bread.

William's jaw set. "I still think you need to go to the doctor."

A small crowd had gathered. Expressions of concern had Emily Jane feeling embarrassed. This wasn't how she wanted to tell her husband they were going to have a baby.

Susanna smiled at them all and announced, "She'll be all right. It's just the heat. Let's give them some room."

Emily Jane offered her friend another weak smile as the crowd dispersed. Susanna shooed people away from her and William.

Once they were alone, Emily Jane smiled at her husband. "I've already been to the doctor, William." The bread was doing its job. Emily Jane stood slowly. She still felt a little ill but not enough to throw up.

He cupped her face in his hands. "Why didn't you tell me you are sick?" His eyes searched hers. Did he think he could see what was ailing her by looking into her eyes?

She smiled. "Because I'm not really sick." Emily Jane enjoyed the confused look on his face. How many times had he shocked her with something wonderful? Now it was her turn to surprise him. "I'm going to have our baby."

His eyes widened. He merely stared at her, tongue-tied. The tenderness in his expression touched her from the tips of her toes to the top of her head. She laid her hand against his chest. He cleared his throat, but his voice still sounded hoarse. "Are you sure?"

Emily Jane nodded. "The doctor says I'm only a couple of months along, but, yes, I'm sure." Her hand moved to her stomach.

"A baby." He whispered the words. His hand covered hers, and a grin split his face. "My baby," William whispered in awe.

She chuckled. "Well, mine, too."

His blue eyes searched her face. "Are you happy about the baby?"

Emily Jane understood his concern. How many times had she said she didn't want to have children? Complained about having to take care of her siblings? It was no wonder he was worried now.

She led him to a hay bale and sat down. Emily Jane took his hands in hers, like he'd done to her so many times, and explained. "Yes, I am very happy. Before I met you I thought children were things to stop you from achieving your dreams, but I was wrong. When God places a dream on your heart, He makes sure you accomplish that dream. Having children is a blessing from God, and I'm thrilled He's allowing me to pursue my dream and have children with you."

William looked deeply into her eyes once more. "Emily Barns, I love you more than you will ever know."

She was breathless at the love reflected in his gaze. Emily Jane saw the truth of his words in the planes of his handsome face.

He stroked the side of her face. "Are you sure you are all right?"

Emily Jane nodded. "I've never been happier."

When he pulled her close and kissed her softly, she felt the deepness of his love. Emily Jane relaxed into his embrace and sent up a prayer of thanksgiving for a man who had made all her dreams come true.

* * * * *

WE HOPE YOU ENJOYED
THIS BOOK FROM

LOVE INSPIRED
INSPIRATIONAL ROMANCE

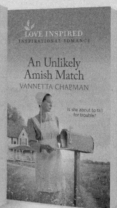

Uplifting stories of faith, forgiveness and hope.

Fall in love with stories where faith helps
guide you through life's challenges, and discover
the promise of a new beginning.

6 NEW BOOKS AVAILABLE EVERY MONTH!

"I'm sorry I was distant before. That was just me being foolish."

Samantha didn't ask what he was talking about; she obviously knew. "What was going on?"

Corbin debated finding some intellectual way to say it, but he wasn't thinking straight enough. "I got turned upside down by that kiss."

"Yeah. Me, too." She glanced at him and then turned to put a stack of plates away.

"It was intense."

"Uh-huh."

Now that he had brought up the topic, he wasn't sure where he wanted to go with it. For him to go into the fact that he couldn't get involved with her because she was an alcoholic... Suddenly, that felt judgmental and mean and not how he wanted to talk to her.

Maybe it wasn't how he wanted to be with her, either, but he wasn't ready to make that alteration to his long-held set of values about who he could get involved with. And until he did, he obviously needed to keep a lid on his feelings.

So he talked about something they would probably agree on. "I was never so scared in my life as when Mikey was lost."

"Me, either. It was awful."

He paused, then admitted, "I just don't know if I'm cut out for taking care of a kid."

Her head jerked around to face him. "You're not thinking of sending him back to your mom, are you?"

Was he? He shook his head slowly, letting out a sigh. "No. I feel like I screwed up badly, but I still think he's safer with me than with her."

She let the water out of the sink, not looking at him now. "I think you're doing a great job," she said. "It was just as much my fault as yours. Parenting is a challenge and you can't help but screw up sometimes."

"I guess." He wasn't used to doing things poorly or in a half-baked way. He was used to working at a task until he could become an expert. But it seemed that nobody was an expert when it came to raising kids, not really.

"Mikey can be a handful, just like any other little child," she said.

"He is, but I sure love him," Corbin said. It was the first time he had articulated that, and he realized it was completely true. He loved his little brother as if the boy were his own son.

"I love him, too," she said, almost offhandedly.

She just continued wiping down the counters, not acting like she had said anything momentous, but her words blew Corbin away. She had an amazing ability to love. Mikey wasn't her child, nor her blood, but she felt for him as if he were.

If he loved his little brother despite the boy's issues and whining and toddler misbehavior, could it be that he could love another adult who had issues, too? He was definitely starting to care a lot for Samantha. Was he growing, becoming more flexible and forgiving?

He didn't know if he could change that much. He'd been holding himself—and others—to a strict high standard for a long time. It was how he'd gotten as far as he had after his rough beginning.

Corbin wanted to continue caring for his brother, especially given the alternative, but the fact that Mikey had gotten lost had shaken him. He didn't know if he was good enough to do the job.

Samantha's expression of support soothed his insecurities. He wanted love and acceptance, just like anyone else. And there was a tiny spark inside him that was starting to burn, a spark that wondered if he could maybe be loved and fall in love, even with a certain nanny.

Don't miss
Child on His Doorstep
*by Lee Tobin McClain, available August 2020 wherever
Love Inspired books and ebooks are sold.*

LoveInspired.com